3—

W9-BRY-522

The Woman in the Cloak

Other books by Pamela Hill:

The Sutburys
My Lady Glamis
Tsar's Woman
The House of Cray
A Place of Ravens
Fire Opal
Daneclere
Stranger's Forest
The Green Salamander
Norah
Whitton's Folly
The Heatherton Heritage
The Malvie Inheritance
The Devil of Aske

The Woman in the Cloak

PAMELA HILL

St. Martin's Press
New York

Library of Congress Cataloging-in-Publication Data

Hill, Pamela.
     The woman in the cloak / Pamela Hill.
         p.   cm.
     ISBN 0-312-03956-5
      1. Margherita da Città di Castello, 1287-1320—Fiction.
   I. Title.
   PR6058.I446W6   1990
   823′.914—dc20   89-27128
                                                            CIP

First published in Great Britain by Robert Hale Limited.

First U.S. Edition

10 9 8 7 6 5 4 3 2 1

To
Father William Bonniwell, O.P.,
in tribute

Author's Note

This is the true story of Margaret of Metola. The original Latin biography and other sources have been carefully studied by Father William Bonniwell, O.P., who kindly agreed to let me make use of his book *Margaret of Castello*, published by Clonmore and Reynolds in 1952.

P.H.

The Woman in the Cloak

1

The child was blind. She moved her sensitive fingers along the rough surface of the wall, foreseeing every jutting part. This was the great passage of the *castello*, with the privy in the corner; beyond that it was less familiar. Presently she would come to the stairs, good foot groping, other following as best it might. But always she could trust her fingers, and the wall. They were thick, the walls of Metola. Enzio of the garrison had told her they would withstand siege-engines and arrows, but since her father had been the castellan there was no war. Margherita let her mind stray over the fact, bringing pride with it; since the Lord Parisio had governed here, there had been peace. Accordingly, the days passed as they would; but today had been different. There was a bustling about the fort, from her mother's solar to the hall to the cellars, something like it would be when the Lord Parisio rode out to hunt, with clattering of hooves and high horns wound, sounding deep into the forests. But there was no hunting today; this bustle was for visitors. They had come, she had heard, from Arezzo, but would not stay the night. She did not know their names. She had remained in her hidden place upstairs, sensing the activity of everyone in the castle, even the journeyings of scullions about the kitchens, deep below; and, nearer and more familiar, the business of *mammina* herself about her spice-chest. The Lady Emilia permitted no one else to hold the key to that; the cooks must ask for what they wanted. Margherita knew that; someone had told her, and she hugged the knowledge to herself like something warm. A gust of spiced warm air, smelling of ginger, had wafted itself to the upper solar today, and that meant that the leather curtain was drawn aside and one could go out, and down the passage. Margherita had sniffed the air, pondering it; but there was no sound behind her, the nurse having fallen asleep in the pervasive warmth.

So she had ventured out; step by limping step, until the privy with its stench was passed and she was on her way to the great hall. There, anyone might be met with; not the garrison or their wives, whom she knew; they only had permission to come in for dinner: not the *padre cappellano*, whom she loved, for he would be at his duties. She reflected that she would go to him later, in the chapel; meantime, her mind reached out towards others whom she might meet. She liked to meet people. Perhaps it would be mamma, smelling sweet from her errands to and from the spice-chest; perhaps, incredibly and fearfully, the Lord Parisio, her father, himself. That was like meeting God in the silence: a God wholly awesome, to be obeyed and feared. She longed to love her father, as the garrison children loved theirs. But a clanking of spurs, a rustle from the rich padded stuffs of his cloak, no words; that was the Lord Parisio, and all

that one could do was to pray for him daily. Mamma
had told her that, when she had also said the other thing
that at the time had seemed cruel.

Margherita halted and her face fell. The bitterness of
that saying still came into her mind at times despite the
priest's assurances; she knew she was different from
other children. Maria and Gian and Beppo, the sons
and daughter of the garrison, with whom Margherita
had twice played, had almost told her. They had been
playing hide-and-seek and Margherita had always
found them, even in the most difficult places. 'That is
because you are blind,' Maria had said. 'It is easy for you
to find your way in the dark.' Then she had drawn back,
because the Lady Margherita was, after all, the
castellan's daughter. Perhaps one should not have
spoken. But what the Lady Emilia had afterwards said
to her daughter had made everything clear.

'You are blind, it is true. The other children are not.
You have a hump on your back and one leg shorter than
the other. You are a dwarf and will never grow to full
height. It is as well that you know of it now rather than
later.'

Margherita had gone to the chapel, sobbing bitterly;
and there had found the *cappellano*. 'Is it true that I am
different?' she had asked him, for he was always kind.
He would not deceive her.

There had been a grave silence while the priest
sought for the right answer; he was a small man,
outwardly timid as a mouse. Margherita knew this as
though she could see him.

Presently he spoke. 'God has visited you, my
daughter, with some of the suffering He Himself
endured. He wants you to suffer with Him. It is a favour
not given to all. I believe that you can understand the

privilege. When something hurts you, think of the Saviour on the cross. Remember what He endured for us, far beyond anything you may ever endure; and offer your sorrows to Him.' And she had done it, since that day she had glorified in doing it. What did it matter that she must limp and grope? The love of God shone through the blindness. It was easier to reach God if one suffered with Him. When she was alone, she prayed to Him. She could pray now, in the passage.

Someone was coming; it might be one of the visitors. Margherita had heard the horses ride in a little time ago; afterwards there had been the sounds of welcome, of talking, the good sound of wine being poured and drunk. It was part of the world she sometimes guessed at when she visited the wives of the garrison as she loved to do; a homely world, full of the shared things of ordinary living, the smells of humanity and leather and steel that was kept sharp and bright by buffing it with sand in a cloth. She knew the women's names, Giannetta and Bianca and Paola and Elena, for they all smelled different. They had rough kindly hands which caressed her, not like mamma's which were smooth and idle, and voices which spoke broadly in their own patois. They mostly came from these parts, from the Metola estate. Sometimes they told her of the great forests which reached as far as man could know, full of bears and wolves, and the rivers which would rise high in spate in autumn, sweeping unwary travellers along with them as readily as they floated cut timber down to the towns. And the mountains were beyond. There was a great world out there, beyond the *castello*. Nobody knew all of it.

But the person who was coming was not one of the garrison wives. She was not the Lady Gemma, the wife of the second commander, who smelt of musk. Lady

Gemma would have come to her, and would have given
her a kiss. Margherita stopped in her progress, the short
lame foot hanging poised above the rough floor, while
her fingers still grasped the stones. 'Lady,' she said
aloud. 'Stranger lady.' It was an alien presence, but
friendly: rich and gentle, with a whiff of flower-essences
and the hushing of silk lined with silk. On her head
would be a linen coif set in gold, like mamma's.
Margherita felt the stranger hesitate. It is because I am
so ugly, the child thought without affectation; she has
not seen anyone like me before. The smell of the saddle
and of horse-sweat conflicted with the essences; the lady
had had a long journey. Her voice was high and soft,
gently bred and hesitant. Margherita grinned cheerfully, showing serrated milk-teeth.

'What do you want, little girl?' the stranger had asked.
This must be one of the servants' children; the only child
of Parisio and Emilia had died at birth. A mercy it had not
survived to be like this! A cripple, dreadfully twisted and
dwarfish; except for the friendly expression, one would
say it should have been stifled when it was born, but after
all a Christian soul ... My lady returned to her own
necessities; she had been looking for the privy, necessary
after the long ride, and the stench was not far off. She
asked the child and the child told her.

'It is along the wall. I am going to the chapel now.'
Her speech was tactful, but she was also full of
happiness. The chapel was above all the place where she
loved best to be; there was the friendly presence of the
cappellano, the scent of wax and incense, and above all
the nearness of Our Lord in the Sacrament. She turned
her face trustingly to the newcomer, seeing her on her
way; if one waited it would be like the surrender of the
fierce hunting-hounds in the hall, their thrusting

muzzles soft as mamma's velvets after the first warning growl. But meantime there was the familiar sound of drawing back; the departing visitor had crossed herself in pity.

Mother of God, she was thinking, the child is a lady from the way she speaks; can it be, after all –? Eyes filmed over as if with milk, and how ugly, how ugly, with that bony face, and the great hump, and the tiny twisted body, and the limp always from the uneven foot! How old was the creature? The thought caused the lady to narrow her eyes. Six years ago Parisio and Emilia had trumpeted the news of a coming child at Metola. The more she thought of it, the more she was convinced the child had not died.

It was a pity. The little creature was confiding and mannerly, as well as intelligent: she had guessed one's rank. A tragedy, best not spoken of at least until one was clear of Metola. 'How do you know I am a lady, little blind girl?' If one had a sweetmeat, perhaps –

'Because you do not speak like the soldiers' wives. Your voice is like that of my mamma, or the Lady Gemma.'

'And who is your mamma, dear?'

'She –'

But running footsteps came; it was the nurse, wakened from her doze and fearful of a beating from my lady for letting the child be seen. Today there were guests and she should not have slept. 'Back to the solar, Lady Margherita! Back to the solar, quickly! *Madama*, do not tell any that you have seen her, I beg. She is supposed to be hidden.'

The visitor escaped to the privy. Margherita followed her nurse; she was obedient, and the limping walk hastened itself until the uneven body rocked between wall and narrow wall of the passage. Her mind was full of disappointment that she could not now go to the chapel, but there was no one left to care. Downstairs the Lord Parisio, Captain of the People like his ancestors, caused more wine to be poured for his guests, and himself drank deep.

The guests continued on their journey, mellow with wine. Later, the castellan of Metola sat at dinner at the high table with his wife Emilia. His handsome brutal face was sullen, for word had reached him that the child had been seen today by one of those who came; it would lead to gossip. From time to time his glance flickered over Emilia's silver-fair, already fading beauty; he was fond of her, she was well-born and had brought him a sizeable dowry, and since his marriage he had not taken another woman. But the truth, that twisted shameful birth after a year of marriage! Deep within himself, Parisio acknowledged that it was perhaps his own fault, which made him the more savage regarding it; what soldier didn't wench a bit before marriage, and must it be a reproach to him for the rest of his life? The physicians had sworn him cured before he laid hands on Emilia as a bride; but looking at their child, which he seldom did, his sins were brought back before his face. Unto the third and fourth generation.... how did it go? At any rate there would be no more children. At first he had desired a son and, when the birth fell due that time, had sent out invitations far and wide to a great feasting, not only here at the fortress but in the town: and then had to cancel everything. He had been made a fool of; he blamed God. His jaw set now and he growled to his wife, lowering his voice in order that the servants might not hear.

'It will not do to keep the monster here any longer. It was seen today by that fool of a woman who came with them in the train; that means the countryside will soon know. We must deny everything; we must send it somewhere.' Mentally he denied his daughter her very sex, as though from the beginning she had forfeited any claim on the human race; it was unusual for him to speak of her. The Lady Emilia coloured, grew white again, crumbled the bread beside her platter with her slim fingers, and stared down at the rings she wore. One was her wedding-ring; she had kept her vows, and always obeyed her husband. It had indeed seemed, since the terrible birth ruined her six years ago, as though Parisio were the only thing left in life; to pass the days obeying him was a just sentence, for she had failed him in his desire for a son. That agony, seeming as if it would never be done, and at the end a creature with a hump! She had thought, in the intervals between the birth-pains, of many things. Among them had been the vision she had had of pale daisies blowing in a field, of pearls, of a single shimmering pearl, a *margherita*. Margherita, a pearl, a daisy; they had christened the poor child that, smuggling her down to the cathedral at Mercatello despite Parisio's ban. Margherita herself troubled them seldom now; the nurse was vigilant. Perhaps another peasant could be found to take the child, rear her secretly in the mountains. Emilia made the suggestion, timidly.

'Pah!' said Parisio. 'Everyone would know the truth in weeks; these peasants talk their heads off in the villages on market day. No, there must be a better plan.'

'If she could only live on here, locked in the room –'

'We've tried that, haven't we? And soon, at maybe twelve years old, it'll be a bitch in heat, going down to

the garrison for more than kisses. No, the business must
be settled, and at once; but how? We can trust none but
ourselves.' As he spoke, his voice was aggrieved; he, the
Captain of the People, had led his men once in the siege
of Metola, had caused that strong fort to fall out of the
hands of the Gubbio who had held it for a generation,
so that they'd given it to him, Parisio, to govern, with the
bit of land beyond with its timber and farms. He knew
himself a fine courageous captain still; the men obeyed
him readily and he had a good second-in-command in
Leonardo di Peneto, who sat with his wife Gemma
further down the table. Otherwise nobody ate with
them except the priest, the *cappellano*; a useless
mealy-mouthed thing, timorous like all his kind. Priests,
monks, hermits, eunuchs; he had no time for them;
weakness should be stamped out.

A memory came to him, in the aftermath of wishing
ill on the priesthood. 'What was that tale you told me
once about some woman who walled herself up for
thirty years and saw nobody, food handed in behind a
black curtain?' he demanded of Emilia. Something of
that kind would be the answer. Already, like a plan of
campaign, he saw the notion unfold itself before him.
Thereafter they could have peace; a man asked little
more.

Emilia had already glanced up from her food. 'That
was a saint, St Veridiana. She renounced the world and
lived all her life in a built-up cell, nearby the Sacrament.
There was a little window which looked on to the altar,
and another let in the wall outside for her food. The
curtain was there so that no one from the world might
see her. To survive in such a way one must be very holy.'
Emilia looked, with regret, at her own white hands; they
had never done a day's work and were kept smooth with

rosewater. 'Such things cannot happen now,' she said sadly.

'Can they not? Can they not?'

'You mean –'

'I mean what I say. I will have a cell built on the forest side of the parish church. Not so many come, and if they should do so they will not see in; we will build the window high.' The Captain grinned. 'For one who likes to pray – you tell me the creature is at it constantly – what more is there to ask of life? And you and I will be free in our minds. We can see to it that the thing does not starve; the parish priest will care for her. He knows what will become of him if he flouts me.'

'But – she is only six years old –'

'I recall the date of the birth very well, and having to silence the bells that were to have rung out for our son, heir to the long line of Captains of Massa Trabaria.'

Emilia fell silent, her failure with her as always. One must obey Parisio. He had been good to her, was still her lover.

Further down the table the *cappellano* sat, taking his food quietly. He had heard nothing of the talk; he had been thinking, as he often did, of the child kept hidden upstairs, and of how among all the sordid sinfulnesses of men and women here she alone had a soul that was clear and shining white and pleasing to God. They could not have named her better. He had not forgotten the trouble over the christening; and the day he had come upon Margherita sobbing her heart out because her mother had told her she was ugly and blind, and he had comforted her.

2

Next day the *cappellano* made preparations for the long ride into town, for he had to buy wax and other necessaries. On the way, he had ridden past the little parish church of Santa Maria di Metola, half-hidden in the forest, frowned on by the great hills that defended the valley, visited by few strangers. Some building had begun there and he stopped to ask the parish priest about it, and to pass the time of day.

The priest, who was an old man, shrugged. 'It is by order of the Lord Parisio, an enclosed cell.'

'Parisio takes little heed of such things. Why should he want it?'

'He did not say.'

Together the two priests stared at the small square of ground which had been levelled; it was at the further end, near the altar. Near them was the hollow for a privy drain. The masons themselves were too busy to talk; they had been told the work must be completed at once, by order of the castellan, lord of the estate; one did not question. The men had brought stones from the hillside and were now spreading and mixing lime, heads bent, shoulders active. The *cappellano* remounted his mule. It was none of his business what went on beyond the fort; his task was to care for the souls in it. He bade the *parroco* Godspeed, and rode off.

He returned late next day, and saw that the building was completed. It was no more than a rough stone box, with a tiny window high above the ground.

The *cappellano* returned to his quarters in the fort, depositing the valuable wax in the place he kept for it; later he would fashion candles. As he disposed his purchases, there came a scratching at the curtain. Leonardo di Peneto stood without, still clad in his mail, face grim beneath the cropped hair.

'I would make a confession, father.' He spoke in a low voice, looking over his shoulder as if fearful of being overheard. This was a common habit in Metola; the castellan could be harsh, even to his immediate subordinate. The priest nodded. Leonardo came in and knelt beyond the curtain. All about them was the hum of busy life in the fort, a little world of its own; the sharpening of weapons, the talk of women and servants about their tasks, the crying of a child; one of the garrison wives had just given birth.

'I have a thing I would say, though you may soon know of it from elsewhere; he cannot keep it hidden.'

'Parisio?'

'The same. All of my men are angry, their wives clamouring; they speak of it more than of this birth. Parisio and Emilia are to shut away the little Margherita in a mountain cell adjoining the church. They are ashamed for her to be seen by strangers, that is well known. But among ourselves it has been different; often she has visited me and Gemma, and the rest in the fort, and her coming brought joy. She is like a little friendly animal.'

'She is more than an animal. She is a Christian soul.'

'I know it. I am telling you in this way lest we are watched and overheard. No doubt they chose the time to make ready deliberately, while you were away, knowing you to be her friend.'

Walled up like a beast, thought the *cappellano*. A rush of unaccustomed anger came to him. 'In the winter it will be freezing,' he said. 'She is only six years old. The Church does not permit seclusion at such an age.' He felt the flush of indignation rise to his cheeks and neck, below the rough cowl. 'You are certain of it?' he said. 'You have evidence that that is what they will do?'

'Ask any of the garrison and their wives. The child is to be taken there tomorrow at Nones, and walled up with lime. It was the nurse who told us. Food is to be handed to Margherita by the window, and there is another inside, by the altar, that she may feel herself near the Sacrament. That will cheer her, it is true, but –'

'God will perhaps have a care to her, more than if she were in the world, with unloving parents.'

'And they are hypocrites. My wife Gemma heard the Lady Emilia tell the child that it was a reward to her, that from now on she would be alone with God. There is much cruelty in the world and I've seen plenty in my time, but not like this.'

'What can be done except pray?' said the priest. He knew that he was helpless against the will of Parisio, as were all at Metola, all beyond; the castellan might hang whom he would.

Leonardo had fallen silent. 'I am not afraid,' said the *cappellano* suddenly. 'I will go to Parisio and his wife.'

'Do not tell them that I have come here. It would

mean trouble for me and torment for my wife. We are in their hands.'

'I will tell them nothing except what they need to be told. If they do not repent I will curse them. Tell your men, and their wives and children, to pray for this poor child. She would have been more fortunate to be born a beggar. Go now, for I will seek the castellan.'

He went, in a flurry of robes, sandals flapping. Anger bore him up and when at last he stood face to face with Parisio and Emilia he still had no fear. Had not Christ Himself cursed the money-lenders in the Temple? And here was greater wickedness.

He tried to reason with Parisio, but the castellan was hard; he told the priest in coarse terms to take himself off. Emilia stood silent, twisting her rings. 'I will visit her from time to time,' she had ventured, timidly, but her lord had bidden her be quiet.

'It is to be forgotten, you hear, forgotten. Many men in my position would have had the creature smothered. As it is I have endangered my reputation with the world; what kind of man sires such? Never a soldier, who can endure wounds, wars, heat and cold. As to that, the winter may finish the business. That is God's will, sir priest, is it not? Never come to me again with your mouthings; get on with your care of souls. Pray for the thing if you wish; it is nothing to me.' He turned on his heel, spurs gleaming; his rich cloak was lined with fur. He was a fine-looking man, growing a trifle heavy now despite the exercise he still took, hunting, tilting. Emilia looked after him like a dog eyeing its master.

The *cappellano* drew up to his small height. 'You are both of you accursed,' he said with stern certainty. 'I myself curse you with all my heart and with the strength of Holy Church. You are inhabited by devils which cannot be cast out, for where your faith and love should be there is a stone. You have cast away a pearl and no good will come to you. You are anathema.' His voice choked in his throat; the image of the blind crippled girl came to him, gentle and merry, devout and undemanding. 'God will requite what you have done to your daughter,' he told the pair. 'He will give you no part of His Kingdom; have you not done evil to a little one? You will burn everlastingly in the torments of the damned.'

'Have you done?' said Parisio thickly from where he stood by the narrow slit in the wall that looked out towards Metola forests. 'Get you gone before worse befall you. I can have your tongue torn out, and none know.'

'God will know, for He knows all you do,' said the *cappellano*. 'He sees you now, and that poor afflicted child. He is with her; He cannot come to you. I will no longer administer the Sacrament to you. I will ask the Bishop that he may free me from hearing your confessions. The spots of sin that stain your souls will not be wiped clean, in this world or the next. I will –'

'You will keep a still and civil tongue in your head, or lose it as I told you. If I find that talk of the matter has spread, I will know where to come, and what to do. Remember it, sir priest.' The thick tones had not altered; it was impossible to make the Lord Parisio afraid. 'I shall go from here,' said the priest. 'You may find another to do your work, for I will not serve the accursed of God.'

'You will lose a fat living. Do as you will, but keep silence. My arm is long.'

The Lady Emilia fluttered towards the *cappellano*, bringing with her the scent of flower-water. 'Do not leave, I beg,' she whispered. 'My daughter knows you and loves you. You will be able to visit her when I cannot. Do not cast us away.'

He stared at her, knowing that he would stay after all. It was true that he could visit the imprisoned child in the forest cell, and hearten her; and the *parroco* could tell him of her needs.

Night fell over the mountains, bringing with it a thousand menacing shadows and sounds; the running of the turgid hill-streams, the thrusting of wild boars in the branches and shallows, the sharp cry of a civet far off. In her cell, the child knelt, staring sightlessly beyond the unseen window to where the sanctuary lamp burned and brought her warmth. It had never occurred to her to be afraid. The cold had deepened, striking her to the bones; she felt her flesh shiver, and offered the discomfort to God as the *cappellano* had told her. What was it he had said? 'When something hurts you, offer it to Our Saviour on the cross.' And Christ was with her, more than ever now in a special way, with the Blessed Sacrament beyond the wall; she, alone here at night, was His guardian, His companion through the long hours, as though at Gethsemane. She would sleep little for the cold, so she could use the time well. The pattern of known prayers came to her and she said them. But beyond and above them, ever near her, was the Presence, comforting and real; more so than the damp smells of drying lime and stone, the rustling of the new straw, the pervading cold. Mamma had said, as the priest had done, that this was an especial favour, an honour; to be alone night and day with God, Who listened always, Who comforted.

She fell into a fitful sleep with the coming of dawn, and woke to the sound of the bell for Prime, rung by the *parroco*. He said the Office and then moved past the altar, his hesitant steps gentle lest he wake her; but she was awake beyond the wall, the pale triangle of her face seen in the faint light at the inner window.

'You are well, Margherita? You passed the night safely? In my little cell I prayed for you.'

'I thank you, father. Tomorrow night I will pray for you. I was too much taken up with myself to think of it. That is a sin, to be selfish. I will try to do better.'

'It was not too cold in the cell? You were not afraid of the dark?'

She smiled, the joy in her face transfiguring the ugly misshapen flesh. It was kind of him to ask, but like many people he did not understand. She was used to the dark. And it was not frightening, but beautiful and welcoming when one was here, alone, with God. 'I am very well,' she said courteously. 'With me it is always dark. I am used to it. You will say Mass soon?'

'Within the hour, and you shall say the responses.' There were not many parishioners who troubled to attend at this hour; they came from scattered places in the hills.

I shall like that, thought Margaret of Metola.

The two priests sat before the stove in the *parroco*'s hut, where a wood fire burned. Steam rose from the *cappellano*'s clothing; he had just ridden in. Outside, the snow whirled down, covering everything in blinding whiteness; soon it would be dark. Both men were silent, thinking of the child in her cell. Presently the *parroco* spoke.

'She makes no complaint, but on the other hand seems happy. It gives her great joy to join in the Masses and the Offices. She seems to need no company.' He downed a small, hurt feeling; he had often tried to talk with Margherita, and had not been rebuffed, he could not say that; as that first time, she was always courteous; but seemed not to require his talk. He stared at the *cappellano*, who was rubbing his hands before the fire.

'A dog would not be out on a night like this,' he said. 'She will have few visitors in this weather. Certainly her mother will not come.'

'She rides across seldom; I think she has to be vigilant that her husband does not know. At first she used to bring comforts, but Margherita would not use them. Only one thing she asked –' He broke off, and his face flushed more deeply than the heat of the fire warranted. 'She asked for a hair shirt,' he blurted out. The other raised his hands.

'That child! You did not give it to her?'

The *parroco* gave a nod, his eyes averted. 'Truth to tell I hoped it would keep the little creature warm,' he said. 'She had not thought of that! All that troubles her concerning it is lest her mother see that her clothes are bulky, and guess the reason. But the mother has noticed nothing.'

'The Lady Emilia sees nothing but herself – and him. They are blind in truth, while the child has the eyes of the soul.'

'We are in company with a saint, I believe.'

'At seven years old! Yet St Agnes, St Reparata were children. They endured martyrdom, and with the kind of cheerfulness Margherita shows daily and has done from the time she could talk. I myself instructed her in the Faith and she was like a thirsty man drinking water. I doubt if any single thing I told her has since escaped her mind. She has the understanding of an old, wise woman. If anyone had told me of such a miracle, I would not have believed them; but I saw it from day to day, despite the coldness of her parents which I am certain grieved her. Yet she accepted even that as an offering to God.'

'She welcomes suffering, knowingly. She fasts the year round. When she came here at first I used to find her weeping in her cell – not, as might be expected, because of her abandonment, her loneliness, but because she said she was not good enough for the honour God had shown her.' He bowed his head, staring into the flames. 'I myself could not begin to show such holiness. It is as though she could spend all her days so.'

'She may survive to do that, despite her father,' said the chaplain. 'She has a passionate nature, which makes it hard for her. What if there is war again, as there was before she was born? I have heard that some mercenaries do not hesitate to burn even churches, for the loot they can provide. Margaret would be trapped, unable to escape.'

The *parroco* shuddered. 'God be thanked, there has been peace in Metola since Parisio came. He is a bad man but a good governor, and a good soldier.'

'He is a harsh landlord. He exacts the utmost from the peasants, whether the harvests have been good or bad.'

'Well, well, there are places beyond the mountains. I must go back now,' said the *cappellano*. 'It will soon be night.'

He rose and went, the muffled sound of the mule's hooves in the snow growing fainter. The parish priest rose to go about his evening duties, unwilling to leave the fire.

3

War did not come for nine years. On a spring day, Lady Emilia sat with a polished mirror in her hand, for once not seeing her reflection in the metal. She was thinking of Margaret, and of how over the years from time to time she had seen her face, upturned from the dark inner place against the light from the tiny outer window where her food and water were handed in and where rare visitors came, Emilia herself, the Lady Gemma, the *parroco* and *cappellano*. The face which had been a child's had altered and broadened, so that now it was wide-browed and aquiline, with a strong nose and strong serrated teeth: the face of a stranger, not one's own daughter to whom – she had not found it easy – must be explained, by her mother, the changes that came with womanhood. Emilia had murmured in a strained way the lore she knew, which was not much, about how one bled with the waxing of the moon; then afterwards realised that Margaret would never see the moon, or a man's face; it was as well, for no man would desire her. Emilia had handed in strips of cloth, and departed; thinking now of her daughter's body, she pictured young breasts under the hump. It was distasteful and she would sooner have turned her mind to other things; yet here the matter was again, troubling her.

The curtain rasped and Parisio stood in the doorway, in full armour. 'It is war,' he said. 'Montefeltro has invaded. You must make ready. It is not safe for you to stay here.'

'Where am I to go?' The sense of disaster whirled about Emilia; she thought of the gown-chest, which would be too heavy to move; the gowns themselves must be put in a bale. And her coifs, some of which were of delicate wire and would not travel well, would be crushed. Well, there it was; one had been, after all, prepared for it to happen at any time. 'Where am I to go?' she asked Parisio, again knowing he would have arranged something; there was no need to trouble oneself overmuch, except that change was always inconvenient. The servants ... the spices, some of them of great value ... her embroidery ...

'You are to go to the house in Mercatello. Take all you need. We will be driving the cattle inside here so do not leave any hangings. No one will remain in the fort except Leonardo and a few old ones. The peasantry are in arms. I have made ready for this for long.' He raised his head, and sniffed the air. 'I can almost smell burning,' he said, 'but they are still seven leagues off. Make haste, though; you must be gone by tomorrow.'

A thought drifted into her mind. 'And Margherita?'

He made an impatient movement. 'Take her with you, well veiled. They may attack the church. When you reach Mercatello, lock her in the vaults; tell her not to cry out or demand anything, except when the servant brings her meals. Give her a pallet, a bench, and a table. That is all.'

'But the Mass? She likes to hear Mass,' said Emilia. She saw him grimace; neither of them had received the Sacrament since the chaplain had cursed them long ago. And Margaret had been the cause of it. Emilia saw her husband's face harden. 'She must learn to do without such luxuries,' he said, 'unless you want to display her with you in the market-place on the way to the cathedral. That would do very well, would it not? Your daughter and mine; a deformed cripple.'

He went out, and Emilia began to run about the solar, directing the servants this way and that; silk and wool clothes, hangings, hose, shoes, everything, were assembled; but she would in any case be able to buy more at Mercatello. There might even be pedlars with luxuries in the market. What good fortune that Parisio kept a house in the town! She would be able to see new faces, the latest fashions.

'Hurry,' she said to the women, and in course of the packing seized a heavy shawl, and kept it by her. It would conceal Margherita's shape in the saddle. The girl would ride behind a servant, and be told to keep silent so that they might think of her as a serving-woman. There was no time to lose.

They had taken picks to destroy the stone wall. Margaret had heard them crashing, heard the swift crumbling of lime and stones, felt the outer air rush in, and then, with hurrying steps, her mother come across the trodden straw, and fling a covering over her. 'We are going to live in town,' she was told, 'while the war lasts.' The *parroco* had already told her there might be war. It was strange to be close to others again, sensing the nearness of mounted men and horses; stranger still to be lifted and thrust in the saddle, told to cling to a servant's back by his belt. She had been alone so long that she had forgotten the warmth of human flesh. She huddled in the protective shawl, and the horses moved off. She was shaken, but kept silent. God would look after her. It had been sad to leave the cell, but the *parroco* would take the Blessed Sacrament away with him to a place of safety. This was safe no longer; as Emilia had not done, Margaret's own keen senses smelled the burning farms as they rode; all of the spring harvest would be lost.

Emilia enjoyed life in Mercatello, which she knew already; she and Parisio had made occasional visits there when matters at the fort were not pressing. It was pleasant not to be surrounded any longer by the everlasting forest and purling hill-streams; pleasant to look out of one's window of a morning and see others like oneself, clad in light gowns and pointed shoes, hair hanging loose below a fillet as was fashionable; she need not have troubled about her coifs. To have oneself dressed accordingly gave one pleasure; then to go down to the market-place where everybody met to gossip. Preaching friars were there, still practising the rule of St Francis and begging; it was modish to go afterwards to the cathedral, with a servant before one carrying a prayer-cushion; and on the way to cast an eye towards the stalls where the servants were shopping, seeing the cabbages and eggs and sucking-pigs and butter, for such things were not all commandeered here in the south. One could greet one's neighbours then and pass the time of day; and, later, company could be invited to the house, and there would be laughter and the sound of lutes. This was civilised living as she had known it before her marriage. She would be sorry to return to Metola.

She bit her lip. The drawback here, as always, was Margaret, who could not be presented to one's friends. There had been no alternative but to do as Parisio commanded and thrust the girl down into the cellars, arrange for food to be taken to her daily, and bid her be silent until then. Emilia found less and less time to visit her daughter. That was an episode in one's life best forgotten; live for the moment, that was all. There was no news of Parisio; the last she had heard was that he was fighting in the foothills against half-trained bands from Montefeltro, and was certain of victory. He had his veterans as well as the conscripted serfs, and they gave as good as they got; Emilia used to mutter prayers for her husband while she lay on her bed, thinking of the pleasant happenings of the day. She was still a fine-looking woman, she knew, and had the maids tend her long silken hair and dye it with saffron, to disguise the grey; and pluck her brows and lashes, to give the fashionable bald look; it made one's eyes larger.

Down in the vaults, Margaret passed her days in increasing misery. This was not like the chapel cell, where she had been always near the Sacrament and had felt that a friend waited in the darkness. God answered her here at first, it was true; but increasingly she felt He had withdrawn behind a muffling veil, like the one they had thrust about her to ride to Mercatello. Gradually the veil had thickened till it was like a mist, and stifled her, till she felt daunted and as though she could by no means beat her way through to God. There was no priest here to help her, not even the *parroco* with his well-meant talk. The servant who came was civil and would tell her such news as she asked for. Yes, the Lord Parisio was still fighting in the war, but as far as anyone knew he was holding his own. That was all he could tell her; and Margaret would try to pray for her father as he rode, basnet lowered, into the thick of a fight she could not see. It was difficult to recall him, a seldom-heard voice from her earliest childhood; he had never come to the mountain cell. It was as though his remembered presence had grown dim together with the figure of God.

She tried to obey the instructions Emilia had given her. She was not to call out under any circumstances; if she wanted anything she must wait till the food was brought and then ask. She had a pallet on which to lie, a bench at which to sit; the cellar was by far larger than the mountain cell had been and the servant found her groping her way about it; next day he brought her a peeled willow wand. 'Feel ahead with that,' he said. It wasn't his business to hold an opinion, that wasn't what he was paid for. But this girl seemed something better than a beast, locked away as she was always after he himself had shot the bolts on the door. He remembered her smile, the charm – she had that, God knew how – shining in her face, as though the soul within were trying to get out. The man went to a tavern that evening and got drunk, nearly losing his employment.

Margaret limped about the underground vault, using her stick to feel ahead as she had been told; it helped. It had been a kindness in the servant; almost, she felt as if a new dimension had been added to her life, enabling her to judge distances, sizes, projections before she stumbled on them. The stick would go with her wherever she went; but where was she going? Round and round, till one was back where one had started, pallet and bench and built groins and pallet again. The days passed so; mechanically, she murmured her prayers. The voices and music and laughter from abovestairs came faintly, something unknown, alien, now and again even longed for; a world from which she was shut out. She was alone in the darkness, would always be alone; and outside there was war.

Pilgrims came once to Mercatello from Rome. Emilia saw and heard them, waiting about in the square as she was with her maid by her, to see the latest marvel; the men wore grey robes and round felt hats and carried staves. They drew away the attention from a troupe of jugglers who for a time continued to toss coloured balls in the air; but the crowd drained away from them towards the silent grey-clad men, marvelling at the crossed keys and cockleshells in their hats; why did they look so grave, was it not joyful to go on pilgrimage? Everyone shouted at once, except for one man who asked steady questions in a clear voice; how was the new Pope faring? He was known to be a lover of peace.

The foremost pilgrim frowned, and traced a pattern on the ground with his stave. 'The Holy Father has fled the city,' he said, ashamed.

'Fled? The Holy Father?' The crowd murmured, heaved, speculated. What could have happened? Such a thing had never been known. Even in ancient times, bad times, Rome had been the seat of the Faith, with St Peter's successor holding his place there. A sign of the times now that all this should be altered! 'Surely there is a curse on the land,' murmured an old woman near Emilia. The latter crossed herself, fashionably. Here came Messer Rainaldo, the chief magistrate; she must be seen in the forefront, listening to the news. Her shallow blue eyes fluttered over the great man's appearance; he wore a saffron gown and scarlet cloak with a hood, trimmed with ermine. He had already raised his arm to speak.

'Let us hear what befell the Holy Father,' he said. 'What is the reason for this disorder?' For Messer Rainaldo was a reasonable man; he did not believe in wildcat scares. The pilgrims surveyed him gravely.

'He asked,' they said, 'for the warring sides to come to terms. He asked that each one should surrender a little of his demands, give way a little; that was all. But none would. The people, seeing that the Pope had failed, turned on him then, and he fled the city.'

'A sad business,' murmured Messer Rainaldo. The jugglers had stopped their antics and held their coloured balls, foolishly. A brown-clad friar who stood nearby said, 'It is a judgement on us. God is angry with us. We have all sinned.'

'You,' retorted the foremost pilgrim, 'are a son of St Francis and should know that we are not so accursed. What of the miracles of your Fra Giacomo at Castello, who makes cripples walk? God is not so angry with everyone.'

'At Castello? So near? St Francis worked miracles there himself, but since then, nothing.'

'You have not heard. News travels slowly over the mountains.'

The crowd was restive; they wanted to know more. The pilgrim raised his eyes beneath his hat's brim, suddenly hopeful.

'Fra Giacomo was a tertiary of the Order,' he said. 'He died lately and since his death the miracles have come. We had heard of it also. They say he can cure many kinds of sickness. To think of the lame cured and the blind restored to sight, as it was in the time of Our Lord!'

Emilia's heart began to beat faster. She looked at the crowd, the friar, the stilled jugglers; suddenly it was as if she stood behind glass and had no part with them. She wanted to go home; she turned away. On reaching the house she thought of going to her daughter, yet did not go; if there was hope in this matter – and why should there not be? – she must discuss it first of all with Parisio. There was no word from him yet. She turned restlessly to the window, looking down at the crowds still gossiping together in the square. Presently she drew away; no gently bred woman would be seen looking out at a window, that was for whores. She had conducted herself with discretion in the absence of her husband. Parisio would be grateful.

Perhaps the Pope's prayers for peace were heard; the aggressor Montefeltro withdrew his troops from Massa Trabaria. He had troubles of his own in the south, in the direction of Perugia; a general must guard his flank. Soon Parisio rode to Mercatello, a free man. He came to his house and was welcomed and sat by the brazier, helmet removed, throat-piece unlaced; the wine was good and his wife more than ever attractive.

'The peasants have gone home,' he replied to her enquiry about matters at Metola. 'The regulars still keep watch, but there will be no trouble now. I am glad to be here, with a little comfort. There was much heat and cold on campaign, and few pleasures.' He eyed her. Emilia came to him, seating herself nearby; the dyed hair swung enticingly. Parisio put his arm about her. A man sweated and fought bitterly, and for what? A few miles gained, or lost. Women and wine were a solace. He groped for his wife's breasts.

'What is the gossip, eh? I wager you know it all, Emilia. Tell me; the past weeks have been like a dry bone.' And she told him, lacing her account liberally with the talk of the town; soon he lost interest and turned his head away. Then he left her, and sprang up and began to turn about the room, like a caged animal. The reason was the last thing she had said.

'A miracle at Castello for the lame and blind, eh?' he murmured. 'I have not the belief I used to have since that priest cursed us: but let us try.'

4

To horse again, with the cold dawn air striking against one's flesh; hearing the restive hooves of the escort, clinging helplessly meantime to a broad back clad in leather which jogged along; going over in one's mind the thing that had been said, very briefly, yesterday. They had put the veil once more about her; but despite this there was a lifting of her misery. It was as though the way were clear to God once more; perhaps it was the thought of the miracle, which Emilia swore must happen.

She had come into the cellar yesterday, without warning from the servant; the perfume she used pervaded the damp, malodorous place. She had spoken from a little way off, not anxious to approach closely. 'Your father is home,' she said, and Margaret turned her head away.

'I know it. He did not visit me. I heard of it from the man. I am glad the war is over.'

'For the time.' Emilia did not comment on her husband's absence. 'We both hope that there is a prospect of your cure; a famous shrine at Castello, a Franciscan lately dead; he has cured many.' The Lady Emilia's voice struck flatly against the dark stones; she felt as though she were repeating a tale by rote; it had been Parisio who believed in the thing. The likelihood of having Margaret returned to them straight, strong and beautiful seemed remote; but stranger things had happened. Emilia stared at the hunched, dwarfish figure of her daughter; there had been hardly any growth from the time she was a child, and the hump was still evident. Margaret turned her face towards her mother again, and the other almost recoiled; that face, with the prominent nose, filmed eyes and strange ridged teeth, attentive as though it saw one! She clenched her fingers against her silk surtout; one must believe that the cure would take place. As Parisio put it, their name was the noblest in Italy. 'We will start early tomorrow,' she said aloud. 'Prepare yourself by praying; it is best to be ready.'

Margaret smiled a little. 'And do you pray too, mamma.' She heard the cell door close. Afterwards the servant came to her; she heard to her surprise that he had been weeping; his voice was thick.

'May God reward you with a cure, lady. They have said little of it except behind closed doors, but I overheard. Remember me in your good prayers; I'm a sinful man, not fit to bring your bread and water on a Friday. It'll be lonely, after; you'll not be back down here again.'

So she had felt happiness, for a time, thinking of the cure, and praying to dead Fra Giacomo. Yet at the same time the words of the *cappellano* at Metola came to her, from long ago. 'God wants you to suffer, Margherita; He has given you especial marks of suffering as an honour, to set you apart.' It would be pleasant, no doubt, to be like other people, and to be invited upstairs to partake of the laughter and the song; to stand by her father, the Captain of the People, and see the pride in his eyes for a beautiful daughter who would make a good marriage. Such things might be hers, if she disowned the setting aside of herself for God. But did she want such things?

The cavalcade did not have an easy journey, for the roads were steep and narrow and bandits were known to lurk in the forest passes. Lady Emilia drew close to her husband in his hauberk and mail. 'How far have we to go?' she murmured timidly. 'I am growing weary.'

'Endure it, for the time; we will be in a comfortable inn by evening, with food and a fire.' He spoke absently, and she could tell that his mind was not on her but on the forthcoming miracle. She downed uneasiness; Parisio always took up one thing or another with enthusiasm, and then if it went wrong his anger was terrible. She bit her lip and jogged on nearby him in the saddle; her thighs were chafed, and she would be glad when they saw the inn. Thank God no bandits had troubled them, even though the escort was no doubt strong enough to deal with an armed band. She did not turn her head to where Margaret rode, arms tight about the leather-clad back of the man who held the reins; best to show no interest which might lead to talk. Everyone thought, no doubt, that the veiled figure was a maidservant. They had not even stopped them at the postern of the south gate leading out of Mercatello.

Castello drew in sight at last, and Emilia drew a breath of pleasure; the city was fair, walled, turreted, and would have shops and palazzos and an inn. A river wound among the great buildings, visible below on the plain. Eager to show interest she turned to Parisio. 'What is the great river?' she asked, and he grunted; he himself was tired, and would be glad of a meal before all this was over.

'The Tiber,' he said, 'which goes on to Rome.'

In her place, Margaret heard him, and through her weariness and stiffness felt anticipation rise. A river which wound to Rome, where the Holy Father lived when there was peace! The sensation of space, of being out in the world, came to her after the time of dim unhappiness in the cellar, and it was as though she had drunk wine. They rode on, down the slope between thick trees overhanging the way. She could feel the sun on her face; it must be afternoon.

They stayed at the inn that night; after supper Parisio had gone out into the town to enquire for further details about Fra Giacomo's cures. He returned triumphant; it was common talk about Castello. 'I found a haberdasher whose nephew was cured of fits, and an old couple whose only child was healed of the itch. They say the lame have been made to walk, as I told you; there are crutches hung before the shrine in thanksgiving.'

'Well will go at first light,' said Emilia. 'Margaret, you must pray.'

It was difficult to enter the shrine; the way was crowded with people, and for an instant she felt as though she were naked, stared at by all. Emilia had taken the veil from her and thrust her forward; there was the smell and press of humanity, of acrid poor sweat, unwashed woollen cloth. She could not see them, but she could feel and know they were there; beggars, cripples, perhaps lepers, the maimed, the blind. She felt the warmth of the candle-flames on her face and limped forward to a place where she could pray. She found it, in a searing blaze of candles; and by it a Presence, sweet, familiar, and long unknown. She fell into an ecstasy; she forgot the people pressing on either side, her waiting parents, the hoped-for miracle, everything. Here was home, and she need go no further. She did not ask for anything more.

'She is still at prayer,' said Parisio. He had waited about with his wife outside the shrine; they had said something to Margaret about taking communion, but had not done so or been shriven; no doubt she herself would, in time. Gradually they began to look about them and in the end took themselves off among the streets of the town to exclaim at its many marvels. Parisio bought Emilia a necklace of silver and coral from a huckster near the river. She was as pleased as a child, and smiled confidently as they returned, her hand on Parisio's arm, the necklace glowing against her ageing throat and breast.

There were fewer folk outside the shrine when they returned. It was beginning to grow cold, with a wind blowing from the northern mountains. Emilia felt a sense of apprehension as she neared the shrine; would there have been a cure, would Margaret come out to them straight, strong and sighted? 'How will she know us when she sees us for the first time?' the woman thought. She did not ask Parisio concerning it. He left her and strode forward and stared among the thinning crowd to where the candles burned low in their sockets. Emilia, standing behind, could see nothing.

'What has happened?' she said anxiously. 'Is there a
cure? Is she –' She glanced up at his heavy face, this
presence which was her arbiter, without whom she
could seldom think or act. His lips sagged; there were
lines of disgust between nose and mouth. Parisio was
staring at his blind hunch-backed daughter, still praying
amid the candles.

He swung about, and dragged Emilia with him. 'Let
us go,' he said roughly. 'There is no cure. There never
will be.'

'But she –'

'The devil looks after his own. Her God may look
after her. We can do no more. Come, I say.'

He took her back to the inn. Once there he paid his
bill quickly, had the horses saddled and, his wife by him,
rode out by the north-east gate, the Porta San Egidio.
Emilia tossed in the saddle breathlessly, as though she
were running. The truth stabbed at her; they had left
the child behind, blind in a strange city. Her mind,
which always smoothed things over, began its task in
her. After all there had been other deformed ones
there, twisted runts, blind beggars, and limbless, the
insane; they would look to each other. Margaret was
better there than returned to the vaults at Mercatello,
where she had not been happy.

Emilia would not forget her daughter. Often, in the
dark hours of the night, for the rest of her life, she
would see that hunched kneeling figure among the
spent candles. But one must say nothing to Parisio;
nothing at all.

5

Margaret came to herself with stiffened limbs; she must have been kneeling for a long time. She had no means of telling the time of day, and the press of people seemed to have withdrawn, leaving her alone; where were her parents? She put out an arm, feeling tentatively about her; there was only the air, still warm with the spent candles. Everyone seemed to have gone.

There were footsteps, strange to her. 'Time to go,' came a man's voice. 'Time to close the door.' He came nearer, and stopped where she was. Had they all gone but herself?

The man peered at her. 'Time to go,' he repeated. He saw the pale shape of her face raised to him above the dreadful hump of the shoulder; she rose to her feet with an accustomed struggle, and he did not help her; cripples, he knew, liked to fend for themselves. Presently she spoke, in a gently bred voice; he gaped at her; this was a lady, who looked like a beggar, and a blind beggar at that; the eyes were filmed over as if with milk.

44

'Are my parents there?' she asked him. He grunted; there was some misunderstanding, not his business. 'You'll be able to find them outside,' he said, 'time to close in here.' She limped away from him towards the door, using her willow stick. The uneven footsteps sounded haltingly on the earth floor. He stood and watched her go, puzzled, and then locked the door.

She went out. The cool night air struck her face; she waited for moments, sniffing the air, searching for the particular scent of her parents; man's sweat, mail and leather for Parisio, flower-like essences for Emilia. There lingered a hundred alien scents from the crowd; but nobody was left here. They had all gone home. 'Home,' she repeated. Where was her home? In the place she had just left; the ecstasy of the experience was still with her.

She sat down on the steps; pointless to stand and wait, they would see her when they came. Where could they be? Had they lost themselves? She began to be troubled, and strained her hearing for a footstep, a presence, anyone to ask concerning it. Perhaps they had been set upon by thieves; such things happened. Somewhere, the body of horse waited; how could she find them to tell them, or had it already been done? For the first time Margaret felt herself helpless in an unknown city; there was nothing she could do but wait.

Waiting, the night grew gradually colder, the lamps in the houses extinguished, the inns themselves silent, the shops closed and shuttered. Margaret huddled in her cloak on the steps and prayed for her parents. It was the only way in which she could help them; and it was a good way. The saints would hear and act; soon, there would be an answer.

She drifted off to sleep; she was less accustomed to

cold stone than most. When she awoke it was to renewed stiffness, and a hand shaking her shoulder.

'Get away from our place, d'ye hear? Waiting to catch our alms, you are; we don't hold with it.' A smell of aged rags came; the speaker was a woman, possibly not very young; a beggar. Margaret spread out her hands. 'I have no money to give you,' she said gently; her wits were still clouded with sleep. She heard the other's laughter, a clear sound against the ugliness. 'Money?' the voice said. 'Who are you that you have money, sitting here on our step?' And, the beggar-woman thought, as the sexton had done, this is a lady. It was a queer coil. Her companion, a man with one leg, hauled himself towards the steps to listen; the two of them were always here early, to pick the cream of the worshippers at dawn Mass. To find someone else before them was unheard of; even the rest of the band were still asleep, curled up in their rags against one another for warmth in the places they found. Who was this?

She's blind, thought the woman, staring at Margaret as she struggled to her feet. And – my God, she was thinking, this is worse than the worst of us; the poor soul, with everything against her, and she seems not to know her way. 'Who is with you?' she asked suspiciously. 'Who brought you here?'

'My parents. We rode in from Mercatello. We stayed at an inn. Then they brought me here for the cure, but it has not happened. I do not know what has become of them. They must be still in the town. Will you help me find them? There is –' she smiled a little – 'money if you do. They have money.'

'You were staying at an inn. Which inn?'

'I do not know. It was near the gate.' The man had drawn closer and the pair stared at the girl; the lightening sky showed them her deformities. Yet she seemed content. The beggar-woman jerked her head at the beggar-man.

'Stay you here, Jacopo, and I will go with this lady to look for the inn.' He would collect the alms, and she the reward; it would be a good day. Also, one could still feel pity. She put her hand under the cripple's elbow, and guided her. 'Mind the steps,' she said, 'and afterwards the street is rough. *Dio!* Neither of us knows where we are going.'

The man watched them go, already crouched as he was into the position of a suppliant for alms. He saw the silhouettes of the two women grow smaller along the street. Some folk are as badly off as we, for all they have rank, he was thinking. He wondered how old the strange girl was. She was no taller than a child, but he thought her older from her very calmness; a child would have been found crying, there on the steps. And she had the face of an old woman.

If he had known, she was seventeen.

They reached the inn at last; by now it was late in the day, and Margaret had not eaten, nor the beggar-woman. 'Trust me for a soft bit,' the woman muttered, 'and missed the price of a day's crust, be sure of it, aiding the likes of you. We've walked far; is this the place?'

Margaret smiled with joy; her fingers had touched the doorway, and she remembered the shape of the lintel. 'I believe it is,' she said, 'and there will be more than a crust for you for aiding me. I will ask the innkeeper if they have been found, my parents; if not, I will tell him to search for them.'

'He'll do that, if he's to get his money.' The woman

stayed within sight; she wouldn't go, anyway, now, till she had seen this young lady claimed. There was something queer there. A sweet girl, a saint; one could tell from her talk. I won't leave her till she finds them, however it may turn out, the woman told herself.

But Margaret had already stumbled out of the inn, face white and drawn; there was anguish in her voice.

'It was the right inn,' she said steadily. 'They have gone. They paid their bill and mine yesterday and rode off by the Porta San Egidio. I am sorry; I promised you money, and now there is none. I will do anything else for you that I can.' The tears had begun to roll down her face; for once she was at a loss, even God seeming to have deserted her. Her own father and mother to abandon her! Yet it had happened.

'We must not blame them,' she said presently, weeping. 'I am as you see me, and all of my life they have had this burden. They hoped for a cure from Fra Giacomo and it did not come. Now I am alone.'

'Not a bit of it,' said the beggar-woman. She came to where Margaret stood and put an arm round her. 'You're one of us now, lady, with no one and nothing like we are. Me and my mate begs for a living, and you can do it as well; they'll give plenty when they see you as God put you together. Come with me and I'll show you a safe place to sleep tonight, though it isn't grand.' She began to guide the blind girl towards town, away from the inn and city gate. What sort of folk could have abandoned her? Noble or not, they must be the scum of the earth. 'You come with me, *cara*,' she said gently. 'It will all be for the best, never fear.'

Margaret tried to smile and blinked away her tears. I will pray for them, she thought, but I will never encounter them again, and I must not mention our name because they would not want it known. This is an angel that has been sent to me; God sends his angels so; I am not forsaken. I will do all I can to help her and others like her. None of us have anything of our own.

For moments it was as though a light shone in her. The woman, looking at her, was confused. How could anyone be so ugly, and yet so beautiful?

'Our Lord had nothing either,' said Margaret.

6

The beggars pervaded Castello. They thronged the streets, writhing their way past market-booths and horses, carts and litters, passers-by in long robes with feet shod high in pattens against the filth in the deep piled ways; against this false strutting height the beggars themselves seemed dwarfish, from another race; not that of well-found striding citizens, the wealthy, the tradespeople with their servants and apprentices laden behind and before. The beggars had all manner of ills, some real and some contrived; there were children with sores which were kept open, legless and armless men and women, the blind, the malformed, the monstrous. They lived from hand to mouth on what the passing crowds flung them, occasionally reaping a rich harvest if a nobleman rode by with largesse. They would be out earlier than anyone at the churches and doorways of palaces, closing in when a visitor alighted from a litter or a great lady emerged in silks and jewels from her door; they were rebuffed often, but not always, for it was against the Gospels' teaching to turn these people away with nothing. What they had they shared, in the underground places where they slept and fed; the disused cellars, the vaults, the sewers themselves; places beneath bridges, unguarded doorways, always to be left by dawn. They wore the rags they had always worn, adding to these in layers as some donor handed them cast-off clothing stained with sweat; wearing it out till it too was ragged and more could go on top. Warmth was life, and the nights were cold even in summer.

They did not starve, or despair too greatly. There were always one's friends, in the same state as oneself, who would share and share alike when it had been a bad day. If there were crusts, or the ends of a banquet the dogs would not eat, they shared, one with another; good fortune was for all, an empty belly to be helped in one's turn. They were a close company, deployed like soldiers to this place and that, with the foresight to vanish quickly should the watch come with fists and staves. They knew the town's lanes and corners better than any, the places to hide, the places to sleep without hindrance.

From the first they took Margaret as one of themselves. At the beginning they guided her on the new unfamiliar ways, wide as the sky to her who had been kept close all her life. There were places to stand and beg, or else make off quickly; they took it in turn to lead her down some twisting street, make her familiar with each doorway, each obstacle where she might stumble. They showed her the way to the freshets of water that gushed up on the way to the young Tiber, where she might slake her thirst and wash. They showed her their own chosen places where she might sleep. They also taught her to beg, though it was long before she would cry out as they did; she simply stood, hands extended, waiting, and when a coin was put into

her palm thanked the giver, and hid the money away to
share with the rest. She got to know each beggar by
name, knowing each footstep, the halting, the pattering,
the wounded, the slow; Gian and Giacomo and Lazzaro
and Elena and Maria and Annina, and the children;
babies born and dying because there was no milk; little
ones who had survived and clung to ragged skirts, thin
as skeletons. Margaret would baptise the dying babies
and beg for food and give it to the mothers, if she could;
she herself had lived on so little for years that she could
contrive with less food than they. She cheered the
hungry, the afflicted; soon they came to her when they
were in trouble. Even the taciturn with their scars who
had resented a stranger melted at last in face of her
undying cheerfulness. For she knew God was with her
again; He had not abandoned her. 'How do you keep
your heart high, Margaret?' they would say, looking at
her deformities.

'God loves us all.' At first they sneered to hear it;
could God love them and leave them as they were? But
gradually they perceived the truth through her, and
many found new faith. 'Let us suffer for Him,' she told
them, as the *cappellano* had told her long ago. She
herself was happy, with her God again and among
friends, as she had been at Metola. She was no longer
singular, to be hidden away as shameful. She was the
same as they were, destitute, with the means to live as
best one could. She begged for them rather than
herself; there were many piteous cases whom she
helped. She became known about the town. Her
deformities were seen, exclaimed on, and then
forgotten; she was the little blind dwarf who was always
cheerful and would creep into the back of the church
whenever there was Mass.

She had begun to make friends who were not beggars. If the pastrycook had leavings over from his dough, he would cook them and save them for Margaret; if the butcher had meat and bones he could no longer sell, he gave them to her for the beggars' broth. In such ways she was kept constantly busy, with little time to remember the past. Of what use to do that? There was much to be done here for the others, and she gloried in it. She was happier than she had ever been; she had her friends and she had the Sacrament, waiting whenever she climbed the church steps. There was nothing more to ask of life.

But the winter was coming and it was soon bitterly cold. Snow lay on the mountains, and in the mornings the very rubble in the streets would be rimed over with frost. On the night of the Feast of St Martin, Margaret slept in a doorway with the snow blown in from outside; the melting flakes soaked her clothes and thin flesh. She endured the cold as she had always done; but the night was still early when one of the beggars came seeking her. He was a diseased man whose eyes rolled up in his head as if he took fits; his limbs were growing paralysed, and he had footsteps she knew, tottering always. She was ready and smiling by the time he came, shaking the snow from his holed, filthy tunic. 'Greetings, Giacomo. Come in out of the snow.'

'It is too cold here,' he said. 'You cannot spend the night so. There is a better place, a stable where I will take you. Some of the others are there. The owner, Piero the carpenter, says we may use it. Come quickly, before the storm grows worse.'

'A stable,' she said wonderingly. He turned his ravaged face to her, mistaking her meaning. 'Oh, we all know you're a lady,' he said. 'But there are worse places. The dung in the straw keeps it warm.'

'I will come gladly. God's Son was born in a stable, on such a night.'

'Maybe,' he said, and stumped off, leading her. The place was not far away, Inside she knew the others waited, huddled in the straw. A great joy was with her; Our Lady, coming in out of the winter weather, would have felt so at the journey's end; would have smelled the good straw, felt the beasts' warmth, their gentle breath. She went to the place they showed her and lay down there. 'You are soaking, Margaret,' said one. 'Let me wring your clothes.'

'Do not trouble; I am warm and happy.'

'You are always happy; tell us your secret.' She could feel the others listening who were not asleep, and smiled. 'You know it already,' she said. 'On such a night, in a place like this, God was born. The good St Joseph had found a place for them, for God and His Mother. It is as though it were happening again. God is always with us. He loves us every one.'

'You are always saying it. Perhaps it is true.'

'He said not even a sparrow falls to the ground without God's knowledge. Of course it is true. Has He not preserved us?'

'The carpenter has preserved us, for this night only.'

'Ah, we have all sinned,' cried another. 'But the rich sin more than we.'

'No, but it is easier for the rich to sin. We are fortunate. But God loves us all, rich and poor. Repent of your sins and take them to the priest, then it will be as though the Tiber water has washed your soul. I know it; it has happened to me also.'

'You say you have sinned, Margaret? But you are always full of charity. You envy no one; you are kind to all. It was a glad day when you came among us.' The diseased man looked about him and for the first time, looking at her filmed blind eyes, thanked God for his sight. Yet she seemed to see what others could not. He crossed himself.

'If it will bring me a tenth of your joy, then I repent,' he said. But she shook her head, smiling. 'You must not repent with any thought of reward,' she said. 'You must do it for the love of God.'

'For God's love, then, let us get some sleep,' called a voice. 'It will be slippery out on the roads by morning; none but ourselves will venture.'

They fell silent, and mostly slept. Margaret lay awake, thinking of the birth at Bethlehem. She felt her happiness pervade her like a glow. By strange ways she had come to these people, who had been kinder than her own. She had friends and a night's shelter. It was better by far than the lonely vault at Mercatello, but even there the servant had been kind. Now Our Lady, St Joseph, and the Child were nearby, as it had been in that other stable long ago. The warmth rose from the straw, and in their places the carpenter's draught-horses stirred comfortably. It was all as it had been long since, and the shepherds and the kings were here in the guise of poor folk. She would remember it always, the carpenter's stable on the night of the snow.

She slept.

7

'Babbo, I want the scarlet gown.'

It was spring again, Mercati the merchant laughed, surveying his pretty little daughter as she moved among the baled stuffs displayed on the booths. 'You want it because it is the most expensive, my Ceccha,' he murmured, 'and thus show yourself to be your father's daughter.'

'And a spoiled little girl,' said her mother Ysachina warningly, but nobody took any notice; Ceccha's wishes were always law. She smiled, pouting her red lips and fingering her red-gold hair; she knew she was pretty and pleased her father, and that he would delight to see her in a scarlet gown when it was made up for next winter.

'I want it because of the worm that lives in the oak-tree that makes the dye,' she said. 'That is why it is expensive.'

'So! And who told you about the worm, child?'

'Domenico.' The parents exchanged glances and smiled. It suited them very well that friendship should

grow between their daughter and the young nephew of
an Easterling merchant, a near neighbour with a
widowed mother, If the young people were to grow up
and marry, Domenico would be away for a great part of
the year on his travels to the north, and Ceccha could
stay with her parents.

They bought three ells of the scarlet cloth, and budge
to line it for the winter; then they looked round the
booths for something to suit Ysachina, for her husband
doted on her as much as on his daughter, minding not
at all that they had no son. They were so happy that
their house, which they shared with cousins, was known
as the House of Peace; and presently, handing their
purchases to the servant, they went back to it.

Margaret had one advantage; she could find her way in
the dark. In winter, this came early, and alone among
the stumbling and lost she could find her way nightly
back from church, or from tending the sick, to wherever
she desired to sleep. One night there had been heavy
rain and the streets swirled with water. She lifted her
skirts with her free hand to keep them from getting
sodden; with the other her stick guided her into the
deserted back ways. A little distance on, it struck soft
matter, which might have been the garbage in the road;
but there came the sound of a groan. She knelt, and felt
for the man's face; it proved to be almost under water,
and he was lying prone; at first she thought he was a
drunkard, but there was no smell of wine. His clothes
were of thick, good stuff; she discovered that he had a
tall broad person, his hands soft and tended. As she felt
him carefully for signs of wounding or broken bones, he
groaned again; she had already dragged him a little way
out of the water, and was kneeling by him now with his

head on her lap, allowing him to breathe and recover consciousness.

'Where ... what ... I was set upon. Where is my purse? Who are you, a beggar?' Awaking, he could tell the thin rags she wore, the thin bones beneath.

'Have no fear, I shall not harm you,' she answered gently. 'Tell me where you live and I will guide you home. It is dark, but I am blind. We can find the way, if you will walk.'

He sat up presently, still groaning, and put his hands to his head. 'My purse,' he said again. 'Whoever they were they have taken it. What is your name? I have to thank you for stopping, like the Good Samaritan.' His voice was pleasant and cultured, like the voices of her parents at Metola.

'My name is Margaret. You must tell the authorities about your purse. It may be that the thieves have not left the city, because of the guard at the gates.'

'I know that well enough,' he said ruefully. 'I was making for Bologna.'

'You cannot ride in your state.'

'No, I must go back home ... to my mother ... she is old and will be distressed. They set upon me when I had gone out to hire a horse for the morning; they knew I had money for that. Since then I have lain here, evidently. Not many pass this way. I am thankful you did.'

She was helping him, assisting him to stagger up on uncertain legs, taking his weight. In course of it his hand touched her humped shoulder.

'You, you are not strong,' he said courteously. 'It should not be for you to support me. Have I not seen you about the city, Margaret? You beg outside the churches.'

'I beg where I can, and give where I can. Steady yourself and we will go slowly.'

'I cannot see; it is too dark. I live near the church of San Francesco. I had best perhaps wait till daylight, and then summon help.'

'You have it,' she said cheerfully. 'I know the city well. When we come to the river, there will be light for you to see.'

'How do you know that, if you are blind?' He tried to maintain his own weight; he still felt that he was dragging at her. When they came to the place where some houses were still lamplit his face could be seen by anyone, handsome but badly swollen about the eye; he might have been thirty-five. His hair was shorn, and he had worn a pointed cap which had been lost in the scuffle. Several times he had to lean against a wall, to regain his senses; they were still dizzy. When he could he looked at the girl who had rescued him. How tiny she was! Yet she had been about the streets at this hour, alone and not afraid. He mentioned it to her and she laughed.

'I have no money to take,' she said, 'and nobody would attack me. They all know me. Even you did so, messere.'

'My name is Orlando,' he said. 'I teach law in Bologna.'

'You must be clever and wise, Messer Orlando. I hope that better fortune goes with you on your journey.'

'I trust it may do so; I cannot wait beyond tomorrow.' As he answered he marvelled; she spoke as a gentlewoman, he thought. What was her history? When he could, he would find out; and help her as she had helped him, if the chance came to do so.

They found his mother's door, and Margaret waited

with him while the servant was alerted. She would not come in, and melted off into the night; he regretted her going so quickly; he would have hesitated to give her money, but she might have had a hot meal, some broth, a place by the fire which still glowed in the hearth. But the night had swallowed her, and tomorrow he must ride to Bologna.

8

Not far off there lived a pastrycook, and he had a
widowed sister-in-law who had been left with a large
family of young children and also an orphan, Annina,
whom she had adopted. As she had nowhere to go the
man permitted her to live in the lower part of his house.
Space was very crowded there and the poor mother had
to work for her keep; she used to roll out the pastry and
clean the vessels afterwards with water and ash; any
time she had left over she would use in laundering for
the rich, who paid her something. Annina was a help
here as her little brown plump hands were magic with
an iron. The flat-iron stood beside the baking-oven and
they would use the wooden table at which they all sat for
meals. That had done well enough while the children
were too young to be troublesome, but now the elder
ones were becoming restive and demanding lives of
their own, and one day the second girl burned a
chemise belonging to the wife of the *podestà*. This was a
catastrophe; the widow would have to pay for it. She
burst into tears, and made so much commotion that the

pastrycook's wife came downstairs, frowning.

'What is the matter?' she asked. 'There is no peace in the house nowadays. We can hear every sound you make upstairs. If you cannot be silent, you will have to go.' She spoke so because she had married, as she thought, beneath her, and despised her husband's family. Her sister-in-law's sobbing grew louder.

'How can you be so cruel! You know nothing of trouble. I must pay for this ruin, and where am I to find the money? All I make goes on the children's food and clothing. And who is to say the same thing will not happen again?'

'You should have given the chemise to me, *mammina*,' said the little brown orphan. 'I would not have burnt it.' The widow fetched her a box on the ear.

'Do not fancy yourself too much, you make mistakes the same as everyone else, Annina!' The original culprit crouched in a corner, her face bleared; she had been beaten, but what good was it? 'I am tired, so tired,' wailed the widow. 'Sometimes I feel it would be better if I were dead and they could all fend for themselves.'

The grubby children crept back to her skirts, and the pastrycook's wife turned up her nose; then she had a notion. It would not do, she knew, for all these children to get out of hand, causing more accidents and mischief: and her husband would not see them put out on the street.

'Why do you not take in a girl to help?' she demanded. 'No, there is no need to pay her; plenty of beggars without a home would mind the children gladly for a roof over their head and a bite of food. You would find it worth your while for the time it gave you to get on with your work; you could make more money.'

'Who wants a filthy beggar about the place? Their

stench is enough to sicken one.' The pastrycook's
sister-in-law had known better days.

'You can insist that she wash,' said the pastrycook's
wife. 'There is one girl who comes here for scraps from
my goodman, and she seems gentle and practical; but
she is blind.'

'What use is that? She won't see where the little devils
hide themselves.'

The pastrycook had come down, shorn of his linen
apron. 'What is to do? Is it Margaret you speak of? She
can find anything; she does not need eyes. The other
day I dropped a ladle and it rolled I could not find
where, but Margaret found it when she came in; it was
behind the rolling-board. The blind have an extra
sense. If you want help, sister, try her for a little while.
She will not ask for money.'

So, for a time, Margaret was given a roof over her
head in the lower part of the pastrycook's. It was not
comfortable, being something like the vault at Mercatello, but smaller; she slept on the floor along with the
poor widow and children, near the warmth of the oven.
The children loved her and after the first day, when she
told them a story, flocked to her; their mother had
never had time for them and it was wonderful to have
this tiny person, no bigger than they were, devote all her
time to them, except when she said her prayers. Even
that was understandable; she had told them about St
Joseph, and how kind he was, and how he answered
prayer. 'When Our Lady was left without a protector he
looked after her and the Holy Child. He will look after
you also if you ask him. You must pray to him for your
poor mother, that she may find help, perhaps money.'

She herself was a help to the widow and besides
minding the children, would limp back and forth with

the iron for re-heating on the stove in the bakehouse, and help the woman fold the linen sheets and smocks when they were done; her fingers were so sensitive that they did not wrinkle the delicate stuffs or drop anything on the earth floor, so that it would need washing all over again. After she had been in the place a week the widow smiled suddenly.

'I am like a different person since you came to us, Margaret. I even manage to love my children again now they are not constantly underfoot. I only wish I could reward you with money, but I cannot.'

'I do not need money,' said Margaret, who loved the children herself and knew each one by his or her footsteps, voice, and ways. 'I am happy with you, Monna Marianna. But soon you will no longer need me.'

Soon this came true, for a relative of Marianna's died and left her a share in a farm in Tuscany. There was great rejoicing when the news was known.

'Think of the grape harvest!' said the eldest, and another said, 'You must come with us, Margaret. There is always enough to eat on a farm, milk and goat's cheese and chickens and eggs.' But Margaret shook her head, smiling.

'My place is in Castello,' was all she would say, though the widow herself pressed her to come with them. 'You are like Annina,' they told her. 'She says she will not come with us either, but will stay in the town.'

Annina herself came and stood before Margaret where she sat among the children. Margaret could not see the deep blush that suffused the girl's face.

'Margaret, will you do me a very special favour?'

'Anything I can, my dear.' She was fond of Annina, who was obliging and ready with her fingers to mend or iron. The girl bent her head and began to pleat her skirt.

'You are friends with the mother of Professor Orlando. Everyone knows how you saved him when he was set on by thieves. She will do anything you ask.'

'I did not save him, alas, only found him afterwards, when by God's mercy he was saved. But in what way can his mother help you, Annina?'

'By putting in a word for me to Monna Annunziata, who is looking for a laundry-maid. I would iron her son Messer Domenico's shirts like a dream, none better.'

Margaret was too unwordly to sense an ulterior motive behind Annina's desire. She knew the girl was good at laundry-work, and accordingly hastened to speak for her to the Professor's mother, who greeted her as always with pleasure, rising from her loom.

'Margaret! My dear! What can I do for you today?'

She was a woman in her fifties, who was still beautiful, with a fine-boned face; she belonged to an old Ghibelline family. She set her work aside and came to greet Margaret, robes hushing. Margaret, smiling, told her of the little maid. Orlando's mother frowned. 'You say she is an orphan?' she enquired. 'Monna Annunziata is a strict mistress; she beats her maids often.'

'Annina is used to blows. But I do not think she will earn many. She is good at her work, and diligent.'

'If you recommend her, I will mention it, certainly. Now let me give you wine.'

The family went and Margaret bade them farewell sadly, but by then the news of her usefulness had spread through the town and there was another offer of shelter, and another. She still kept in touch with her friends the beggars and managed often to give them scraps of food she did not eat, and sometimes clothing. But there was not so much of either to be spared despite her own continued fasting; the families she worked for were poor.

She loved her work, but would have liked a place to be quiet and alone in sometimes; the cell at Metola had given her a need for solitude and peace. Often when the inmates of whatever house she worked in were asleep round her, she would lie awake, despite the fact that she was tired with the day's work, and listen to God in the silence. He gave her strength for the new day; she would devise games for the children she minded, little tasks with which she could help them; she entered easily into their minds, having herself a great simplicity. Often when the adults in the house would spurn or shun a child and it came crying to her, she would whisper the word of Our Lord and his love for children. 'And unless you have the heart of a little child you will not enter the kingdom of heaven. God loves children as He loves fools. Neither were ever reproached by Him.'

'Are you a fool, Margherita?'

'Maybe, maybe.' She was always good-natured with them; she loved their company. Gradually she had learned ordinary household tasks, like preparing vegetables, washing plates, tending the stewpots as they steamed on the fire, gauging the heat with her fingers and finding the long metal spoon for stirring. Sometimes, too, a child was sick, and she would wrap and carry it carefully away from the rest and tend it, feeding it milk or wine and feeling its forehead for abating of the fever; but many children died, and then she would kneel and pray with the others for its departed soul, feeling as much sorrow as if it had been her own. Every priest in town knew her, visiting as they did with the Viaticum, or meeting the blind girl with children clustered about her on the church steps as she assembled them all for Mass. When she could, she would go alone to this, early while the households were still asleep. All Castello knew her and spoke well of her; it was known that the lawyer Orlando and his mother were her friends, and any house she had been in had a lightening of its troubles, its quarrels. The pastrycook's wife was less proud nowadays, and used her husband kindly; others had ceased carping and complaining, suspecting their partners, beating their wives. It was as though everywhere she went the blind cripple sowed seeds of peace and kindliness; yet she said little, only speaking when addressed, and then cheerfully. If any asked the reason for her cheer, the answer was the same.

'God loves us.'

9

Ceccha, Mercati's daughter, sat at a small table, with her newly affianced Domenico seated opposite; he was teaching her chess, and the intricately carved red and ivory set had come from the north and was a betrothal-gift. Mercati and his wife Ysachina looked on from their fireside, well pleased. The young couple made a handsome picture; Ceccha's scarlet gown, no longer new, flattered her figure which had grown pert little breasts; her red-gold hair hung down beneath a gold fillet. Domenico himself, only son of a doting mother, was remarkably handsome, pale and black-haired, with the blunt agreeable features of a boy; his body was tall and slim and his hands sensitive. He moved the chessmen knowledgeably, instructing the young girl in a gentle voice about the various moves. He had been well educated by his uncle, the Easterling merchant, who saw to it that the things of this world were made known to Domenico and that he would have every opportunity of bettering himself. Yet the boy was not conceited with it all: he had a natural and pleasing air and modest manners.

Ysachina regarded him with open pleasure; it had been a favourable opportunity to acquire such a bridegroom for their daughter. 'How beautifully your shirt is laundered, Domenico,' she remarked, her eyes on the manifold tucks and embroidery in the snowy linen at the boy's throat. 'Ceccha will have to learn a good deal before she can do as well as that.'

Domenico smiled pleasantly. 'We have a little orphan maid, Annina, who pleases my mother greatly by the way she irons and mends linen,' he told them. Ceccha laughed. 'We had better take the orphan into our household,' she said, 'and then I will not need to learn to iron at all.'

'Why, for shame!' said Mercati. 'Every wife strives to do the best she can for her husband; your mother does so for me,' and he fingered his own rich linen; yet it was not finished as superbly as Domenico's, and they both knew it. He had not been altogether pleased by Ceccha's response; she must learn to appreciate her future husband. After their meal, when Domenico had gone back to his mother's house, he would speak to his daughter, and reprove her. But in the meantime they talked about the journey Domenico would shortly make with his uncle to Antwerp, to see the warehouse there. It was an opportunity for the young man to make his way in the world, and the Mercati approved of it; also, it meant they need not part with Ceccha for a while, for they loved her dearly and she was like a light in their house.

It so happened that the next day, Domenico was out riding in the town and when he dismounted, pulled a thread of his tunic sleeve on the housing of the horse's apparel. He looked at it ruefully, for the tunic was of new green stuff and his mother had woven it especially for him to wear for the long journey to Antwerp. Then he bethought him of the little maid Annina, who could sew and mend. When he reached the house he took it straight to her; she was making his bed, shaking out the feather mattresses and pillows so that dust rose in the room. He looked at her with pleasure; she reminded him of a little brown plump quail, and her eyes were bright and dark like a bird's; her curly hair had been shorn close to her head to keep the lice from it. She was full of work and energy, but stopped and smiled when she saw him. 'You are home early, master,' she said. He showed her the torn sleeve.

'Never fear,' said Annina, 'I will go and get a needle, and put it right; it will not show when I've finished with it.' And she returned with the needle, made Domenico take off his tunic and hand it to her, and herself sat down in the only chair, so that he mounted the *predella* and went and lay on his bed in his shirt and trunks. While he did this he talked to her, watching her handstitch the torn cloth. When she had finished it was as good as new, but by that time he had launched into a story.

'You asked me about the journey I am to make,' he said. She raised mournful eyes; how empty and dark the house would be while he was away! 'It is the old journey that my ancestors used to undertake along the trade rivers, when they would trap beaver and sell the skins for hats, and later sweep the dust from the bottom of the barge to make into felt, for even that was valuable. Afterwards they traded in other things than beaver, but that was the beginning.'

'Nobody has ever talked to me like that before,' said

Annina. 'I love to listen to you, Messer Domenico.' She loved to look at him too, he was so handsome; wasted on that little cat of a Ceccha. If she herself had her way she would disguise herself as a page and go to Antwerp with him, or anywhere else in the world provided he asked her. Meantime, she listened; and nothing loath, Domenico talked on.

Next time he saw Annina there was a bruise on her arm; when he asked her what had happened she lowered her eyes. 'Your lady mother beat me for idleness while I listened to you,' she told him. He was horrified. 'But you were not idle, you were mending my coat!'

'Do not say anything about it,' she begged. 'It will only make more trouble, and I do not mind being beaten if I can listen to you.'

But Domenico went to his mother, very angry, and told her never to lay hands on Annina again. Monna Annunziata was thunderstruck: a woman to be instructed never to beat her maids! Domenico had never spoken to her before in such a way, and she was made to realise for the first time that beneath his gentle temper lurked a ring of steel. 'I mean it, mother,' he said. 'I am master in this house now, and I give the orders; pray heed them.'

She had to do so, accordingly, for the time; but she bided her own. Soon he would be gone to Antwerp, and after that she would put the little minx in her place; not that the girl was anything but a good linen-maid. Meantime, her neighbour Professor Orlando's mother had a new plan for the blind cripple Margaret; she ought to be accepted into the convent, and the Prioress had been informed that they would visit her and tell her more.

*

'But who were her parents? Our postulants here are as a rule well-born.'

Monna Annunziata glanced briefly at the mother of Orlando, who as the older of the two visitors spoke first, setting down the little almond cake at which she had been nibbling though her teeth at her age were sparse. Wine-cups sat on the board which divided them, the outsiders, from the Prioress of St Margaret's Convent and her subordinate, who sat regarding them, not partaking. The room in which they all sat was small but elegant; it had folding chairs and the walls were hung with tapestries, some of them secular. Nevertheless on one wall was a silver crucifix.

The Prioress moved her plump hand, staring at her rings. She was uncertain about accepting this young woman they spoke of whose life, so many reliable witnesses had already told her, was exemplary and holy. In fact, the life in the Benedictine convent was no longer either; a fact one could hardly set forth in front of these formidably determined ladies. The lawyer's mother had begun to speak.

'She brings blessings with her. My son thinks very highly of her. I myself have not had her in my house except on brief visits, but madonna here will tell you, for Margaret lived below her for a little while, that by the time the girl left troubles had calmed themselves and good fortune come to those who had given her refuge.'

'We felt,' then explained the pastrycook's wife, 'that she should be with you in the shelter of the convent, with peace to pray when she will and no more need to look about her to know where she will sleep.'

'She may bring great benefits to yourselves in the way of pilgrims and visitors, who already flock to see her in the town,' put in Orlando's mother eagerly. 'Think how

Castello has benefited from the shrine of Fra Giacomo! And here you have a devout young woman who is still alive, who has many years, we hope, before her, and – is it not extraordinary? – bears the same name as your royal patroness. You ask about her family's name; but she will never reveal it. We think they were of the aristocracy, for her manners show this. Whoever they were they abandoned her. I think they need not trouble you.'

'But a dowry? She could bring none.'

Both women smiled. 'Those who came here to make their submissions would surely leave enough silver to compensate for such a lack. And Margaret is useful and active; she can do many household tasks.'

'Then I will see her.'

As the two women left they heard the sound of raucous laughter coming from one of the upper rooms. Both checked their steps; it was not a sound which should have been heard in a convent of holy women. The laughter rang out and then stopped abruptly, as if a hand had been laid over the perpetrator's mouth. They looked at one another, then went on; it had perhaps been a deranged serving-woman. By the time they had reached town their minds were full of the news to tell Margaret herself, and they had forgotten, or glossed over, the ugly sound. Would it not be by far the best thing for her to enter the convent? No more crowded unsavoury nights, no more begging, only prayer and the ordained life! She would hasten to it if she knew what was good for her.

Behind them, the Prioress had already forgotten about the crippled woman's coming interview. She sat for a while looking out at the river and thinking, as she often did, how conveniently the convent was placed, near the Santa Maria gate where they could always be sure of the pick of choice melons and pumpkins from the south, brought in on the weekly market-carts. It was a pleasant life, not too demanding; on the face of it they adhered to the Rule of an ascetic saint who had lived long ago on a mountainside, but everyone knew that that could be adapted, nowadays and for women, by whatever bishop happened to be in charge of the diocese; and this bishop liked to drink the convent wine.

Domenico was making his way home on foot from the Mercati house, and found himself a trifle flown with wine; they had had dinner with the Offrenducci cousins, who had made a night of it, and the young man's footsteps were uncertain now along the rough way; but the sight of the flickering torch at his own door cheered him. He went in, glad to be home; as always nowadays he had not felt at home with Ceccha, who was inclined to giggle at the sallies of her young cousin, who would have liked to marry her except that the Mercati parents had preferred himself. He, accordingly, was considered unpopular and too dull; the Offrenducci boy had made loud sallies and told rough stories, at which everyone burst out laughing except Domenico. Nobody, therefore, would think of listening to any of his own tales, as Annina did constantly nowadays at home; he did not know what he would do without the presence of her cropped curly head, bent over her mending, and her slow smile that meant she was listening as Ceccha would never do. He knew that he must marry Ceccha, as their families had arranged it; but how much more comfortable he felt with Annina, and how he wished that she belonged to his own class, with a family who would have made arrangements for her to have a dowry!

He stumbled into the hall; his mother, he remembered, was away for two nights, visiting a sick old relative on the other side of town. He pulled off his cap and coat; a servant took them. 'Bring me wine to my room,' said Domenico thickly, knowing he had already had quite enough; but it aroused the need for more.

Annina was waiting, as he had known she would be. The bed was turned down and he suddenly felt a longing for it. 'Was it a good evening?' asked Annina softly. She was wearing a stuff gown he had not seen before, perhaps new; it outlined her plump little breasts and her arms and waist. He reached out for her suddenly and she came to him.

'Not so very good an evening, *cara*,' he told her. 'I needed you to listen to me.'

'I am here now,' she said softly. Her nearness warmed him after the walk he had had through the cold night; he could smell the woollen stuff of her gown, sense the flesh beneath; it smelled of soap and cleanliness. She slid her arms about his neck; the gesture was entirely warm and natural.

'I love you so much, Domenico,' she said quietly. 'Let me show you how much I love you; here, in your bed.'

The glow came and pervaded him: they lay together. Afterwards they stood and watched the flicker of the torch die out below the window with the coming of dawn. A figure limped past in fluttering rags; it was the blind woman Margaret, making for the convent, her bundle of belongings below her arm. 'Poor soul, she cannot love as we do,' said Annina. And they turned to one another

again, as though the night were not long enough to
show their love.

'And so, my dear daughter, we will welcome you as a
postulant among us. I have no doubt your humility will
bring us many blessings.'

Margaret knelt, hearing the Prioress's languid voice
as if in a dream; was it indeed possible that she, humble,
deformed, blind, ignorant as she was, should be
accepted as a holy nun? 'I will do my best to be worthy,'
she breathed, almost overcome with awe and with a
strange excitement; it would be, a little, like her
mountain cell, always with God, yet also with a
sisterhood who prayed as she did, who lived as she
would try to live. How fortunate she was! God had been
cut off from her at Mercatello, in the lonely vault; now
he was everywhere; she had already been led to the
great crucifix which hung in the parlour and had kissed
the nailed silver feet.

All this was commendable; the Prioress smiled and
extended her hand, and then, remembering that this
extraordinary creature was blind as well, said mean-
ingfully, 'You may kiss my hand, Margaret; how
pleasant that you are named for our royal patron! Saint
Margaret of Scotland was a most revered queen.'

Margaret came to where the smooth idle fingers lay
and kissed them; as she did so a shock of bewilderment
shot through her. Surely a nun did not wear rings with
jewelled settings? The only ring should be the gold
wedding-ring to Christ. But it would not do to ask. She
knelt on, as the Prioress had not bidden her rise; shortly
a silver bell rang to summon the Mistress of Novices.
This was the personage who would instruct Margaret,
blind as she was, in the psalms, the writings of the holy

fathers, the Rule itself. Joy lit Margaret's face; she followed the Mistress at last out into the scrubbed passage,
alert for the scent of the life lived in these holy surround-
ings. She smelled beeswax, incense, linen laid in laven-
der, wine. She promised herself that she would learn to
scrub and clean the holy place, listen to everything they
might tell her; she was avid to learn. The Mistress murmured constantly, close by her side; but already Margaret knew she could find the way alone. There was the
chapel, where she knelt in thanksgiving; later she was led
down further passages to the dorter. How blessed to have
one's own pallet again, after the crowded places she had
been in! Nevertheless the folk in them had loved her, and
she them; it had been hard to part, but now she could
pray for them all. 'How fortunate I am,' she said aloud.
The Mistress of Novices looked down from her tall
height; here was another of them, she was thinking, full
of early fervour. It soon wore off in easy company.
However this creature would be willing to help in the
kitchens, and that was a mercy; most of the sisters considered themselves too well-born.

The light from the refectory window was warm on
Margaret's face. Here they would all eat, after grace, in
silence, listening to a reading from the fathers. She said
something of it to the Mistress, who shrugged unseen.

'Sometimes that is still done,' she said, 'but there are
always those who would rather talk than listen.'

'But the Rule says "In much speaking thou shalt not
escape sin".' The blind face was aware and puzzled.

'You do not know the Rule yet. Wait till you are taught
our ways before commenting on them.'

Perhaps the trouble had started then; or perhaps it began
when Margaret, set to work in the kitchens, first smelled

the good smell of roasting meat. Had not the flesh of four-footed animals been forbidden, and had not they spoken of it only yesterday in her hour with the Mistress of Novices? She was still exalted with the rapid broadening of her knowledge; her mind was filled with the beauty of the psalms which she learned quickly by heart, almost at the first hearing; and with the humility of the saints, in particular Thomas Aquinas who had made everyone believe he was stupid when he was not, so that the credit should not make him puffed up. And there was St Joseph to whom she never failed to pray, or he to answer. She would reflect on all these while she carried out the tasks that were given her, scrubbing the long passages, preparing vegetables brought in from the garden, washing plates and scraping the leavings into a bucket for the swine. The beggars she had known would have been glad of such leavings; but she had already curbed her own talk. She longed to be as the others; her swift grasp of direction helped her to do everything the sisters did, and more; she gloried in following every aspect of the Rule, being first in at Prime, last out at Vespers; denying herself always for the glory of God, careless if her portion of food at collation should have been taken, leaving her with the scrapings of the dish. All her life she had fasted and it was no great trial to continue with it now. At first she did not realise that she was being whispered about. Only, one day, with her sensitive ear, as she cleaned a window, she heard two of the sisters talking.

'That blind cripple does penance constantly. It makes the rest of us look foolish.'

'She is supposed to bring pilgrims to the convent. At first they came, it is true; but now they have fallen off.'

'It is the way of the world.'

'Well, we deserve our respite also. All she does is create a nuisance and show us up by her silences and her discipline; we were happy enough before she came, doing as we would.'

'There is no need to copy her.'

'No, but she is into everything. Sister Assunta was basting lamb, and the cripple came up and told her it was forbidden, and when the time came to eat it with us all she pushed away her plate and would eat nothing but bread. Are we never to enjoy our food because Margaret is so holy?'

'Wait till Lent; she will excel all of us then, with her mortifications and penances. Perhaps she will finish herself off. She is nothing but a bag of bones, and coughs often.'

Margaret drew away from the window, tears in her eyes. She had not meant to offend; but what could she do other than live as the Rule said? If one did not, one should not be a nun. She pondered over it, and could find no solution; in the midst of this thought, Lent came, with its penances.

10

On the day before Ash Wednesday, Margaret stood with the rest outside the Prioress's door with her list of mortifications. She would scourge herself, take no meat and no fish, only bread and water, between now and Easter; but that was customary with her. She craved to be given further penance. She had waited already an hour, but it was not her turn yet and the door did not open. A sound of laughter came from inside; should that be so, at such a time? Death lay at delight's door, the Founder had written. She bowed her head and prayed, and a voice from the passage taunted her. It was one of the idle sisters who took pleasure in teasing Margaret and ridiculing her in all things. 'Well, dwarf, what do you here? Is not your very existence a penance? What more would you?' And the unseen hands laid hold on her and spun her round, so that her head reeled and she fell against the passage wall. The others laughed.

'What does she here?' they asked again. 'Does she think our Reverend Mother has leisure to take to do with her, a beggar? Some here are of the blood of princes.'

'So was not God's Son, but born in a stable, of poor folk.' She had her answers always, gentle enough, but they made the rest angry. The nun who had spoken flounced off, and presently one came out and said, 'Do you suppose Mother Prioress has all day to waste? Her door is closed now; the Bishop is with her.'

'But tomorrow is Ash Wednesday, and I would give her my deeds for Lent. The Rule says we must not embark on our list without permission from the Superior.'

'The Rule says, always the Rule says! Hark at the wise woman who has never read a book! Know you not that rules were made to be bent, little hunchback? Think of your own spine, and go back where you came from and leave us be. Who thinks nowadays of penance, getting up at dawn to draw blood, except yourself? You disturb all of us from a comfortable night's sleep.'

'She thinks she is better than any of us, this beggar,' came another voice. 'Let her go back to the world she came from, and leave us be.'

'I beg your pardon,' said Margaret. 'I had not meant to offend.' She was near tears; why did they use her so? She only wanted, more than anything on earth, to come close to the saints, and find God. Surely a convent was the place to do it. But when she tried, her sisters were angry with her. She stretched out a hand from where she stood, hoping that someone would take it; the other still grasped her willow cane. None took her out-stretched hand. 'It says in the Rule that we must not touch each other,' mocked a voice.

'I am sorry.' She drew away, knowing that perhaps she acted wrongly as so many seemed opposed to it; and yet the blessed Benedict, the blessed Jerome, the blessed Thomas, had all said the same thing; one must mortify

the flesh to be pleasing to God. These women here
played the lute for their diversion, tunes that they had
heard from the town; they entertained male friends; they
feasted on fast days. It could not be right, but she herself
was the least among them and could not say so constantly.
She felt the Mistress of Novices brush by, and waited to
see if there would be any word about penances; inside the
room, the Prioress drank with the Bishop. The former
looked up peevishly; they had been in the midst of a very
good story, and now the point was lost. 'What is it?' she
asked sharply. The Mistress, who had no illusions, stared
at her superior coolly, noting the half-empty cup.

'Only the little Margaret, waiting with her list of
penances,' she murmured. 'The rest can wait.'

The Bishop, who as usual was enjoying his wine,
smiled affably. 'The little novice,' he murmured. 'How
fares she? Are they kind to her? Much good is still spoken
of her in the town; the *podestà* asked about her only the
other day.'

Then I would he'd come here, and bring his silver,
thought the Prioress. She made a sign to the Mistress to
go. 'Tell her they are acceptable,' she said of the
penances, which she had not heard. 'Sister Margaret will
take to heart our drinking wine together on the last day
before Lent, Bishop,' she said roguishly. 'She is strict with
herself and others.'

'Well, well, we have till tomorrow,' said the Bishop
comfortably, and held out his cup for more wine. Outside, the cripple's halting footsteps had dragged away.

It was recreation, and through the long room echoed the
sounds of talk and laughter. Margaret sat in her place,
answering quietly when spoken to; her fingers moved
over her rosary beads. As she told them, a nearby sister

quizzed her.

'This is the hour for relaxation; you need not pray all the time.'

Margaret smiled. 'I must do something. The Rule says idleness is the enemy of the soul. I cannot read or sew as you do. If I am given a task I can carry out I will do so gladly, but when there are none I say my rosary.'

She continued the decades; the fingers faltered for only a moment, as though aware of the shrug her neighbour gave. In fact, no one was sewing or reading; they were gossiping, as they usually did. Two were discussing Margaret.

'She prates constantly about the Rule; it becomes tedious to listen to her.'

'She is up early in the morning for Prime when the rest of us would lie abed. Nobody now takes the good Founder's words as uttered; times have changed, we are in the fourteenth century.'

The nun who had been sitting by Margaret made an excuse and moved away, her head joining the others like a cluster of magpies, chattering. The blind woman continued to tell her beads, taking comfort in them. But she was not as happy as when she had first come.

'I have sent for you to tell you that your keeping of the Rule is excessive. The others are made uncomfortable by your insistence on things, observances no longer kept. At the beginning we thought of it as the early fervour novices show, but by now you should be settled into our ways. We are a happy community here and have no wish to alter. Remember that you were taken in as a favour, with no dowry.'

'Reverend Mother, I cannot disobey the Rule. It is written down and the Mistress reads it to me. I have memorised all of it, and the psalms.'

'That is very commendable,' yawned the Prioress, looking at the long barred shadows the grille cast on the floor. She was expecting company, and wine and biscuits were again laid out. 'Remember what I have said, Margaret; be reasonable, that is all. You must try not to upset the sisters as you do. It is not hard; only a little giving way here and there; that is all we ask.'

Margaret was near tears. 'But I have asked the confessor, and he says that I am justified in the things I do, like not eating meat and keeping a sober mien at Lent. It is not right to laugh, surely, when we remember Our Lord's forty days and nights in the desert, without food or aid.'

'I am well enough instructed in the Gospels; do not be impertinent. You may go now; I have other business. Remember what I have said.'

It might have been after that that the persecution started. It began with little things; mislaying of her rosary so that she could not find it, hiding of her veil so that she could not come bare-headed into church; putting sharp stones where she knelt, so that she gave an unexpected cry of pain in the silence at the Elevation; such things persisted, and she neither tried to find the authors of them nor did she report them, taking them as extra penance sent to her by God. Presently the others began to mock her openly whenever she spoke, so she kept silent. She was no longer happy in the convent; it was as difficult to find God here as it had been at Mercatello. She considered this as a fault in herself, and during the hours when she should have been asleep wept and worried over it, then rose as usual earlier than anyone, at the hour the Rule prescribed; at the collation afterwards someone had put salt in her bread, making it uneatable except as further penance. Margaret said nothing, and endured all of it. If she prayed for the sisters who mocked her, that was obeying Our Lord, and perhaps would bring them back to the Rule. The priest to whom she confessed steadied her; he himself was well aware of the laxity in the convent. But if he spoke to the Prioress it would no doubt mean more persecution for this devout cripple. He took pleasure in Margaret's ready mind, and tried to give her as much support as he could; but the real strength lay in herself.

Christmas came, and the feasting started well before the day; crowds of friends invaded the convent, bearing rich presents for their relatives or particular friends. At recreation the recipients would show them off; a silver girdle, a lawn veil, a lute, a box of sweetmeats, opened to be gobbled at once.

'A sweetmeat, Margaret? Do not refuse. We do not have our feast till Christmas.'

She knew the box was offered to tease her and would be swung away if she reached out for it; she did not. 'It is not right for us to eat such things yet,' she heard herself saying, knowing how they would mock her continued observance. The nuns laughed. 'There she goes again, casting sour looks, dropping improving words from those lips of hers! May we play Assunta's lute, Margaret? Does the sound offend your ears?' They strummed with careless fingers at the lute, using a melody heard in brothels.

'You should be out in the world,' said Margaret. 'Such things here should be the property of all, for the good of God. That is the Rule.'

'Away with her and the Rule! She will spoil our merriment with her sour-milk face. Put her out! Let her go and teach the world to be sorry, if we are too gay for her.'

'It is intolerable. She is like a death's-head.'

'Life would not be worth living without a little cheer.'

'Why did you take vows?' cried Margaret. 'Was it not to offer yourselves to God in penance and prayer? To be sure we may be merry on Christ's birthday, but not sooner; it is gluttony to act as you do, gluttony and false pride.' She turned away. 'The devil has come in.' She heard them laughing, some the worse for wine; another expected a lover this evening. They had come here for their convenience, to practise shame secretly; not all were so; but the good women among them kept silence for fear of trouble.

'Hark at our judge!' said one of the revellers. 'Maria Dolorosa, have another sweetmeat. These are good; there is marchpane in 'em. Margaret will have none; well, well, that leaves all the more for us.'

'Take your ugly face out of here,' said another. 'We are sick of being lectured as to what we should and should not do. I'll do as I please, and that goes for the rest of us, eh, Dolorosa?

'It is not even as if crowds came flocking to her piety, as we were promised they would do when we took a beggar into our company.'

'She came with nothing, and she can leave with the same. That is justice, is it not?'

'I will speak to the Prioress,' said Maria Dolorosa, and flounced out.

'She ought to go. We have all had enough of her, mouthing her prayers and doing her penances as they used to be done in old time, and criticising us always. She was

better in her hermit's cave where they tell me she lived
for ten years. No wonder her parents abandoned her
after; imagine a long face like that about the place
constantly! And she is so ugly one cannot bear to look on
her. She is grown thin as an anatomy as well with her
penances and fasts, and has the impudence to tell us it's
for us also; who asked her to take responsibility for our
souls?'

The Prioress considered the angry young nun who
had come. Within herself she knew that Margaret was
right, but affairs in the convent had gone too far now to
be rectified; and many, like Maria Dolorosa here, had
come from Arezzo and nearby towns because of scandal,
so that they might not marry suitably. The money had
come in useful; and if they left, so did the dowry. The
ways were easy here and suited them. The Prioress
briefly consulted her Maker, reminding Him that the
price of meat had lately risen, and then nodded.

'It is as you say,' she told the other. 'I will see Margaret.
Bid her come to me after Terce, and not to be late.'

The last was unjust; Margaret would never be late. Part
of the complaint was that she was always too early. The
Prioress downed a martyred feeling that the world was
misusing her; when she first took vows she had felt as this
child now did, but matters had come between; it was too
late now, too late, to go back to what she had been. She
rose and poured herself wine and tried to make clear in
her mind what she should say to the girl; in the end she
found a book of the despised Rule and, opening it at
random, found a phrase that would suit. She smiled a
little; that would answer Margaret in her own way. In any
case there was no alternative.

She was coldness itself when the girl came, hardening her

face even as she heard the dragging footsteps outside her door. The twisted figure entered and knelt, then fell prostrate. 'Get up,' said the Prioress coldly. 'You will know why I have sent for you?'

'Reverend Mother, I –'

'Do not say anything; reports have been made to me constantly. The sisters find you a disturbance; you have already been reprimanded for it.'

'Mother, only for obeying the Rule.'

'Do you think yourself alone in knowledge of the Rule! I have a phrase here, written by our very founder. It deals with those who though often corrected will not amend. I have refrained from using the rod to you because of your condition.'

'Mother, I have myself –'

'Do not interrupt me; you are in a state of error. Our Founder as you will know, knowing the Rule so well, recommends all kinds of prior punishment for an inmate who continues contumacious; last of all saying *But if he be not healed in this place ... banish the offender from your company.* You will leave here, taking only what you brought; the convent cannot again be a contented place till you have left it.' She did not add that the expected silver from the crowds who were to have flocked to behold Margaret here had been, in themselves, disappointing.

They put her out in the street, carrying only what she had brought. At first when she felt the bitter wind blow through her rags, lacking her habit, she felt as though she were naked. The Prioress's cold parting seared her mind, for ice can burn; was she indeed so ungrateful, so stiff-necked? She had obeyed the priest, had told him everything in the confessional. She had honestly sought

to understand the words of the founder, and to obey the
Rule. Yet the words themselves seemed to have lost
favour in the community. Margaret ran over the
remembered Rule in her mind. Where had she erred?
At the same time, from habit, she was hobbling down
the streets as she had used to do, using her stick to help
her find the way; but where?

'Margaret! Margaret! Help me! Help me!'

The cry came from behind her; someone, a girl, was
running after her. She paused, turning her blind face
towards whoever came. How could she help them now,
she, the outcast? Yet she would do what she might.

'Margaret, it is Annina.' The girl paused for breath.
'You remember the pastrycook's house; we used to
share the floor. I used to do the ironing; oh, dear!' And
she burst out crying. 'Nobody will ever give me ironing
to do again,' she wailed. 'Monna Annunziata has
dismissed me without a character.'

Here was somebody whose troubles were worse than
her own. 'Why should she do that, *cara*?' asked Margaret
gently.

'Because Domenico has ridden off on his journey,
and she wasted no time in getting rid of me.'

'But why should she want to be rid of you? You were a
good laundry-maid.'

'Because I am going to have Domenico's child,' said
the girl defiantly. 'Oh, I know you will say I sinned. I'd
do the same again, any time. We loved one another. If
he knew I'd been brought to this pass he would help me,
but I am afraid of the servants' staves at the Porta San
Egidio; they'd beat me back. Margaret, would you go?
Ask for him by name; tell him what has happened. Will
you do this for me, for old days' sake?'

'I am concerned for the child,' said Margaret. 'For

that reason I will do as you ask, if I can. But the staves may beat me too.'

'They will let you past, because you are as you are.'

'I will try what may be done. Wait for me at the Carità. I will bring you news there as soon as I may.'

'I will wait. God go with you, Margaret.'

The crippled figure limped off, its rags fluttering. Annina leaned against a wall, her hand to her breast; she thought of Domenico, and how he might ride off without ever knowing about the child, and he would not be back for a year.

Margaret made her way through the town to the north gate. It always hurt her to come here because this was the place where her parents had last ridden through, leaving her behind. There was a bustle about it as the Easterlings prepared to start on their long journey, and their escort was like a prince's, guarding the valuable bales of dyed stuffs and embroidery and jewellery to sell in the north. The servants with long staves would protect the party from being robbed in the hills; the ponies were sturdy and chosen for the rough ride. Domenico sat on one, nearby his uncle, a florid man in a wide beaver hat. As Margaret approached the uncle thought she was a beggar and waved his hands in disclaimer, saying, 'No, no.' But others whispered to him that it was the holy woman, and that she would speak with his nephew.

'Make it short, then,' he said grudgingly. 'We are about to start.'

The young man bent down to listen to what Margaret had to say, and when he straightened his face was white. He reached into his tunic and brought out his purse. 'That is all the money I have,' he said in a low voice. 'Tell

Annina that I will acknowledge the child when I return.'
He looked about him defiantly. 'Tell her I love her,' he
said clearly.

'And the lady Ceccha?'

He flushed scarlet. 'She is my betrothed.' There was a
jingling among the ponies. 'I will tell Annina,' Margaret
called, 'and I will deliver the child when it is born.'

'God bless you, Margaret.'

'God go with you for your journey.'

She waited while they rode off, through the gate;
after they had gone the street was quiet. She thrust the
purse safely in her bodice, intent on taking it to Annina:
and evaded her friends the beggars who might call out
for a portion of what it contained. She made her way
back to the Carità, found Annina there, and felt the
young woman's tears on her hands.

'I knew you would not fail me; and I knew he would
not. Now I can pay for a lodging, perhaps look out for
some work.'

'Let me know where you lodge. I have promised to
deliver the child.'

The prospect cheered her; it gave purpose to her life
which had seemed empty.

The task for Annina done meantime, Margaret was at a
loss what to do next, or where to go. For months now
she had let her days and hours be regulated by the
convent practices, and despite everything she found
herself still clinging to them. One thing that had always
helped her was the daily hour with the Mistress of
Novices, when she had learned many of the psalms.
Their comfortable words came to her now as she
paused, tired and hungry, in the shelter of a wall. *He
shall give his angels charge over thee that thou dash not thy foot*

against a stone ... do I fly to the uttermost parts of the sea, thou art there ...

God was here, then, with her; God would not forsake her. The thought gave her strength; she knew now where to go. The parish church of the Carità, where Annina had waited, was a little way down the street. Margaret stumbled towards it, and dragged herself inside, for she was tired; it was empty, with the smell of doused candles. Margaret knelt there a long time, and when a priest came in at last, made her confession. 'Was I wrong in what I did?' she said piteously. 'Should I have given in, said nothing in order that I might please them? I did not feel that I could, yet this may be due to pride in me.'

'You were right, my child,' said the priest, who had heard certain things about St Margaret's convent of late. 'Continue as you have begun, honestly and well; but, as you yourself say, guard against pride. It can undo the best of us when we least expect it; it is the subtlest weapon in all the devil's armoury. Keep guard constantly, humble yourself always, and all should be well.' And he absolved her.

She had early opportunity for humility.

It was not long before gossiping tongues told the town what had happened at the convent and how at last Margaret had been put out into the street. Now whenever she went abroad there were mocking cries following her. 'There goes the hunchback who thought she was a saint!' 'Who could not stay a nun?' 'Take your stick to your own back, cripple!' 'Fool with no name, who are you now?' 'Beggar!' 'Bat!' 'Serpent!' So they would call after her, and imitate her limp while whistling a tune; even the children who, when they were

younger, had loved her, now fancied themselves grown
and beyond childish things; accordingly, they would set
obstacles for her to trip and fall, then call obscenities as
she struggled to raise herself. It was as hard as anything
she had yet had to endure, and often she found herself
near tears; but God was with her, and when they saw no
answer came from her, they began to leave her in peace.

But she did not regain her peace of mind even after the
cries of mockery grew silent and the mockers had found
other targets. She had returned perforce to her old
habits of begging and sharing, and the beggars had
welcomed her without comment, but her heart was not
with them as it had used to be. It seemed to her now that
the whole of mankind had rejected her; she would crawl
to her place in the Carità, kneeling hunched there by
the hour, her lips moving in formal prayers; but she
could not pray. This was the dark night of the soul, the
agony Christ Himself had endured on the cross when
God at last forsook Him. She herself was no one and
nothing, could never attract the love of man; her
parents and now her very sisters had abandoned her. It
grew bitter the more one thought of it, but she could not
rid her mind of the memory of the nuns' hostile voices
urging her out into the street. Was there to be nothing
more for her than beggardom, all her days? If so, she
must accept it; but it was hard, and for the first time in
her life she felt the darkness about her, covering her;
one groped for a light that had gone out.

One day she was in the church, sobbing quietly; a
beggar's child had died and she had not been able to
save it for lack of food. She had felt the small fingers
growing cold and lax, and heard the mother's wailing.
She herself would never know motherhood; but the loss

might have been her own. Presently she must go out and wait by the door for alms, to take to the poor mother.

There was someone else in church; someone whose hushing robes were not of silk, like those of the rich, nor of fluttering rags like those of the poor. This woman – Margaret knew her by her light step – was clad in a white wool robe, a black mantle, and a white hood. She came closer to where the girl knelt. 'You are crying, Margaret,' she said quietly. 'Perhaps I can help you: tell me your trouble.'

'If God cannot help me, none can.' She did not speak churlishly, or feel surprised that this person, whom she did not know, should have heard her name, no doubt all her affairs and that she had been ejected from the convent. She heard the stranger seat herself by her, and turn her hooded head; the great cloak's warm folds fell against Margaret, thawing her chilled flesh.

'God sends His angels to do His will.' There was a smile behind the words; the woman did not lightly, blasphemously call herself an angel. Yet she had come, and offered help. Margaret began to talk to her, telling her in a low voice all she had done and endured, the trying to keep the Rule that had led to her expulsion. 'And yet what else could I have done?' she said again and again. 'What else could I have done?'

'You could have done none other, being honest. Perhaps God has other other work for you.' The girl turned to her eagerly.

'Other work? I would do anything to serve God. But as you see I am blind; I have to be guided in strange places, and am a burden to others. I would not want that. If I can work for God and trouble nobody, that is my desire.'

'You were troubled by the others' lack of truth and of idleness, in the convent; the truth is out about town. You would be better under your own direction, but in a sisterhood which fortifies itself by doing good and by visiting the sick, wearing the mantle I wear.' The woman took a fold of the stuff and put it into Margaret's hand; she felt the warm felted texture with her fingers. A great wonder filled her.

'A *mantellata*? But it is for women who have been married only, when they are widows. I have heard of you and the good you do. It would be great joy to me – but they would not take me, I believe.' She was trembling; the other put her arm about her.

'I and others will speak for you, and we will ask the Prior of the Order of St Dominic to admit you provided you yourself are willing.'

'I am willing indeed; I thank you for coming to me.'

'Do not be hopeful yet; the Prior may raise difficulties for a time because of your age and your single state.'

'I shall never be otherwise,' said Margaret.

The Prior did indeed raise difficulties; it was as Margaret had herself said, and only older women had hitherto been acceptable to become *mantellate*. But the clamour of Margaret's friends at last convinced him. 'She is young, but her way of life is holy and pure, like Our Lord's; she has no possessions, and when she obtains money shares it with the beggars, and tends their sick. She is leading the life of a *mantellata* already, except that she has not taken the vows and does not wear the cloak and hood and gown. It would comfort her greatly to be among our number. They were cruel to her in the convent, though she would never speak of it. The sight of her interfered too greatly with their life of ease.'

The Prior spread out his hands. 'What you ask is still irregular. If this girl is admitted to our number, other young girls will flock to join; and that would soon cause scandal.'

'Margaret is exceptional. There will be no scandal. Think of her deformities.'

He nodded; he had seen the blind cripple limping about the streets. 'I will appoint seven good women to enquire into her way of life,' he said, 'and then we will see.'

The seven good women found Margaret blameless, and at length the Prior gave his consent. 'She must present herself on Sunday for formal admission,' he told them. 'Tell her to make her confession first and do penance.'

On the day, the church was full of hooded women, friars in the black habit of St Dominic, priests, beggars, some rich from the town. A hush fell as the blind girl was led in and limped towards the altar. Lying on it was the habit which was to be given to her. Its simple folds were of white wool. The Prior stepped forward.

'What do you seek?' He was reciting the order of service.

'God's mercy and yours,' said Margaret. Her voice was strong and clear and rang through the church.

'You are about to become a member of the Order of St Dominic. Henceforth, though you live in the world, you will not be part of the world. Your habit will at once be a pledge and a reminder that you have dedicated yourself to the service and love of God without reserve or conditions other than those expressed in the written Rule.'

She smiled; she knew the Rule already, as she had known that of St Benedict. The Prior was still speaking from his place by the altar.

'From now on, my sister, your greatest concern must be to serve God and your fellow man, in the love of God. This is possible only if you make your life one of prayer, continual penance and cheerful sacrifice.'

I can do that, she thought. I have always done it. It is comforting to be joined with others who do likewise. I will try not to be proud, to anger anyone.

The Prior had turned to where the white habit lay. He raised it and blessed it. 'May it be preserved by you without stain till death,' he said. Two of the cloaked women stood on either side of Margaret, and he handed them the white habit and the great dark cloak. The watchers burst out into the *Veni Creator Spiritus*, their voices soaring with the bright day beyond the windows. The warm folds of the mantle enveloped Margaret's small body; it was as though she were clothed in armour. A great joy pervaded her.

'You must go up to the altar to make the vows,' whispered one of the women. Haltingly, using her stick to ascend the steps, the blind woman went, while the others sang on. The Prior reached out for her hands, placing them between his own. She heard a voice which must be hers, reciting the prescribed vows; she did not falter.

'To the honour of Almighty God, Father, Son, and Holy Ghost, and of the Blessed Virgin Mary, and of St Dominic, and in the presence of you, Reverend Father, Prior of the Order in Città di Castello, I, Sister Margaret, do make my profession. And I do promise that henceforth I will live according to the form and Rule of the same Order of Penance of St Dominic until death.'

The Prior's voice was deep. He had been moved to experience the earnestness with which this crippled creature made her vows. God moved mysteriously. No doubt her condition was His will. The women had crowded forward to greet the new *mantellata* and kiss her. Tears were running down Margaret's face.

'May He who has begun his good work in you perfect it,' intoned the Prior, 'until the day of Christ Jesus.'

11

It was an honour to have a *mantellata* under one's roof, and among others the Offrenducci gladly offered Margaret a home with them and with the Mercati. She chose to live with the two families because their house, two-storied and built of stone, was near the Carità. She would disturb nobody when she slipped out through the night to the church to recite Matins and Lauds.

The house, Domus Pacis, the House of Peace, held its inmates easily. Offrenducci and his wife and son lived in one half; the other, reached by the same entry, held the Mercati. Ysachina and Offrenducci's wife Beatrice were sisters. It was not possible to live in the house and avoid meeting any member of it; everyone met to gossip on the house-stairs, in the rooms, on the steps outside leading to the courtyard. There was much friendship, laughter and love. Meals were shared by both families.

The news of Domenico's unfaithfulness had hurt Ceccha; in some way, not through Margaret, the family had become aware of his seduction of a maidservant. Mercati himself viewed the matter lightly; it was the

natural action of a lusty young man waiting for
marriage. 'He will have had one or two plump Flemings
by now as well; the way to stop it is to please him
yourself, let him know there's no one like his wife to
come home to.' Ysachina was less pleased, but said
nothing that would disturb her daughter. Such matters
as town gossip and dress occupied her; she was always
attired fashionably. At meals, and at other times,
Margaret and the girl Ceccha talked together, though
Margaret's vows bound her to speak of nothing but
God.

'You talk of heaven as if it were here,' said Ceccha.
She bit her red underlip. One must be careful not to
hurt this cheerful cripple, who bore her dreadful
deformities as if they did not matter, and wielded her
stick as though she could see. How fortunate I am to
have been born straight and strong, thought Ceccha;
and yet my bridegroom does not love me. She felt
increasingly unwilling to marry Domenico; but her
father would be angry if she said so. Instead, it was a
refreshment to talk with Margaret about the saints,
about God, heaven and the sacraments.

Margaret smiled, having guessed everything that
went on in Ceccha's mind. She found herself nowadays
with an increasing insight into people, in the same way
as, when she prayed often, she came to a place beyond
prayer. But it was not yet time to speak of that to
Ceccha. 'Heaven is near us,' she said. 'It is not so far
away as people think. Our Lord said that if one had the
mind of a little child, one would gain the kingdom. You
have such a mind, Ceccha; there is no guile in you.' She
made no movement, standing there in the sun, but it
was as if her fingers reached out to touch the flesh of
the lovely girl; Ceccha trembled suddenly. Margaret was

so holy that she must be a saint. 'Tell me more of what
you know,' she said. 'I love to hear you tell the stories of
the saints. It is as though they were alive today.'

'But they are indeed alive, though no longer in the
body, and answer our requests.'

Ceccha considered it; it was true that when one lost
anything, St Anthony would find it; even Mamma knew
that one. The idea of the communion of saints had not
yet been borne in upon her; the fact of an unseen legion
of helpers, ready to respond to prayer in different ways,
as they had been different on earth. Margaret tried to
explain it to her; her face shone with joy. 'And Our
Lady is the greatest of them, and St Joseph is a very
great saint. I pray often to St Joseph. He was never rich,
yet he was contented. And he taught Our Lord how to
become a carpenter. Think of the privilege that must
have been! St Joseph would be a good craftsman. And
he cared for Our Lady all through the time before her
Child was born, although others would have cast her
away; and he found the stable at Bethlehem. Have I
ever told you of my night in a stable here, and of feeling
Christ had been born again? I could smell the hay, and
the animals' breaths; it is said their breaths warmed the
little baby, born into the cold. I never tire of thinking of
it, and about St Joseph; he has answered many prayers
for me.'

'You are always so happy; is that because your prayers
have been answered?' Ceccha put the question almost
hesitantly; it seemed so extraordinary that this woman
who had nothing at all should be as full of joy as oneself
if ... if there were a new gown, or sweetmeats after
dinner. How false those things seemed! 'I would like to
be like you, Margaret,' Ceccha said, and it was only
afterwards, when she was alone, that she thought how

extraordinary a thing that was; to want to be like a blind hunch-backed cripple, who had no possessions!

Time passed, and Ceccha did not forget her wish; being discreet, she said nothing of it to her parents, because she knew they wanted her to marry Domenico when he returned, and she did not think that would help her towards what she really wanted; but it would hurt them, especially her father, if she told them so. She went about her days outwardly as usual, and listened whenever she could to what Margaret had to say; it was incredible to think that the blind woman spent each day in prayer and reciting all the psalms, then got up during the night to go to church and pray. All *mantellate* did not do this; Ysachina spoke of it sometimes.

'She will wear herself out with the life she lives; she is not strong and has a cough. But when I said to her that she ought to take care of herself, she only smiled with that sweet smile, and said she was happy as things were. I feel such a worldly woman when I speak to her or see her; I have never felt like it before.'

Beatrice, her sister, laughed. 'Be careful that you do not take the vows also.' She meant it as a jest, for Ysachina was the last person who would ever do that. Mercati, who was seated in his chair with his accounts by him, laughed loudly also, his jolly face rubicund. He was a man who liked his food, his wife, his wine. It seemed as if he had nothing more to wish for, except to see Ceccha well married. He looked at the two women with indulgence; what a pretty creature his wife still was, with her fair head covered by a veil of the finest lawn and a narrow gold circlet he himself had given her, when Ceccha was born! Other men wanted sons, but he was content. His wife's chatter pleased him; he enjoyed the busy life in the family house, with the cousin – who of course would not be permitted as a bridegroom for Ceccha, the relationship was too close.

'Come here, *carina*, and talk to your old father,' he said to Ceccha, who had come into the room. She came, and Mercati cast his arm about her and drew her on to his knee, as he had done when she was a little child. 'When do we see you a bride, my daughter?' he asked gently. Ceccha drooped her eyelids; he could not tell what she was thinking. Ysachina broke in, still laughing at Beatrice's joke. 'You are in a great hurry to lose our darling,' she called over. 'The day you take Ceccha to church to be married you will be miserable at losing her; wait a while, the child is young.'

'But the bridegroom has waited a long time,' riposted Beatrice. They smiled at her, all three, but did not answer; in truth they were such a united family that it was difficult to picture a bridegroom, however eligible, being welcome among them. They were complete in themselves.

'I do not think that it will be long now,' said Annina. '*Dio mio*, he kicks so hard he can only be a boy!'

She placed her hands on her gravid body, her face merry. Margaret had managed to find her enough laundry-work among the *mantellate* and she was surrounded with it, the piles of snowy linen rising nearby two heating irons.

'You look grave, Margaret,' said Annina. 'I am well, I assure you. I am not afraid of the labour. I can hardly wait to hold my son in my arms, and to hope that he resembles his father. Whichever it is, boy or girl. I can look after it now, with your good work.'

'Annina, Domenico's mother Annunziata was found

dead in bed this morning.'

'So?' Annina sketched the sign of the cross. Then she paled. 'There will be the less reason now for Domenico ever to return to Castello,' she said.

'There is Ceccha, and his promise to her.'

'He would not return for Ceccha. He always wanted to see strange places. Antwerp promised much; he spoke to me of the great waterway the merchant ships use, and the trade with England and Russia. He would talk by the hour of such things.'

'Meantime, poor Monna Annunziata died before the priest could come with the sacraments; pray for her soul.'

'I do not grudge her soul its prayers,' said Annina. The iron was hot and she spat on it, watching the bubble of spittle hiss and disappear on the ready metal. Then she got on with her ironing. Margaret went quietly away, promising to return for the birth. 'He vowed to acknowledge the child,' she reminded Annina, and the young woman's dark eyes suddenly filled with tears. 'Then perhaps,' she said. 'I shall see him again.'

Domenico sat in his Antwerp office, whose fine glass windows rattled as they overlooked the estuary with its ships rocking at anchor; they never had gales like this at home. In the streets the women's great linen coifs were blown awry as they returned from market with fresh fish, which likewise one never saw in Castello; he had developed a taste for it. The office itself was set about with elegantly carved wooden furniture, and Venice glasses sat on a table ready for drinking wine. At the moment, however, he expected his uncle; they were to discuss his mother's death, news of which had come lately. Domenico was not overcome with grief; he had been a good and obedient son to the formidable widow, only on that one occasion crossing her about not beating Annina. He thought of the girl with affection now, troubled still that she had been turned out of the house immediately on his own departure; but he trusted Margaret to see to it, if one might, as he pondered, use such an expression about a blind person. He had been unable to write to Annina because she could not read, and in any case he did not know where to reach her; but he hoped all went well.

His uncle came in, wearing his long robe. He went to the Venetian glasses and poured wine for himself and for Domenico, and they drank. 'Your mother's death,' he said, 'has made a difference to your prospects. There is no longer any reason for you to return to Castello.'

'There is one, a private one.' The young man had flushed; he had in fact hoped for an offer to remain here, but he must see Annina first and also Ceccha's family. He could not picture Ceccha as his wife here; she would not want to be separated from her father and mother. Now that his own mother was dead there was no reason to adhere to the betrothal. The whole situation had changed. He listened to the older man speaking.

'That is as may be; you are of age and can decide for yourself. But here we need a young man on whom we can rely to see to the written work and bills of lading. You would have clerks under you to manage the drudgery; the books need only be inspected, and this you are well able to do; I have had my eye on you, as you know, since coming. You are interested in the merchandise and get on well with the ships' captains. In other words you could be of great value to us in Antwerp.'

'I would like to do it,' said Domenico without hesitation. 'But as I said I must return to Castello, very briefly, soon.'

The merchant shrugged. 'If you must do it, you must,' he said. 'It is to do with your betrothal, perhaps? I ask as your relative.'

'With breaking off my betrothal, uncle. I no longer want to marry Ceccha Mercati.'

The other's tongue clicked. 'That is a good dowry to lose. But you will have plenty of choice, once you are established as our representative here.' He smiled. 'There are plenty of Flemish heiresses who would be glad of you.'

'I do not intend to wed an heiress,' said Domenico firmly. And there they left it, though his uncle was unwilling.

12

'Where are you going, Margaret?'

'I am going to confession.'

'But you were there yesterday.' Ceccha's light footsteps ran to catch up the cripple, who was hurrying on, stick well forward, twisted body a dynamic hastening shape, cloak eddying about her. But she slowed for Ceccha, smiling. 'I go every day,' she said, 'and hear Mass afterwards.'

'But you can have nothing to confess. You are not sinful.'

Margaret laughed. 'There is nobody in the world who is not sinful. Only Our Blessed Lady was free of sin.' She began to use the guiding stick again gently, her limp slowed now to a walking pace. Ceccha pouted, making a pattern in the dust with her foot.

'I must be very sinful,' she said. 'I have not been to confession since I was confirmed, as a little child. You know my parents do not trouble greatly with church, except perhaps at Easter. My *babbo* thinks that if one does good and is loving in this world it is enough. You know our house is called the House of Peace, though that is partly due to my cousins. Yet ever since you came I have watched you, and felt differently.'

Margaret's face was grave. She knew well enough that it was Offrenducci who had offered her a home, and that Mercati, though friendly, would have no truck, as he would have put it, with religious observance as she herself professed it. 'You should go to confession,' she said to Ceccha. 'Think for a little while and your sins will become clear to you. The priest will help you. It is sinful in itself to remain unclean and unworthy to receive Our Lord when He comes; and we do not know when that may be.'

'I have been happy enough,' said Ceccha. 'Does the Sacrament mean so much?' Her clear eyes brooded over Margaret. This creature, so ugly and deformed, had an inner happiness that made her the envy of oneself; nothing to do with pretty gowns, with combing out one's hair, with giving pleasure to others. She listened to what Margaret was saying.

'Ceccha, I lived ten years in a little cell in the mountains when I was a child, with the near company of the Blessed Sacrament, summer and winter, night and day. During that time He became everything to me in a way others cannot know, and even I myself cannot fully describe. It is terrible to me to think that you are cut off from that grace because you will not do this little thing, and confess. Yet I will not ask you to do it to please me; you must do it to please God.'

She bowed her head in its white hood, and limped slowly off. Ceccha stood where she was for a moment and then caught the other up, saying breathlessly, 'I will do it, Margaret. I will go to confession. You have shown me the way.'

'Take time to think,' said Margaret again. 'You are impulsive, Ceccha. It is one of the charming things in you. God loves the warm-hearted, but do not come back to Him and then leave again when the next fancy takes you. God demands all or nothing.'

Ceccha's eyes had filled with tears, but she was not sad; a strange joy and strength were rising in her, and at the same time she thought of Margaret, frail, afflicted, disciplining herself, rising in the night to pray, spending the days on her knees or else hastening to visit the sick and dying. She is worth so much more than I, the girl thought, and it was the first time such a thought would have occurred to her. I can never be quite like Margaret; perhaps no one can. Already she is the wonder of the town; everyone talks of her, reverently as if she were a saint. She has done so much good, comforted so many people! God in His turn must comfort her, for she seems always cheerful and content. It must be very blessed to be so. If I could be more like her! If I could!

She found herself crying in the street, and in order not to be remarked on wiped away her tears with her embroidered sleeve. At the same time she knew a change in herself; she was no longer the heedless Ceccha who had run out to say, 'Margaret, where are you going?' I myself, she thought, knew where I was going yesterday, even today, till now; I was about to make a rich marriage. Now, I would rather be like Margaret, as much as I can.

Ceccha's parents noticed that she went oftener to church, but at first thought that it must be in preparation for her betrothal; young women became emotional at such a time. Yet still Ceccha said nothing to

Mercati about the marriage, and he was too loving a
father to force her to it. It was good, no doubt, that she
had made such friends with the *mantellata*; a holy
woman would do the child no harm, and the
bridegroom might be glad to have a pious wife. He
shared his thoughts with Ysachina, who laughed in her
merry way. 'You were not afflicted so,' she teased him.
He smiled at her.

'I would not have you any other way than you are,
my dove,' he told her. 'Nor do I want to lose Ceccha. But
it is time she was married; I do not want to be unjust,
and keep her too long with us.'

'Perhaps we should see more company,' said Ysachina
vaguely; there was nothing in life that could not be put
right by a little laughter and company. She perched on
the arm of Mercati's wooden chair and discussed with
him whom they might invite to a meal. The Offrenducci
would be present, of course. 'We have seen less of the
cousins lately,' Ysachina noted. 'We have become too
greatly wrapped up in ourselves. Now, shall it be a roast
of lamb? But Margaret will not eat it.'

Mercati sighed; he had more difficulty than his
daughter in living up to Margaret's ideals. 'Have what
you will, wife, and she may eat what she will,' he said
placidly. He sat back in his chair and scanned the
familiar view of the river; there was a boat on it. How
pleasant life was, and how happy they had all been! Why
did he think of it as being over?

13

Word came that Annina had fallen in labour in the small hours, and Margaret slipped out of the house and went down to the place near the river where the girl lodged and did her laundry. It was still piled up in the room, for Annina had not stopped working until the pains were well started. She lay now on her pallet, and the two other young women who shared the room with her lay on theirs, complaining that her cries prevented them from getting any sleep. They were servants at a nearby house and had to be out in the morning, but there was no room for them there. Margaret took off her cloak and fetched water, and busied herself about the birth.

'Oh, oh,' moaned Annina. Margaret comforted her. 'Have courage,' she said, 'it will not be long. I can feel the head coming.'

Sweat had broken out on the young woman's forehead; her hands clenched on the pallet. The girls in the next beds began to imitate her moans. 'Get on with it, Annina! Do you mean to keep us awake all night?'

'Do not mock her,' Margaret told them. 'You will be in the same way one day yourselves.'

'Yes, but we'll get ourselves a wedding-ring, holy woman.'

Annina screamed; the head was coming through. Margaret pressed on it and let it come slowly; presently it was born, and she twisted away the body from the mother; a fine boy, with black hair. 'Here is your son,' she whispered. The child cried. '*Dio*,' said the young women, 'now we will have him to listen to as well as her,' and they rolled over and yawned. 'Do not trouble yourselves,' said Margaret, 'he will sleep, and so will the mother.'

She left mother and child wrapped and washed, and hastened back to the Offrenducci house. On reaching her room a presence disturbed her; Ceccha, her hair loose over her shift, her eyes dark with lack of sleep.

'That was Domenico's child being born, was it not?' she whispered. 'Was it a son?'

Margaret did not ask how she had heard; no doubt the servant who came with the news had spoken clearly. 'It was a fine son,' she answered gently, 'and they are both well.'

'He should marry her,' said Ceccha, 'the mother of his son.' She went away with shoulders drooping. Margaret went into her room, said her prayers, lay down on her pallet and slept.

Margaret was praying for Ceccha, who now loved herself less and God more. She came to church every day. At first the cripple had thought it was an easy fervour, such as girls sometimes showed, and would pass off in time: but Ceccha now had been faithful for three months. Margaret was conscious of the sweet-scented presence constantly about her, the soft hair washed with birch-bark, the smooth skin fragrant with oil. But Ceccha talked less than she had done, and she had been diligent in learning the prayers Margaret had taught her, the Little Office of Our Lady, the psalms, the Office of the Cross. It was as though she had fallen deeply in love, but not with her earthly bridegroom. Margaret kept silence on the matter for long; she would not force Ceccha to a decision any more than her father had done. During her prayers a shining clarity came to her that all would be well.

One day Ceccha came to her and said, 'Margaret, may we talk in private? I would not have my mother overhear.'

'You must not deceive your mother, Ceccha.'

'I will not – I would not – but how can I tell her what is in my heart? I – I do not want to marry.'

'Then what will become of you?'

'I would be like you, a *mantellata*.'

Margaret put out a hand to her. 'Child, it is not so easy. Could you mortify yourself? Could you say the prayers, day and night, without full sleep? You are young, and sleep well.'

'I can do all that. I have been saying them. I know that it is right for me to join you; I asked my confessor about it. He counselled me to wait, and tell no one; and I have done that. Now I must tell you, and I ought to tell my parents. But I have not the courage to do it. They will not be pleased. It is not what they planned for me. But I know Our Lord said one must leave parents, brothers, sisters – though I have none – for Him. I would do it gladly. I have never been so happy as in the past months. I would like to do everything you do, visit the sick, comfort the dying, pray nightly and daily. Please help me, Margaret; please tell my parents.'

Margaret frowned a little. 'The Prior of the Order may not accept you. It would be useless to tell your parents and then be refused. They made an exception for me, though I am young, because – because there could be no scandal about me. But you, you are young and pretty –'

'How do you know that I am pretty, Margaret? You cannot see me.'

The cripple smiled. 'I can feel the warmth of your presence and the love others have for you. You are like a flower, a jewel, to be cherished by those who love you and would make you happy in this world. Do not forsake all of it until you are sure, quite, quite sure, that what you want is above all other things to you. You have a place in the world, as I had none. It may have been easier for me.'

'Easier! You were left abandoned, and –'

Margaret raised a finger. 'Hush; I do not speak of myself and of the things that are best forgotten. If you will that I speak to your parents, I will do it; but we must wait till the right time.'

'I want it more than anything in the world.'

'Then I will speak.' She did not tell Ceccha of the curious clarity that had already come to her, making her certain that this was the right way. She could not explain it, and would wait for God's good time to tell the Mercati the truth. They might be angry; they would certainly be hurt; perhaps they would ask their cousins to tell her to leave the House of Peace. Well, if that were so she must go; it was in any case a mistake to become too greatly attached to worldly things, and she had grown to love Ceccha's family as well as Ceccha.

14

The roast lamb had been made ready, fragrant with rosemary and spices; there were tarts and honeyed conceits and much wine. The four guests were seated at table with the two families; a jolly merchant and his wife, a notary and his, all friends of the Offrenducci and Mercati both. The women compared head-dresses and gowns and whispered to one another. Ceccha sat quietly in her place, not taking part in the talk, eyes downcast. Margaret was at the further end, seated beside the Offrenducci son, a loud-mouthed impulsive lad who was all his parents' joy. He wore parti-colour as was the fashion, red and yellow checked, short tunic and tight hose setting off his dark good looks flamboyantly. He did not address Margaret, who did not interest thoughtless young men; but eyed Ceccha, and for once kept his thoughts to himself. She had used to be good sport, his cousin, they had known one another from children, but now she had grown silent and dull. Was it the fault of this repellent cripple who sat by him? He dismissed the matter, bolted his food and longed to be out among the young men and women of the town. Beside him, the blind cripple was still mouthing grace over the bread which was all she would eat. Young Offrenducci reached for a handful of sweetmeats and crammed them into his mouth.

At the head of the table Mercati was sharing jests with the notary, who had a lawyer's sly wit. The two men often gave vent to bursts of laughter and Beatrice Offrenducci, Ysachina's sister-in-law, in the end looked down the table at the silent *mantellata* and reproved the men. There should not be unseemly mirth in presence of such a one. Mercati looked at her and winked.

'Say no more, we honour and revere the cloaked ladies and the good works they do. They are known far and wide for their charity.'

'And their penance,' said Beatrice. 'Three times a day, like the blessed St Dominic, they scourge themselves for the sins of the world.'

'Monna Beatrice, please say no more,' whispered Margaret. 'Once a day is the required practice, but one may do it oftener.' She would have gone on to explain that once was for one's own sins, the second for the salvation of one's fellows, the third for the souls in purgatory. But Mercati and his friends had grown noisy again and she relapsed into silence. The host's rubicund face shone with good cheer and good fellowship. He loved his friends, he loved his wife, he even loved that poor little twisted blind thing who coughed and would never permit herself a square meal; impossible not to pity and admire her.

'Forget penance,' he said. 'It is well known the *mantellate* do much good in the world. Where would we be without their ministrations in time of sickness? I tell you, many who were ill in this town would not have recovered without their tending, for the physicians care nothing unless they are paid.' He raised his wine-cup. 'Let us drink to the holy women, and may they grow from strength to strength.'

The others drank. In the moment's silence Margaret interposed quickly, 'If you have so great a love for us, let your daughter become one of us.'

'My –' The mouth in the great red face was suddenly agape. Silence grew and enfolded the room, the guests, the courtyard beyond the arches. 'Ceccha a nun, my Ceccha a nun?' repeated Mercati, incredulously. 'My Ceccha – never, never!'

'You are wrong,' said Margaret calmly. 'Before very long I can tell you that not only Ceccha, but your wife Ysachina also, will have become *mantellate* of the Order of St Dominic.'

But this was too much, and the laughter rang out from all sides; Ysachina a nun! Mercati reached out his arm to embrace his pretty wife; even the sullen Offrenducci boy smiled. Ysachina! As well put crows' feathers on a hen!

The meal continued, with the subject which had been raised allowed to die quietly, as everyone thought. Afterwards they rose from their places and Ceccha was told to fetch her lute. Passing by Margaret she whispered, 'You tried. I knew very well *babbo* would not agree. Do not say any more or he will grow angry. We must wait.'

Mercati returned to his great chair, and beat his hand in time to the melody Ceccha played. Unseen, the cripple made her way out to her own place. Nobody remarked her going except Ceccha, seemingly intent on the lute. The guests hummed the melody and, had they been younger, would have danced together. Young

Offrenducci slipped away early to town, and did not see what followed, there in the room.

Ceccha had at last fallen silent; she knew no more songs. She looked at her father for his approval; he liked to hear her play. Then she gasped and clutching Ysachina's arm, looked again at Mercati. He was seated askew in his great chair, coloured like lead, his face flaccid, the loose mouth gasping sideways, a bead of saliva trickling down the chin.

They got him to bed. When they tried to undress him they found that one side of his body was powerless. Ceccha, weeping, hastened to find Margaret. 'You must help us,' she said. 'Oh, Margaret, my father is taken ill; I do not understand it, just when he was so merry.'

'He may not want to see me yet,' Margaret replied. 'I will pray for him.'

'For his recovery?' The girl's face was blotched with crying.

'No, for his soul.'

Afterwards Margaret took turns in the sickroom, wiping the helpless man's face with cool cloths, feeding him, for he could no longer eat except awkwardly. The merry House of Peace had changed in a moment; now there were only sounds of grief, and no music. Ysachina at first had taken to her bed, and wept long; when she rose again she was a changed woman. She tended her husband lovingly, Ceccha also. Once when Ceccha was with her father the older woman came to Margaret, who had just come in; the light from the archway fell on the great cloak, hunched round her body, and on her white hood. Her face was calm and grave; she might have been an old woman. She had been to another sick-bed, in a hovel near the river, and had delivered a poor woman's child.

'Will he recover?' asked Ysachina piteously. 'He has never been ill. He has no patience, and frets at it.'

'If he has no second seizure, he may grow a little better; the use of the hand may come back, and afterwards he may walk with a stick. But if there is a second, prepare yourself, Ysachina; he may not recover then. I have seen it happen often, in the town.'

'Then I shall be alone, quite alone,' moaned Ysachina. 'Ceccha will go with you. Do you suppose I do not know how obstinate she is, once she has made up her mind? It would have given her father pleasure to see her married, to hold his grandchildren, but she put it off again and again. Now she may be orphaned and I a widow. What are we to do?'

'Trust in God.'

'You talk always of God. Why did He allow this thing to happen to us? We had done Him no harm.'

'Think a little. I know you are in grief. What was the last thing your husband said before we rose from table that day? You do not remember? He said that Ceccha should never be a nun. If God has called Ceccha, it is a disservice to Him to refuse her.'

'How hard you are! Ceccha is all we have.'

'You will not lose her by giving her to God.'

Ysachina burst into tears. 'We have given you a home, and you repay us with bitterness. Before you came Ceccha was a happy child, about to be married, and my husband a big hale man who loved me. Now –'

'He still loves you, Monna Ysachina.'

'And cannot say it, or do other than take pap from a spoon, like a child. I had as soon see him dead as like he is. I had as soon see him dead.'

She had her wish; Mercati had a second seizure, and died

soon after. The house was hung with mourning; Ysachina and Ceccha clothed themselves in black, and did not go out of the house after the funeral. Only the *mantellate* came and went, aiding them in ways in which they could not at present help themselves; marketing, preparing vegetables, making light custards which might tempt them to eat. One day Ceccha came downstairs, her face pale with confinement away from the sun. The sad eyes looked at Margaret steadily.

'I am to tell you that my mother gives me permission to join the Order,' she said in a low voice. 'And – Margaret – she would like to be admitted also.'

15

The Prior had made no difficulties about accepting Ysachina; widows often joined the *mantellate* and at their age were sober and practical. Ceccha was a different matter; as he had done with Margaret herself, he demurred. 'She is young,' he said. Margaret herself came to plead the girl's cause.

'I know,' she told him, 'that Ceccha will make one of us. Do not cast her out, good father; let her come with her mother. The two console one another.'

'There should be enough consolation for Ysachina in the sisterhood, and at the weekly conferences,' said the Prior, hands folded in the sleeves of his habit, white hair lit by the daylight which came in at the round-arched window. His room was almost bare except for a crucifix, a chair and table, and some books. He had the uncanny feeling that Margaret saw everything in the room; she moved with certainty to where he stood, avoiding obstacles, and knelt to him. Pity stirred in him; what a tragedy for a woman to have been born so!

'I ask it of you, reverend Father. I will be responsible

121

for the good behaviour of Ceccha.'

'You cannot be everywhere,' he said, at the same time knowing he would yield to her. So great was the fame she had acquired for doing good works that there was no quarter of the town which did not know her and watch for her coming, Had they been less isolated, he knew, her fame would have spread by now beyond Castello.

He laid a hand briefly on the hooded head. 'If you will promise it, then I have no further doubts,' he said kindly. 'And now tell me of yourself and of how you fare in our company.'

'I am happy in it, though unworthy. God has granted me many favours.'

'Tell me of them,' he said. After she had gone his sub-prior entered and found his superior deep in prayer. He waited, and presently Don Luigi rose to his feet. 'I have had a most marvellous experience,' he said, 'the conversation of blind Margaret. Do you know that she can recite all the psalms by heart?'

'She would need to, for she cannot read,' said the sub-prior practically. 'Some she would learn in her time with the Mistress of St Margaret's.'

'Half a dozen, perhaps. She was not in the convent long enough to learn them all. She herself says she completed the knowledge the day after becoming a *mantellata*. And there are other things. She has been granted understanding of matters such as geometry, the placing of the stars which she can never have seen, much Latin which she can never have heard or read. It is, I am convinced, an instance of the direct intervention of God. In fifty years of life in the Spirit I have encountered nothing like it.'

The sub-prior had turned his head away towards the window; beyond was a murmuring, which increased as they stood there together. A crowd was coming down the street, shouting and gesticulating; prominent among the leaders was a young man in red and yellow. 'It is the Bianchi faction,' muttered the sub-prior, and crossed himself. 'Their leaders have sworn to overthrow the government. There will be trouble.'

'It is not our concern,' said the Prior quietly, moving away from the window as the crowd passed on. Later there were other cries, the sounds of struggle and some arrests; he heard none of it, for he was back again at prayer before his crucifix, remembering Margaret and the strange way knowledge had come to her.

There was no more trouble about Ceccha; she joined the Order and continued, like her mother, a faithful *mantellata*. The three were walking home together after a tiring day's work among the sick; Ceccha recited the rosary and the two other women made the responses. The shadows lay long across the courtyard and as they passed, flung striped patterns on their cloaks and hoods.

'How quiet it is,' said Ysachina. She had given up painting her face and looked like an old woman, but a happy one. She had taken to charitable work and prayer at first perhaps as an opiate, to let her cease brooding on Mercati's death. As time passed the grief faded, but her strength remained. Ceccha was a comfort to her; it was better this way, they did not have to part company. She pushed aside the leather curtain which led to the stairs. Seated on them was Beatrice, silently weeping.

'What has happened?' cried Ysachina, and ran to her. The other woman sobbed out her story; early today, before most people were about, the law-officers had come and taken away her son. 'They say he is in league

with the Bianchi,' she wailed, 'and it is true enough; he
has been out almost every night, plotting and coming in
boasting of it. He is such a fool he will not keep quiet, it
is a wonder they have left him free so long. Perhaps they
were waiting to see who else he would blame.'

Ysachina paled; the penalties for such plotting were
terrible; they might torture and execute the boy, or fine
him heavily. 'If we do not pay,' moaned Beatrice, 'they
can flog him through the streets of town and brand him
with red-hot irons, or cut his hand off. And besides all
that, we as his parents may be banished from the
district, and where are we to go? Offrenducci has few
friends in other places; we have always kept to
ourselves. What shall I do, what will become of us?' She
raised a tear-blotched face, its red eyes staring at
nothing. The others waited in shocked pity. Suddenly
Margaret said, standing a little apart, 'Do not fear,
Monna Beatrice. There will be no banishment, no fine,
no torment. Your son will be set free.'

'How can you say it? You do not know how cruel the
law can be. You should keep silent when you can do no
good. Pray that he may have courage, that is all.'
Beatrice's anger made her bosom heave; she had
stopped crying. Ceccha and her mother drew together
in silence. There were things they did not understand;
but had not Margaret foreseen their own entry into the
Order? She had not spoken idly then. Now, it would
remain to be seen; they themselves did not think there
was hope for the boy. He had plotted too flagrantly, as if
to be revenged on something. Ceccha herself had met
him returning home one night drunk. He had looked
sullenly at her and said, 'Pretty Ceccha, with your hair
cut off and your smooth shoulders scarred; what is the
use of it?' And he had almost daunted her, for she was

sensitive to pain and feared the discipline; but she had prayed, and the doubt had gone away. Perhaps Margaret now had prayed for her cousin. If only it were true that he would be released! Surely after such an experience, he would not be such a fool again.

The Offrenducci boy was released, though no one seemed certain why. In the midst of the rejoicings as he came home was still fear; they had best leave town after all. They would go meantime to one of Offrenducci's few friends elsewhere, who lived in Mantua. 'It is far enough away for all this to be forgotten,' said Beatrice. She looked with compassion at Ysachina, Ceccha, Margaret. 'The house will have to be sold to provide us with money,' she said. 'Where will you three go?'

It was Margaret who answered. 'Do not fear, there are places for us,' she said, 'homes will be offered to us all.' She seemed a calm centre in the storm of upheaval; even Ysachina ran about the house distracted, looking out this and that that she owned. 'Do not trouble with them,' said Margaret, as if seeing the piled cooking-vessels and jars and tapestries. 'A *mantellata* has no property. Our Lord had the sensible view; it cannot go with us when we die, and while we live moths may eat it.'

Ceccha's eyes rested on her lovingly. 'Margaret, you will not go away from us?' she said hesitantly. 'You will stay in the same house, wherever we go?'

The blind woman shook her head gently, smiling a little. 'No, Ceccha,' she said slowly. 'It is time for me to be alone again. You and your mother will come to no harm now you wear the cloak; you have many friends.'

'None like you! None like you!'

'I will not forget you in my prayers,' said Margaret.

16

'But naturally you must come and make your home with us. The house is large, and although my boys are full of high spirits, they will not trouble you.'

Lady Gregoria was a serene well-born woman who had joined the *mantellate* some years earlier. She had leisure to do much good work, for her husband Venturino was very rich, and high in the city councils. When she said her house was large it was no exaggeration; it was a palace, the grandest in Castello.

Afterwards the other women clustered about Margaret, congratulating her on her new home. They were joyously certain that at last she would have comfort; in all her life she had never known it. 'And the Venturino boys are little devils, but you're good with children; remember how many you have minded in your day, and how glad the mothers were.' That had been while she had lived in the houses of the poor.

She slipped into the Venturino house with her rosary, her discipline and her stick; she had nothing else to bring. Gregoria took her by the hand and guided her to

126

the room that was to be hers. The boys were out at
school in the city. Afterwards she met them, at first
sensing their wide eyes at her appearance; but they were
civil and well brought up, and respected her, playing
their pranks elsewhere.

Gregoria had led her round the room. It was
sumptuous, and had a view of the river. Scented rushes
lay on the floor and Margaret's feet limped through
them with a muffled sound; there was no filth mixed
with them as was usual in the houses in which she had
been. The bed had curtains thick with embroidery,
and a mattress of feathers. There was a chest for
holding clothes. Gregoria stepped back and regarded
the blind woman, smiling. 'You will sleep soundly here,'
she said, 'and if you want to go out to church privately
there is a door to the street; I will show you.' She led the
way down flat steps to the postern, opening it so that
Margaret could assess the placing of the bolts. They
proceeded back to the room in silence. Gregoria stared
at the cripple's thin, humped back. Margaret had grown
even more emaciated this past year; the kindly woman
looked forward to persuading her to break her fast
sometimes, to eat well and restore her health; she
coughed often, sometimes bringing up blood.

Left alone, Margaret limped about the room. She
could find everything now, and there was the blessed
door to the world she knew. For this other world was
strange. Not in all her life had she slept in such a bed.
The soft mattress would caress her tired body, the thick
rushes soothe her feet. She could summon servants for
her slightest need; she need want for nothing. She stood
in the centre of the luxurious room, and hated it. But
she must not be ungrateful. She could still mortify
herself, to atone for the comfort. She knelt down at the

predella, and loosening the robe over her shoulders scourged herself, as she did daily three times. The sting of the whip against her thin flesh brought her back from the moment's urge, the moment's joy and thankfulness that at last, in this, she could be as others, no longer condemned to sleep on a hard floor, in chilly doorways.

The boys came home from school each day in time for the meal. They ate heartily and between mouthfuls, told Margaret, of whom they were no longer shy, what they had learned. She questioned them eagerly. 'I was never at school with other children,' she told them. They gazed at her round-eyed.

'Did you never play?' It was impossible, now one thought of it, to picture her as different from what she was now; in a way, she was still like a child, simple and tiny.

She smiled, and told them of the garrison children with whom she had played hide-and-seek. 'And I always found them, because it is easier when one cannot see.'

'Who taught you lessons?' For they knew that she was not ignorant.

'The *cappellano*, and life. Now tell me of your geometry. Which proposition did you learn?'

They told her, and she corrected them; there had been two mistakes. 'After supper, fetch me your exercises; I cannot see them, it is true, but I will tell you where the errors are. And your Latin. Bring that, and we will revise it together. It is not yet perfect.'

She was joyous, as though the inner knowledge she had were a shining jewel, ready to be uncovered. The boys clustered about her, brows puckered, then clearing as she gave them the right answers instead of what they had written. She knew quotations she could never have read; she knew musical terms. 'Where did you learn, Margaret?' they asked, knowing the answer would always be the same.

'From God.'

She was never mistaken, they knew from experience; tomorrow, the schoolmaster would be astonished and would ask if their father had helped them, and they would say with truth that he had not. Venturino in fact would have been small help with learning; he had not applied himself when a boy, and was the more determined that his sons should profit by a good education. He watched the lessons, indulgently at first, then in growing amazement.

'Where did she learn it all, alone and blind?' he asked his wife. Lady Gregoria smiled wisely.

'Margaret has access to sources we know nothing of. It is like the coming of Pentecost, when the disciples began to speak in unknown tongues. She is close to the Holy Spirit, who aids her.'

'She has a particular devotion to St Joseph,' said Venturino. 'I hear her talking of his virtues to the boys. Even the priests pay that good saint small attention; it is singular that Margaret should prefer him above all saints except Our Lady.'

Gregoria told him the tale, for she had heard it in the city, of how Margaret had once slept with beggars in the carpenter's stable, and had felt the Incarnation come again. 'Well, at any rate she sleeps in comfort now,' replied Venturino. He was proud of his rich tasteful house, and took as much interest in its tapestries and embroidered hangings as a woman. Gregoria, despite her duties among the *mantellate*, ran his house perfectly. He was glad that his wife was a member of that sisterhood; it brought her friends, and if anything should happen to him while the boys were still young, Gregoria would not be forsaken.

One of the servants left the Venturino house to be married in her own valley, from which she would not return. On her going, Margaret asked if she might speak with Venturino. He came, and listened courteously; but was soon perturbed.

'Sleep in a servant's room, with no mattress, a garret cold in winter and stifling in the sun? Why so when you are welcome and comfortable downstairs? If you dislike the river room, we can change it for another. We cannot allow a guest to live like –' he had been about to say 'a beggar' then remembered that that was in fact what she had been. He flushed at his own carelessness, and to cover it up began to speak of other rooms; one had a brazier, another a tiled stove, a third thick tapestries from France. 'They keep the walls warm,' he said. 'You must be careful of your health for all our sakes, Margaret. We cannot have you fall ill in our house. Accept a little comfort, I beg.' He saw that she was looking thin and drawn, a little bag of twisted bones. She smiled, and shook her head.

'You have been kindness itself to me, you and Gregoria; more than kind. But I cannot be happy in a rich room when our Saviour often had nowhere to lay his head. I try to be like Him; I do not need riches.'

Gradually she persuaded him, but he was not happy about it; often he would complain to Gregoria that the wind was howling above the roof, and would keep Margaret awake and cause draughts in her cold garret room; or the snow was falling, and would seep through joints in the wall; or the sun was too hot, and would stifle her. 'Let her be,' said Gregoria. 'She herself knows what is best for the way of life she has chosen. I myself, and the other women, would not have the courage to endure it.'

'I would not permit you to do so,' said Venturino. And she smiled; he permitted her, in fact, anything she chose.

Gregoria's sister-in-law had given birth to a little girl, and she asked Margaret to be its godmother. The blind woman held the small warm bundle in her arms, blessed and kissed it; the child had been christened Margherita. From time to time over the next three or four years the mother brought the child to visit her, then when Margherita grew strong enough to climb the stairs she came alone; her hurrying footsteps stumbled with eagerness. She brought joy to the house; she was a beautiful child, like an angel, Gregoria said; certainly she was seldom naughty. When word came one day that she had been taken ill, both women hurried round to the child's home. The physicians had been; there was not yet cause for concern: it was a fever, and would pass.

Next day it was different. From tossing in fever the little girl had grown very quiet; she no longer cried out with pain, but appeared sunk in torpor which was like death. The doctors came again, prescribed other remedies, and these were brought, to no avail. Soon, it was felt, Margherita would stop breathing.

The mother and Gregoria sobbed by the bedside; Margaret herself knelt in the passage, praying. She seemed oblivious of the passing to and fro of doctors and well-wishers; she might have been in a trance. Night fell, and nobody left the house; it was considered a courtesy to witness the exit of the child's soul. The priest had already been with the Viaticum. There was nothing more to be done except pray.

Midnight passed, and a bell sounded; it was the call to Prime. Suddenly the little girl opened her eyes, and smiled. 'I am better,' she said. They clustered about her; it was true, colour had returned to her cheeks.

'Margaret prayed for me.' They turned to watch the kneeling shape of the blind cripple, still rigid in prayer. Gregoria's sister-in-law made her way to the twisted figure and knelt also, kissing Margaret's hands. It was as it had been in the Bible; the child grew better from that hour.

After that, Margaret's fame spread beyond Castello. It became difficult for her to find peace for her prayers; if she were seen in the street, or even in church, folk flocked to her to beg for cures. She began to stay more and more in her attic room, going through the prescribed prayers and Offices: until she found out about visiting the prison.

17

The Venturino garden was a hive of sound that day. Above the splashing of the fountain, which sounded continually, came the clacking of looms; Gregoria and her maidservant were busy weaving cloth. Further off the boys, released from school, were kicking a ball about, shouting with pleasure. The only one idle was Venturino himself, seated in his great dagged head-dress, enjoying the sun and the company of his children. Into the scene came Margaret, in her cloak; it wrapped her humped form, making her like a great black bird against the light. The boys smiled when they saw her.

'Here is Margaret,' they said, 'and she will ask us about our geometry again.' The blind woman still amazed them by not only asking questions about all they had learned at school, but putting them right if they erred: whether Euclid, the placing of the stars, rhetoric or Latin grammar, it was all the same to her. Nobody knew how she learned all she did. 'She knows far more than those who have sight,' their mother told them.

But Margaret did not ask them about geometry today. Her face was grave.

'Gregoria,' she said, 'I have just met Venturella. She has been to the prison. Why do we never go?'

Gregoria flushed a little. 'The conditions there are terrible,' she told the other. 'We have constantly pressed the city authorities to improve them, but to no purpose.'

'Some of the cells are underground without fresh air or light,' said Margaret. 'Many of the prisoners have no mattresses, not even straw, and must sleep on the stones. Some are starving; they receive no medical care if they are sick. Some go mad. They are chained to the walls like beasts. How can they believe in God if they are treated so?' Margaret was passionate: her fists clenched over her stick.

'The jailers are paid very poorly,' said Gregoria. 'That means they make money where they can; if a man would be unchained for a little, he must pay. Even the food given by charity is sold to those who can pay for it.'

'And what of those who cannot pay?'

'They starve.'

'We must visit them, Grigia! We must do something for them!'

'There is the stench of the prison, which is frightful; and the risk of jail fever.'

'And you are afraid of bringing it home to your family.' She turned her head to where the boys were playing again with their happy shouts. 'I cannot ask Venturino to risk letting me bring the fever home,' admitted Gregoria unwillingly.

But he had heard his name spoken and came and towered over them. 'What is this you speak of?' he asked them. Ever since Margaret had deserted her rich room for the garret he had had an affection for her and noted everything she did: her help with the boys' lessons was not the only matter that had not escaped him.

'Messere Venturino, let us visit the prison,' said Margaret now. The filmed eyes gazed at him as though she could see.

He stared at his garden; at the green calm of the trees and plants. 'When I die,' he said suddenly, 'I do not want our good Lord to say to me "Venturino, on earth I was hungry and you gave Me not to eat; thirsty, and you gave Me not to drink; sick in prison, and you visited Me not".' He turned to his wife. 'If it is your wish, my dear, you shall visit the prison, you and Margaret both,' he said. 'I no longer withhold my permission.'

So Margaret and Gregoria, like others of the *mantellate*, began to visit the prisoners with food, clothing and bedding. If the men were sick they got them doctors; if they were dying they persuaded them to make peace with God. 'The Son of God was a man,' said Margaret. She helped to make their lives less squalid: she prayed that they might find peace.

There was a man lying in prison whom none of the *mantellate* dared face, so great were his blasphemies.

His name was Alonzo of San Mario. He had been arrested on the escape of his brother, and tortured to try to find evidence concerning the latter, His wife and little son had been reduced to destitution because of his imprisonment. Lately the little boy had died of starvation.

'You must not mention God to him,' Margaret was told. She came to the place where the man was, lying on the stones; his skin was a mass of ulcers, and Gregoria began to bathe them with warm water. Margaret knelt at her prayers nearby. Presently she rose to her feet. The man Alonzo turned his head; he could hardly bear to look at Margaret, he turned away. Then the sound of cries came through the prison. 'Mother of God! Look at her! Look at her! It is a miracle!'

He made himself turn again to look: and held his gaze in wonder. Margaret had risen twenty inches off the floor, her face tilted upwards as if in rapt contemplation of a heavenly vision. Her hands were still joined in prayer. Everyone saw it. Her face was radiant as if in sight of divine love. Alonzo stared. 'Will you not love our Lord?' whispered Gregoria to him.

The tears blinded the chained man. He had seen what he had seen. Henceforth he would believe in miracles, and that his little son was now with God: it comforted him.

Winter came, and with it the bitter winds down the mountain passes; Venturino went daily to his office wrapped in furs. During the Christmas holiday season he used to take his sons with him; it was good, he felt, for the boys to see how matters were run and to be able to oversee the clerks at their work. 'Keep up the fire,' he would say to Gregoria, 'we will soon be home to warm ourselves.'

She piled logs on the hearth, keeping the house snug against their coming; but one day a spark caught. In no time there was a blaze, and Gregoria cried out for help; in the town everyone would drop whatever he was doing to man buckets, or the fire would spread.

'Help! Fire! Help! Help! Fire!'

The echo spread. 'Venturino's house is afire!' Men came running from all directions, each carrying a full bucket; soon two lines formed, one to pass up the full buckets and one to return the empty ones to the fountain and the cisterns. Soon the great bell of the town hall sounded, warning all citizens of danger. 'Fire!' they echoed. 'Fire!' And more and more came to fight the blaze, but the wind spread it.

The fire had broken out on the ground floor. Smoke bellied and flashes of flame shot among the smoke; it was hard to see. Neighbours began to remove their own belongings, fearful lest the fire spread. The Anziano, the senior warden, ran up and down to urge the men to greater effort; but in vain, the flames grew beyond control.

Gregoria cowered in a doorway, thinking of her precious possessions; the tapestries, the woven cloth, all gone, all to be done again. 'Luckily my husband and the boys are away,' she told a neighbour. 'There is nobody upstairs —'

Suddenly she placed a hand to her mouth. Margaret! Margaret had not left her attic room. She was up there praying. She would not see the flames; they would engulf her.

Gregoria ran. She ducked in her own blazing doorway, and two firemen turned her back. 'Margaret!' she screamed. 'Margaret!' Suddenly a figure appeared above, beyond the smoke and flames. It was Margaret, wrapped in her cloak. 'Hurry,' called Gregoria. 'The house is on fire. Come down to me.'

She heard the other laugh. 'Have confidence in God,' called Margaret. 'Take my cloak. Cast it in the flames.'

She removed the black mantle, and rolling it in a bundle threw it downstairs. She was quite calm, even smiling. Terrified, Gregoria caught the cloak. 'Spread it out over the flames,' said Margaret again. Then she turned away towards her attic room.

In full sight of the crowd of men who had come to fight

the fire, when the cloak of Margaret was thrown into the flames the blaze was instantly extinguished.

That news could not be concealed; nor could the healing of Sister Venturella's eye.

Venturella was a middle-aged *mantellata* who was well known in the town. She had been visiting the prison long before Margaret went there, and went about everywhere doing good, her basket of food and bundle of clothes on her arm, her cloak about her. Lately she had been troubled by a tumour over one eye and the doctor to whom she took it, the son of Maestro Imberti, said he doubted if he could save her sight, and would in any case charge so high a fee that she could not pay it. She had already paid much money for an operation for her son; now she was poor. She hurried to Margaret; someone who was blind would understand.

'I cannot bear it,' she sobbed. It hardly occurred to her that the young woman listening had never known sight. Margaret smiled.

'God is offering you a means of grace,' she told the other. Venturella shuddered.

'To be blind! Never again to see the faces of my family! I could not endure it! I would rather die!'

Margaret sighed a little. How well Our Lord had known weariness at the numbers who pressed on Him to restore sight, to make them whole! 'Take my hand,' she said, 'and place it over your eye.'

She wants to know the size of the tumour, Venturella thought. She took the blind girl's hand and did as she asked. At once the tumour vanished and her sight was whole.

Above on the hills, a party of horsemen was riding

towards Castello, looking down on the spreading town
and the Tiber. Among them was a young man with a
black beard. Domenico had grown it during the year he
had been away: he thought it made him look more of a
man and less of a boy. But his features were unchanged,
grave and handsome: he wore rich clothes, for he had
made money during the journey to the northern towns
and still had the opportunity to return if he wished, with
a place in the Antwerp warehouse. He had decided to
accept it and to take Annina back with him as his wife;
there, there would be no ugly gossip to follow her,
nobody to call his son a bastard. It remained to find her,
and to clear his affairs here in the south. Of Ceccha he
did not think; such matters could not be helped. No
doubt her parents would make other arrangements for
her.

He turned to the others, who waited on his order to
ride. 'Let us go,' he said, 'if we are to be in before dark.'

And they rode on down the path towards town.

18

Margaret heard the paved floor echo to the faint tap of her stick; the church was empty, as so often at this hour. She limped on towards the confessional and paused for a few moments; she was tired, so tired. She began to cough and felt the familiar warm sticky blood, tasting of salt, on her hand and tongue. She knew well enough that she would not live much longer now. The thought of death was joyful to her and her lips smiled as she advanced to where the priest waited. He saw her come and thought, as he had done for some time of late, that it was like watching a skeleton move. He would grieve when Margaret died; she was the perfect penitent and came to confession daily. Moreover he had heard certain things of her and frequently examined her regarding them. But he had found no falsehood in her and she enacted no drama. Things had happened as they had; that was all.

Once she had said to him, 'I used to want greatly to be loved, and when my parents did not love me I was hurt by it. That was a sin of pride, for I had much of it. I have

since learned that all one need do is love, love others,
love God with the whole heart.'

'Much has been granted you, Margaret.' He reflected
that it might also have been said that much had been
taken away; her sight, her shape and bodily strength,
her right to live as a woman. But she would never
regard herself as pitiful, and accordingly was not.

She began to tell him of a thing he had heard from
her previously, namely that she had again beheld God at
the altar. 'You have been blind from birth,' he told her.
'How can you know what it is to see?'

'I know, that is all. I see Our Blessed Lord at the time
of Elevation.'

'What else do you see then?'

'Nothing.'

'You do not see the altar itself, the candles burning,
the priest as he says Mass?'

'I see nothing but Our Lord.'

'Describe Him.'

'How can you ask me to do what cannot be done? He
is beauty infinite. Words cannot tell it.'

'Nevertheless try, Margaret.'

Her tongue stumbled; then she felt it move in spite of
her, felt her mind and body drag at it, trying to hold it
down; but they could not. It was the same as when
others had told her she was lifted up from the earth; she
willed nothing then, only was caught up, as now, in an
awareness beyond awareness, a state that could not be
described by earthly means. She herself was borne
above her tongue's confession and did not know how
long a time went by while her tongue spoke. She heard
the priest answer at last; how long had they been here?
It did not matter.

'The pure in heart shall see God,' he told her. His

voice was trembling. 'Go in peace; your sins are forgiven.'

She went back to her attic bed and this time lay down; she had no longer the strength to kneel. Presently, as she had not appeared for their meal, Gregoria came to her.

'Are you well?' she whispered, and knew that it was not so; she could see the dried blood about Margaret's mouth.

The sick woman smiled. 'I am as well as I have ever been, for I know of God's love and can think of nothing but that I am going to Him.'

'You are ill,' said Gregoria, her tears rising. She turned away. 'I will fetch the priest.'

She felt the straw pallet, the shrunken body lying on it, the bloodstained clothing, the illumined face. The tears started to spill over and she found it difficult to see her way in the partly rebuilt house; what would any of them do without Margaret?

The priest said he would come, and bring the Unction. By that time all of the household, servants, round-eyed sons, Venturino himself, knew that Margaret was very ill. They knelt on the stairs and in the passage, praying, remembering the things she had said and done; remembering that quiet presence limping among them cheerfully.

The *mantellate* had come, filling the house and street with their presence of white and dark; their prayers made a murmuring. The Prior himself came then, carrying the Sacrament, his escort of friars chanting the gradual psalms. The sound of chanting grew louder and then stopped; a body of horsemen had ridden into the street. Their leader pressed forward as they reached the dying woman. The Prior took the Unction and anointed her; there was hardly any flesh to touch. He held up the Host in his hands before her blind eyes.

'Do you believe that this is the Christ, the Saviour of the world?'

Her face was serene with radiance. 'I believe it,' she whispered. It was as if all the bodily strength left in her reached out to the small white wafer. The prayers for the dying began and swelled, repeated through the house and down into the street where others knelt, many crying openly.

In the room above, with the wafer on her tongue, Margaret's eyes had closed. As if they could watch it pass, they sensed the soul leave her body. Many looked up into the sky, as if hopeful of seeing it open to receive her, as had happened with God. But they saw nothing.

It was the second Sunday after Easter, 1320. She was thirty-three years old.

They washed the body lovingly, exclaiming over the scarred shoulders and cadaverous thinness. They dressed it in the religious habit of the Dominicans and laid it on a wooden frame, to serve as bier for carrying to the Carità. She would have the privilege of being interred there, but otherwise would be buried as the poor were, without a coffin and with no embalming. The great cloak shrouded her. The bier was lifted and they carried her out into the street.

The body of horsemen had ridden into the street. Their leader pressed forward.

'I would speak with Margaret.'

They murmured at him. 'She is dying. She can speak with no one.'

'She will not refuse me.' How could he find Annina
without being told where? Only Margaret knew where
she lived now, with his son.

He looked despairingly about him, encountering only
hostile faces. Suddenly he saw Ceccha, kneeling in
prayer, her hair cropped beneath her hood. He scarcely
knew her; it came to him with incredulity that she had
become a nun. He went to her, flinging the reins to his
man.

'You will not refuse me,' he told her. 'Go to Margaret
for me, and find out from her where Annina lives now.
She has cared for her all these months, and saw my son
born. I do not know where to begin to look for her.
Please help me, Ceccha.' He stared at her, wondering if
she resented his request. It was not as if she had ever
loved him. Presently she rose, her eyes still downcast,
and hurried into the house. Nearby was her mother, still
praying; Ysachina had ignored him.

He waited, while all about him sounded prayers for
the dying woman. Presently the Prior came with his
procession, bearing the Blessed Sacrament. Despair
took Domenico; after receiving that, Margaret would
have no further contact with anyone on this earth. But
Ceccha came hurrying back, thrusting her way through
the crowd.

'She is in the fourth house by the river, on the upper
floor. Margaret sent the child her love.'

'I cannot thank you enough,' he told her. There
seemed nothing more to say. Still with the sounds of
their prayers in his ears he took horse again and rode
towards the river.

He found the house; it was huddled among the rest.
He strode upstairs. A young woman opened the door to
his knock and he took Annina in his arms. She was a

little fatter, brown as ever, shedding tears at the sight of him.

'Domenico! Domenico! I thought that I would never see you again. Come and look at our great rascal. Is he not like you? And now you have a beard.' She rubbed her cheek against it: he might never have been away. Suddenly fresh tears sprang to her eyes and she said, 'Margaret is dying. The whole town knows it. She was good to me here. Do you know that they say she was of noble birth? But she would never tell anyone her name.'

The Prior had anointed the body, which would have no coffin: the *mantellate* followed, each one holding a candle which burned pallid against the bright spring day. As had happened to Margaret in the last days of her life, crowds came; the street was packed, and on the church steps more people thronged, unable to join the press already within. It might have been the burial of an empress.

The crowd parted to let the pall-bearers go in with their burden; the Mass for the Dead began to be chanted and was heard by those waiting without; presently the sacring bell rang. Soon thereafter there was a stirring in the crowd and someone said, 'They are bringing her out. They are taking her to be buried in the cloister with the rest, with everyone.'

Voices began to protest. 'Bury her in the church,' they shouted. 'She is a saint.'

The friars who were bearing the body out looked back towards the Prior. Don Luigi shook his head; it was not for every *mantellata* to expect to rest in the church; the service had been held here, that was enough. But the crowd thought otherwise. By now the cry had spread to those who waited in the street and to the others beyond them again, so that it seemed as if the whole city shouted that Margaret must be buried in church, Margaret was a saint. The people surged forwards and sideways, blockading the way to the cloister; the friars could go no further and set down their burden on the floor. The corpse with its open eyes lay peacefully, removed from the uproar. 'Do not tread on her,' someone said. Behind, at the altar, the Prior had begun to wave his arms for quiet. Soon the noise stilled; they respected him.

'Content yourselves,' he said, his deep voice reaching to the furthermost in the church. 'Margaret was a holy woman, a good woman, we know. But if she is a saint the Church alone must decide it. We will mark where she is buried; bury her in the cloister, in a marked place. When the time comes the question will be resolved.' If the body was to remain incorrupt, it would do so, despite the lack of a coffin and the embalmer's art. 'Give it due time,' he said, and again, 'give it due time.' He was thinking of others who had been lately canonised; the blessed Francis, the blessed Anthony. But the crowd howled him down.

'We all know how long the Church takes! We ourselves will be dead and buried by the time they remember little Margaret! Bury her in the church, in a tomb!'

There was a little pool of silence; a well-dressed, handsome man of perhaps fifty years held up his hand. Those round about whispered concerning him; this was Professor Orlando, who taught civil law at the university in Bologna. He had been a friend of Margaret, had admired and helped her, seeing her go to and fro about the town. 'Thomas Aquinas, Margaret of Hungary, Albertus Magnus are not yet made saints by Mother

Church, and they are dead these fifty years,' he said
calmly. 'We in Castello do not want to wait so long. Bury
our Margaret in the church here, where she will be
remembered and all can come and pray to her.'

The Prior shrugged mentally. He himself was not an
enemy of Margaret. But how had the crippled outcast
gathered to herself such powerful friends? Professor
Orlando had the finest mind in North Italy; he could
not be ignored.

Meantime the crowd called on. The women were
perhaps the most vociferous; they had had Margaret
come to them when they were in labour, in want, in
sickness, in distress. They besieged the friars about the
bier; behind them the deep voices of their menfolk
growled and swore. It was beginning to resemble a
fight, a street brawl. 'Mother of God,' lamented
Gregoria from where her candle guttered in the
draught made by the stirring crowd, 'she would not
have wanted all this! She effaced herself always.'

The woman Venturella, whose eye had been cured,
turned a calm gaze on her, shading her own candle with
her palm. 'I think they will listen now,' she said quietly.
'They cannot resist so great a press of people, and the
Professor's plea.'

She turned back to stare at the crowd and to reflect
again on the delight it was to see them clearly. Soon she
saw another thing; a man and his wife had brought their
daughter, a mute cripple who could neither stand nor
walk. 'Let us in!' they begged. 'Let us go to Margaret!'
The mute's head lolled; her father carried her on his
shoulder. Out of pity, the people let them pass.

They came to the still body, where it lay on the floor
on its pall. The woman knelt and the man, still holding
his daughter, lowered his eyes and began to pray.

Presently he crouched down with the cripple on the floor and took her hand and stretched it out so that the fingers touched Margaret's cheek. The mother still prayed and wept. 'Help us, you who were crippled yourself,' she begged. 'You had a tongue which could tell of the things of God; she cannot speak. Do not refuse us, where you are now in full sight of God's face.' And the crowd pressing round began to pray also, their attention diverted from the matter of burial. 'Help, Margaret, help this child! From where you are now, hear their prayer! She is afflicted like you!'

Suddenly there was a cry. On the floor the corpse had lain still; now slowly, as they watched, the left arm rose, reached out, and touched the crippled mute. The child scrambled to her feet, wide-eyed, and spoke. 'I am cured,' she said. 'I am cured through Margaret.' She turned to her father and they embraced. The mother rose to her feet trembling with joy. 'She is cured,' she said. 'She can walk and speak. It is like Our Lord come again.'

The news spread rapidly. The crowd began to shout 'A miracle! A miracle! A cure, like Our Blessed Lord! They cannot refuse Margaret now!'

The Prior bowed his head. He was in the presence of a force stronger than his own will, stronger than decorum, than the regulations. He spoke to the priest at his side and the latter thrust out between the pressing bodies of the crowd, and shortly returned. The thing was done; they had sent for a coffin. Margaret would be buried in church. With so great a miracle before so many, who could refuse?

19

The city council met in the Palazzo del Podestà, in a medley of long gowns and grave faces. The unpopular governor, Guelfucci, was present, but said little in the discussion, which in any case was short. It was evident, and witnesses were not lacking, that a mute cripple had been cured by a blind cripple after the latter's death. 'There we have the stuff of miracles,' murmured a member of the company, and no one disagreed; there was silence, as if every man present realised that something beyond their understanding had happened, making them humble.

It was decided that the body should be embalmed at public expense. 'It is certain that she will be made a saint one day,' said the councillor who had spoken of miracles. The rest nodded. It would be necessary to approach the Bishop to provide lay and clerical witnesses. The viscera would be placed in one urn and the heart in another. That business settled, the council turned to other matters, but with their minds only half on them.

The Dominican church had been crowded since Margaret's death. Now that she had a tomb in one of the chapels folk knelt all day in prayer, crowding past one another to light candles; these blazed in company, shedding warm light on the tomb which contained the coffin. As in life, the crippled, the blind, the diseased came; among these a girl named Bernadina and her father. The man, Jacopo Cocci, had taken his daughter to many physicians, but none could cure the spreading cancer which obscured half her face. One eye was blinded with it. They lived near Margaret's homeland at Massa Trabaria; word had long ago spread there of the wonders done by Parisio's daughter from Metola, whom he had abandoned. 'We will go there,' said Cocci, and they had taken the rough path over the mountains, the same Margaret had travelled long ago; now, they were moved to see the crowds about her tomb, the candles burning. 'Go forward and kneel, and pray,' whispered Cocci, and they made way for Bernadina; she advanced fearfully, a hood pulled over her face. Cocci in his place prayed for her; he watched her go forward and touch the tomb. She knelt for a little, then threw her hood back with an expression full of joy; the cancer had gone, the eye could see. The crowd murmured in gratification; they expected cures from Margaret now. 'Go to a notary, and swear it,' said one. 'We must collect evidence, that she may be canonised as soon as it can be done.' Jacopo and his daughter went to a lawyer, Ser Giacomo, and swore to the cure, and it was written down. They went home, in great gladness; news of the cure spread like wildfire, and another afflicted person, Federico Binoli, who lived near Sant' Angelo in Vado, heard of it. He could not go to Castello, he had lost the use of his arms long ago, and now he could not walk. He prayed to Margaret where he was; if she was in heaven she would surely hear him. She heard, and he was cured. He swore to it also before a notary, in the presence of witnesses.

Near Borgo San Sepolcro, a man named Muzio had a five-year-old son, Ceccolo. The father had been proud when he was born, but the boy grew up a cripple. Physicians could achieve nothing. 'We will see what Margaret can do,' declared the father. He carried the boy on his shoulders all the way to Castello and laid him by Margaret's tomb. He himself knelt in prayer. He did not need to pray long; the boy rose and walked back to him.

Giovanni Cambi lived at Monte Santa Maria. He had a disease of the spine and could not turn his head without turning his body. Lately he had also had a fever, which made him weak. A friend returned from Castello and told him of Margaret's cures. Giovanni prayed, and while praying fell asleep; when he woke, he had been cured.

The fame spread. A noblewoman named Zinocia, from Paterno, had a son Narni who had a painful ulcer between his shoulders. Again, physicians had failed. The great lady arrived in a litter with the boy, and swept her bright silks through the church till she came to Margaret's tomb; again the cure was immediate. Lady Zinocia in gratitude hastened to a lawyer, and made her deposition as the rest had done. Evidence was piling up in many offices of law. Castello had almost forgotten Fra Giacomo and his earlier miracles, and hastened to Margaret. The convent which had ejected her was left without novices. The city was proud. Rich and poor still remembered; among the poor was the cripple, Aldobrandini. He could not climb a flight of stairs and on level ground had to drag himself. He prayed from where he lay near the Porta Santa Maria, and Margaret cured him. 'I was her neighbour,' he said proudly to the notary. 'She could not refuse me, could she?'

Worse than all these was the fate of a woodsman, who was killed and mangled by bears. Friends found the remains in the woods and carried them home. He was the breadwinner, and without him his wife and children would starve. They knelt round the bier, and implored Margaret to restore the man to life. He was restored, and his wounds healed.

Children were cured. One boy fell into the Tiber and was drowned, and his mother begged Margaret in her prayers to give him back his life; it was restored to him. Another child fell from a balcony and was killed, and Margaret gave him back to his mother, unhurt. There were others; so many others, among the crowds who rode into Castello to visit the places Margaret had known; the church where her parents had abandoned her – no good had come to them – the Offrenducci and Venturino houses, and the house of the baker; the ways she had known, the priests to whom she had confessed, and above all the Carità, and the tomb. They came from all parts, from Bologna and Padua and the other great cities, even Venice which had its fill of saints; from other lands, from ships which waited at Genoa or Cività Vecchia, so that the visit must be made in haste to catch the tides; from all places, marvelling, hoping, wondering; going home with a tale of the blind crippled girl on their tongues, who had not herself been cured.

But she was not yet made a saint. As the years passed, and the interest did not wane, the Prior – no longer Don Luigi – had the thought of preserving the heart in a reliquary, if it were still intact. They dug up the urn in which it had been placed at the time of the embalming. The heart was sound, but evidently contained some foreign matter. It was opened, and inside they found what looked like three pearls. On examining these, they were astonished; one showed a picture of the Incarnation, one a crowned woman, one an old man before whom a girl knelt, with a white dove nearby.

They looked at the marvels. One old monk, who remembered Margaret, said softly. 'She used to tell us "If you knew what I carry in my heart, you would marvel". How could she know? And that is St Joseph to whom she kneels. She always had a devotion to St Joseph.'

The new Prior spread out his hands. 'Knowledge is sent to such people,' he said. He went away thoughtful. The cause for canonisation should proceed at once; he would do everything he might to hasten it.

But haste was not forthcoming.

20

The time had passed; it was two hundred and thirty-eight years since Margaret's death. An assembly of persons, all of them important, stood in the chapel where her coffin had rested since her death. It had been noted of late that the coffin was rotting away, and the Bishop had ordered a new one to which the remains were to be transferred. In the slanting June sunlight the new wood showed, planed and unsullied.

The Bishop kept his thoughts to himself. He was aware of the history of events that had prevented the cause of Margaret from receiving attention in Rome. First of all there had been internecine wars and the regrettable handing over of the government of Castello to a Ghibelline faction. That had meant that all Church matters had had to lie low for a century. And then ... and then there had been the plague, the Black Death, which had decimated peoples and had put all idea of the next world out of their heads while contemplating the ruin of this. The carts, with their stinking bodies, rumbling along the streets ...

This body did not stink. The Bishop himself, as an acolyte, had often prayed before it and had emerged comforted. Nevertheless it was unlikely that there would be anything left now but the bones. He felt excitement rise as the workmen appointed came to open the frail coffin; they could rend it apart without tools, but the matter had to proceed with decorum, and the churchmen waited in grave silence while the nails were removed, the lid opened.

The workmen stood back. The churchmen came forward. There was a silence which could only be due to reverence. Inside the coffin lay an incorrupt body whose coverings had rotted away. Amid the remains of her Dominican habit the body of Margaret lay as those who had been at her death-bed must have seen it two and a half centuries before. The left arm was raised a little. 'The embalming,' murmured an old priest near the Bishop. 'They knew about such things in the old days.'

'Not so,' said the Bishop. 'In those times it did not preserve a body more than a few days. God is at work here. They cannot ignore Margaret now.'

He stared at the tiny, dwarfish body, the face with its broad forehead and aquiline nose and white serrated teeth, the latter easily seen as the lips had parted. The head was large by comparison to the small twisted trunk, the hands and feet narrow, the right leg shorter than the left. Here was Margaret of Metola as those long dead had been used to see her. Despite himself the worldly churchman felt deep emotion. War, plague, the passing of history, had delayed the cause of this woman's recognition as a saint. But the common folk still prayed here daily.

The Bishop remembered his duty and issued an

order for the body to be examined for chemical preservative. None was found. When the physicians had finished their probing the body was clothed in a fresh habit and placed in the new coffin.

News of the marvel leaked out. There was an intensifying of prayer to Margaret, a new recurrence of miracles such as had happened earlier. The Church was at last forced to act, though it took a further fifty years. An investigation into Margaret's life and miracles followed; the Sacred College of Rites declared Margaret a beata in 1601, with a feast day on the anniversary of her death, April 13th.

Her canonisation should have followed, but did not. There were always wars.

The shrine of Blessed Margaret of Metola reveals her body in a glass reliquary, beneath the high church altar which is reached by a flight of steps. One day a little blind girl named Elena came with her governess, who had studied Braille. Elena's keen hearing sensed the murmuring of prayer in the church, and she hesitated to go up to the altar, though she had been dressed for it with especial care, her dark hair combed and threaded with a blue ribbon to match the sash on her muslin dress.

'Take my hand, and climb the steps,' said the governess. 'Those are the little blind children from Margaret's Asylum for the Blind in Castello. They come here to pray to her.'

'Are they cured?' asked the child.

'Some, but not all. You must ask Margaret to cure you, and if not to send you her own humility; remember she spent all her life blind and no one cured her.'

They went together up the steps and knelt at the

reliquary inside which the calm dead body lay, as the Bishop had seen it when the first coffin was opened three hundred years before. The child touched the reliquary and prayed; the governess gazed on the dead woman's face, thinking that it had in any case been worth making the long journey from Florence to see it. Such things could not be explained.

Elena finished her prayers and rose. She was still blind. Tears began to make their way between her eyelids and she wept silently, while the governess guided her down the steps.

Outside she said, 'Blessed Margaret was always blind. Yet she was happy. You see, it is not so important that the eyes of the body should see, as that those of the soul should be clear. The blind make many friends. You will have consolations, Elena.'

They came out into the sunlight and made their way to the place where the hired car waited to take them back to Florence.

Tales from
Oregon State Sports

**Jeff Welsch and
George P. Edmonston Jr.**

Sports Publishing L.L.C.
www.SportsPublishingLLC.com

Director of production: Susan M. Moyer
Project manager: Greg Hickman
Developmental editor: Erin Linden-Levy
Copy editor: Cynthia L. McNew
Dust jacket design: Kerri Baker

ISBN: 1-58261-706-6

Printed in the United States.

SPORTS PUBLISHING L.L.C.
www.SportsPublishingLLC.com

*This book is dedicated to the memory of
Jon Christian Edmonston (1973-1995)*

Acknowledgments

The stories selected for *Tales from Oregon State Sports* came together over a 10-year period, during which both authors had jobs requiring them to cover current OSU news as well as the history, traditions and achievements of Beaver athletics and athletes.

Where possible, those athletes and Beaver fans who lived or witnessed these great moments were consulted and interviewed. In addition, Oregon Staters with a reputation for vast institutional memory were sought for stories and information. In both instances, we are especially indebted for the help given by the following individuals:

Jimmy Anderson, head basketball coach, 1991-1995 and assistant under Ralph Miller for many years; Dee Andros, former head football coach and athletic director, whose affection for his former players, particularly the 1967 "Giant Killers," has kept his memory sharp; Paul Andresen and Kip Carlson of the Fielder Jones Society, whose knowledge of OSU baseball, both past and present, has to be experienced to be believed, and whose devotion to the career of Fielder Jones has kept the story of this legendary Chicago White Sox player/manager alive into the 21st century; Darrell Aune, radio "Voice of the Beavers" for 30 years and the play-by-play announcer who called the upset over the Washington Huskies in Seattle in 1985; Thomas Bennett, freelance writer, whose stories in the *Oregon Stater*, OSU's alumni publication, remained an inspiration throughout the writing and compiling of the manuscript; Charles "Chuck" Boice, longtime editor of the *Oregon Stater* and dean of Beaver sports historians; Bert Brown of Tacoma, Washington, former member of the OSU Mountain Club, who first made us aware of Willi Unsoeld and his conquest of Mount Everest; former head football coach Dennis Erickson (1999-2002), in many ways the great architect of the new level of respect now enjoyed by OSU football and Beaver athletics in general; Helen Gill, wife of basketball coaching legend Slats Gill, who passed away in 2003 at age 98.

Also, the late Crawford H. "Scram" Graham, former OSU alumni director and a veritable walking archive of OSU history; Tom Huggins, OSU alumnus and former high school buddy and running mate of Steve Prefontaine; Larry Landis and Elizabeth Neilsen of the OSU Archives; Jess Lewis, a rare two-sport All-American in wrestling and football, for his honesty about himself; Ralph Miller, Hall of Fame head basketball coach from 1972-91 who, along with his predecessor Slats Gill, put OSU hoops firmly on the national map; Ken Munford, the widely acknowledged "dean" of Corvallis historians; Alex Petersen, original member of the 1947 "Thrill Kids" and teammate of Olympian Lew Beck; Dan W. Poling, whose institutional memory as former student, faculty member and longtime dean of men spanned from the 1920s until his death in 1998; Cliff Robinson, OSU's No. 1 basketball fan for more than 80 years; OSU's legendary former wrestling coach Dale Thomas, for his insights into the personalities and wrestling techniques of Olympian Robin Reed and All-Americans Howard Harris and Jess Lewis; Bill Tomsheck, last surviving member of the 1933 Iron Men and forever a grateful alumnus for the education he received at his alma mater; Paul Valenti, head basketball coach from 1965-72 and Slats Gill assistant for over 20 years, for his memories of the Harlem Globetrotters game; Donald S. Wirth, OSU Alumni Association executive director from 1975-1999; and Stephen T. Smith of the association for his support and encouragement throughout the project.

Pat Filip, managing editor of the *Oregon Stater*, and Sherry Moore Welsch, an OSU alum, deserve special thanks for applying their amazing and spirited talents of proofreading and editing and for their words of encouragement.

Finally, we want to thank our wives, Lucy Edmonston and Sherry Moore Welsch, for their patience during the long hours it took to produce this book.

Few of the accounts included in these pages have been published as they appear here. Each story has been pieced together using oral interviews, archived printed materials, photographs and, in some cases, simple good fortune.

Contents

Introduction

At first glance, Oregon State University and its host town of Corvallis seem like remote outposts on the American landscape.

The nearest major population center, Portland, is 90 miles to the north. To the south, if one sidesteps Eugene, which most Beavers do on impulse, it's some 400 miles to Sacramento or San Francisco, California. Downtown Corvallis has stayed within the confines of a five-block area for more than 150 years. On some Saturday mornings, the most exciting thing happening is the farmer's market.

In the broad plain of the Willamette Valley east of campus is the area's largest industry, companies that develop and produce grass seed for lawns and golf courses around the world. To the west, a 50-mile wide mountain range extends to the Pacific Ocean. Since its founding by pioneer Joe Avery in the 1840s, Corvallis has only had one television station.

On closer examination, however, Corvallis and its land grant university have been historically and inextricably linked to mainstream America.

OSU is the alma mater of Linus Pauling, one of the world's preeminent scientists and still the only person to ever win two unshared Nobel Prizes. Another graduate, Miles Lowell Edwards, co-invented the artificial heart valve, a miracle device responsible for saving thousands of lives since its introduction in the early 1960s.

For more than 30 years, OSU has been the leading wheat-breeding university in the country. Scientists at OSU were the first to develop the maraschino cherry and the flea collar for dogs and cats. Oregon Staters Vance DeBar "Pinto" Colvig and George Bruns composed songs that have become American cultural icons, the former for "Who's Afraid of the Big Bad Wolf" and the latter for the "Ballad of Davy Crockett."

In 1986, Oregon State student Stacy Allison became the first American woman to conquer Mount Everest. She was following in the footsteps of another OSU alumnus, Willi Unsoeld, who in 1963 was a member of the first American team to reach the summit of the world's tallest peak.

Reaching for still greater heights, OSU has produced some of the nation's best-known astronauts, including Donald Pettit, one of three crew members left circling the globe in the space station as the world mourned the loss of the space shuttle Columbia in February 2003. Looking on with much interest as a graduate student in OSU's College of Oceanography was Scott Corrigan McAuliffe, the son of Christa McAuliffe, the nation's first teacher in space and one of the seven astronauts to perish in the Challenger shuttle disaster of 1986.

At the turn of the last century, OSU president John McKnight Bloss (1892-96) was the same John Bloss who, as a sergeant with the 27th Indiana Regiment before the Civil War's Battle of Antietam in 1862, is credited with finding Gen. Robert E. Lee's Lost Order 191, still one of the greatest security leaks in American military history. A Bloss contemporary, John Letcher, taught mathematics at OSU in the 1880s and was the son of the man by the same name who served as governor of Virginia during the Civil War.

Before moving in 1878 to Corvallis, where he quickly became a member of the Board of Regents for the university, Wallis Nash was a London attorney with a client list that included evolutionist Charles Darwin and steel magnate Henry Bessemer. OSU was the first school in the west to establish a College of Home Economics, the first in the west to offer what we know today as ROTC, and the first to instruct students in the science of agriculture. In 1870, OSU became the first public university in the west to award college degrees.

To be sure, these accomplishments and many others connect Oregon State University to the larger world through historic people and events worth remembering. The same can be said of OSU athletics, and herein lies the chief purpose of this book: to share some of the memorable moments in Beaver sports history that connect the reader to the athletes, the teams, the games, the achievements and the near misses that collectively show that OSU is one of the nation's storied NCAA Division I programs.

Included are some of the greatest names and teams to ever wear the Orange and Black. On these pages you will meet the 1933 basketball team, which probably saved a legend's job; the 1933 "Iron Immortals" football team that dethroned a No. 1 team using only 11 players; the team that won the only Rose Bowl played away from Pasadena, California; a wrestler who defeated all but one of his fellow Olympians and would've happily broken every one of their arms; the high jumper whose revolutionary approach was considered a flop by U.S. coaches until he won Olympic gold; the women's basketball team that fashioned the greatest upset in school history; courageous national champions; the cross-country team that ran barefoot in the snow to the school's only national team title in any sport; legendary head coaches Bill Bloss, F. S. Norcross, Slats Gill, Sam Bell, Berny Wagner, Paul Valenti, Ralph Miller, Dee Andros, Paul Schissler, Tommy Prothro and Dennis Erickson. And of course, there's a chapter about how a personable PR man helped bring the Heisman Trophy west of the Pecos River for the first time.

Although we've tried to include something for everyone, the authors acknowledge the impossibility of compiling a series of stories inclusive of every single greatest moment in OSU sports history. So let us apologize now to those readers who look to these pages for a favorite athlete or game or season only to come up empty. Such a book would be encyclopedic in length and far beyond our resources to produce in a single volume. Rest assured, any future versions of *Tales from Oregon State Sports* will likely include stories on the likes of Gary Payton and others who made Beaver athletics what they are today.

Any journalist is always looking for an interesting story to tell, and we kept this theme uppermost in mind when the time came to prioritize and finalize the book's contents. We also placed high value on producing a publication that would play a small but hopefully important role in preserving institutional memory, that is, featuring certain people and events critical to an understanding of OSU's athletic program.

With this in mind, we gave special attention to choosing stories rarely told or not at all, such as the chapter that describes the birth of Beaver football and the players responsible for its beginnings, and the story of Notre Dame's Knute Rockne and the circumstances surrounding how this legendary football coach became a summer faculty member at Oregon State during the 1920s.

A few of our selections are from well-known events on which a closer examination through research provided a new twist, such as the account of Willi Unsoeld's ascent of Mount Everest in the company of a faculty member from the University of Oregon, or the bizarre circumstances surrounding the firing of promising basketball coach Bob Hager in 1929, which opened the door for Slats Gill's hiring.

Along the way we've included a few Civil War pranks and pages of the unusual, the rare, the spectacular, the intriguing and the controversial, the stuff that makes the history of college or university athletics, at OSU or any other school, such a fun topic for the journalist to share.

OSU is a charter member of the Pacific Coast Conference, which years later would become the Pacific-8 Conference and then the Pac-10. The first year of competition for the PCC was 1916, and the schools that joined to make history were OSU (known then as Oregon Agricultural College or OAC), the University of Oregon, the University of California-Berkeley and the University of Washington. This, however, was not the beginning of Beaver sports. Football began as an organized sport at OAC in 1893, along with track and field, and women's basketball followed in 1899. The men picked up the sport in 1901, refusing to participate any earlier in what they felt was a "sissy game."

The historical record shows that even these three sports were late arrivals on the Corvallis campus. As early as April 1883, OSU had a baseball team under the supervision of faculty member Bruce Wolverton, who encouraged the formation of the squad and scheduled its games. Newspaper accounts at the time show that OSU (named State Agricultural College or SAC until 1907) played two games against Christian College of Monmouth, Oregon, losing both contests by fairly hefty scores.

After Wolverton's departure in 1884, athletics at SAC continued for a few years, with baseball and "field sports" among the most popular.

Sometime around 1890-91, a group of men and women students formed what they called the College Athletic Association, an organization that is generally considered the genesis of everything we associate today with Beaver athletics. Sporting activities, including boxing, fencing, and gymnastics were conducted in a crude gymnasium on the second floor of Cauthorn Hall, the school's first dormitory for men known today as Fairbanks Hall. Of the 17 young men who made up the roster of OSU's first football team, seven were officers in this association of athletes.

In the final analysis, it is the legacy of these students that is the subject of this book.

—*George P. Edmonston Jr. and Jeff Welsch*
March 2003

1

Birth of Football

From January to September 2001, OSU enjoyed heady times in foot-ball: Fiesta Bowl champs, preseason No. 1 ranking in Sports Illustrated *magazine, first true Heisman Trophy contender in four decades, sold-out stadium, game tickets treated like gold bullion, conference and school records falling like rain. But where did all this Orange and Black football madness begin? The first season? First game? First coach? First stadium? First quar-terback? First touchdown? The saga of the people and events that sit at the historical taproot of Oregon State's most popular spectator sport begins with William "Will" Bloss, the first head coach, the great organizer, the opening spark of a century-old athletic tradition.*

In a sense, the birth of OSU football was probably at the Battle of Antietam during America's bloody Civil War. It was 8 a.m. on the morn-ing of September 17, 1862.

This is a moment in time military historians know well. The place name still sends chills down their spines: *The Cornfield.*

At this opening phase of the battle, it was the 27th Indiana's turn to enter Farmer Miller's 40 acres of ripe, head-high corn to face the loaded Enfield rifles of two Georgia regiments formed in line of battle at point-blank range.

Their volley went off like a bolt of lightning, sending thousands of "minnie balls" into the ranks of the 27th. Still looking sharp in their new blue uniforms, the Indiana boys were cut down like blades of mown grass.

Amid the smoke and hailstorm, amid the sounds of friends and comrades screaming and dying all around, was a future president of Oregon State University: John McKnight Bloss (1892-1896).

A sergeant at the time, Bloss would survive both Antietam and the war to become one of the country's top public school administrators. He would also father a son, William. The two would join forces in 1893 to start football at OSU, known at that time as State Agricultural College, or SAC.

The lesson of Antietam is that the football riches OSU enjoys today came within a Confederate bullet of happening some other way.

Bloss would spend the rest of his life as one of the nation's most celebrated soldiers. Three days before Antietam, it was Bloss and Corporal Barton Mitchell who found what today is known as "Lee's Lost Order."

Handwritten on a sheet of paper wrapped around three cigars, the document showed the disposition of Confederate Gen. Robert E. Lee's army, the kind of information an opposing commander could use to develop a strategy of divide and conquer. That Lee's counterpart, Union Gen. George McClellan, failed to cash in on his prize remains a source of endless debate among Civil War buffs.

Still considered among the greatest security leaks in American military history, the fame this event brought to John M. Bloss served him well as he climbed the ladder from school principal in Kansas and Indiana to college president in Corvallis.

Bloss has often been credited as the "father of intercollegiate athletics" at Oregon State. This is only partly true. That title should be shared with two others: Benjamin Lee Arnold, OSU's second president (1872-1892), and a faculty member named Bruce Wolverton, who taught at SAC for about a year (1883).

In April 1883, and with President Arnold's blessing (difficult to get from one so dead-set against any college activity not involving scholarship), Wolverton, an alumnus of Christian College in Monmouth, talked the two schools into facing one another in a game of baseball, written at the time as "base ball."

This game, probably the first intercollegiate athletic contest in OSU history, was played on April 14, with the "farmers" from Corvallis on the short end of a lopsided score. On Saturday, April 28, the farmers traveled north to Monmouth for a rematch. Same result.

After Wolverton's departure, athletics at SAC continued for a few years, with baseball and "field sports" the most popular. Then sports went dead until 1890, when SAC was back in Monmouth to avenge its earlier losses, to no avail. Final score: 32-22.

At about this same time, an unknown number of men and 30 women students at SAC formed what they called the College Athletic Association, a forerunner to the OSU athletic department. Sporting activities such as boxing, fencing and gymnastics were staged in a crude gymnasium on the second floor of Cauthorn Hall, OSU's first men's dorm (known today as Fairbanks Hall). Funding came from the students. From this earliest training facility emerged many of the athletes who figured prominently in the birth of football and track and field.

Will Bloss arrived in Corvallis shortly after his father took over the SAC presidency in June 1892. It is not certain if Will made any attempts to organize a football team. What is known is that he had been a star player at his alma mater, Indiana University, and had brought to Oregon a keen understanding for playing the rough-and-tumble sport.

In addition, he would not be the first to introduce Corvallis or SAC to football. Oregon's Willamette Valley has never been that isolated from popular culture. Portland's Multnomah Athletic Club, along with the city's Bishop Scott Academy, had been fielding football teams since 1887. Some evidence suggests football had been tried as a collegiate sport in Corvallis in 1891 or even earlier.

An April 29, 1892, article in the *Corvallis Gazette* reports that "football was all the rage for awhile but as soon as the boys found out there is considerable hard work mixed in with it, and saw some of the handsomest and strongest men limping around and their faces all bruised from the effects of too much hard playing, they decided to leave it alone for awhile...and to play base ball."

What Will Bloss did do was to reintroduce the campus to the sport. The result was the appearance in 1893 of OSU's first school-sanctioned, collegiate-level football team. Bloss transformed a club sport indulged in for exercise and macho bragging rights to one involving contests with other schools in a crude league. Yes, football had been tried, but nothing with the excitement Will Bloss was giving it.

At this time, SAC's mascot was a coyote named "Jimmie" and the school color was navy blue, a holdover from the days when the college was known as Corvallis College. A baseball diamond had been fashioned on Lower Campus as early as 1890, and it was here that Will and others selected the ground for the first football field.

Today, the site of this original field would be on that plot of ground that sits between Ninth and 11th Streets, just south of Madison Street.

At this location now sits the Oxford House and the Dixon and Avery co-ops. The original "stadium" was an open grass lot with yardage marked off using long, wavy lines cut into the surface of the playing field. In 1896 or 1897, bleachers were constructed for the south side, the home side. Around 1899-1901, a similar bleacher section for visitors was built on the north side. The field ran east and west.

In selecting his first team of 17 players, Bloss became both head coach and quarterback, not a bad move since he was the only one who had played at the collegiate level. Team morale was boosted by the start of several traditions that still spice up home games today.

On May 2, 1893, the SAC faculty voted to begin using orange to represent the school at all official activities, particularly athletics. Black was added later as the backdrop, the campus community possibly remembering the classy-looking, all-black baseball uniforms town clothier J. H. Harris had donated to SAC in April 1892. Though his gift was generous, there was a catch: Mr. Harris had put his initials "J. H. H." in big white letters on the fronts. "Hope you college boys won't mind," he said when they were delivered.

For such gorgeous uniforms, the college boys didn't mind a bit.

Not content on stopping here in starting new school traditions, President Bloss appointed a faculty committee to confer with students in the writing of a "college cry" or "yell." Thus the cheer, "Zip Boom Bee, Zip Boom Bee, O-A, O-A, O-A-C!" was born, the first such in school history and quite a departure from the old days, when such utterances were looked upon as undignified. Whoever created this three-line ditty remains a mystery. Some credit Gordon C. "Don" Ray, an engineering student in the class of 1896, while others claim it was Coach Bloss.

During the season, the school also introduced a mascot, or maybe he introduced himself. A Presbyterian minister named John Robert Newton Bell replaced Jimmie.

"Doc" Bell, as he was often called, would remain the official athletic mascot for 35 years. OSU's football stadium from the early 1920s until 1953, located where the Dixon Student Recreation Center is today, was named Bell Field in his honor. For years, Bell lived near the north corner of Ninth and Madison streets, a stone's throw from the original field. He only had to walk across his back yard to attend games.

Three names were used to identify athletes: "Farmers," "Agrics" or "Aggies."

After workouts that stretched to mid-October, Bloss settled on an eclectic group. No stranger team has ever been assembled to wear the

Orange and Black. The starting left guard was a high school junior. One of the substitutes was John Fulton, an alumnus and SAC faculty member assigned to a department called the "Chemistry Station." He would spend the rest of his career at his alma mater and become one of OSU's most beloved professors.

Two members of the starting lineup were brothers; their father was the secretary of the Executive Committee of school's Board of Regents. The head coach played quarterback. He was not a student. Neither were three other members of the squad, all substitutes.

Bloss made many of these acquaintances through contact with members of the already mentioned College Athletic Association, now meeting in the "new" SAC gymnasium, which had been moved from Cauthorn to a room in the school's new Mechanical Building, constructed by his father directly behind the Administration Building (now Benton Hall) in 1892. Seven of the 17 original players, including three starters, were not only members of the association but officers on its board of directors: the president, vice president and secretary. Three subs were also members of the board.

There were other similarities. In the short time he had lived in Corvallis, Bloss had watched these guys in other club sport activities, from baseball and track and field, to workouts in the college gym. By the fall of 1893, he knew who could get the job done. Bloss also realized that most of his players were from farming backgrounds, replete with the mental and physical toughness that goes with that lifestyle, and knew this would serve them well when games got tough.

Following are the 11 players and five subs that Bloss took to the field on November 11, 1893, to face nearby Albany College, in OSU's first-ever football game. Spellings used for positions were in popular usage at the time.

Left End: Charles Owsley of La Grande. He was a sophomore and sergeant at arms of the Athletic Association. He graduated with a degree in mechanical engineering in 1896, then returned home.

Left Tackle: A. Desborough Nash, brother of SAC starting left half Percival Nash. Born in 1876 in London, England, Desborough was 17 and not enrolled as a student. His father, Wallis Nash, was a member of the SAC Board of Regents and had, early in his career, worked as an attorney in London for Charles Darwin and other English and American luminaries. Desborough survived a scarlet fever outbreak that claimed the lives of two brothers and two sisters in one week. He played first base on the SAC baseball team.

Oregon State's first football team, 1893-94.
Will Bloss (holding football) was head coach.
(Photo courtesy of Orange & Black.)

Left Guard: Daniel Harvey Bodine of Albany. He was vice president of the Athletic Association. In 1893, he was enrolled in the "preparatory" department, meaning he was still in high school, probably a junior. He did eventually graduate from Oregon State in agriculture in 1898 and became the city recorder for his hometown. He lived at 819 W. 9th Street in Albany.

Center Rush: Harvey "Pap Hayseed" McAlister or McAllister. Originally from Lexington, Oregon, McAllister played one of the toughest positions in early football. Anchoring the center of the line, it was this freshman's job to clear a hole for the popular "wedge play," which meant one guy running the ball with 10 blockers out front. He typically wound up at the bottom of the pile. His personal scrapbook, which includes numerous newspaper clippings of the 1893 season, was his gift to the OSU Archives and is one of the primary research tools school historians use today to recall the first season.

Right Guard: Henry M. Desborough. He was a senior and graduated in 1894 in mechanical engineering. In 1925, the Alumni Association's Student Directory lists "no record" for this pioneer.

Right Tackle: Thomas Beall. He was a junior and graduated in 1895 with a degree in agriculture. In 1904, he was the first player from the 1893 team to die. He was president of the OAC Athletic Association and played center field for the baseball team.

Right End: Charles Small. He was a freshman and class secretary. He graduated in 1897 in mechanical engineering but spent his career as a farmer in Benton County.

Quarter Back: William H. "Will" Bloss. He left after the 1893 season to return as coach in 1897. In two years Bloss lost one game, to the University of Portland. Many SAC fans said the loss was a fluke, since the UP had sent "spies" to campus and had practiced by scrimmaging a team that had played SAC earlier in the year.

Left Half Back: Brady F. Burnett. He was probably Bloss's favorite player. He was team captain and scored the first two touchdowns in school history, back-to-back fumble recoveries, the second for 60 yards. He had already graduated in agriculture and was listed in *The Hayseed* below the senior class as a "special student." He was a member of first track and field team. He eventually became an attorney in Roseburg with the B. L. Eddy law firm. He was the younger brother of Ida Burnett Callahan, legendary English teacher at OAC, graduate of the class of 1881, and namesake of Callahan Hall.

Right Half Back: Percival Nash. He was the older brother of Desborough Nash. Like Burnett, Percival had graduated in 1893 in agriculture and was listed as a "special student" for the fall of '93. He became a federal probation agent in Reno, Nevada. He played right field on the baseball team.

Full Back: Ralph Terrill. The sophomore graduated in 1897 with a degree in mechanical engineering. For years he worked at the Acme hardware store in Wilmington, California, and lived at 315 Canal Ave.

The "subs" were: A. Lambert (not a student); W. Abernethy (not a student); Arthur E. Buchanan, who graduated in 1896 in mechanical engineering and died in 1916; John Fulton, an SAC alumnus and faculty member; Harry W. Kelley, a graduate in agriculture in 1896; and Clem Jones (not a student), who moved to Athens, Tennessee, and quickly disappeared from alumni records.

When the big day finally arrived, the Albany team appeared on the field as scheduled at 1:45 p.m. for a 10-minute workout. The "farmers" arrived at 1:55 p.m. The game would begin at 2 p.m. with the toss of a coin at center field.

At that moment, team captain Brady Burnett would make a decision that would help define the spirit of OSU athletics for all time.

November 11, 1893, 1:58 p.m. Overcast skies, no rain.

As Burnett walked to the center of College Field he was astonished at the scene.

It was bedlam. More than 500 spectators had paid a dime each to see this inaugural gridiron clash. That would equal the "take" of many of the popular literary societies on campus at their annual fund-raisers. This was some accomplishment, since these groups enjoyed top billing in the social life of the school. It was the biggest crowd ever to watch a sporting event in Corvallis.

And the noise! Horns of various sizes were scattered throughout the assembled spectators, many decorated with the school colors of the two participants.

Honk! Squeak! The brass cacophony grew louder as fan emotions were pushed to fever levels. Off to one corner of the home side, the south side, some of Burnett's classmates were trying out their school's new cheer. They were desperately trying to be heard over the noise of the Cadet Band, which was also trying to be heard over all the other racket that seemed to concentrate in the center of the field into one giant ball of chaos. The new cheer also reflected the growing popularity among students and townspeople of referring to the school as the "Oregon Agricultural College," a name that would not be made official until president William Jasper Kerr made it so in 1907.

Burnett saw two others approaching. One was a fellow named Washburn, captain of the Albany side. They had first met that morning at 11 a.m., when the Albany team had arrived riding a bunch of hacks they had used to travel the 12 miles between the towns. He and Bloss had accompanied the visiting fellows to the Cauthorn men's dorm, where all had enjoyed a meal and had swapped horrible tales about what they were going to do to one another once the game was under way.

This welcoming act would one day be the spirit that would help form the historic "30 Staters" organization at OSU, which from the 1920s through the 1950s performed similar services for visiting teams.

The other person to meet in the center was the referee, I. N. Irvine. He would later be accused by the newspaper in Monmouth of "home cooking" a game for SAC against the Oregon State Normal School (now Western Oregon University).

Washburn, as visiting captain, was given the call. The crowd grew quiet as Irvine's right hand flipped the silver dollar into the autumn sky.

"Heads," Washburn cried out.

It was.

"We want the ball," he quickly told Irvine, who just as quickly informed the crowd with crude hand signals that Albany College would receive the opening kick.

Now it was up to Burnett to decide which side of the field his team would defend.

There is an old axiom in warfare that says when defending something precious, you put it to your back: King Leonidas and his 300 Spartans defending the high frontier pass at Thermopylae; Lee at Petersburg; the French at Verdun; the Russians at Moscow...war is full of examples. Maybe Burnett had some of this in mind that day. Or maybe it was just pure instinct.

"We will defend the West goal," he said loudly. There was no hesitation in his voice. He had not checked the direction of the wind. Nothing weather-related really mattered.

He had decided they would put their college to their backs; it was time to defend this most precious thing called "alma mater."

And defend it they did.

After receiving the kickoff, Washburn tried a "V" wedge play over Pap Hayseed's center rush position. SAC stood like a wall of granite. Washburn fumbled. In a flash, Burnett scooped the ball off the ground and ran unopposed to the Albany goal for the first touchdown in OSU football history. The extra-point try, for two points, was wide, and the "farmers" were ahead 4-0, the number of points allowed for a TD at the time.

Furious they had fallen behind so quickly, Washburn and company tried another wedge on their next possession. Same result. Again there was a fumble and again Burnett was Johnny-on-the-spot, taking in the ball and carrying it some 60 yards for the second TD. It remains the only time in school history an OSU player has scored TDs on back-to-back fumble recoveries.

The score at half was 38-0. It would be much worse by game's end. Officials and coaches agreed to a 10-minute intermission. As was customary, the two squads retired to opposite ends of the field. Students from both schools took the opportunity to form serpentine-type formations that circled their champions with shouts of encouragement about "fighting the good fight." Albany, playing short-handed that day, approached Bloss with a request that he might send over a few of his subs. He obliged.

The second half produced OSU's first-ever trick play. On the kickoff, Bloss carried the ball about 30 yards. Just as he was about to be tackled, he tricked the Albany side by handing the ball off to Burnett in mid-stride. The fleet-footed captain ran 70 yards down the sidelines past a confused defense for yet another score. Final: SAC 62, Albany 0.

Bloss, Burnett, Pap Hayseed, the Nash brothers and their teammates posted a 4-1 record that season, with away and home wins over nearby Monmouth College, 36-22 and 28-0, and a 6-0 win over the Multnomah Athletic Club. SAC's only loss was to the University of Portland, a controversial 26-12 setback in which the Corvallis faithful accused the UP of using spies and cheating to win. The only points SAC's defense allowed were on the road.

After 1893, Bloss left and Guy Kennedy took over, beginning a string of annual coaching changes that would span almost a decade. Kennedy was the first to play the "Dudes from Eugene." This inaugural Civil War game, initiating the longest-running football rivalry in the west, resulted in a 16-0 SAC victory.

Bloss would return in 1897 to coach the team to a 2-0 season and its first championship of the Pacific Northwest, accomplished with wins over Washington and Oregon. A measure of national recognition would come in 1907 under the direction of coach Fred S. Norcross, a University of Michigan alumnus who would lead the Agrics to their first unofficial championship of the West Coast.

Little is known about Will Bloss after the '97 season. John Bloss stayed on as OSU's third president until 1896, when failing health forced him to resign and return to his home, "Blossom Acres," in the township of Hamilton, Indiana. He died on April 26, 1905. To historians in his home state, John Bloss is still known today as the "father of the consolidated school movement." He doubled the size of the SAC campus from two to four buildings. He increased budgets and faculty and instructed young minds as a professor of ethics and moral science. Bloss Hall is named for him. On the former president's grave, only one thing about his life is mentioned: "Finder of Lee's Lost Order."

2

Birth of Basketball

Go out of bounds! Get a hatpin in your butt! Five points in 10 seconds! The referee leaves at the half and suits up to play, for the other team! Sleeping in the snow in Pasco! OAC Agrics 104, Winlock A.C. 5! In some ways, the mark of a great basketball season rests with how much it recalls seasons of the past, stored-away memories of the fantastic, the incredible, the improbable, the interesting, the stuff that sets one team or year apart from another. This is the story of the troglodyte period in Oregon State's storied basketball past, a time of the two-handed set shot and YMCA rules, players barnstorming for bucks and getting thrown out of train stations for unruly behavior, and young students in the infant years of college basketball playing out their passions in every crackerbox gym from Salem to Seattle, Boise to San Francisco.

In the beginning, the sport of basketball at Oregon State was often referred to as a "sissy game."

In 1899, an Oregon Agricultural College alumnus named William H. Beach formed a women's basketball team to represent the school. It was the first basketball team in OSU history.

Beach left OAC in 1901 and returned to Corvallis only once during the remainder of his life. This was on June 7, 1952, to meet old classmates at an Alumni Association Golden Jubilee Reunion. He had driven the family car from Racine, Wisconsin.

At one of the reunion gatherings, Beach met his former player Fanny Getty Wickman, a Portland homemaker. Together, they remembered that turn-of-the-century basketball at OSU was exclusively a women's game.

"The boys wouldn't play," Wickman said. "They thought it was sissy stuff."

It took the young men of OAC about two years to see the light. When they did, they put together an eight-year record that arguably may be the best of any similar time period in Beaver basketball history.

From 1901 to 1903, when the college sponsored its first men's team, to the 1908-09 campaign, OAC won 61 games, losing 15. Eleven defeats occurred in only three of the seven seasons. The 1906 squad went undefeated and was led by six-foot-five Walter "Shorty" Foster.

To say OAC dominated its opponents during this early period is an understatement, topped in 1906 by the 104-5 shelling handed to the Winlock Athletic Club of Winlock, Washington. The Aggies also defeated Albany College 74-0. It remains the only game in the program's history in which a Beaver opponent didn't score. Pacific College managed to put in a single bucket in a 74-2 loss.

In 19 games, the 1911-12 team gave up an average of 9.37 points per game, a school record that won't be broken. Three teams that season failed to record a field goal against the Beavers, scoring only "penalty shots."

The 1906 team made history in another way, becoming quite possibly the first college or university basketball team in the west to travel on an extensive barnstorming tour to play non-conference, non-collegiate pick-up games.

The trip took place during the Christmas holidays. The boys from Corvallis were to play nine games in 12 days and be back when classes started in January. They were excited about the possibility of testing their skills with other players from around the Northwest. They knew they were good; now they wanted to see just how good. There was no better way than to take on all comers.

The guys also believed they might pick up a few bucks in the process, so they spent several weeks before the trip lining up "guarantees" to help meet expenses. Just before leaving to play their first game against the Evergreen A.C. of Vancouver, Washington, head coach W. O. "Dad" Trine fell sick and had to back out. The team was on its own.

They didn't miss Trine a bit, beating Evergreen 58-18. Then came the amazing 104-5 victory. Winlock jumped to a 4-0 lead, then OAC called time out. At the half, it was 59-5.

The "Agrics," as they liked to be called, finished the trip undefeated. Their closest margin of victory was a 40-30 win over a group representing the Seattle YMCA, a strange contest in which the referee quit the game at halftime only to play the second half as a Seattle forward.

On the trip back home, the schedule called for a tight connection in Pasco, Washington, which they didn't make.

There they were, stuck in Pasco for the night, with no place to stay. And it was snowing. Quickly, the guys decided to split into small groups and hang out in the downtown shops that stayed open late. They would pretend to be customers. They would be warm.

When the last store closed, it was back to the depot. The waiting area was full, but a sympathetic station manager told them they could bed down in his office till morning, provided they behaved like gentlemen.

They didn't. Once the lights were out, a shoe flew through the air, hitting a player on the forehead. Blankets, jackets and belts began cutting the darkness as more and more team members entered the fray. Curses and laughter quickly poured through the little station, waking everyone in the next room. In 10 minutes, OAC's "gentlemen" basketball players were outside on the loading platform, bags and baggage in hand. It was 3 a.m. When their train arrived the next morning, they were blocks of ice.

Even into the 1920s, the Beavers played on unusual courts, some with stacked wood or coal stoves close enough to the court to serve as a constant menace.

In Livermore, California, an opera house was used as a gym. The place was so small that one of the baskets had to be attached to the front edge of the stage. Spectators were so close to the floor their legs hung out on the hardwood, waiting to trip the unobservant. Flying into the crowd for a loose ball might get you a hatpin in your butt.

In Idaho, fans took BB guns to a game. One OAC player remarked, "A sharp sting on the leg was not conducive to winning ballgames." Another said, "How we got out of some of those towns without being mobbed, I'll never know."

In 1913-14, Billy King scored every OAC point in a 29-10 loss to the University of Washington. Not to be outdone, teammate Ad Dewey, several games later, dropped in all 17 points in a 17-10 thumping of the UO. The next year, Dewey put in all 14 tallies in a 26-14 loss to UW.

Old-timers still talk about the game in 1949 where Tommy Holman scored five points in the last 10 seconds against Oregon at McArthur

*OAC's fabled 1906-07 men's basketball team was
led by six-foot-five center Walter "Shorty" Foster.
(Photo courtesy of* The Orange, *1908.)*

Court in Eugene. With a minute to go, Holman sank a basket, cutting the lead to five. With less than 10 ticks on the clock, he scored another. Now the lead was three. On the UO throw-in, Holman intercepted the pass and scored again. And he was fouled. He converted the free throw just before the buzzer, sending the game into overtime.

Oregon State went on to win the double-overtime game 79-72.

3

The Wall

The Oregon State football team's defense in the autumn of 2000 was considered one of the finest the school has ever had, a relentless and ferocious pack of 11 that hunted down opposing quarterbacks and running backs with merciless resolve. Yet these Beavers and their gaudy statistics paled next to the greatest defense in school history, a group so impenetrable that it was, quite literally, perfect during a 1907 season that almost certainly will never be matched.

At first, the kick seemed wide.

Twice earlier, Willamette University had attempted field goals against Oregon Agricultural College and had failed. This one would surely suffer the same fate.

All the guys from Corvallis knew it.

Launched from OAC's 23-yard line by a young man named Curtis Hamline Coleman, the son of WU president John H. Coleman, the football sailed through the uprights with inches to spare.

Inches or not, it was good for four points.

The Salem crowd went wild.

The OAC Agric rooters, along with the team and coaches, stood in stunned silence. Up to this moment, in this, the last game of the season, no opponent on the 1906 schedule had scored a single point on the Beaver defense. The last time the Orange defense had cracked had been in a 6-5 loss to the Multnomah Athletic Club to end the '05 campaign, 32 quarters in the past.

The game ended in a 4-0 Willamette victory. It was Oregon State's only loss that season, against two ties. Afterward, 200 OAC students marched as a unit along State and Commercial streets in downtown Salem, singing college songs and giving OAC yells.

History has not recorded how each member of OAC's '06 team personally handled the Willamette defeat. It's also silent on how many individual promises for revenge were made over the course of the next winter and summer.

If, however, results are indicative of resolve, the Willamette loss formed a deep impression, one that carried over into a performance the following season that remains one of the most outstanding in northwest football history.

Using a squad of 18 athletes, and with a head coach only a few years older than his players, OAC finished the 1907 season undefeated, untied and unscored upon. The perfect, the pristine, and the unblemished had been achieved—the only one in OSU history.

In fact, it would not be until the Oregon game of the '08 campaign that the OAC goal line would be crossed, this in an 8-0 loss six games into the schedule.

Except for the Coleman field goal in the Willamette contest, the Agric defense was an impenetrable wall for three years...17 games...72 quarters...numbers unthinkable in today's modern game. The highlight of the streak was an 11-game run with flawless defense.

The architect of "The Wall" was Fred Stevenson Norcross. Known as "Norky" during his playing days as quarterback for Fielding "Hurry Up" Yost's famous "Point-a-Minute" squads at the turn of the century, Norcross helped the Wolverines to a combined 25-1-1 record from 1902-05; the average score of a Michigan game for Yost's five years was 50-1. And touchdowns were only worth five points then, field goals four.

In the years Norcross played for his alma mater, he saw Yost's defenses give up all of 42 points. No other coach and no other football team so dominated an era as Fielding Yost and his Michigan teams did during the first decade of the 20th century.

It was while coaching during this early period that Yost invented the position of linebacker, and Norcross used what he learned from his mentor to incorporate ways for his Beaver defenders to rush the ball and smother plays, often as the offense was in the middle of its execution.

This was the trademark of the Yost defense, and for three years Beaver opponents seemed befuddled by the whole thing. Not until the last three games of the '08 season did other teams catch on, and only after Norcross watched two of his best players rendered inefficient by injuries.

Norcross was hired during times of uncertainty for OAC football. After the 1905 season, head coach Alan Steckle, a medical doctor, had resigned without warning to take a job with the North Bank Railroad in Collins, Washington. Quickly, the school hired Fred Herbold to replace Steckle, but Herbold also resigned, leaving OAC again looking for a head coach.

It took until after the middle of September to have Norcross on board. Even after his arrival, OAC had little to offer its new coach in the way of facilities or experienced players.

Using a gruff teaching style, replete with put-down expressions that raised eyebrows even in his own day, Norcross took a team of mostly green recruits (Norky's "Green Bunch" as they were called) and molded them into one of the best teams in OSU history.

This was an era when the drop-kick and surprise punt were two of the principal offensive weapons used in the college game. Because a kicked ball was a *free* ball, teams could fall on their own punts and start with a first down from the point of recovery.

Teams with great kickers usually finished with winning seasons. In this regard, Norcross had one of the best in the west in Carl "Tubbie" Wolff, who could not only run with authority but could also punt the ball an average of 40 yards.

Even though the forward pass had been legalized in '06, it took several years after Norky's departure for the team to fully incorporate the hand-thrown ball as an important part of its offense. Norcross stayed in Corvallis for three years and amassed a record of 14 wins against four losses and three ties, a truly envious record for someone who was in Corvallis for so short a time. It was also during his tenure that the name of the college was changed from State Agricultural College to Oregon Agricultural College.

The highlight of Norcross's career at OAC came at the end of the 1907 season. The team returned to Corvallis after winning the unofficial championship of the western United States on November 28 with a 10-0 whipping of St. Vincent's College on its home turf in Los Angeles.

More than 1,000 people showed up at the train depot in Corvallis to greet the team, including the entire student body and faculty. A student reporter that day made it a point to mention that it must have been an important moment in the history of the school because OAC president William Jasper Kerr had brought his whole family down to the station to watch the boys arrive.

Head coach F. S. "Norky" Norcross (1906-08), architect of "The Wall."
(Photo courtesy of The Orange, *1909.)*

During the game, emotions were so high the local newspaper reported: "Every telephone in the area was in use with inquiries. From four o'clock until the college cannon boomed out the result about seven, one person was kept constantly busy at the *Times* office answering inquiries for news. The calls came not only from Corvallis but from throughout the countryside."

And the reporter went on to say, "A peculiar feature was that women were even more anxious questioners than were the sterner sex."

Hitless Wonder

As age-old home run records are shattered, another of baseball's venerable trophies sits waiting to be toppled. It dates from 1906 and belongs to the Chicago Cubs. That year, they won 116 games. No major league team chalked up that many victories in a single season until the Seattle Mariners matched it in 2001. In 1998, as national sports shows concentrated almost exclusively on the historic home run chase of Mark McGwire and Sammy Sosa, the New York Yankees had 100 victories and were quietly closing in on the Cubs' 92-year record. So good was that Yankee team, many baseball analysts assumed the Bronx Bombers were a cinch to set the record and win the World Series. Fortunately for the Yanks, they didn't have to contend with a former Oregon State baseball coach named Fielder Jones.

Baseball is a funny game, full of "maybes" and "maybe nots," a game that promises nothing and where the underdog sometimes comes away with the prize. Just ask the '06 Cubs.

Or, better yet, ask Fielder Jones.

In 1906, the Cubs were huge favorites to defeat their cross-town rivals, the Chicago White Sox, for the World Series title. And why not? They had finished 20 games in front of the New York Giants. They had led the league in batting, fielding and pitching. Three Cub starters—Brown, Pfiester, and Reulbach—had combined for 65 wins and a team earned run average of 1.76. The Cubs entered the World Series confident of quick victory, especially since they knew the White Sox had finished their championship season as the American League's poorest-hitting team. Sportswriters called them the "Hitless Wonders."

But the Sox had very good pitching, and they had a player/manager named Fielder Jones, a master motivator who would not only engineer one of the greatest upsets in World Series history but would, just four years later, coach a college baseball team in Corvallis to its best season ever.

Jones, a native of Pennsylvania, had started his baseball career in the Pacific Northwest in 1891 with the Oregon State League. Seven years in the majors followed. In 1904 he was offered the job of player/manager of the White Sox, leading the team to a respectable third-place finish in the standings. In 1905 the Sox were second. Now they were going for the whole enchilada.

Jones's style of play was "short ball," an aggressive approach that was perfect for the "dead ball" era in which he played and coached. He told his team that to beat the Cubs they would have to rely on good pitching, executing timely steals, exploiting mistakes, and stringing together singles and doubles to produce runs. (Ironically, Jones led his team that year in home runs—with two!)

His suggestions were followed to the letter and resulted in a stunning defeat of the heavily favored Cubs, four games to two.

Exploiting mistakes: Game 1 was lost on a Cubs pitching error in the seventh.

Good pitching: Game 3 was lost by the Cubs' inability to hit Chicago White Sox ace "Big" Ed Walsh, who two-hit the NL champs and struck out 12.

Combining hits: In the final two games, the White Sox scored 16 runs on 26 hits to lock up the Series victory.

Jones managed the White Sox for two more years, enjoying only moderate success, then left the organization after the 1908 season over a salary dispute with owner Charles Comiskey.

Remembering fondly his playing days in Oregon, Jones moved to Portland and began investing his baseball earnings in timber interests.

But he didn't stay away from coaching long. In 1910 he accepted an offer at Oregon Agricultural College to serve as varsity baseball coach.

Often seen strolling the diamond before a game like a well-dressed bulldog, his right hand clutching a bat as if he were about ready to smash something, Jones instilled in his young OAC players the same play-hard philosophy he had used in Chicago to win a world championship. The result was the best record ever recorded by an OAC nine, a 13-4-1 mark good enough for the Northwest Championship.

*Former Chicago White Sox manager
Fielder Jones on OAC's lower campus.
(Photo courtesy of* The Orange, *1911.)*

About Jones, the 1912 OAC yearbook *The Orange* proclaimed: "Fielder Jones needs no introduction…and it was indeed a happy moment when Orange supporters learned that this man, acknowledged to be one of the greatest generals in the baseball world, ex-manager of the famous 'White Sox Hitless Wonders,' had been secured to coach the team.

"Coach Jones was with the team from the very first, and, though he had important business in Portland, he was present at every important game. From the major leagues, the Coach brought a complete knowledge of the scientific end of baseball, and to his generalship, his constant hammering of the fine points of the game till they became almost second nature to the men, OAC owes much of the credit for the privilege of flying the Northwest Championship banner from her spires."

It was the last championship at any level Jones would ever win. By 1914, he was back managing in the big leagues, this time with the St. Louis Federals. When the Feds joined the American League a year later as the St. Louis Browns, he stayed on as skipper, but the best the team could do was a second-place finish in 1915.

In 1918, after watching his team lose a 5-1 lead to the Washington Senators in the ninth, Jones quit baseball for good. He moved back to Portland and remained there the rest of his life.

In late February 1934, the famous player-coach took ill in a meeting with a group of baseball boosters at the Elks Temple on Morrison Avenue in Portland. On March 14, he was dead of heart failure at age 62. More than 300 people attended his memorial service, many of them prominent baseball personalities.

Among these was Billy Sullivan, catcher for the "Hitless Wonders" of 1906. Billy moved to Newberg after quitting baseball and lived there until 1964, where he passed away at age 95. Sullivan and Jones were partners for a time in a Yamhill County, Oregon, filbert orchard.

Jones is buried in Sellwood, a suburb of Portland.

5

The Greatest Ever

The greatest athlete in Oregon State history? The debate could last for hours, with arguments on behalf of at least a dozen athletes. Terry Baker. Gary Payton. Dick Fosbury. Jess Lewis. Joy Selig. And no list would be complete without wrestler Robin Reed, one of the most dominant athletes his sport has ever known. The orneriest athlete ever? No question. It's the ill-tempered Reed, whose genius and toughness on the mat were matched only by his nastiness.

In his era, he was the Ty Cobb of his sport.

Oregon State wrestler Robin Reed was as loathed as he was respected. Reed would just as soon break your leg as pin it. Even teammates despised the brooding, aloof, distant 134-pounder from Arkansas with the gangly arms and square shoulders.

Yet there is no disputing that Reed, who won a gold medal in the 1924 Olympics in Paris, France, is one of the greatest wrestlers in American history and, pound for pound, perhaps the best ever.

"It is a matter of record that he never lost a match at any time, at any place, to anybody," marvels the *Encyclopedia of American Wrestling*. "He is generally regarded as the most feared and punishing wrestler of all time, a man who would break an opponent's arm if the mood struck him to do so."

Reed, whose family moved from Arkansas to Portland, where he attended Franklin High School, was the national freestyle wrestling champion for Oregon Agricultural College in 1921, 1922 and 1924.

What made him unique was that he would wrestle anyone of any weight. A Seattle sportswriter once wrote, "Seattle fans fail to figure out why coach Guy Rathbun does not use Reed at all weights except the 125-pound class, for which he's too heavy. He would be sure to win them all and this would save the coach the trouble of having to train a whole team. Reed is calm, cool and collected, and is entitled to be called 'The champion of all amateur champions!'"

At the Pacific Northwest Olympic trials in 1924, Reed entered four weight classes and won all four. On the boat ride to France, he wrestled every member of the U.S. Olympic Team and pinned every one—except 167-pound Guy Lookabaugh, whom he either tied or defeated, depending on who was asked. Among the vanquished was heavyweight Harry Steele, who would win gold in Paris.

In Paris, Reed won every match by fall at 134.5 pounds. In the finals, he pinned archrival and OAC teammate Chester Newton of Portland.

"They hated each other's guts," remembered longtime Corvallis resident and OSU fan Cliff Robinson, who knew both.

Reed's strength made him too tough for smaller wrestlers. His flexibility frustrated the larger ones.

"He had a genius for knowing how to handle the human body in wrestling," former OSU wrestling coach Dale Thomas said. "He was tremendously flexible and quick. He had great balance, was a keen competitor, and his ingenuity was so remarkable that he would figure out a way to beat you."

Reed's meanness gave him a psychological edge akin to Cobb's, the universally hated baseball star of the era who was known for sharpening his spikes before games.

"He was ornerier than the devil," recalled Robinson, who traveled with Reed on many of his professional wrestling excursions to Albany and Portland. "People didn't like to wrestle Robin. He'd say, 'Give in or I'll break your arm.' Coaches would have to race down to the mat and say, 'Lay off, Robin, for goodness sakes!'"

Reed started wrestling in high school so that he didn't have to participate in regular gym class.

"I needed gymnasium credits to graduate from high school, but I didn't want any gym because I was already getting all the exercise I needed operating an air hammer at the shipyards," he once said. "I was only 125 pounds and could barely hold on to that hammer, so that was all the gym I needed."

After winning gold, Reed retired from amateur wrestling with a perfect record and donated his medal to the National Wrestling Hall of Fame. He became student-coach of OAC's team and led them to the Amateur Athletic Union national championship in 1926. But after he was accused of cheating at a tournament the school hosted, the program was dropped for a decade.

A devastated Reed then turned to professional wrestling, where he became one of the sport's best-known "hookers," the term for applying a wrestling submission or concession hold on a hapless opponent. Hookers were considered the most dangerous fighters in the world because of their ability to administer punishment while absorbing it as well. Choke holds weren't unusual; neither were disfigured participants.

Reed was proficient, but he was never happy with the carnival atmosphere of pro wrestling. It was a completely different world from amateur wrestling, as he quickly learned upon visiting the greyhound farm of fellow "hooker" John Pesek in Ravenna, Nebraska, one summer day.

According to accounts, Reed attacked Pesek with his usual unbridled ferocity when they met on a mat in the farmer's barn. The roof leaked, allowing a puddle on the mat, which Reed instantly saw as advantage. He angled Pesek to the wet spot, causing him to slip. But as Reed went for the takedown, Pesek responded with equal or greater intensity, exhibiting moves his foe had never seen.

"After I took him down," Reed said later, "I never saw so many elbows and knees in my life."

Reed quit wrestling, started a real-estate business and moved to Lincoln City, Oregon. Thomas said he was the most astute businessman he's ever known.

Despite all their trips together, Robinson said he never gained much insight into this quiet man.

"He was very pleasant," Robinson recalls.

"He didn't say much. We talked about politics and things of the time."

Reed would occasionally return to OSU to speak at wrestling camps, and in 1971, at the age of 72, he came back to Corvallis to finish his degree. He was the oldest member of the class of '71.

Reed died in 1978, but not before leaving a lasting legacy not unlike Ty Cobb's.

*Robin Reed is considered one of the greatest amateur wrestlers
in history and won gold at the 1924 Olympics in Paris.
(Photo provided by Barry Schwartz.)*

In 1950, the Sportswriters of America called him the greatest wrestler of the first half-century in the lower weights, with Henry Wittenberg getting the nod for the upper weights. He is still regarded in his sport as one of the four or five best of all time. The National Wrestling Hall of Fame and Museum in Stillwater, Oklahoma, lists him as one of the "giants" of the sport.

"He was," Robinson wholeheartedly agreed, "an extraordinary wrestler."

6

Schissler's Boys

In 1999, it was the question every Beaver fan wanted answered. After 28-straight losing seasons in football, would this be the year OSU finally turned the corner? The faithful believed it was. For several years they had watched OSU raise itself up by degrees: improved football stadium; new playing surface; best coach in decades; super sophomore on the roster; high expectations for a winning season; a program that had inched its way back to respectability and now sat poised to make its move. As November turned to December, Beaver fans finally had their wish—and more: a winning season and a bowl game for dessert. In a way, 1999 was a mirror image of another time long ago, when Paul Schissler was the coach and Jim Dixon, Webley Edwards, Dallas Ward, Howard Maple and Wes Schulmerich were the stars. The time was the mid-1920s.

By the end of the 1923 football season, Oregon Athletic College fans had seen enough of R. B. Rutherford. The Beaver head coach was likeable and had his supporters, but back-to-back losing seasons in 1922-23 spelled his doom.

Particularly distasteful to alumni were the two defeats his team had suffered in Hawaii (to the University of Hawaii and the Hawaiian All-Stars) to close the '23 campaign. It was the first time the school had ever sent a team outside the continental United States to play football, a big step for a small agricultural college in Oregon—and expensive. Rutherford, they felt, had thrown their pride to the wind.

Disgust in the program, however, wasn't strictly limited to the coach. The last decent team the Beavers had fielded was in 1914. World War I had decimated athletics at OAC, but now the war was over and alumni wanted to be competitive again. Fund-raising for Oregon State athletics reached historic levels after 1920, and the first place they put their money was in the remodeling and enlarging of the football stadium, Bell Field.

It was a big undertaking, but the work was accomplished by Charlie Parker, a graduate of the class of 1908. Included in the job was planting a grass field, which before the rains came looked a sight better than the sawdust fields of earlier years.

Better facilities or not, Rutherford's 4-5-2 season in '23 did nothing to ease a growing mood of impatience. And so he resigned and a call went out for a new coach. More than 55 applicants responded; all were rejected. Soon after, a member of OAC's College Board of Control was sent to the Midwest to look for suitable candidates.

Five possibilities were identified, including Paul Schissler, the 31-year-old head coach at Lombard College in Galesburg, Illinois, a school of 350 students.

In three years, his teams had only lost once, a 14-0 defeat a year earlier to Notre Dame. After the game, Notre Dame coach Knute Rockne was so high on Schissler that he wrote the young man a strong letter of recommendation for the OAC job. So did Major John L. Griffith, football commissioner for the Big Ten, and legend Walter Eckersall, sports editor of the *Chicago Tribune*.

All referred to Schissler as a real "catch," probably the best offensive coach in the country. They were not lying. In the 24 games Lombard had won under Schissler, his teams had outscored their opponents 800-69. In the 11 years he had been coaching, his combined losses numbered only 12. Quickly, Lombard's coach became the coach OAC had to have.

Schissler didn't officially apply for the job and was not looking to leave the Illinois school. But Corvallis could pay a lot more, and in short order it was a done deal. Schissler came west. Without question he was the best gridiron coach OAC had ever hired. With a newly refurbished Bell Field, the school's first big-time coach, and renewed alumni support for athletics, a lot had been invested in the program.

Now it was expected to pay off.

Once Schissler accepted the job, some silently wondered how long he would stay. Since 1913, his first year in coaching, he had been at four different institutions and had never stayed at any place longer than three years. But he had won 81 percent of his games, so fans were willing to take a chance on his longevity. The gamble paid off. He stayed nine years, amassing a 40-30-2 overall record. In his first three seasons, he took a team mired in the Pacific Coast Conference cellar and led it into contention for the conference title.

Maybe Schissler's most important contribution to OAC was the expanded vision he gave Beaver fans of what the football program might be—a team known and respected nationally, and willing to go outside its own region to play some of college football's best teams. His 76-0 defeat of the Multnomah Athletic Club on September 25, 1926, would be the last time OAC would play a club opponent. Now universities like Detroit, Marquette, New York, West Virginia, Colorado and Fordham appeared on the schedule. Most were away games, and two, against New York and Marquette, were stunning upsets of national powers.

Winning didn't happen right away. In his first year, 1924, Schissler went 3-5. But his losses were by close margins. One victory that seemed to point to the future was a 7-6 win over the Multnomah Athletic Club, a team that had given OAC fits for 25 years. It would be the first of only two losing campaigns he would record during his time in Corvallis, the other being his last, a 4-6-0 finish in 1932.

Over the next two seasons, 1925-26, the future finally arrived. Losing only three games (twice to USC) and winning 14, Schissler compiled a two-year winning record at Oregon State that has rarely been equaled or surpassed.

In 1925, the Beavers finished 7-2 behind a stingy defense and a powerful, high-scoring offense. In 1926, Schissler's best season, the team finished 7-1, with a loss to USC the only blemish. Yielding but 30 points during the year (17 to USC), Oregon State led the nation in defense. The Beavers also finished 10th in total offense.

As much as facilities and coaching make a difference, quality athletes are also necessary to turn a program around. Here Schissler was blessed. Operating with a two-quarterback system to run his punishing ground game, he used both Webley Edwards and sophomore sensation Howard Maple to call the signals. Edwards showed great poise and maturity when leading the team, while Maple had the ability to turn a game around with one play. His interception and long return during the Idaho game in 1926 set up the game-winning field goal and saved OAC from certain embarrassment. He also ran back a 65-yard interception in the Oregon game to seal a 16-0 victory. In 1928, Maple would receive first-team All-America honors, only the third Beaver ever to be so recognized.

Tackle Jim Dixon anchored the line. Known for his ability to dart through defenders to block punts and extra-points, he received national recognition by placing on the third team of Rockne's combined "All-America" squad of 1926 and won more All-Coast first-team honors than any other teammate. All-Coast honors also went to end Dallas Ward and to fullback Wes Schulmerich, OAC's short-yardage special-ist, who bulldogged his way into the end zone for 15 extra-points dur-ing the '26 season. He was also the team's field goal kicker and best "smoocher." It was his boot that had provided the only points in the 1926 3-0 squeaker over Idaho. After a Howard Maple touchdown against Oregon, Wes put a smack on young Howard so animated that it sparked laughter all over Bell Field.

Ultimately, the true measure of a team lies in its total history, a combination of its achievements both on and off the field. In this light, Paul Schissler's early teams rank among Oregon State's all-time best.

Today, Webley Edwards is considered one of OSU's most distin-guished alumni. After graduation, the former quarterback moved to Hawaii, where he both created and hosted one of radio's legendary music variety shows, "Hawaii Calls."

From 1935-52, more than 400 radio stations throughout North America carried "Hawaii Calls." Cultural historians generally credit the show as a major contributor in establishing Hawaii as one of the world's great tourist destinations.

From 1941-45, Edwards was one of America's best-known war cor-respondents. On December 7, 1941, he was the first announcer on the radio in Honolulu to report news of the attack on Pearl Harbor. Five years later, he was aboard the battleship USS *Missouri* to broadcast to a worldwide listening audience the proceedings of the ceremony between the United States and Japan that ended World War II. He finished his career as a member of the Hawaii state legislature.

Dallas Ward stayed in football, and the people of Colorado have been forever grateful.

When the University of Colorado won recognition as the nation's No. 1 football team during the fall of 1990, the name Dallas Ward kept cropping up as writers traced the relatively brief history of the Buffaloes in big-time college football.

Ward was the head coach at Boulder from 1948-59 and finished with a 63-41-6 record. He established the school as a legitimate Big Seven Conference power, something no other Buffalo coach had been able to do. He also gave Colorado its first-ever bowl victory, a 27-21 win over Clemson in the 1957 Orange Bowl.

Ward died of cancer in Boulder in 1983. He lived long enough to see himself inducted into the Colorado Sports Hall of Fame, the third person named in the first group. He did not live long enough to know that the athletic administration complex at the University of Colorado now bears his name.

Jim Dixon also chose coaching, but closer to home. Leaving Corvallis only once during his career, to serve in the navy during World War II, "Big Jim" coached at OSU in three sports: football, track and wrestling, the latter as head coach. A dual appointment as an assistant professor in physical education kept him close to intramural sports and student recreational sports, and he devoted much of his teaching time in later years to these areas. In 1947 and again in 1956, Dixon served as a member of the NCAA Rules Advisory Committee. The Dixon Recreation Center on campus is named in his honor.

Wes Schulmerich, known during his playing days and throughout his life as "Iron Horse," left OSU to become one of only a handful of former Beaver greats to enjoy a career in professional baseball. He eventually returned to Corvallis to live out his life.

7

The Bare Facts

Sometimes history turns on one seemingly innocuous moment. Just ask Wally Pipp, the New York Yankees' first baseman who got a headache one day and was replaced by a youngster named Lou Gehrig. Such was the beginning of a basketball dynasty at Oregon State. The Beavers' journey to becoming one of the winningest programs in collegiate history started, curiously enough, in the campus swimming pool. The story was revealed publicly for the first time on the eve of Gill Coliseum's 50th anniversary in 1999.

In its day, the swimming pool at Langton Hall was a campus showcase, a shining monument to modern architecture of which William Jasper Kerr was unabashedly proud.

Small wonder.

When Kerr assumed the presidency of Oregon Agricultural College in 1907, he was driven to see the lightly regarded "farmer's school" evolve into a major West Coast university. He commissioned a 25-year master plan that included all aspects of the campus scene, including athletics.

And the 43-year-old Utah native was just the kind of no-nonsense man to see it through.

Born and raised a Mormon, he was a natural leader whose imposing frame and dignified air instantly commanded respect. He expected to be saluted when met on his brisk morning walks across campus, and he usually was. He was intimidating and aloof, devoted and generous, colorful and controversial, a nattily dressed ultra-conservative who didn't drink liquor, abhorred foul language and banished smoking from campus.

He held his people to the highest of standards while elevating the school's.

Kerr immediately raised OAC's entrance requirements. He created 10 diverse major colleges and selected deans for each. He started a museum, a radio station and the agricultural extension service.

He masterminded a 20-year era of construction that saw a 225-acre campus worth $229,000 grow to a 555-acre land-grant giant valued at $7.5 million.

No single person has had a longer reign as president or greater impact on the university than William Jasper Kerr, and to this day the campus—as well as Corvallis—reflects the pride and prestige he instilled.

Amid this unprecedented expansion was construction of the pool, which was quietly carved out of the dirt behind Langton Hall six years after the building was completed in 1914.

It would be the site of a little-known scandal that would change the face of OAC athletics forever.

******

Success at OAC wasn't limited to the academic arena.

In 1924, the wrestling program produced an Olympic gold medalist in Robin Reed and a silver medalist in Chet Newton. Football had winning records from 1925-31. The pool was the home to Hap Kuehn, Olympic springboard diving gold medalist in 1920.

But perhaps the most successful program was coach Bob Hager's budding basketball power.

After succeeding Dick Rutherford before the 1922-23 season, Hager began a streak of unprecedented success.

Captain Art "Pug" Ross's surprise ineligibility cost OAC the Northwest Conference title in Hager's inaugural year, but the team still won 19 games. Hager produced the school's first 20-win season in 1923-24 en route to the league crown and he won a whopping 29 in 1925-26. The "Agrics" won 19 the next year.

Hager employed what he labeled the "Percentage System of Offense," which limited field goal attempts to layups and short set shots.

Without a shot clock, Hager's teams spread the court in an early version of the Four Corners offense and would control the ball for 30 of 40 minutes, waiting for a defensive breakdown.

Scores were predictably low. The year OAC won 29 games, nobody scored more than 39 points. Two teams were held to fewer than 10.

The balding, smallish Hager reloaded after the 1926-27 season with gifted young players and overachieved for two years, finishing a respectable 15-16 in 1927-28.

After six years, Hager was 115-53. His average record was 19-9. He had nearly all of his key players returning for a promising 1928-29 season.

And on August 11, 1928, some 10 weeks before the opening of practice, Bob Hager resigned, offering no clue as to why.

******

Unlike today, where Langton Hall is a dark snapshot of yesteryear, the pool was a buzz of activity in the 1920s because graduation requirements mandated that all students be able to swim at least one length.

Kerr often hosted the Board of Regents and other dignitaries, and he liked to show off his crown jewel. Visitors would enter and stroll immediately to the balcony, where they had a view of all the activity below.

But it was also tightly policed.

Because of the unique filtration system, pool users had to swim in the nude. Men had their times, and women had theirs.

Kerr, who forbade dating among his faculty and staff members, had staffers assigned to the pool to ensure privacy, particularly for women. Coed swimming was, of course, strictly prohibited.

One day in the summer of 1928, Kerr dropped by with some friends to see the pool.

He led them through the front doors to the back of the building and onto the balcony. Moments later, the visitors blushed while the president's face went flush with ire.

Below them, a man and a woman were frolicking, *au naturel*, in the water.

The man was Bob Hager, OAC's head basketball coach.

The woman was not his wife.

******

Kerr had little patience for such behavior.

He had divorced one of his two wives and left the Mormon church because its ideology conflicted with his strict values. He had fired Reed as wrestling coach and abolished the program temporarily because of suspicious officiating at a national meet on campus.

Kerr had Hager's resignation on his desk immediately, and the man who was building a dynasty suddenly became a tiny footnote in OSU basketball annals.

Meanwhile, the president had a vacancy to fill. He didn't look far. He had heard good things about a wiry, clean-cut, hard-working, fiery Rook (freshman) coach who had earned All-America honors while playing at OAC from 1922-24.

Never mind that the No. 1 candidate was a mere 27 years old, had coached the Rooks for only two years and was a head coach for just one season at a high school in Oakland, California.

Kerr, who had vision unlike any leader in school history, never flinched in announcing his choice to carve a basketball legacy befitting his master plan: Amory Tingle Gill.

Friends simply called him Slats.

You know the rest of the story.

8

Knute Was Here

On January 1, 2001, Oregon State's surprising football team recorded its greatest season ever, winning 11 games with a smashing victory in the Tostitos Fiesta Bowl in Tempe, Arizona, against the most storied college program in any sport: Notre Dame. No team is more shrouded in mystique than the Fighting Irish, and to land them on your football schedule is considered a coup of great magnitude. Indeed, in more than 100 years of competing, OSU and Notre Dame had never met on the gridiron until the Fiesta Bowl. But in 1933, the two schools came ever so close, thanks to OSU's unique relationship with the game's most famous coach ever... a man who also happened to be a part-time Oregon State professor.

For a few summers during the 1920s, the most powerful man in college football shifted his headquarters from South Bend, Indiana, to the most unlikely place in America.

Corvallis, Oregon.

Lecturing in room 323 on the third floor of Strand Hall, Notre Dame's Knute Rockne taught his famous "Knute Rockne's Method" football course two weeks each summer during the years 1925-28 as a member of OAC's summer session faculty.

That's right. Faculty. His name is right there in the session bulletins issued at the time by the office of M. Ellwood Smith, dean of the School of Basic Arts and Sciences and summer session director.

That Notre Dame's most famous coach was once a teacher at OSU—not once, but numerous times—remained the most important historical connection the Beavers and the Fighting Irish had until they squared off at the 2001 Tostitos Fiesta Bowl.

And Rockne wasn't a has-been at the time.

In 13 seasons (his first year was 1918) at his alma mater, he won enough games to finish at .881, still tops in college football. The majority of his 105 total Notre Dame wins were racked up during the '20s.

Upon his tragic death in 1931, he had only been defeated 12 times, had tied five times, had won three national championships, and had compiled five undefeated seasons. The Four Horsemen graduated in 1926. Numerous All-Americans called him coach. He watched his boys crush Stanford 27-10 in the '26 Rose Bowl.

He was as well known as Babe Ruth. His name was synonymous with his sport. He lived to see the expression, "I may be a coach, but I'm no Knute Rockne" become a pop culture expression. In all his 43 years, this Norwegian-born (Voss, March 1, 1888) football genius was never a has-been.

The truth is, Rockne was at the height of his career during the years he taught at OAC. He was one of the most sought-after public speakers in America, commanding $500 for a single speech.

Almost addicted to trains (and later airplanes), he spent his off seasons traveling around the country conducting football clinics, coaches' clinics, motivational workshops, promotional films, sales promotions, banquet and graduation keynotes, and on and on. Around it all, he had time to be Notre Dame's athletic director, design and build the football stadium still in use, and raise a family. His annual salary from his university was $12,000.

Everywhere he appeared, people flocked to see him. He loved to hold court and was always quick to indulge someone in the crowd with a friendly jab or share a joke or story. He was a wonderfully gifted communicator and seemed particularly pleased when he could get under someone's skin or bring the house down with laughter.

After teaching at Bell Field, Rockne would trek over to coach Paul Schissler's office, his desk just a cuspidor away from his Beaver friend. As Schissler would attempt to write a letter or do some other little office chore, Rockne would entertain the many coaches and players who would beat a path to the room (each afternoon between 3-5 p.m., his published office hours) with non-stop conversation about anything and everything. Loud talk and laughter would fill the air. Schissler would only grumble, look at Rockne and say with a smile, "Are you trying to pick a fight?"

All this, of course, begs the question. Why Corvallis? Why Oregon State? Why not a school in Los Angeles or San Francisco? If you're going to travel 1,500 miles to somewhere, wouldn't it be to a big city with all the amenities?

The full answer may never be known, but it is almost certain that most of Rockne's motivation centered on three special friendships he enjoyed with members of the OAC athletic department: Schissler, former head football coach Sam Dolan and head track coach Michael "Dad" Butler.

Dolan, who coached the Beavers from 1911 to 1913, was a star at Notre Dame in the early 1900s and was still well known in Rockne's circle of friends. Rockne loved to pick at Dolan and always affectionately referred to his fellow Irish alumnus as "Rosie."

Butler knew Rockne as a boy and had served for a time as the young man's coach at the Chicago Athletic Club, where Butler was a manager (The likeable track coach would later leave OAC to go to Detroit; in 1939, Butler was one of three ringside judges at a Joe Louis world heavyweight championship fight held in that city.)

The primary reason Rockne taught his summer football clinic at OAC (the only campus in the west where he said he would work) might have been his relationship with Schissler. The young Beaver mentor was one of his favorites.

The two first met in 1923, when Schissler's Lombard College team lost a hard-fought game to Notre Dame, 14-0, the only defeat Schissler would suffer at the small Illinois school of 350 undergraduates. A short time later, a Rockne letter of recommendation helped Schissler land his Oregon State coaching job. Then, in 1926, when the Beavers traveled to play New York University in Yankee Stadium, Rockne made the 180-mile round-trip from South Bend to Chicago's Soldier Field to visit Schissler during workouts scheduled for midway in the trip.

In 1928, Rockne taught his final clinic at Bell Field, though no one knew it at the time. Scheduled to be back in the summer of '29 and listed in the program for that year as "faculty," the famed coach was kept from traveling by a severe case of thrombosis.

His condition improved in 1930, and he made plans to return to Corvallis. Again, his doctors said no.

On February 21-22, 1931, Rockne paid his last visit. He was on a 25,000-mile tour sponsored by the Studebaker automobile company.

*Notre Dame's Knute Rockne (center) pauses to have
his photo taken with coaching colleagues at OAC's Bell Field.
(Photo courtesy of OSU Archives #22.)*

Schissler picked him up at the train station in Albany. That weekend, the two old friends reached an agreement for their schools to meet on the gridiron in 1933. Notre Dame would do the traveling.

Rockne also told Schissler to expect him back for the summer term, that he had missed everyone on campus and in town. He said he was again looking forward to working with those coaches willing to travel to Corvallis from all over the West to hear what he had to say about football.

He never made it back. About a month after his meeting with Schissler, Rockne was killed in a plane crash near Bazaar, Kansas. The 1933 game was never played.

Just two days before he took off on his tragic flight, he sent word back to Dean Smith that his doctors had forbidden him to engage in any work for the summer and he would not be able to travel to Corvallis.

OSU head archivist Larry Landis says he has a theory why the contest was never played: "I suspect the 1933 Oregon State-Notre Dame game fell through because the agreement the two men reached was only verbal. As Rockne was the one pushing for the game, there was no one around to see the deal through after the plane crash. The new Irish coach didn't. Plus, Schissler was replaced by Lon Stiner after the '32 season. Nonetheless, it's interesting to speculate on OSU's football future had that game been played."

Upon hearing of Rockne's death, the flag on the Oregon State campus was immediately lowered to half-mast.

9

Starting Point

February 9, 2003. What a special Sunday it was for OSU men's basketball, as 90 former Beaver players descended on the campus to enjoy Homecoming activities celebrating both their respective teams and their collective role as architects of the eighth winningest program in NCAA history. All the championships, the All-Americans, the Olympic gold medalists, the No. 1-ranking in 1981, the great upsets and the near misses, the spirit of all this success was in great abundance. Fans attending the Stanford game that afternoon had a chance to meet many of the great players responsible for firmly entrenching OSU as one of the nation's storied basketball schools. Four players in particular deserved special attention. Three were at the game. All were in their 90s, or close to it, and their achievements during the early years of the Great Depression, when the game was played with a center jump after each basket, still reverberate across the years. All-American and team captain Ed Lewis of Salem headed a list that included forwards Merle "Humpty" Taylor of Albany and Clarence "Jiggs" James of Tillamook. Reserve center Fred Hill of Walla Walla, Washington, could not make the trip.

They are what's left of one of the most revered squads in OSU history, historic for what could have happened that didn't, historic because a surprising performance in 1933 set the tone not only for seven decades of success but also for all the wonderful moments, players and teams OSU's basketball faithful hold dearest to their hearts.

The year 2003 marked the 70th anniversary of coach Amory T.

"Slats" Gill's '33 squad, and its place in the record books is easy to explain: They were probably the first OSU team in any sport to win a Pacific Coast Conference championship. Earlier years had produced players with impressive individual credentials and even a few Olympic medal winners. But no group of Beaver athletes had won a major trophy.

Football had ventured the closest in 1907. Finishing the regular season with a 5-0 record, the Oregon Agricultural College Agrics of coach F. S. Norcross traveled to Los Angeles to defeat powerful St. Vincent's 10-0 to keep their perfect record intact. Shortly after, OAC felt it had earned the right to call itself "Champions of the Pacific Coast," but it's uncertain just what this meant. In the days preceding conference affiliations, of which 1907 is a case in point, schools enjoying success in athletics routinely assigned themselves lofty titles when convenient. Schools like Cal-Berkeley, the University of Washington and other gridiron powers of the West Coast are conspicuously absent from the '07 Agric schedule, leaving us to wonder what their reaction was when learning that OAC had suddenly emerged as "champions" of the region.

Oregon State College's 1922 basketball squad also came close. Led by All-American Marshall Hjelte, on a team that included Slats himself, the Beavers finished 21-2 overall, 10-2 in the Pacific Coast Conference. But Idaho was declared champion with a 7-0 record.

In 1925, after the PCC had been divided into Northern and Southern Divisions, Oregon State and Oregon ended the season in a tie for the Northern crown, with OSC winning an exciting three-game tie-breaker series to earn the right to play USC for the title. But USC won two of three, and that was that.

As the 1932-33 season approached, the experts had Gill's Orangemen picked to continue their mediocre ways. His 1929-30 club had finished next to last with an 8-8 conference record. In 1930-31, Oregon State did slightly better for a third-place PCC finish. Another third place was OSC's reward in 1931-32. By 1933, Hec Edmundson's Washington Huskies had won five PCC crowns in a row. They were favored to repeat.

Of the 36 years he coached Beaver basketball, Slats Gill would look back on the early '30s as among the most difficult seasons of his career. During the '29-30 campaign, a stay in the hospital after a sudden illness forced him to miss the first six games of conference play, including four losses. With a veteran team returning the next year, plus the arrival of an amazing sophomore center named Ed Lewis, the Beavers were expected to be a conference terror. But food poisoning on a trip south to California, combined with a season-ending knee injury to Lewis, left OSC no better than 9-7 in the PCC.

Could things get worse for the boys from Corvallis? Absolutely.

The 1931-32 season would be one of Gill's biggest nightmares. It began when Forrest "Skeet" O'Connell shattered his ankle in practice. Next, Lewis broke his hand in a game against San Francisco. As Northern Division play got under way, veteran Jerry Thomas had to be hospitalized. He missed four critical games. Returning to the lineup, Lewis gamely played with a special protective cast on his hand. Adversities aside, Gill had his guys on top of the division with a 4-1 record.

Their success would not last. Two heartbreaking losses followed and then lightning hit the team again. Lewis hurt his shoulder, thus limiting his playing time. Now Gill was forced to add both a football player and the catcher from the baseball team to shore up his bench. On a trip to Washington and Idaho, Lewis re-injured his shoulder and couldn't play. Everett Davis, a reserve, had to leave the Idaho series with a broken ankle. Against the Vandals, a minor riot ended the first game. In the second, the lights went out in the gym, delaying the contest for 30 minutes.

What else could go wrong? Plenty. On the trip home, their train missed its connection. The team ended up snowbound. Back on campus, Carl Lenchitsky took sick and missed the last five games of the season.

Unknown to his players, fans and family, Gill was also battling a Portland group that wanted his job. Injuries and the perception that Gill's growing list of missed opportunities was not just coincidence were more than some alumni could take.

Ed Lewis, whose jersey No. 25 was retired by OSU in 1999 and who has often been described as the Pistol Pete Maravich of his generation, remembers the incident, although he admits he found out about it much later.

"There was a movement in Portland to get rid of him in 1932," Lewis said. "I'm not sure who was responsible but I've always heard it was a former OSC student body president. I remember something about it in the newspapers, and it made a real impression on me. It forced me to change my mind about what I wanted to do for a living. I had decided I wanted to be a coach, but after watching what Slats had to go through, I changed my major to business."

Many of these same alumni had already forced the firing of football coach Paul Schissler. A "clean house" atmosphere had taken hold.

One can only imagine what might have happened had Gill fallen to the same ax that ruined his football counterpart: no five PCC Conference championships; no West Regional championship trophy in 1963; no opportunity to coach 12 All-Americans; no 599 wins, the most in school history; no eight consecutive Far West Classic titles; no Naismith Hall of Fame induction; no Gill Coliseum; maybe no Ralph Miller or Gary Payton.

In a very real sense, Slats Gill's 1933 team and its championship performance saved his career and saved OSU from a men's basketball legacy that could have been dramatically different.

Washington, which by 1933 had won five Northern Division titles in a row, was again the overwhelming favorite to win it all. When Oregon State split its first series with the Huskies in Corvallis, halting a

15-game UW Northern Division winning streak, a new level of confidence began to descend on Gill's charges. The new mood, however, was somewhat shaken by a split with Idaho, in a road trip still remembered by Ralph Hill, who played backup center to Ed Lewis.

"When we played Idaho, the crowd up there was really getting on Ed Lewis, calling him 'Turkey Legs' and making fun of him," Hill recalls. "Now, Ed was an extremely good passer, and we had a great starting five. Those guys handled the ball real well. The first time Ed passed the ball behind his back, the crowd got real quiet and stayed that way the rest of the game."

At season's end, with the divisional title on the line, the Beavers took two from Washington on the road to finish on top with a 12-4 conference record. It was only the third time in a 100-game series dat-

1933 Pacific Coast Champions, coached by "Slats" Gill (far right) and led by All-American Ed Lewis (No. 25, center). (Photo courtesy of Orange & Black.*)*

ing to 1904 that OSC had won both games in Seattle. Now Gill prepared his team to face the 10-1 Trojans of USC, champions of the Southern Division. It would prove to be one of the greatest series in Oregon State history, all played at the old Men's Gymnasium on campus, known today as Langton Hall.

In the first game, Lewis led his team to a 35-33 decision. Coach Sam Berry's Trojans won the second contest 39-28. For both schools, it was down to one victory to win it all. In a carefully played third game, with the state of Oregon tuned in like never before, OSU prevailed 24-19.

As sports historian Chuck Boice would write for OSU's alumni newspaper the *Oregon Stater* in 1987: "OSU would win numerous other championships, but this was the first."

Above all else, those teammates who remain—Lewis, James, Taylor and Hill—credit Gill with the success they enjoyed as athletes and what they became later in life.

Shared Merle Taylor, a retired VW dealer living in Albany:

"The thing I remember most about Slats is how great a man he was. After my first year, in which he talked the freshman coach into not dropping me from the program, I had no money to continue in school, so was planning to leave OSU. My folks were farmers. One day, while working in the fields, I saw this man walking across our place headed toward me and wearing a suit. I asked myself, 'Who can this be?' It was Slats and he asked, 'Merle, do you want to go to school?'

"I answered him 'yes' and he said that if I would come back he would give me a scholarship and a job. It changed my life."

From his assisted living facility in Tillamook, Clarence "Jiggs" James said in a telephone interview that, although he liked everyone on the '33 team, he "liked Slats Gill the most. He was an outstanding human being, was able to handle our players and never had to get nasty with us."

Born in 1910, James said with pride that he still follows the Beavers and considers it a blessing that he was able to attend the Homecoming.

Lewis cherishes similar feelings about Gill: "I lost my dad when I was young and so I grew up without a dad. Slats was the closest thing I ever had to a father. He was a great man."

10

First Lady of Basketball

Behind most of history's great basketball coaches was a supportive and understanding wife, a woman hidden in the shadows who privately wore the thrill of victory and the agony of defeat on her heart. It was a lonely life, filled with empty days and quiet nights while husbands traveled, recruited and coached. They absorbed the adulation during winning streaks and cringed at the detractors during losing streaks. For nearly four decades, that woman in Corvallis was a pillar of strength named Helen Gill, who reflected on her life as a basketball wife in a 1999 interview. Mrs. Gill passed away on July 22, 2003, at the age of 98.

The front door to the old bungalow-style home on historic Fifth Street in Corvallis opens, beckoning visitors into a rapidly vanishing era.

Old-growth mahogany frames the doors and entryways. Hardwood floors creak underfoot. Black and white family photographs cover the top of family heirlooms, an old RCA Victor television and every other available space.

The diminutive figure of Helen Gill, standing no more than four feet eight, reaches up with an extended hand and reaches out with a warm smile. At 95, the first lady of Oregon State University basketball no longer has a bounce in her step, but she still has the soothing maternal voice, grace and zeal for life that made her the belle of the ball in Corvallis for nearly four decades.

Gill turns and gestures across the living room.

"There's the master right there," she says, pointing reverently to a large framed portrait over a piano.

The gesture wasn't necessary. The familiar face of Amory T. "Slats" Gill is prominently displayed. The eyes are quickly drawn there upon entering a home that has been touted for inclusion in the city's historical register as simply "The Gill Residence."

The Gill name is synonymous with the city's history. It ranks with Avery, Dixon, Kerr and a handful of other families whose contributions and vision have made Corvallis what it is today—a bucolic, highly educated college community of 50,000 with a passion for good basketball.

Slats Gill is to Oregon State what Phog Allen is to Kansas, Adolph Rupp to Kentucky and John Wooden to UCLA.

From 1929 to 1964, he won 599 games and nine titles as head coach, finishing with a losing record only eight times in 36 years. He was the architect of what was, as recently as 1991, the fourth winningest program among NCAA schools.

He was so revered that in 1949 Oregon State College built a basketball palace—an engineering marvel considered then to be one of the finest arenas on the West Coast—for him, and unofficially named it after him.

Was it really 1949?

It hardly seems possible to Helen Gill, the way time passes.

Has it been 33 years since her legendary husband passed away? Fifty since the arena opened? And 67 since they had to be married in the living room of her family home because in those days a Catholic couldn't marry a non-Catholic in the church?

"It's hard to believe," she said.

But then, Helen Gill doesn't live in the past. The present and future still have too much to offer.

She is cheerful and witty, enthusiastically giving tours of the home where she has lived "for more than 100 years." She shows the kitchen where she cooks, reads magazines and newspapers, does crossword puzzles and occasionally watches a small television—usually *Jeopardy* or *Biography*, but always a "thinking show."

She takes visitors to the downstairs bedroom where their son, John, a 60-year-old retired OSU employee, has lived since Slats died in 1966.

Helen Gill is always busy and never bored, but 33 years later she admits to missing one link to her past: her husband. Her life then, as now, was defined by Slats. She even divides it into two eras: Before Slats Died and After Slats.

"I was a coach's wife—basketball was number one and I was number two," she says without a trace of resentment. "That's the role I played."

They met on a blind date at what was then Oregon Agricultural College in the Roaring '20s. She was a home economics major who had moved to Oregon to be near a sister after their father died in Tampico, Illinois, where she had been an older childhood playmate of the second most famous person in her life, one Ronald Reagan.

Amory Tingle Gill was the youngest of eight children. His father had died when he was a child. His mother passed away when he and Helen were courting.

She knew him as Amory. Everyone else had a different moniker.

When Amory was 12, he went swimming at a local pond. When he emerged, buck naked, a neighborhood friend scrutinized his scrawny, bony body, with ribs protruding, and said they looked like slats in a picket fence.

The name stuck.

Slats became the head coach at OAC after a scandal involving former coach Bob Hager in 1928. He and Helen were married in 1932, and they bounced from house to house during the Great Depression, living in homes of professors who were on sabbatical. They were too poor to buy their own. His annual raises often arrived in unique ways, one of which was to allow Helen on road trips.

"Basketball coaches didn't make as much then as they do now," Helen recalls. "Even [my son] John made more money at OSU than Slats did."

In the 1930s, they finally bought the house on Fifth Street behind what later became the Big O Restaurant, purchasing it from the city's postmaster. They raised two children, John and Jane.

OAC won immediately and Slats quickly became a local icon. Nearly every morning he would stop at Wagner's, one of the town's watering holes, where people gathered around to praise or critique the Agrics or, as they later became known, the Beavers. He always listened and sometimes even took suggestions.

Winning wasn't the only reason Slats was adored. He was also a member of the school board and involved in charitable causes.

Meanwhile, Helen could walk into Nolan's department store and not have to introduce herself, because everybody knew the woman who had swiped the town's most eligible bachelor.

"He was affable and charming," she says. "We always sat when we went out and people gathered around him instead of him going to people. He was very good about meeting people. He put them at ease."

Slats was different on the bench. He never smiled, frequently stood with his arms crossed and a scowl on his face, and often erupted into tirades at referees.

"He ranted and raved at the officials," Helen remembers.

By 1948, Slats had won six Pacific Coast Conference crowns and was a hot commodity. After the season, UCLA approached him with a generous offer to take over the program in Westwood.

While Gill considered the move, the town mobilized. Students rallied outside his house, then marched him to the Memorial Union, where he was presented with a shiny new DeSoto automobile. With the region in a post-World War II building boom, plans were formulated to construct an expansive new pavilion for his team, a state-of-the-art coliseum that would have no rival on the West Coast.

Gill turned down UCLA. The Bruins started over in their search, eventually settling for a young Hoosier named Wooden.

In 1949, a sparkling new 10,400-seat arena opened. Though legally no building could be named after a living person, and it was officially called simply "The Pavilion," Oregon State fans instantly called it Gill Coliseum.

Gill continued his dynasty for 16 more years. He missed a chance at 600 victories because he suffered a heart attack midway through the 1959-60 season. He missed 14 games that year, deferring to assistant Paul Valenti.

Slats returned for four years, coaching the Beavers to the Final Four in 1963 and closing his career with a 25-4 mark in 1963-64. His overall record, spanning portions of five decades, was 599-392.

"He was a very dedicated man to his profession and very honest," says Valenti, who played and coached under Gill for 18 years and can never remember seeing him smile. "Everybody knew where their place was. He worked at the job of basketball very, very hard and expected a lot out of people not only as players but as citizens, too.

"I've got three great experiences in life: Playing and coaching for Slats, raising a family and going to war."

Gill turned over the reins to Valenti and became athletic director, but he didn't last long, not even long enough, Helen quips, "to get him on Medicare." He died in 1966, and "The House That Slats Built" was officially named in his honor.

"I've struggled ever since," Helen says quietly.

Helen was there for most of the games, and she still is whenever possible, though surgery prevented her from attending in 1998. When she can't go, she listens on the radio, admitting she turns down important social events because the Beavers are playing.

"He told me once that if I didn't like the outcome, to leave town, to get away from it," Helen says of the pressure associated with coaching. "But I went to all the games."

As the House That Slats Built celebrated its 50th anniversary in 1999, she was aware of a movement underfoot to change to name to honor a corporate sponsor. Already, football's Parker Stadium has given way to Reser Stadium, and former OSU athletic director Mitch Barnhart had contacted her to see how she felt about selling the coliseum's name.

He told her that the venerable old building needs upgrades. The halls are dark. The locker rooms and basement are dingy. Repairs are needed. It is no longer the palace it was when Slats was patrolling the sidelines in his business suit.

It's the type of work corporate sponsorship can remedy and can help OSU compete the way it once did, when Slats was king, the Beavers were the fourth winningest program in NCAA Division I history and the facilities led the league.

As of winter 2003, there were no changes afoot. Former OSU star Gary Payton had committed $3 million to build a Gill Coliseum annex, but for now, the name endures.

"I don't want to change that, but I think it's inevitable because whoever gives a big lump sum like they did with Reser Stadium is going to get it," Helen says. "But I think this is quite different. Slats was a coach for 36 years, and that's unheard of these days. And he had a good record."

Valenti agrees: "I wouldn't like to see it change. It might be OK if they kept Slats's name on it somehow. I think that's something most people would accept."

To Helen Gill, as long as she is in Corvallis, the master's name, like his portrait in the historic house on Fifth Street, belongs in the most prominent place as a link to a cherished and glorious past.

11

Iron Immortals

It is one of the most lopsided series in college football. In more than 100 years, Oregon State has defeated powerful Southern California only eight times. So when the Trojans came to Multnomah Stadium in Portland for a predicted pushover victory in the autumn of 1933, they had little concern for the Beavers. USC had won 25 consecutive games and appeared destined for its third consecutive national championship. What happened on that gray afternoon remains unparalleled in the annals of college football. It forever branded 11 stout OSC players with one of the school's most fabled nicknames, of which fans are reminded each time they sing the words to the Fight Song.

Part of the drama that would surround Oregon State's October 21, 1933, game against No. 1 Southern California started nine months earlier, on New Year's Day.

OSC coach Paul Schissler had resigned, leaving the program with no one to guide it through recruiting and no leadership to organize the team for the approaching season.

To make matters worse, the university and its alumni had used up most of spring practice to find his successor. They finally settled on an ex-Nebraska Cornhusker tackle named Lon Stiner, but only after there were fewer than 10 days left for spring drills. Until the team reassembled in August, conditioning would take a back seat to organization.

At the start of the fourth quarter, in the "Ironman Game" of 1933 against the defending national champion Trojans, before 21,500 fans in Portland's Multnomah Stadium, the nation's best team was beginning to wear OSC down. The lack of a full spring season was beginning to show. You could see it on the faces of the Orangemen, hear it in the words they shouted to one another.

Many Beaver fans still know their names by heart: Vic Curtin and Woody Joslin at the ends, Ade Schwammel and Harry Field at the tackles, Bill Tomsheck and Vern Wedin at the guards and Clyde Devine at center. The "backs" were "Red" Franklin, Hal Pangle, Pierre Bowman and Hal Joslin.

After the game, *The Oregonian* sportswriter L. H. Gregory would refer to them as the "Iron Immortals." Two players—Franklin and Schwammel—would be named first-team All-America, and many decades later, these same lads (and their teammates) would be the first football team inducted into the OSU Sports Hall of Fame (1980). But all this was still to come.

Their immortality still had to be earned.

They had been out there the entire game, playing both sides of the ball, with no substitutes. Team captain Curtin, who would one day become an outstanding detective with the Portland police department, seemed especially tired.

After each play, he would mumble something about a replacement. He was giving out, he said. He was going to motion to Stiner to get him some help.

"Just hang in there, Vic, hang in there. You can't quit now."

It wasn't a single individual giving encouragement, but everyone on the squad. "Just hang in there" became their rallying cry. After each play, they would pat each other on the rear, say the words, and get ready for more.

There was something else, a special dynamic, unspoken, determined. Each player took personal responsibility for his assigned space. Each vowed to the others that if points were scored, it would not be through his position.

The third quarter was rough. USC pushed the ball deep into Oregon State territory twice, once to the 13-yard line, another to the eight. Franklin was brilliant during this quarter, turning two intercepted passes into defensive gems. His runback on the second interception was for 48 yards. At one point, only a single Trojan defender stood between Red and a touchdown. The way Stiner's boys were playing defense, Franklin's score would have been enough for an outright major upset.

*Creators of the "Pyramid Play" (featured on cover) and the 11 teammates
who tied defending national champion USC using no substitutes.
(Photo courtesy of* The Beaver.*)*

On the offensive side, Oregon State found USC in the third quarter to be an immovable object. Throughout the period, Franklin had to
kick the ball on second or third down. The Orangemen didn't have
much playmaking left in them.

As OSC punted to start the fourth quarter, a new mood began to
settle over Trojan coach Howard Jones.

Content with playing mostly his starters during the first half, Jones
began substituting freely after intermission. He would wear OSC into a
score if it were the last thing he did. To beef up the line in the fourth
quarter, he returned to the lineup the great All-American Aaron
Rosenberg, his brilliant "running" guard who had been knocked out of
the game in the second quarter with a leg injury. OSC fans all over the
stadium saw this as a sign that USC was desperate.

They were. Much was at stake. Jones had the nation's longest winning streak. He was the most victorious coach in USC history. There
were all those national championships and the No. 1 ranking.

He had brought 80 players to the game, almost three times the
number Stiner had carried up from Corvallis, and he would use as many

as it took to keep the streak going. He had seen enough of a tight conflict and was ready to put the opponent in its place. It was unthinkable to him that Oregon State had played the entire game with just its starters. Most schools around the country believed that to beat USC you needed "substitutes for substitutes." So why was Stiner not showing any respect for USC's reputation?

He would answer his own question with the power of his running backs. They began taking cracks at Oregon State's six-man front, designed by Stiner especially for this game, in droves. Griffith, Warburton, Watkyns, Powers…all got their shots as the Trojans tried one power sweep after another, hoping to break the Aggie boys like an egg. The crowd was deafening, a constant roar that never let up, a wall-to-wall sound that became almost unbearable the last five minutes of the game.

Warburton from the OSC 40…Warburton twice more…First down on the 29…Now Watkyns for 10 yards and another first down, ball on the 15…Warburton again, power sweep to the right, five guys blocking out front, this time for a pickup of five yards to the OSC 10.

First and goal.

Warburton again…One yard gain…Second down.

Curtin is finally convinced to stay in the game. His OSC team-mates tell him they're a family, that they're clicking, that to take one out might upset the whole thing and they might end up losing.

It was a war zone on the field, a heart attack zone in the stands. No one could hear anything. The next day, L. H. Gregory wrote of this moment that all the OSC players were patting one another on the be-hinds and shoulders, giving encouragement, talking to one another, sticking together.

You gotta hang in there.

Third down…the snap…the rush of human flesh…the grunts and screams.

The ball is given to Watkyns. For a split second there's an opening in the line, gaping huge at first. Watkyns dashes through it. At about the five-yard line he looks as if he will score standing up. From out of nowhere Ed Pangle attacks from his backfield position, hitting Watkyns so hard he is knocked cold and has to leave the game. Griffith replaces him and has the ball on the next play, a fourth-down, off-tackle slant with four blockers in front. He gains two to the five. OSC takes over on downs.

But Stiner's offense can do nothing, and USC is given back the football. Three minutes to go. Now USC's Jones begins pulling out all the stops. Keeping the ball on the ground will no longer do. They will win it or lose it with passing. There are seconds left as the ball leaves Red Franklin's foot heading for the outstretched arms of USC's Howard. He bobbles it momentarily, then races up field for 13 yards to the USC 39. Howard stays in at quarterback and tries a desperate pass downfield. Franklin intercepts again.

The game ends with OSC in Trojan territory, on offense, going for what many believe would have resulted in a score. As the sound of the game-ending gun cracked the air, over half the crowd of 21,500 began streaming onto the field hoping to get close enough to their "Ironmen" to shake their hands, pat them on the back. To the Corvallis faithful, this was no 0-0 tie; this was a victory. Their Beavers had achieved what no team had been able to do for almost three years—play USC and have the Men of Troy leave the field without a victory. At the hands of 11 Oregon Staters playing the full 60 minutes, Southern California's three-year dominance as the nation's best football power was over.

Today, the starting 11 who played in this historic contest are known as the "Ironmen." What they did that October day, and the joy they brought OSC fans across the nation all those many years ago, remain immortalized in a song still heard at every Oregon State athletic event: *"Watch our team go tearing down the field, those of iron, their strength will never yield."*

Were the USC players impressed at the performance?

You bet.

At the time, football custom ruled that, in case of a tie, the visiting team would receive the game ball. In this case, USC's star end and team captain, Ford Palmer, offered the ball to OSC's team captain Vic Curtin, saying, "Here, Vic, you take it. You guys earned it. You played like winners."

Later, Stiner's boys would find out they had accomplished something even bigger than the unseating of a three-year champion. They were and still are the only team in college football history to unseat a No. 1-ranked, two-time defending national champion using no substitutes. Notre Dame had tried two years earlier against Army but had fallen a point short, 7-6.

In addition, one historic milestone was not enough for this team. This is also the group that created and perfected the infamous "Pyramid Play," used twice during the 1933 season to block field goal and extra-point attempts.

In the maneuver, OSC center Devine would be lifted into the air by teammates grabbing both legs and hoisting him suddenly skyward. The idea was that he could block almost anything if he threw his arms above his head as he leaped. Why Devine? He was six feet six.

The first try of the Pyramid Play was against Washington State. It worked, but drew no attention. That would come on November 11 in a game against the Ducks in Portland. Photographer Ralph Vincent of the *Oregon Journal* was walking behind the back of the end zone and happened to see the Ducks lining up for an extra-point try. The rest is history. Snapping a photo of OSC's attempt to block the kick, Vincent noticed later in the darkroom an image of astonishing drama. A lot of other papers noticed, too, and soon Vincent's image was on virtually every sports page of every newspaper in the country.

The picture also found its way to the NCAA rules committee. They quickly banned the play. Vincent's "Pyramid Play" remains the most famous photo ever taken of an Oregon sporting event at any level.

Statistically, OSC was the big loser in the game, gaining two first downs to 14 for the Trojans. The yardage was also lopsided: 80 for the Orangemen, 257 for USC.

History also shows us this '33 OSC team was not a one-game wonder. Stiner's charges finished 6-2-2 that year, with marvelous victories over Washington State, national powerhouse Fordham (played at the Polo Grounds), and a close victory over West Coast power San Francisco—an away game the week before USC in which Stiner used only 12 players.

Of the original 11, only guard Bill Tomsheck of Corvallis is still alive. In an interview in 2001, Tomsheck was asked if his teammates ever showed any jealousy over not playing in one of the truly legendary contests in OSU history.

"You know," he said, "that's an interesting question. I remember my teammates showing no animosity at all. We were down in the dressing room [after the game], and many of them came over to where we were sitting and they undressed us... helped us take off our gear. I guess they felt we needed a little help. I know I've never been that tired in my life."

12

War of the Roses

Say this for the Oregon State Beavers: They have won the Rose Bowl only once in 111 years of football, but the one they did win has had no equal in the long and storied history of the event. On January 1, 1942, OSC defeated Duke 20-16 in the famous "transplanted" Rose Bowl, which was moved from Pasadena, California, to Durham, North Carolina, to strip Japanese bombers of a potentially appealing target. It's the only time the game has ever been played away from Arroyo Seco.

Oceans away, the world was unraveling one grainy black and white newsreel at a time in the autumn of 1941.

In Europe, Adolf Hitler's forces were plundering the countryside, marching over one nation after another in search of *lebensraum* for Aryan Germans. In the Far East, the Japanese were pillaging China and raising their flag over hapless South Pacific islands.

In the Willamette Valley of Oregon, a group of football players and their coaches barely noticed, their innocence insulated by distance and primitive technology.

The Oregon State Beavers were focused on school and football, and there was little to suggest an extraordinary autumn when the team entered its stretch run with an inauspicious 2-2 record that included losses to Southern California (13-7) and Washington State (7-0).

As what would become known as World War II intensified in both the European and Far Eastern theaters, reaching a point of unprecedented crisis by November 15, the Beavers moved into sole possession of first place in the Pacific Coast Conference by blanking California in Berkeley.

They were 5-2, ranked 17th nationally and needed only to defeat archrival Oregon in Eugene to earn their first trip to Pasadena, California, as the league's Rose Bowl representative.

Little did they know even then that the next month would go down as one of the most extraordinary in the school's athletic history.

The Beavers took care of business at Hayward Field, downing the hated Webfoots 12-7. It was their first league title of any sort since 1906 and ignited celebrations in the streets of Corvallis.

"This victory gave me, and probably many other Oregon Staters, the greatest thrill," OSC coach Lon Stiner said later.

As the PCC's host, it was Oregon State's privilege to extend an invitation to the party in Pasadena.

The Beavers chose undefeated Duke, which featured a "southern gentleman" quarterback from Memphis, Tennessee, named J. Thompson Prothro Jr., who would one day be known simply as "Tommy" when he'd prowl the sidelines as OSU's most successful coach ever.

Duke (9-0) had outscored its opponents 311-41 and was one of six unbeaten teams nationally, but the Los Angeles media was unimpressed. They preferred either Fordham or Missouri, which would later agree to play each other in the Sugar Bowl in New Orleans.

OSC athletic director Percy Locey quickly moved to defuse the ire of fans in Los Angeles, who were particularly eager to see the Beavers face Missouri. Locey announced that some of OSC's 15,000 allotted tickets would be available for purchase in the southland.

Meanwhile, 3,000 miles away, in Washington, D.C., negotiations between the United States and Japan broke down as December approached.

Corvallis was too busy celebrating to notice events that seemed so far away. Hotel reservations were made. A train was arranged to carry 500 boosters and the band to Los Angeles. Approximately 35,000 programs were printed, a Herculean task given that there were no printing firms in Los Angeles with paper, thanks to the war. New uniforms were ordered because the others, made of silk, shrank after the third washing.

"Jingle bells, jingle bells, jingle all the way; oh what fun it'll be to ride in a bowl on New Year's Day," the coaches sang.

The innocence was abruptly shattered on the morning of December 7, 1941, when a squadron of Japanese Zeroes bombed Hawaii's Pearl Harbor. A day later, Congress declared war.

OSC officials held their collective breath. What would happen to the Rose Bowl?

The same day that the United States declared war on Japan, the Rose Bowl committee announced that the game would go on as scheduled.

In Corvallis, it was back to business as usual—with a wary eye directed toward the Pacific shores 50 miles away.

The Beavers returned to practice. The varsity worked out against a promising Rook (freshman) team that simulated Duke's offense.

"Those are my fondest memories, playing against that Rose Bowl team," recalls Bill Gray, a lineman for the Rooks. "That was a great team we played against. We stayed out there in the dark sometimes playing those guys. We were eager Beaver freshmen, and we were better than blocking dummies—just a step above that."

Little changed immediately on campus.

OSC quickly reported that Beaver end Jack Yoshihara, an American citizen of Japanese descent, would not be subject to restrictions. He would not be sent to an internment camp.

Then came December 14, exactly one week after Pearl Harbor.

The U.S. Army announced during a meeting in San Francisco that it was canceling the Rose Bowl, declaring a national emergency. The army said that the setting in Pasadena was an attractive bombing target.

"We were too young to think about that," remembers Quentin Greenough, a Corvallis resident. "The main thing was that we made the trip. I think we wouldn't take no for an answer."

Undaunted, Oregon State publicly began to consider the option of relocating. Bids poured in from Atlanta, Chicago, Spokane and Norman, Oklahoma.

The Beavers decided on Duke's home campus in Durham, North Carolina, and the army gave its OK.

"It's still the Rose Bowl game," Locey assured the fans. "The only change is the location."

Recalls Greenough, the team's center, "We knew the Japanese wouldn't go back there to bomb."

The move wasn't as simple as changing street addresses.

More than $64,000 in tickets had to be refunded or reissued. New arrangements had to be made for the team to travel by train. Hotel reservations were canceled and remade on the other side of the country.

The psychological obstacles were even more daunting. While the Beavers tried to concentrate on football, public service advertisements in the *Corvallis Gazette-Times* reminded readers "WHAT TO DO IN AN AIR RAID."

Duke was a three-to-one favorite when the Beavers left December 19 for Durham. The team stopped en route for practices in Chicago and Washington, D.C. A total of 31 players were selected by coach Lon Stiner to make the trip. Jack Yoshihara was not one of them.

Scalpers were asking $15 per ticket in the days before the teams were to tee it up January 1, 1942. The tickets were snapped up in three days, and the teams played in front of a packed house of 56,000. The crowd gave the schools hope that they would still net $75,000 from the game despite the losses incurred by the move.

The game was close throughout. The Beavers led 7-0 in the first quarter on a 15-yard run by halfback Don Durdan, only to see Duke knot it at 7-7 by halftime.

The 1941 team went to the transplanted Rose Bowl in Durham, N.C., where they defeated Duke, 20-16. (Photo courtesy of Barry Schwartz.)

A 31-yard pass from Bob Dethman to George Zellick made it 14-7, but the Blue Devils evened it again on a one-yard run by Winston Siegfried and the extra-point by Prothro.

The Beavers finally prevailed when Dethman hit reserve running back Gene Gray on a 68-yard touchdown pass in the third quarter, making it 20-14.

Oregon State fans listening to the game back home on NBC radio were ecstatic, though a bit miffed by the lack of respect shown the Beavers by announcer Bill Stern. He repeatedly referred to the "Blue Beavers" and their "scarlet" uniforms, and he also frequently praised the performance of "Ohio State."

A fourth-quarter safety by Duke proved meaningless.

Final score: OSC 20, Duke 16.

"Just too much western football in general and Don Durdan in particular," Duke coach Wallace Wade lamented afterward.

OSC, which had already proclaimed itself national champions after downing Oregon, staked another claim, though it went unheeded by the pollsters.

Nevertheless, the Beavers received a hero's welcome upon their return to Corvallis. Impromptu parades and rallies broke out throughout town.

Only about half of the players were on hand to see the support, however. Many had stopped off at their homes in California and elsewhere for the holidays. Even Stiner was absent. He stayed with family in Nebraska.

One who did return was Gene Gray, the five-foot-ten, 165-pound reserve running back from Portland who caught the game-winning touchdown pass.

For Gray and his teammates, life would never be so innocent, so carefree again. The wars "oceans away" quickly changed their lives.

The 1942 season was canceled. Many players entered the military.

Less than a year after his Rose Bowl heroics, Gray joined the service and eventually flew 53 missions against Germany in A-2 bombers. He became a hero of a different kind.

After the war, while flying an F-80 on a training mission, his fighter crashed in the jungles of Panama. Gray survived, but his injuries were severe.

The arms he used to give Oregon State a scintillating victory—still the only Rose Bowl success in school history—had to be amputated.

13

Thrill Kid

In many ways the story of college athletics is the story of individuals overcoming adversity and how the spirit of competition—the constant striving to be the best—sometimes triggers in certain athletes the will to beat the odds and the ability to perform miracles. No Oregon Stater's life and career exemplify the test of courage that remains so much a part of what is fun and exciting about college sports better than one of OSU's all-time basketball greats: Lew Beck.

More than 56 years ago, a gifted athlete from Pendleton, Oregon, was coming off what was possibly the greatest two-year span of his entire life.

Bucking all the preseason predictions, Lew Beck had captained his 1946-47 Oregon State College team to a 28-5 record, capturing the Pacific Coast Conference championship and earning a fifth-place finish in the NCAA tournament.

In addition to being chosen first-team All-Coast, All-PCC and All-Northern Division, Beck made several All-America teams. Shortly after, he was invited to join the Philips 66 Oilers of the American Athletic Union, whose league of corporate-sponsored teams attracted the best college players in the country. According to the fans, the league played the highest level of basketball in the country. Only two years in existence at the time, the National Basketball Association was still several years away from the caliber of competition that would eventually spell doom for the AAU.

In June 1948, Beck was invited to the Olympic basketball tryout for the London Olympics. To make the team he had to perform well enough to impress the two best basketball coaches in the country, both of whom would guide the team in England: Oiler boss Omar Browning and Kentucky's Adolf Rupp. Beck made the team and was selected its captain, leading the Americans to a first-place finish, thus becoming the first of four Oregon Staters to win Olympic basketball gold.

Today, the old-timers still talk about Lew Beck with awe and respect. Few realize or remember, however, that his greatest moment, his Olympic medal, almost never happened.

In 1943, 10 Beavers from Slats Gill's '43 squad departed Corvallis for the war. Beck ended up in California, at Camp Luis Obispo.

In July 1944, Beck took part in a judo combat training exercise. Caught off guard, the young athlete's knee was so severely twisted he had to be hospitalized for three months.

When the cast was removed, Beck was stunned. The limb had shriveled to the size of a pipe stem. His doctors delivered another blow: they told him his basketball days were over.

He couldn't believe it. Did they have any idea who they were talking to? Did they realize he had made All-Coast in '43? That his 23 points against Idaho that year were a team high? That he planned on returning to Oregon State after the war to complete his final year of eligibility?

Determined to prove medical science wrong, Beck put together, on his own, a program for rehabilitation. Through sheer guts and determination, he crawled at first, then hobbled and limped. After many weeks of hard work, he was finally able to run.

By 1946, he was back to his prewar form, only better, as his numbers that season would indicate. His performances against Washington played a key role in why Oregon State, and not the Huskies, claimed the Northern Division crown.

After one of Beck's displays against the men from Seattle, legendary Husky basketball coach Clarence "Hec" Edmundson, who was in his final season, said of Beck: "He does everything but take up tickets, lead the cheers and answer your correspondence."

Edmundson's view of Beck again rang true in the two-game conference championship series with UCLA.

Ignoring a Bruin lineup that featured two All-Americans, Beck scored 30 points, exhibiting ball-handling skills on fast-break plays that had the Southern Division champs dazed and bewildered. OSC took both games, each by 17-point margins.

Olympic gold medalist and All-American Lew Beck in 1947.
(Photo courtesy of the Oregon Stater *photo collection.)*

All season, Beck and Co. had played this way. Beaver fans called them the "Thrill Kids," and they delighted in watching their team run Gill's fast-break "weave."

"Beck was quick, quicker than most guards in the country, and he was probably the best fast-break player we've ever had," remembers retired OSU coach Paul Valenti, a teammate of Beck's in the early '40s. "I played against him in practice when I was a freshman. To be honest, I always had to get help to guard him."

The record also shows that Beck's achievements his senior year were not accomplished in a vacuum, for that 1946-47 squad included Beaver greats Red Rocha, who also made All-American, five-foot-seven guard Morrie Silver, who may have been Slats's best dribbler, and playmaker Cliff Crandall, another component in Gill's three-guard "weave" offense. Rounding out the group was Alex Peterson, a most deadly shooter from the corner.

Together the lads from OSC set 50-year offensive records with 2,087 points and a 63.24 points-per-game average. Beck and Rocha received numerous regional and national awards, and Silver and Crandall received several regional honors.

"Thrill Kid" Rocha, who has lived in Corvallis after retiring as head basketball coach at the University of Hawaii in 1987, recalls that Beck's all-around quickness stemmed from his great feel for the game. "Beck wanted to be good," Rocha shares, "so his entire mind was always on the game. He was great on both offense and defense, a complete player."

Both former teammates also remember some of the qualities that made Beck a natural leader.

"He had great morals, great values," Valenti says, adding, "Beck was always the one you could count on to follow the rules, a 'hell-of-a-guy' kind of person who was always very considerate of other people."

After leaving basketball in the early 1950s, Beck returned to campus in 1953 to participate in an "alumni game" with former teammates Valenti, Rocha and others against the Harlem Globetrotters. They lost, in a contest Valenti says today they tried very hard to win. Beck, who spent much of his career working for the company that gave him a basketball job, died of colon cancer in Great Falls, Montana, at age 47.

14

The Day Harlem Came to Town

Before the Washington Generals and the New Jersey Knights became stage fodder for their slapstick comedy routines, the Harlem Globetrotters enjoyed mixing serious basketball with merry pranks. In the 1950s, it wasn't unusual for the Globetrotters to defeat strong NBA teams and rout collegians. In 1953, the 'Trotters came to Corvallis to entertain a crowd that wanted to laugh. A competitive bunch of former Beaver stars, however, had other ideas.

In the half-century history of Gill Coliseum, this may have been the only basketball game ever played in OSU's storied arena in which the home crowd came to cheer the visiting team.

The date was January 13, 1953. The "visitors" were the Harlem Globetrotters. Often traveling from town to town smashing one quintet after another, this group of extraordinary athletes would find something a little different in Corvallis. Their opposition would be a squad composed of some of the biggest names to ever wear the Orange and Black, arguably the greatest alumni team ever to take the floor at OSU for an exhibition match.

For starters, there was Lew Beck, OSC All-American and Olympic gold medal winner. Alex Petersen also suited up; in 1948, "Pete" led the nation in field-goal percentage with a .476 average. Arriving by train from San Francisco was Bob Payne, along with OSC All-American Cliff Crandall. The two had led the Bay Area's Stewart Chevrolets to the AAU national championship in 1951.

Crandall also held the distinction of being the only Beaver up to that time to score more than 1,000 points in a career. Petersen, Beck and Crandall had all starred for the famed "Thrill Kids" of 1946-47. They were delighted when it was announced that teammates Erland Anderson, "Mushy" Silver and Doug Martin would also be there for the game.

Others participating included John Mandic, Paul Valenti, Don Durdan (of '42 Rose Bowl fame) and Bill Harper. A year earlier, Slats Gill, OSC's head basketball coach for 24 seasons, had named each of them to his list of the greatest players ever to play for the Beavers. Not only did Valenti suit up to face the 'Trotters, Slats gave him the responsibility of putting the team together.

Both Payne and Petersen had competed against the Globetrotters in previous years and had a good idea of what to expect. The rest only knew of their opponents by reputation. No matter. Everyone braced for a tough game.

Led by center Bob Hall, team leader Louis "Babe" Pressley and dribbling sensation Leon Hillard, the Globetrotters in 1951-52 had won 325 games against eight defeats. In their 25-year history, they had recorded 4,233 wins against 260 losses. Their winning percentage was an astronomical .941.

Under the direction of ace promoter Abe Saperstein, the Globetrotter organization in the early '50s was different from what we see today.

Sure, the crowd-pleasing skits and dribbling and shooting exhibitions were included in many of the games they played. But they also enjoyed playing "real" games against legitimate competition, consistently beating the nation's best teams.

In a series against a team of college All-Americans in 1952, for example, they had taken eight of 11 games. Their success against the pros was just as impressive.

Most members of that 1953 alumni team are still alive, including three Corvallis alumni who enjoy reminiscing about this special game. As they like to tell it, a Globetrotter representative came down to their dressing room before tipoff to explain how the game would be conducted.

"They said there were certain skits and things they wanted to perform for the crowd and asked us to go along with the show," Payne recalls. "I had already played against them four or five other times so I knew what to expect. But it was Valenti's first experience with something like this, and after their guy left, Paul's competitive nature took over. He told us he wanted us to go out and try to win the game."

As Petersen remembers it, that's exactly what they did.

"The Globetrotters liked to weave in and out and around their pivot man, Bob Hall. I worked closely with John Mandic in the first half to make sure Bob got no easy passes."

The rest of the Beaver team played tight man-to-man defense. Until the last half of the third quarter, it was a strategy that kept the Globetrotters out of their routines.

"We knew it was just a game for fun," Payne said, "but deep down inside we wanted to see if we could really beat this team."

As Petersen remembered: "We weren't there to play an exhibition. We were there to play a basketball game."

With 4:55 to go in the third period, the Beavers were within two points of taking the lead. By this time, however, fans were getting restless. Satisfied their Oregon State heroes could still play the game, they were ready to see a little slapstick. They were ready to laugh.

"When the crowd got restless for comedy, it all but took away our desire to win the game," Payne said. "When I think about it, I believe we were probably the wrong group for the Globetrotters."

The shift in the crowd's mood also turned out to be a blessing in disguise for OSC's alumni team. From a conditioning standpoint, the former Beaver greats were starting to breathe pretty hard.

"Most of us were not in real good shape, so the game was a bit overwhelming," Harper said. "And let's give the Globetrotters credit. They were exceptional athletes who had been playing together for a long time. They were good enough to have played for any college or professional team in the country."

"It was a very positive experience," Payne added. "Everyone had a lot of fun."

Always deadly serious about basketball, even on this evening of make-believe, Slats let his guard down once during the action, when a back-peddling Don Durdan tripped over his own feet and fell to the floor. The crowd of 8,012 roared. So did Slats.

Later he told *Corvallis Gazette-Times* sportswriter Brian Storm: "I think Durdan tripped over the center line."

Before the main event, the crowd had watched the Philadelphia Sphas defeat the Hawaiian Surfriders, two teams that were traveling with Saperstein's Globetrotters as a warmup act. To ensure no one left during halftime, Saperstein's show included entertainers whose acts to-day speak to a simpler age, including two tap dancers and a ping pong match for the first game, later followed by two hula dancers, "straight from Hawaii," and a French unicyclist for the alumni contest. The audience stayed captivated.

Newspaper accounts of the evening reported that everyone said it was the best time they had ever had at Gill. Well, almost everyone. The next day, Storm reported in his *Gazette-Times* sports column, "Between the Lines," that a fan told him he thought the hula dancers had "faced the general admission seats too much, neglecting the reserve seat customers while they danced."

By the way, the final score was 57-38, in favor of the Globetrotters.

15

Kidnapped!

Once upon a time, in a more innocent era, pranks between rival schools were as much a part of the college football scene as Homecoming, marching bands and cheerleaders. For nearly 80 years, students from Oregon State and Oregon would play an annual game of one-upmanship in hopes of producing the most creative, clever and memorable prank. That honor, even the most jaded Beaver had to grudgingly admit as yet another Homecoming approached in 1998, must go to Oregon's Theta Chi house for its masterful performance in November 1957.

The four young men seemed genuine enough.

They wore white shirts and ties. Their haircuts were trim and neat. The tall one sported a tan trenchcoat and thick-rimmed black glasses. He used a large camera to take photos.

Another carried a reporter's notepad, asked questions and smiled with faint embarrassment every time he wrote something.

They looked every bit the part of who they said they were, reporters for the *Seattle Post-Intelligencer*, sent this November 1, 1957, to Oregon State College to interview homecoming queen Pearl Friel and her court.

After a brief meeting, Friel was asked if she would accompany the *PI* team out to Corvallis's Avery Park for a few photos. She agreed without pause. As part of her Homecoming responsibilities, she had met with many reporters and photographers during the week. This seemed no different.

They also insisted the rest of the court be invited, but only two of the four could be found. The young men seemed eager to get going. They had deadlines to meet, they said, suggesting to the young ladies that their story might be a full-page feature in the Sunday edition.

The three OSC ladies were escorted outside, where two cars waited to whisk them away. No one noticed the vehicles sported Oregon license plates. If they had, they may have suspected something, the beginnings of one of the most daring pranks ever staged in the long rivalry between the UO and OSU, the kidnapping of Oregon State's homecoming court.

Pranks between the two schools, especially during Civil War Week, extend back to before the turn of the last century. At any time during the year, but especially Civil War Week, students from both schools would try to outfox each other with a variety of innocent deeds that ran the gamut from stealing or destroying the "O" atop Eugene's Skinner's Butte to setting off the OSU Rook bonfire early.

Rioting between fans of the rival schools around Seymour's Restaurant in downtown Eugene began after the 1937 game made national news. In 1953, several UO students were captured as they tried to burn a giant "O" on the grass in front of Benton Hall. As a memento of their visit, they were held down and given a good dousing of orange and black paint all over their stripped-to-the-waist bodies.

No one, however, had ever tried anything as bold as a kidnapping. But bold action was needed, retaliation necessary. That Monday night, pranksters from Corvallis, following a generations-old tradition, had not only stolen the "O" from Skinner's Butte but had cut it up into little sections, where it now lay scattered, according to rumor, in a half-dozen Portland basements.

Several days later, at the Theta Chi house on the UO campus, a prank of historic proportions began to take shape. The four who elected to attempt the feat were all UO student-athletes: Jim Grelle, a star miler; his friend Steve Anderson, a sprinter; Bob Prahl, a member of the golf team; and Ron Dodge, a baseball player.

In a November 1998 telephone interview from his home in Gig Harbor, Washington, Anderson remembered the planning of the kidnapping and said with a smile in his voice: "We really didn't care that much about them cutting up the 'O', but we all agreed that some kind of response was in order. That's when the idea of a kidnapping was discussed, but we agreed it had to be done in the name of fun. We phoned our president's office and were told that the prank was OK, provided we didn't break any laws and if nothing 'physical' happened.

"We all thought that if we could just con them out to the cars, the prank would be a success. It was all we could do to keep a straight face."

Not only did the young Oregon State coeds walk to the waiting vehicles, they got in. The four Ducks were delirious. Homecoming princess LuAnn Mullen joined Friel, who was from Kaunakakai, Molakai, Hawaii, and a descendent of Hawaiian nobility. Mullen, from Albany, was a home economics education major who had run for class vice president as a junior.

Into the other car went Verle Pilling of Portland, a transfer to OSC in her sophomore year from Lewis and Clark College. At the time this story was researched, she was Verle Weitzman and lived near Sisters, Oregon.

"I remember driving away from the Kappa Kappa Gamma house with these young men who said they were reporters from Seattle," she said. "But we headed north, out of town, and it didn't take long for me to realize something wasn't right."

She also admitted she didn't ever remember being scared or concerned and that once she realized she had fallen victim to a college prank, she had a great time.

"They were all very nice young men, acted like gentlemen the entire afternoon and treated us with great respect," she said. "And we all thought they were very good-looking."

One of the two "reporters" accompanying Verle was Grelle, who in 1960 became a member of the U.S. Olympic Team and set an American record in the mile at 3:55.4. Later, Jim and Verle would become very good friends, even date.

On this day, however, as his car sped north to Salem for a rendezvous with the others at Bob Prahl's house, where Bob's mom was waiting to chaperone the group and entertain them with homemade cookies, the future Olympian could only think of one thing: What if one of the girls panics?

"Well, that would have been the end of it," Prahl shared from his home near Gearhart on the Oregon coast. "We would certainly have turned them loose."

But it never happened. Not even close.

"They were so convinced we were reporters from Seattle, they didn't believe us when we told them we were from the UO," Grelle said.

By this time, however, news flashes on the radio were beginning to report the "kidnapping" of OSC's Homecoming court, which finally convinced the women their captors were telling the truth. There were

*OSU's 1957 "kidnapped" Homecoming Court, from left, Verle Pilling,
Queen Pearl Friel, Sandra Ferrell, Nina Gollersrud and LuAnn Mullen.
Pilling, Friel and Mullen fell victim to the notorious UO prank.
(Photo courtesy of* The Beaver.*)*

even reports that the Hawaii media had picked up on the story and
were demanding the release of Queen Friel.

Arriving at the Prahl house, the group settled down to refreshments and a good time. Phone calls were made, including one to OSC
Dean of Men Dan W. Poling, who was assured the young ladies were
fine and would be returned to Corvallis in time for the Homecoming
rally and parade that night. Poling insisted he meet the group, not on
campus but out of town, at the Benton County line. It was so agreed.

But Grelle's anxiety remained high. During one of the calls, someone mentioned that the entire OSC football team was out looking for

the kidnapped court, led by the captain of the team, who just happened to be dating Friel.

"We heard they were out looking for us and were going to beat the crap out of us," Grelle recalled with a laugh. "Later, it was rumored the team was going to come to Eugene, hold us down and cut our hair off. I spent the next three weeks looking over my shoulder. I even took buddies to class with me as bodyguards.

"In the end, everything turned out in a very congenial way," he said. "It was a fun party for everyone, a very enjoyable afternoon."

Campus observers agree there has not been a major prank committed by either school in over 25 years. The feeling is that community standards for college town behavior have stiffened; pranks are simply not treated as pranks anymore. In the mid-1990s, during Civil War Week, OSU students conducted a round-the-clock vigil over the cast iron Beaver that sat on a stand in the northeast corner of the end zone at what was then Parker Stadium. A rumor out of Eugene said an attempt would be made to steal Benny, stand and all. In the climate of the '90s, this rumor turned out to be nothing more than wishful thinking.

For the record, Oregon State won both its Homecoming game in '57 *and* the Civil War game to finish its season at 8-2.

The Beaver victory over the UO left the schools tied for the conference title; however, the Beavers had been to the Rose Bowl in '56 and since the Pacific Coast Conference (now the Pac-10) had a no-repeat rule, the Ducks went to Pasadena.

16

Beginner's Luck?

OSU has been competing in organized collegiate athletics since 1893. Baseball, track and field, and football are the oldest sports, in that order. Think of the years. Think of the athletes, the coaches, the teams—Farmers, Agrics, Aggies, Orangemen, Beavers, Lady Beavers, Orange Express, Men in Black. Think of the games, the tournaments, the matches and meets, the bowl games, the winning seasons, the national rankings and major upsets this cast of characters has turned in for the Orange and Black. Collectively the number is in the tens of thousands. After all this time, with competition in intercollegiate athletics going back more than a hundred years, Oregon State has won exactly one team national championship sanctioned by the NCAA—in any sport. This is the story of the athletes who turned in this singular achievement, written on the 40-year anniversary of their historic accomplishment.

Oregon State has, of course, suited up more than its share of individual NCAA champions, but team titles have been difficult to come by. The Pacific-10 Conference may be the self-proclaimed "Conference of Champions," but you wouldn't know it by the Beavers. Look to Southern California, with 70 men's team titles alone, or Stanford or UCLA for the schools that put the conference where it is.

OSU's lone claim to NCAA fame came in November 1961. And it wasn't earned in one of the marquee sports. It was cross country, and the team, coached by the likeable Sam Bell, consisted of five outstanding athletes led by the amazing Dale Story, still known for competing without shoes.

Barefoot was Story's style, and he stuck with it all through his brilliant running career, both at Santa Ana (California) Junior College, where he set a world age group record at eight minutes, 36.9 seconds over two miles, and at Oregon State, where he set 13 course or meet records. He set school records in the two-mile (8:46.9) in 1961, the mile (4:03.4) in 1962 and the three-mile (13:37.2) that same year.

Not that he hated shoes. Sometimes he had to wear them, particularly on track surfaces where he needed traction to build speed.

But barefoot was his choice on November 27, 1961, on the campus of Michigan State University in East Lansing, as the huge group of collegiate runners began to take their marks to start competition for the national team title.

"He even tried to talk the rest of us into doing the same," team member Cliff Thompson recalled from his Kings Valley, Oregon, home in November 2001. "Jerry Brady said he would, and did. A mile into the race, he regretted his decision in a big way."

Without the support an athletic shoe provides, a nagging tendon problem became worse. Jerry Brady was going lame. He threatened to stop and drop out. Teammates begged him not to and he didn't. Had he quit, OSU would have zero NCAA team national championships.

Story was having troubles of his own, dealing with 30-degree weather, a 25-mph wind blowing in his face, and pressure by some of the nation's best distance runners. His performance remains one of the best ever at OSU. Story captured the individual NCAA crown and then joined his four teammates to capture the overall NCAA title in a composite time of 1:43:15.9. Not only was this a big day for the runners from Corvallis, they were even more delighted when they learned they had become the first West Coast team ever to win the title.

In clocking the four-mile championship course, Story dashed through the first two miles at an impressive 10 minutes, 4.4 seconds. The third mile was 4:48.6, the home stretch 4:53.6. He finished 11 seconds ahead of Finland's Ratti Matti of Brigham Young University. Other big-name runners that day included future Olympians Billy Mills of Kansas; Pat Clohessy and Al Lawrence, a pair of Australians competing for the University of Houston; and Tom O'Hara of Loyola of Chicago.

This was OSU's first appearance at the national meet. Story and teammates Thompson, Brady, Bill Boyd and Rich Cuddihy defeated a field that included outstanding squads from runner-up San Jose State, Houston and traditional power Kansas.

Beginner's luck? Perhaps. But it was good enough for the title.

Today, all five team members, along with Bell, are enjoying second or third careers or retirement.

Bell still turns in a few hours a day at Indiana University, where he holds emeritus status with the university's track program. Boyd lives in Coeur d'Alene, Idaho, and is an attorney with his own firm. Story recently retired as a high school educator in Wallowa, Oregon, where he trained 53 state champions in track and field and, yes, cross country. Brady moved back home to Oklahoma in 1971 to teach and coach. He's still there, drives a school bus in retirement and has eight grandchildren. Cuddihy lives outside Yamhill, Oregon, and has a vineyard. Thompson does a little farming.

Four of the five former team members were contacted for this chapter; all still enjoy talking about this special moment in their lives. The last time they were together was five years ago, when they all returned to Corvallis to be inducted into the OSU Sports Hall of Fame.

Story, who lives in a new log home he built just outside Richland, Oregon, remembers well the confidence the team had going into the championships: "We ran and trained year-round. I loved cross country because it was such an individual sport. We identified a lot with the wrestling team because it was both an individual sport with rigorous training and also a team sport. I had great feelings for our team and didn't want to let the other guys down.

"We trained in the hills out in the McDonald Forest. We would see if we could run all the way to the top without stopping. We usually did, and it was interesting that when we got to East Lansing and saw the course and saw what they were calling a 'hill,' we laughed and said, 'You guys have no idea of what a hill is.'"

Why no shoes?

It was the result of a polio attack when he was 11. Amazingly, the effects of the disease lasted only a few years. As he was healing, he developed the idea that "less material is better," and later, as a runner, "less material is faster."

The 1961 OSU cross country squad, still the only Beaver team in school history to win an NCAA national championship. Coach Sam Bell is far left, standing next to All-American Dale Story.
(Photo courtesy of The Beaver.*)*

"I just felt better and healed faster when I was outside. So I would go around wearing fewer clothes and barefoot," he remembered. "I just felt more comfortable and felt like it was helping me."

Still an avid outdoorsman at age 60, Story is one of the finest bow hunters in the Northwest. He has registered 32 "kills" over the years hunting black bear, deer, elk, moose and mountain goat. Part of his technique, he said, is taking off his shoes at the right time and finishing his stalking of the animal like he won the national championship— bare flesh right on the ground, although he admits his feet are not as tough as they used to be. "I just grin and bear it," he said with a laugh.

From his law offices in Coeur d'Alene, Boyd remembered the trip to Michigan and a story about Bell.

"We flew in to East Lansing, and when we got to where we were going to stay, it was already dark. Then Sam came up with the idea that we should all keep on West Coast time, should be on the same schedule just as if we were in Corvallis. Sure enough, we went out and ran in the dark! The next day, the day before the race, it was a 'bluebird' day, real warm. That night, it turned really cold—below freezing. The next day, when we got to the course, we were all wondering if Dale was going to run without shoes, as he always did. He kept worrying that the ground might be too cold or too hard to run barefoot."

It was then, according to Boyd, the team made a fateful decision, one that, in retrospect, may have contributed enough of a difference to give them the title. "All the other athletes were showing up wearing warm clothes for the race, long sleeves and such. We decided right there we would keep things light and go with our regular clothes, the ones we wore in warm weather."

Brady still winces when he remembers the race. An Achilles tendon problem had kept him from working out for two weeks before the championship. During the race, the problem came back to haunt him, threatening to force him out of the race, threatening, in a way, to alter Oregon State's sports history forever. But he stayed the course and today says he thinks more about his finish than the pain it took to get him through the race.

"I'm still disappointed on how I performed," he shared, "especially with my finish, because I had demonstrated all through college that I was much better than I was showing at the race. I finished 51st, not real good, but, in the end, good enough to help OSU win the championship."

Like Story, Brady became a track coach, employed at Norman High in

Norman, Oklahoma, where from 1985-1993, his track teams won five state titles. He did so by adopting early in his career a philosophy that he saw Bell use at OSU. He remembers him as having a sort of "mountain man" attitude about everything, that "nothing ever bothered him."

"He was always confident, and this gave me and the rest of the team the belief that we could go to East Lansing and at least be in the hunt for the title."

He also recalled with passion the role Bell played in keeping team members feeling good about themselves and their chances of doing something big.

"Sam Bell was a real personable guy and still is. He was a man with a strong character who cared about everybody and a personable guy who was really kind of a father figure to us. You always knew what he was doing because he always had such a good system for how he managed things."

17

Heisman Hype

Today, college football's annual race for the Heisman Trophy begins soon after the final day of the previous season, when the first of mass mailings, e-mails and colorful notebooks are shipped to media types across the nation. Until 1962, no such hype existed. Players quietly compiled their statistics, rankings and victories, and in the end voters quietly announced whom they had selected as the top player in the land. All that changed with a clean-cut All-America quarterback named Terry Baker and a congenial sports information director named Johnny Eggers, both of whom achieved the impossible and forever altered the face of the Heisman Trophy derby. That was evident 39 years later, when OSU tailback Ken Simonton became a Heisman contender months before his senior season even began.

For Ken Simonton to have won college football's most coveted player award in the autumn of 2001, a lot of stars had to line up in just the right way.

A great offensive line, a winning team, ending the season with a bowl bid, a national ranking, enough TV exposure on the East Coast—everything had to connect if the Heisman Trophy was to make its way back to Corvallis in December.

That's right, *back* to Corvallis. OSU remains the only school in the Northwest to have a player win the Heisman. The magical season was 1962. Everything connected.

OSU was nationally ranked and bowl bound. The Beavers had finished strong the previous year. By midseason, no school had produced a clear front-runner. It was anybody's prize to win.

OSU coach Tommy Prothro, with a keen eye for talent, knew this. Suddenly, his interest in the Heisman race became less professional, more personal.

His quarterback was Terry Baker, clearly the best athlete that the "Gentleman from Tennessee" had ever seen lace up a pair of cleats.

Baker was capping a legendary college career. The ambidextrous quarterback was well on his way to 4,979 total yards for three seasons, placing him second to Drake's Johnny Bright on the all-time list of ground gainers.

He was averaging 5.5 yards per play and ended the campaign with 16 touchdowns running and 23 passing to give the Beavers a shot at Villanova in the Liberty Bowl.

There, Baker electrified the nation by running 99 yards from scrimmage on frozen turf for the game's only score in a 6-0 victory.

Not bad for a gifted athlete from Portland's Jefferson High School who had no intention of playing football at Oregon State University.

Raised by a single mother, Baker was an intelligent, gifted student and athlete destined to succeed when he arrived in school as a two-sport athlete in 1959. At Jefferson, he played alongside brothers Mel and Ray Renfro on a football team that many believe is the best in Oregon high school history.

Baker's dream at OSU was to play point guard on coach Slats Gill's basketball team. He also wanted to pitch for Ralph Coleman's baseball team. Football? He didn't care for Prothro's single-wing formation.

But the baseball season in 1960 was a forgettable one for Baker, who was placed on the freshman, or Rook, team.

"It seemed that every game we were supposed to play got rained out," recalls Baker, now a successful lawyer for Tonkin Torp in Portland. "Well, Tommy Prothro could be quite persuasive. He knew how to punch my buttons. He finally got me to come out for spring practice. And they say the rest is history."

Prothro had a great athlete and he knew it. Before the 1962 season, he wanted others to know it as well, particularly sportswriters who figure in the Heisman voting.

After all, no player west of Texas's Pecos River had ever won the Heisman Trophy. Texas A&M's John David Crow in 1957 was the only

*Running back Ken Simonton poses in 2000 with former Heisman Trophy
winner Terry Baker as the Beavers kicked off Simonton's Heisman campaign.
(Photo courtesy of Barry Schwartz.)*

player west of the Mississippi River to nab it. It was a virtually impossible task in an arena dominated by eastern media.

Sometimes, a magical season reaches a crossroads. The right person has to come along at the right time to keep the magic going. In this, Prothro was lucky.

To get the word out, Prothro turned to the guy whose job was to tell the world about the Beavers.

His name was John Eggers, but everybody just called him "Johnny." He was Prothro's sports information director, an old-school kind of journalist who had graduated from OSC in 1950 and who couldn't remember, he would always say with a grin, exactly what he had majored in.

No matter.

His place in history is secure.

He is generally credited as the person who engineered the public-relations campaign it took for Baker to win the Heisman. Through an almost Herculean effort, Johnny Eggers carried out a simple but effective media campaign that year that helped convince the nation's experts that a quarterback from a small aggie school in the remote Northwest was qualified.

Eggers had been around Oregon sports for more than 10 years, after a brief stint at *The Oregonian* newspaper in Portland. He had spent his early career honing his skills on what he did best: cultivating and keeping good one-on-one relationships with members of the state and regional media so they would want to cover OSU sports.

Current sports information director Hal Cowan, who watched the 1962 football campaign while finishing his undergraduate degree at Linfield College in McMinnville, came to Oregon State in 1976, as Eggers, in failing health, was finishing his career.

"He was a real friendly guy," Cowan recalls. "In an era in our business when we didn't have all the computers and promotional campaigns and all the other things we use now to get the word out, John was the right person for the right time.

"He was great at one-on-one relationships and everybody liked him. He was a guy you liked to be around, who knew sports and who knew how to approach his friends in the business to get the Beavers in the news."

There's an old axiom from the world of business that applies here.

If your thinking is expansive and out-of-state, don't attempt anything new until you're doing a good job closest to where you live. This was an Eggers trademark, for he had only the strongest of support from the media at home.

For Baker's campaign, he only had to take his talents and personality for dealing with home folks and use them to make new friends among strangers. Soon, a lot of sportswriters around the country knew who Johnny Eggers was. And they knew where he worked. Still, he would not be able to help Terry Baker win a Heisman on grins and good times alone.

Cowan has heard many stories about how his predecessor conducted the Baker campaign. In a sense, it was a grassroots effort, a down-and-dirty, in-the-trenches, one-on-one approach that's the most taxing and time-consuming way an SID can spend a season, but probably the one, if the persistence is there, that's most successful.

"Without the benefit of having seen John work, what I have been told is that he set up a system where he routinely sent out a lot of personal notes or postcards around the country to a set mailing list of sportswriters, and then would follow with personal phone calls," Cowan remembers. "The cards usually had game stats and some quotes from the opposing coach.

"Everything was put together on Sunday, something he informally called 'Terry Baker Notes' or a 'Terry Baker Page,' and it was nothing fancy, just an effective effort at a time when SIDs didn't have electronic communications, TV clips, none of the devices that we have today."

Back then the approach was a novelty. Today, such campaigning is the norm—and we can thank Johnny Eggers.

Eggers didn't breathe a word of his plan to Baker. Newspapers said nary a word about the Heisman all season, even though Baker was giving Eggers plenty of fodder.

In Prothro's new T-formation offense, No. 11 accumulated 1,230 yards total offense, owned 14 career records already and was the team's Most Valuable Player his junior season. That winter, he played guard on a 22-5 basketball team that was runner-up in the NCAA Tournament's West Regional.

All the while, he continued to pursue a degree in the school's demanding mechanical engineering program.

The next year, behind an offensive line known as "The Light Brigade," Baker passed for 1,738 yards and ran for 538 more. His combined yardage led the NCAA and his career total of 4,980 was second in NCAA history behind Johnny Bright of Drake.

The Beavers finished 8-2 and were ranked 15th nationally.

One morning in December, Baker woke to learn he had won college football's most prestigious award.

"I was surprised by it when it was announced," he said. "It wasn't really anything I was focusing on. Nobody had ever won it from the West."

Afterward, Baker met President John F. Kennedy, was awarded the trophy by Attorney General Robert F. Kennedy and was invited to appear on *The Ed Sullivan Show* and *The Tonight Show.* Today, Baker still gets "stuff" in the mail daily asking for autographs.

Baker then played on OSU's Final Four basketball team in 1963. But he's forever remembered for the Heisman.

"It's kind of like getting a tattoo," he said. "People identify you with it and it becomes a part of you."

That it worked goes without saying, for whatever it might have done to bring football fame to his alma mater, he set a standard for success still not equaled—not even in 2001 by Simonton, whose bid was hyped early but short-circuited by a leaky offensive line.

Johnny Eggers turned football heads topsy-turvy. If he had to do the job with a million phone calls and postcards, that's what he did.

Somehow, some way, men and women of destiny—and in no small measure John Eggers was one of these—find a way to get the job done. They just do.

Actually, he must have done even better than we can imagine.

More awards and accolades came Baker's way. He was named to the first squads of 11 All-America teams and was named Sportsman of the Year by *Sports Illustrated* magazine.

"He was," former OSU coach Bobb McKittrick once said, "a hero."

The reference was to Baker. It could've just as easily have been to Johnny Eggers.

18

A Beaver and a Duck at the Top of the World

The early 1960s were banner years for OSU athletics. Quarterback Terry Baker won a Heisman Trophy. The basketball team made it to the Final Four for the only time in history. The cross country team won the school's only NCAA team championship in any sport. And halfway around the world, renowned OSU mountaineer Willi Unsoeld was making history—not to mention a memorable photo op—on the world's highest mountain.

It was 3:15 p.m., May 22, 1963. Lute Jerstad and climbing companion Barry Bishop could finally see the top of the mountain, clearly marked by an American flag flapping briskly in the almost hurricane-force winds that whipped the summit.

The flag was planted three weeks earlier by expedition team member "Big" Jim Whittaker of Redmond, Washington, marking the first successful climb of Mount Everest by an American.

Now, in just a few minutes, it would be Jerstad and Bishop's turn to stand where Whittaker had stood, plant their own flags, take a few photos, gaze at the world far below and reflect on what it meant to be standing at the highest place on earth.

They had started their final ascent two hours before daylight, from Camp VI at 27,450 feet. The way they had chosen to the top was the one route Everest gives you: the South Col, pioneered in 1953 by the mountain's first conquerors, Sir Edmund Hillary of England and Sherpa

Tensing Norgay. In 1956, a team of four Swiss climbers had retraced Hillary's path.

Thirty-year-old Barry Bishop lived in Washington, D.C., where he was a staff photographer for *National Geographic* magazine. Once on top, he would have work to do: taking the photos the magazine needed for its story on the climb.

Jerstad, 26, was a doctoral student and speech instructor at the University of Oregon. His passion was mountain climbing. He had cut his teeth by tackling most of the higher peaks in the Rockies, the Cascades and Alaska's Mount McKinley.

Now on the summit, the two spent the next 45 minutes celebrating and taking photos. When they were done, there was one more assignment to complete: wait for the others.

The plan that day was to put four climbers on the top—teams of two using separate routes to the objective. After meeting, they would descend together to Camp VI. As they stood alone at 29,000 feet and watched deep shadows begin to form in the valleys below, Bishop and Jerstad looked toward the west face of the mountain, hoping to see some sign of their friends.

Nothing.

They waited.

Still nothing.

With daylight fading, the two decided to ditch the rendezvous idea and start back. To stay after dark on top of Everest was an invitation to disaster.

The missing climbers were extraordinary athletes. What separated them from everyone else was their daring, the lengths they would go to prove a point. On this expedition, they had nixed the idea of following Jerstad and Bishop up the South Col. It had been done at least four times, so why bother? Instead, the intrepid climbers were attempting what the experts said was impossible: conquering Everest by climbing its West Ridge, which featured almost sheer cliffs to the top.

Raised in San Diego, Thomas Hornbein was a 32-year-old anesthesiologist who designed the oxygen masks the four were wearing. He talked the Maytag home appliance company into making the equipment at no charge.

His companion was William Unsoeld, who, at 36, was the oldest of the four. A year earlier, he took a leave of absence from his teaching position in the philosophy department at Oregon State College and moved his family to Nepal for a two-year assignment as that country's deputy director of the Peace Corps.

Unsoeld and wife, Jolene, were Oregon Staters, he finishing in 1951 and she in '53. The two helped start the OSC Mountain Club and announced their engagement during a club outing atop Oregon's Mount Hood.

Arriving at the summit of Everest some three hours after their teammates, Unsoeld and Hornbein quickly set about completing their own celebration. Then, with nightfall rapidly approaching, Unsoeld had one final ceremonial act he wanted to perform. Handing Hornbein his camera, he pulled from his pack a large, triangular flag sporting the circular logo of the OSC Mountain Club.

Jolene and classmate Jeanne Neff hand-stitched the banner in the early 1950s as an *esprit de corps* item for the new club. It quickly became popular with the members and went with them on all their outings.

As Willi Unsoeld began attracting attention for his climbing skills, he was given permission to take the flag on his travels. And so, when he joined an American-Pakistan expedition in 1960 to climb Mount Mashabram (25,660 feet) in the western Himalayas, the flag was there. The banner's history also included a trip in 1960 to Antarctica, the world's most southern point. It was carried there by Cmdr. Edward W. Donnally.

Moving off the summit, Unsoeld and Hornbein could still see well enough to find the South Summit, a short distance below. It was 7:15 p.m. The last light was gone from Lhotse, Makalu and other nearby peaks. Now the sun's rays lingered finally on the summit of Everest itself.

Darkness closed in with a swiftness that caught the two veteran climbers by surprise. To that point, they had loosely followed the tracks left by Jerstad and Bishop. When failing light made this impossible, they were suddenly without a clue about where to go next.

A moment of truth had arrived.

Hornbein, who was having trouble with his oxygen supply, wanted to stay put and start again at first light. Unsoeld voted no. His opinion was that they would never survive the elements at that altitude. An argument ensued. In the end, Unsoeld got his way. His prize was a nightmare, a descent down the South Col in pitch-black darkness.

Cutting across what seemed to be a large snow slope, the two began moving in the direction of Camp VI. Having only a flashlight, and tied to one another with a 60-foot piece of rope, they groped their way

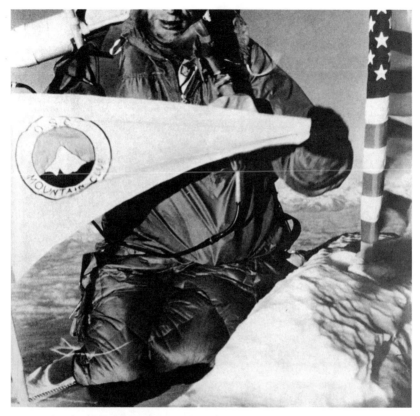

Willi Unsoeld unfolds the Oregon State College Mountain Club flag atop Mt. Everest, May 22, 1963, on the first American expedition to successfully scale the world's highest mountain.
(Photo by Dr. Thomas Hornbein.)

downward, looking for track marks or ice ax holes left by their friends. To fight back fear and exhaustion, the two began to yodel. They were hoping the noise would arouse someone from camp.

They were heard. In the distance, faint shouts were somehow cutting through the frigid, howling wind. Human voices were calling out to them. It was Lute and Barry.

They pushed on. Finally, figures began to emerge. The night had turned to total blackness, rendering the climbers completely blind. Jerstad had to reach out to "touch" the nearest voice to identify who it was.

Then Unsoeld arrived. The teams were together at last. It was 9:30 p.m. With their oxygen supply almost exhausted and a weak flashlight their only source of light, their situation was serious. The four continued down the mountain.

At 30 minutes past midnight, the decision was made to bivouac. Altitude: 28,000 feet, more than 2,000 feet above the highest previous emergency bivouac in history. Temperature: 20 below.

Lying snug against an outcropping of rock, with arms, legs and bodies intertwined for warmth, the four prepared to die. But Everest was merciful. The winds stopped their raging gales, and in five hours, the sun was once again touching the slopes.

The next day, the group was at last at base camp. For Willi Unsoeld, Lute Jerstad and Barry Bishop, a new ordeal was about to begin: the ill effects of frostbite. After being carried a full day on the backs of Sherpas to reach a rescue helicopter, they were whisked off to the United Mission Hospital in Katmandu, where all would live to see another day—and climb another mountain.

Unsoeld and Hornbein were particularly pleased with what they had done on the climb. In addition to setting a world record for an emergency bivouac, they became the first climbers to scale the West Face of Everest. The two were also the first to "traverse" the summit of the mountain—going up one way and coming down another.

Unsoeld averted tragedy that day, but eventually fates caught up with him and his family. He was killed in an avalanche on March 4, 1979, while leading a group of students from Evergreen State College across Mount Rainier's often-dangerous Cadaver Gap. He was a founding member of the college.

In 1976, while attempting to climb Nanda Devi, India's highest peak, he watched the high-altitude death of his daughter, a gifted and talented climber whom, ironically, Willi and Jolene had named after the mountain that took her life.

Jolene Unsoeld eventually became a resident of Washington State, where she was elected to Congress in the early 1980s.

Hornbein served for many years as the chair of the anesthesiology department at the University of Washington's School of Medicine. Today, he is an emeritus professor with the school. On February 13, 2003, he delivered the 2003 Willi Unsoeld Seminar Series lecture at OSU, where he has been an ardent supporter of the series since its inception in 1986.

Jerstad operated Lute Jerstad Adventures in Portland until his death from an apparent heart attack on November 1, 1998, while trekking in the Everest region with his stepdaughter and grandson. According to news reports, he was cremated and his ashes spread over the Thyangboche Monastery on the route to the great mountain.

Bishop lost his life in a one-car accident near Pocatello, Idaho, in 1994. He had only recently retired from *National Geographic* and had moved to Bozeman, Montana.

Unsoeld may have been the first from the Corvallis area or OSU to scale Everest, but there have been others since.

On September 29, 1988, another Oregon Stater, Stacy Allison, became the first American woman to reach the summit. In addition to serving as a motivational speaker, the 1984 OSU graduate owns and operates Stacy Allison General Contracting, a residential building company. She lives in Portland with her husband, David, and their two sons.

In 1996, Corvallis High alumnus Jon Krakauer made it to the summit in a climb that ended with the tragic loss of eight members of the expedition, a dramatic story captured in his book *Into Thin Air*.

19

The Flop

Oregon State has had its share of athletic invention—The Pyramid Play, the football huddle, Heisman Trophy hype. But among Beaver Believers, there's no debate about whose accidental entrepreneurial genius most revolutionized a sport. In the mid-1960s, a gangly Medford native named Dick Fosbury, unable to grasp standard forms of the high jump, as a last resort tried a newfangled approach: going over the bar backward. The resulting Olympic gold medal took the track world by storm in 1968. More than two decades later, the man who put OSU track and field on the national map was trying to put it back in Corvallis. He revealed his feelings in an interview while the 1991 NCAA championships were contested 40 miles to the south in Eugene.

Day after day, Pacific breezes surge gently through the rickety bleachers at Wayne Valley Field, pushing leaves, weeds and an occasional hamburger wrapper into the surrounding chain-link fence.

If you listen closely, you can almost hear the ghosts of Beavers past, wailing over the decaying facility and the loss it symbolizes.

When it was dedicated in 1974, Wayne Valley was billed as the nation's most modern track and field facility. Seventeen years later, it is a weather-beaten remnant of Oregon State's once-proud track program, which was purged in 1988.

Weeds nearly a foot tall dot the long-jump pit and infield. Thorny blackberry vines have run amok, wrapping themselves around the first two rows of bleachers. Rust has eaten away at the high-jump supports. The press box and storage sheds are boarded up tight.

In this track and field wasteland, it's hard to imagine that 40 miles away, in the so-called "Track Capital of the World," the grandest spectacle in college track, the NCAA championships, are under way in front of thousands of track-hungry spectators at Eugene's Hayward Field.

Somehow, track without a team at OSU is like Florida without sunshine or Jay Leno without Dan Quayle jokes: still pretty good, but just not the same. In other words, OSU without track is downright unfathomable.

"It hurts," says the most famous of those ghosts, Dick Fosbury. "It hurts bad."

Dick Fosbury, architect of perhaps the most revolutionary change in track history, lives in Ketchum, Idaho, but his thoughts are never far from Corvallis. He's still a Beaver, using "we" when discussing his alma mater.

Moreover, though his professional life has long sine been devoted to Galena Engineering, the small civil engineering and land-surveying company he co-owns in the famed winter resort area of Sun Valley, track remains a passion. Small wonder. Of the many Oregon Staters who have competed in the Olympic Games, Fosbury, above all, continues to capture the imagination of those who love Olympic history.

Fosbury won a gold medal in Mexico City in 1968 with a benchmark performance by which all high jumpers are measured. His gold came between his junior and senior years at OSU, and it happened at Games made famous by the clenched fists of U.S. sprinters Tommie Smith and John Carlos as well as the barrage of track world records broken (26 out of a possible 30).

Yet only Bob Beamon's incredible world record mark in the long jump and the unforgettable black-glove display overshadowed the performance of the young high jumper from Corvallis.

Fosbury didn't set a world record, though he leaped into the books by breaking the Olympic mark held by the Soviet Union's famed Valery Brumel, the defending gold medallist from 1964. He soared to seven feet, four and a half inches, nearly three inches better than Brumel, to give the U.S. its first gold in the event in 12 years.

What made it the most-watched high-jump competition in history was the OSU star's style.

Everyone wanted to see Fosbury and his "Flop," the newfangled way the 21-year-old had developed of going over the bar backward instead of the traditional face-first straddle technique that was still used by all others.

"The crowd of 80,000 that day paid Fosbury the ultimate compliment," OSU historian Chuck Boice recalled in a 1987 story in *The Oregon Stater* alumni magazine. "It is an understandable tradition at the Olympics that when a marathon leader re-enters the stadium after his or her grueling hours out on the course, that they will receive undivided recognition through the final lap. The Olympic men's marathon champion, Mamo Wolde of Ethiopia, ran his final lap practically unheeded because Fosbury was starting his jump at the winning height."

Concluded Boice: "Dick Fosbury did revolutionize the high jump, writing a dramatic chapter in the Olympic Games and in Oregon State history."

Not bad for a guy whose unconventional style had OSU coach Berny Wagner thinking he made a mistake by offering the Medford native a track scholarship. After all, he already had sophomore Steve Kelly and freshman John Radetich, both of whom had better technique than Fosbury.

Kelly and Radetich used the straddle method. Fosbury was struggling to learn the straddle after years of using the archaic scissors technique.

Fosbury appeared to be going over the bar almost backward.

"We had two great straddlers and then we had this guy doing this weird jump," Wagner told the *Corvallis Gazette-Times* in 1999. "I thought, 'We still need a triple jumper.' I was like, 'Dick, maybe you better find another event, too.'"

Fosbury wasn't trying to invent the Flop. He and Wagner worked constantly on trying to correct his form.

They both laugh years later as they recount the evolution to the Flop.

"He and I differ on this story," Wagner says, chuckling. "He told me he wanted to be a good jumper and he was tired of being laughed at. I said, 'Well, we'll start working you on the straddle.'"

Fosbury spent his freshman year working on the straddle—facing the bar, leaping and then swinging one leg over the bar followed by another—but couldn't perfect it.

Exasperated, his coaches let him use his own style at the first meet of his sophomore season. Fosbury leaped six feet, 10 inches and won. Later that spring, he won the Pacific-8 Conference championship. A year later, he set an NCAA record at the championship meet.

Brian Jackson reacts to a three-pointer against Southern California in Los Angeles. Oregon State won 83-74.

AP/WWP

WINE QUIZ

1 What Oregon Winery was recently selected by *Wine & Spirits* Magazine as one of the "TOP 20 VALUE BRANDS" *in the* COUNTRY?

2 Which Oregon Winery was nationally syndicated columnist and noted wine judge, BROOKS TISH referring to when he stated, "No one in the United States makes a complete stable of dessert wines that competes with these wines"? ...No one!

3 In a recent judging of 174 "Gold Medal" winning wines by *Wine Press Northwest*, which winery's Chardonnay was selected as a "PLATINUM" WINE ...in other words, whose was "Best of the Best"?

4 HARVEY STEIMAN of the *Wine Spectator* Magazine wrote about Oregon Pinot Noirs in a recent issue. "Some of Oregon's top Pinots," he said, "are getting up there in price, topping $50 and even $100. This wine sells for less than $30 [a lot less], yet still offers distinct character—it has a personality that sets it apart from the competition—sheer excellence." Whose Pinot Noir was Mr. Steiman talking about?

5 Over 1,500 wines were entered in the recent *Taster's Guild* International Wine Competition, but only a handful won the prestigious "DOUBLE GOLD" award. Can you guess who?

6 What Oregon Winery does a Sunday Brunch every Sunday that has been widely acclaimed as "*The* BEST SUNDAY BRUNCH ...not just in wine country...but anywhere in Oregon?

7 Oh, by the way, guess which Oregon winery regularly hosts "ROADTRIPS" to OSU's away Football games.

ANSWERS

A small group of investors, spearheaded by six college fraternity brothers planted a vineyard in the hills just west of Salem over 20 years ago. That operation eventually evolved into Eola Hills Wine Cellars. Guess what college those Fraternity brothers were from? That's right...OSU! Go Beavs!

Tailback Steven Jackson runs into the end zone for a first-quarter touchdown ahead of Oregon defender Steven Moore during the Civil War game on November 23, 2002, in Corvallis. The Beavers beat the Ducks 45-24.

Then it was on to Mexico City.

Fosbury's winning leap in the 1968 Olympics wasn't celebrated by everyone, even in his own sport. Some track and field veterans weren't happy about such a dramatic change from someone so young.

U.S. Olympic coach Payton Jordan publicly criticized him, saying the Flop was a dangerous example for kids.

"Kids imitate champions," Jordan said. "If they try to imitate Fosbury, he will wipe out and entire generation of high jumpers because they will all have broken necks."

Today, every high jumper in the world uses the Fosbury Flop, which he perfected at OSU, not far from where Wayne Valley Field sits idle.

With such history there, Fosbury couldn't believe it when the school dropped the sport, can't believe it's still dormant and refuses to believe it can't come back.

To that end, Fosbury has spent much of what little free time he has dedicated to a seemingly futile cause. He writes, phones and meets with OSU administrators in a passionate and ambitious drive to reinstate a program that was ranked fifth nationally in 1974.

"I can't understand it," Fosbury says. "They say they don't have the money, don't have the resources. Well, listen, all it is is a question of priorities. You either rank it as important or not important. If there were people concerned with the tradition at Oregon State, they would make it a high priority. Bu apparently those people aren't the decision makers."

Indeed, restoring track is such a distant dream that Fosbury's attention has been focused more on the facility in which he never competed as a Beaver. He cringes at the very real prospect of Wayne Valley becoming a soccer complex.

"Wayne Valley Field was constructed for track, and I don't want to lose the opportunity if it can possibly return us to track in the near future," he said.

Which is not likely, given that part of a recent tuition-waiver deal at OSU contained a clause prohibiting the start of new sports or reinstatement of suspended programs. Fosbury also knows there hasn't exactly been a clamoring for track's return.

"I don't hear a lot of people who are very concerned about it," he concedes.

Yet Fosbury is determined. He understands that the state is suffering from a budget crisis, that OSU's biggest money maker—football—has been suffering from a 20-year win-loss crisis and that track is suffering from a public interest crisis, but the fight goes on.

"I love all sports, and I feel that it's very important to have that aspect of life available to students," he says. "I think it's a glaring omission at OSU."

So the letters, phone calls and meetings will continue.

Meantime, Wayne Valley Field remains a silent and endangered reminder of ghosts of Beavers past—Fosbury. Kasheef Hassan. Ed Lipscomb. Tim Vollmer. Hailu Ebba.

Day after day, the Pacific breezes blow in, occasionally splattering the stately facility with rain.

And if you look closely, you can almost see tear drops.

Note: In 1996, five years after this story was written, Wayne Valley Field was indeed dismantled in favor of the plush new soccer facility named Paul Lorenz Field at Patrick Wayne Valley Stadium. School officials say track and field has no chance of returning to OSU until its athletic budget is balanced. On the once-vacant lot next to the old track is a new softball complex and a Hilton Garden Hotel. Still, from his Sun Valley home, Fosbury fights on, refusing to allow his sport to become a permanent flop at OSU. (Women's cross country and track were reinstated at OSU in July 2003 to help comply with Title IX.)

20

Giant Killers

If there is a common thread bonding Oregon State football over a century-plus, it's the story of gritty, mud-splattered underdogs rising on gray autumn Saturdays to smite their glittery, glamorous opponents. Beaver historians can easily recount many such upsets, including The Ironmen's 0-0 tie with No. 1 USC in 1933, the 20-0 shocker over the top-ranked Michigan State in 1915 that prompted a famous poem by renowned sports writer Grantland Rice, and a 25-13 stunner over powerful New York University in 1928 that put West Coast football on the map. Yet none have the mystique of the 1967 team known simply as "The Giant Killers."

An extraordinary energy permeated the gray, damp air when the normally serene community of Corvallis awoke on the morning of November 11, 1967.

For the first time in memory, the eyes of a nation were focused on a community, a university and an overachieving football team that had captured the nation's fancy in a way that transcended the playing field.

Though they weren't aware of it then, Oregon State University was one of the last vestiges of an era of innocence, a slice of a dying Americana epitomized by such TV shows as *Father Knows Best* and *Leave It To Beaver*. The Vietnam War, the Beatles, riots, drugs and the legalization of the birth-control pill were rapidly altering the social landscape of a dazed and confused republic.

In Corvallis, the Beaver football team was still a clean-cut group of Joe College boys who wore crew cuts, dressed in button-down shirts and dated pretty Betty Coed. They were unwavering in their devotion to rotund and gruff coach Dee Andros, a marine disciplinarian who was awarded the Bronze Star for valor at Iwo Jima and sold his players on the idea of "death of self." They were a classic American success story: Rockwellian athletes who overcame glitzy opposition by combining just enough talent—11 would be drafted by National Football League teams—with heart, grit, determination and self-sacrifice. They were the ragtag colonists who would rise against the polished British, the Little Engine That Could in cleats and shoulder pads, a team so tightly knit that it seems, 30-plus years later, as if it all happened yesterday.

"There was a love there that I've never known with any other club," recalls John Didion, the team's center and a longtime NFL star. "It's impossible to describe, but those of us who went through it together have a common bond that's so meaningful and important to all of us we'll never let it die.

"It was just wonderful."

Small wonder that a popular national general interest magazine called *Look* would produce a rare sports feature on the Beavers.

By then, OSU had earned the attention of the sports world by shocking second-ranked Purdue 22-14 on October 21 in West Lafayette, Indiana, and by mustering a 16-16 tie with the new No. 2, UCLA, two weeks later in Los Angeles.

It was then that the national media dubbed them "The Giant Killers."

Now, as Veteran's Day dawned a week later, a flashy team some described as the best in college football history was coming to town. Top-ranked Southern California was undefeated, boasted five future first-round NFL draft choices and the nation's leading rusher in a tailback named Orenthal James Simpson, better known as "O. J." or "The Juice."

An estimated 10,000 supporters had packed the Memorial Union quad around a bonfire the previous night. California Gov. Ronald Reagan had flown up for the game and was so confident in a USC victory that he vowed he'd handpick a crate of oranges for Oregon Gov. Tom McCall if the Beavers won.

The largest crowd in Parker Stadium history (41,494) was in attendance, though many didn't find their seats until almost halftime because of the worst traffic jam the mid-Willamette Valley had ever experienced.

Oddsmakers favored USC by 11 points over 13th-ranked OSU. The Los Angeles media, unimpressed by the previous week's tie with UCLA, dismissed the Beavers. The only hope, they said, was for rain to give the speedy Trojans a soggy turf. Washington State coach Bert Clark agreed, suggesting that OSU "water the track."

Andros shrugged it off in the *guaran-damn-tee-ya* style that had become his trademark.

"We're tired of foolin' around with No. 2," he growled in his rugged Oklahoma twang after tying UCLA. "Bring on No. 1."

Corvallis was abuzz with an electricity that would've lit the entire city of Los Angeles.

What happened next on that blustery afternoon is etched as the single greatest moment in OSU's checkered football history, and not just because it was a monumental victory.

OSU's improbable 3-0 win that gloomy afternoon epitomized the triumph of human spirit.

It also signaled the abrupt end to that era of innocence for 50-odd football players, a university and a community.

******

Not even the most optimistic Beavers had envisioned anything special at the beginning of the 1967 season.

Three years removed from what would be their last Rose Bowl berth, OSU was laden with sophomores and juniors. The media guide described it as a rebuilding season, and indeed, the coaches played musical positions so much that few players wound up in familiar spots.

But they brought an intangible quality to the field that couldn't be measured with a stopwatch or tape measure, and an ex-marine named Demosthenes Konstandies Andrecopoulos had the personality to coax it to the surface.

Dee Andros joined the Marine Infantry Battalion out of high school and became a sergeant. He volunteered for two combat patrols against a Japanese resistance pocket on Iwo Jima, where his troop had been sold on the nobility of death the night before the famous assault.

Andros later would sell his players on such a complete commitment to team. It isn't a sin to get knocked down, he would bellow in pregame Rockne-esque pep talks, it's a sin to *stay* knocked down.

He would charge down the ramp at Parker Stadium wearing an orange windbreaker—hence the nickname "The Great Pumpkin"—and keep pace with athletes half his age despite his ample girth. His only training rule: "We will not tolerate a player who will embarrass me or the university."

Andros was not an Xs and Os man, instead turning that role over to a highly regarded staff that included Sam Boghosian, Rich Brooks and Bud Riley, all of whom went on to greater glories in college and the NFL.

The head coach simply blew volumes of flammable air on a fire that already raged in 50 bellies. By the end of the season, he would frequently have his coaches, players and himself in tears.

"Dee was the greatest motivator I've ever, ever played for," said Didion, who two years later would play for a coach of some inspirational renown named Vince Lombardi. "I respect him more than almost any other coach I've ever played for. We all loved Coach Andros. I've never been around anybody quite like him."

Andros's speeches had an immediate impact. Junior guard B. J. Jeremiah leveled Stanford's returner on the opening kick of the season, and the tone was set.

The Beavers won their first three games in classic three-yards-and-a-cloud-of-dust style, but were out-muscled by Washington and crushed 31-13 by pass-happy Brigham Young. They were 3-2 entering their date at No. 2 Purdue, which had whipped former No. 1 Notre Dame and had just demolished Ohio State 41-6, impressing Buckeye coach Woody Hayes enough that he described the Boilermakers as the best team he'd ever seen.

That week, the national rankings looked like this: 1. USC; 2. Purdue; 3. UCLA. All three loomed on the Beavers' schedule.

OSU arrived in northern Indiana on a Thursday, a day earlier than normal, as 19-point underdogs. The Beavers had a full day to wander the sprawling campus. Students jeered the players, and tombstones with their names scrawled on them were conspicuously placed.

"No one was giving the Beavers a chance," remembers Gary Houser, the tight end whose booming punts would play a huge role for OSU in the coming weeks.

Never one to miss a motivational opportunity, Andros stood in the locker room before the game and waved newspapers containing derisive remarks about OSU.

"That kind of ticked us off that we were given no respect at all," placekicker Mike Haggard recalls. "I think that angered our team as much as anything."

Another teeth-chattering hit, this one by sophomore linebacker Wally Johnson, put touted Purdue tight end Jim Beine out of the game early and quickly quieted the crowd. Near the end of the game, Houser was so consumed by the emotions that he hyperventilated and fainted on the field.

Afterward, Andros and his assistants sat in the locker room and wept.

"The Purdue game was really fun," quarterback Steve Preece recalls. "It was more special [than USC] because nobody expected it."

After an easy win over Washington State, the Beavers headed south to play another glamour team, UCLA, the new No. 2. They were again heavy underdogs against their former coach, Tommy Prothro, but by all accounts they pummeled the Bruins.

A field goal by Haggard with 1:14 to play tied it, and tackle Ron Boley blocked a field goal to preserve the deadlock.

"They tied us," Didion says flatly. "We didn't tie them."

Afterward, the Beavers again wept in the locker room. A reporter from Los Angeles surveyed the scene and was stunned.

"Coach," he said to Andros, "you just tied the No. 2 team in the country. Why are they so down and crying?"

It was then that Andros uttered his most famous quote.

"I said, 'Dammit, because they wanted to win!' and then one thing led to another and I finally did say, 'You know, I'm tired of screwing around with No. 2 teams—bring on No. 1!'

"It sounded a hell of a lot better than it looked in the papers the next day."

On the plane ride back from Los Angeles, Andros read the headlines and told his staff to call an emergency meeting of the players back at Gill Coliseum. Damage control was in order, he figured.

He was wrong.

"We all had a good laugh when coach said he was tired of messing with No. 2s," Didion says. "We knew he was setting us up for success."

During the meeting that Sunday, Andros explained his comment and reiterated his belief in his players.

"I think so much of you guys that I did say that, and there's no way I can back out of it," he told them.

"But I said it because I believe it from the bottom of my heart that you guys can meet a hell of a challenge and get the job done, and I wanted to tell you that personally."

No. 1 was coming.

******

A light rain fell throughout much of the morning on Veteran's Day, ensuring a quagmire on the grass field at Parker Stadium.

Andros has long been accused of taking the advice of WSU's Clark and lending Mother Nature a hand with sprinklers the night before the game. He jokingly says he never considered soaking the field—"I can promise you that, because I'm not that smart"—but he swears he wouldn't have watered the track even if he'd thought of it. After all, he had seen Simpson score six touchdowns on a muddy field in junior college. He also figured, despite assertions to the contrary, that a soupy track might help a straight-ahead running team like USC more than the rollout-oriented Beavers.

"I thought the field was fairly good for all the water that was on it," Andros recalls.

The buildup was enormous.

Simpson entered the game with a national-best 1,050 yards rushing even though he sat out the previous week's game against Oregon with an injury. USC's defense had yet to allow more than 128 rushing yards and 262 total yards despite a rugged schedule.

Only once had OSU drawn more than 30,000 spectators, but now officials were bracing for more than 40,000. Police pleaded for fans to arrive early to avoid a traffic mess, to little avail.

"It was wild beyond belief," Preece recalls. "I remember what it felt like at that game because of the crowd and how noisy it was and how dark it was. You were kind of in a little bowl."

Ironically, Andros didn't give one of his patented speeches. He spoke in hushed tones about his pride in the team, what the game meant for the state, and how little respect USC had for them.

"When the meeting broke up," linebacker Skip Vanderbundt remembers, "there was no Knute Rockne cheering, yelling and charging. We left that locker room like men on a mission."

Back and forth they went on the worsening turf, neither penetrating the end zone. Passing games were nonexistent as both teams relied on their star running backs: Simpson for USC and Bill "Earthquake" Enyart for OSU.

On the first play of the second quarter, Simpson broke free around left end and had one man, safety Larry Rich, to beat. Rich was tied up by a blocker.

The crowd held its collective breath. The Juice was loose.

"I had watched him enough on film, so I said, 'Well, we're going to have to score,'" Andros said.

*USC star O. J. Simpson is tackled by three
Beavers in the 1967 game at Parker Stadium.
(Photo courtesy of Barry Schwartz.)*

It was then that a legend was made.

Simpson shifted from his toes to his heels momentarily while deciding which route to take around his blocker. Out of nowhere flew defensive lineman Jess Lewis, an All-American who had chased O. J. from the opposite side of the field.

Down went Simpson at OSU's 32. It was the Trojans' last serious threat of the day, and Lewis's tackle was almost instantly immortalized.

"Right then," Vanderbundt says, "I knew we were unbeatable on that day. I knew there was no way that those 11 offensive players were going to beat our 11 defensive players. It was a moment I will never forget—and a feeling that I have had very few times in my life."

In the second quarter, Haggard kicked a 30-yard field goal that nobody believed would stand up. But by the second half, as the bloodied and muddied Beavers made stop after stop, the players and crowd began sensing the upset.

And when the teams caught their breath while switching sides between the third and fourth quarters, thunder radiated across the gray skies.

"It was like being able to share a team feeling with everybody who came to the game," Didion says. "I guess everybody felt it. It was almost like an animal roar coming out of the stands when we changed. It was almost visceral, like they all got it, they all understood how hard we were working and wanted to be a part of it.

"It wasn't like they were cheering for us, it was like they were cheering with us. It was incredible, really difficult to describe."

Finally, the Beavers drove for the crucial first down that sealed the game late in the fourth quarter. Haggard's field goal withstood the test of time, and though Simpson ran for 188 yards, he and his teammates never crossed the goal line.

"USC was out of timeouts, and we stood in our huddle looking at their defense," remembers Houser, whose 41-yard punting average pinned the Trojans deeper and deeper on an unforgiving field.

"It was a 'Who's Who of the NFL Draft'—Tim Rossovich, Adrian Young, Fred Gunn, Mike Battle—and they couldn't stop what was about to happen. We stood in our huddle and yelled, laughed and went crazy, and they stood in their huddle and watched our celebration.

"It was a great moment for us and our university."

When the gun sounded, bedlam ensued. The players hoisted Andros onto their shoulders so that USC coach John McKay would have to reach up to shake his hand.

Though the Trojan players and coaches tipped their caps to the Beavers, the Los Angeles media and fans weren't so kind. They ripped OSU for the poor field conditions.

"I can assure you," USC athletic director Jess Hill said, "that there will be a conference rule that all Pacific-8 institutions have a tarp and use it the week before a game."

USC boosters took up a collection so that OSU could buy a $15,000 tarp. Reagan contributed the first $1 to a fund to replace the grass with a newfangled synthetic grass called AstroTurf.

Nothing could spoil OSU's party.

"It was the most electrifying game I've ever been around in all my years of athletics," The Great Pumpkin said. "It's a part of history I don't think any of us will ever forget."

The Beavers would be seventh in The Associated Press poll the next day, their highest ranking until they reached No. 4 at the end of the 2000 Fiesta Bowl season.

******

Afterward, the Beavers celebrated long into the night, minus one player.

Jeremiah, whose hit set the tone for the season and who was given the official game ball, had enlisted in the marines and was supposed to leave for Vietnam before the USC game. But his ex-marine coach lobbied to keep him one more week.

At 5 a.m. the morning after the win, while many of his teammates were still partying, Jeremiah boarded a bus and left for what the Beavers almost unanimously agreed was a noble cause.

The others continued to celebrate until the sun rose over the Cascades.

For many, the hangover would last for years, for when the cheering stopped, many of the Giant Killers were lost.

The 1968 team was ranked No. 1 in the preseason poll by *Playboy* magazine, but an injury to Preece and three losses by a combined six points shattered OSU's dreams.

OSU went 7-3 and stayed home for the holidays.

After the season, an African-American linebacker named Fred Milton, who had played so well against Purdue, grew a goatee-type beard called a Van Dyke, which was against team rules. When ordered to shave it off, Milton refused and was kicked off the team.

The Black Student Union staged a protest and asked the school's 17 black athletes to boycott OSU teams. A student protest lured 4,000.

The scandal hurt recruiting. Combined with a decreasing commitment to football, it started a downward spiral from which the program wouldn't recover for three decades.

They wouldn't beat mighty USC in Parker Stadium until their magical 2000 season. The Veterans Day game is still referred to simply as "the 3-0 win."

Meanwhile, drugs and alcohol began to permeate the locker room. They would stay with many members of the Giant Killers for years.

OSU coach Dee Andros reaches down to accept congratulations from
USC coach John McKay after the Beavers' 3-0 win in 1967.
(Photo courtesy of Barry Schwartz.)

Some battled alcohol addictions and have been through treatment at places like Serenity Lane. Others became lost in a swirl of cocaine and speed. Another has chronic fatigue syndrome and believes the Type A behavior needed for success in football is a factor.

One hitchhiked around Europe and Japan in search of the meaning of life. Others went through several marriages. Cornerback Jim Scheele and Jeremiah have both succumbed to Lou Gehrig's disease.

Some found themselves drawn to empty Parker Stadium, where they heard the echoes of glory years suddenly lost.

They were, as it turned out, human.

Happily, though some of the Giant Killers haven't recovered and perhaps never will, today most who struggled through the 1970s have become remarkable success stories.

The epitome was Lewis, the All-American who would win an Olympic gold medal in wrestling in 1968, then battle alcohol for 22 years before recovering. Now a facilities maintenance supervisor at OSU, Lewis gives talks about the evils of drugs and alcohol.

Eleven Beavers were drafted by NFL teams. Most are successful in such businesses as real estate, insurance and law, while many stayed in the game to coach.

"I think for some kinds of businesses there's no better training than football," Preece says. "You get what you put into it; it establishes a winning attitude."

Never was that attitude so apparent than with a group of 50 crew-cut, Joe College, corn-fed football players in the autumn of 1967.

They were so close that at least 80 percent keep regular contact today and have regular reunions. In the 1970s, many would congregate at Lewis's farm and ride his bus to the beach, where they would build bonfires and reminisce.

None have ever known anything like The Giant Killers since, in any endeavor.

"There was just something almost magical about that team," Didion says. "We have reunion after reunion to keep those feelings in the present, so it's not like a distant memory at all.

"It's something that keeps happening again and again."

21

Andros at Iwo

To most Beavers, he is known affectionately as "The Great Pumpkin." His first name, Demosthenes, is a mouthful, so over the years, everyone has simply shortened it to "Dee." For the last 30 years, he has been treated, especially by former players, as an OSU legend; at a minimum, he truly embodies the spirit and tradition of Oregon State football. And yet, there's another side to this former head football coach that he waited until late in life to share with people beyond his circle of family and close friends.

Before the 1967 "Giant Killers," before his picture on the cover of *Sports Illustrated*, before his tenure as OSU athletic director, and before his induction into the State of Oregon Sports Hall of Fame, Dee Andros had another life, one as far away from the gridiron as the moon is to the stars.

Andros had a Marine Corps life that almost ended 57 years ago on a small island known as Iwo Jima.

His regiment, the storied 28th of the 5th Marine Division, landed with the third wave in a massive assault to silence one of the deadliest fortresses in warfare history. The brilliant Japanese general, Tadamichi Kuribayashi, spent months preparing for this day, February 19, 1945, turning the small volcanic island of eight square miles into a massive killing field.

In more than 6,500 strategically located bunkers, rifle pits, and mortar and artillery emplacements, 22,000 of Japan's finest and bravest troops sat waiting, ready to force the invading Americans back into the Pacific. Failure to do so would result in yet another island falling into enemy hands, putting U. S. forces one step closer to the Japanese homeland.

They were ordered by the emperor to succeed or die.

Kuribayashi's plan was to let the marines land unopposed for one hour. Little known to Andros or any of the other 30 men riding with him toward a piece of Iwo known as Green Beach, Kuribayashi's grace period would end just about the time they were disembarking from their landing craft. Even though Andros was a field cook, he would cook nothing over the five weeks it would take to secure the tiny island. The 28th was told in briefings to expect the worst, that every man was needed as combat infantry once ashore. What food the men ate came from tin cans.

"Our regiment's assignment," he said in an interview from his office in Gill Coliseum, "was to take Mount Sarabachi, the place where we raised the flag and where the famous picture was taken by Joe Rosenthal. They gave me a box of hand grenades and told me my job was to get the box ashore."

The grenades never made it. A maelstrom of fire suddenly erupted from Sarabachi. Every square yard of Green Beach was enveloped in exploding steel, pinning his regiment belly-down in the island's thick, sucking volcanic ash. All around, marines were screaming and dying.

"When we touched the beach, I ran like hell for cover," Andros said, his face suddenly taking on that far-away, long-ago look. "I realized either me or the grenades wasn't gonna make it. So I threw 'em away."

An explosion behind him forced him to turn around just for an instant. The landing craft that had been his ride to the beach had received a direct hit from an artillery shell. In an instant, it was gone, along with its coxswain.

"On the trip to Iwo, I really didn't know what we were getting into or what it was all about. As soon as we hit shore I knew the Japanese were playing for keeps. There was no safe place anywhere. Everyone was the same."

For the next two days, Andros and the 28th worked to maneuver around all sides of the 556-foot ancient volcano. More than 18 hours had passed since they landed and already the casualties in his and three other regiments were in excess of 2,300 killed or wounded. For the shy, but tough, 18-year-old from Oklahoma City, the scene was a nightmare. One thought kept flashing through his mind, slowly forming a mental state that he admits kept him from going crazy.

"I figured, if I got wounded they would ship me home. If I got killed, I wouldn't know anything about it." He would soon come closest to the latter.

"I remember seeing our commanding officer, Colonel [Harry B.] Liversedge, stand up, look at me and shout: 'Get two men and go down to Green Beach for some fresh water.'

"I looked around and saw Lumpkin, my best friend, and another fellow. I motioned for them to follow and off we went. I was the only one who made it back. Lumpkin and the other guy got a direct hit from an artillery shell. They were not two feet from me. I didn't know what had happened, so I yelled, 'Let's go, Lump,' but he was dead. I stopped for a minute and then figured the only thing I could do was stick his rifle in the sand next to his body. I wanted to be sure he was found."

Though he came close to dying by following orders, he never questioned anything he was told during the entire campaign, a discipline he quickly added to his small list of survival strategies.

"When they told me to do something, I did it," he said.

Most times, however, he didn't wait for orders, opting rather to volunteer for any job. Andros served as stretcher bearer (Iwo's most dangerous assignment), infantryman, runner and lookout. For his courage under fire, he was awarded the Bronze Star at battle's end, a memento he cherishes today as much as he does his many successes in football. The commendation for his medal hangs framed in his office, next to the picture he took in 1967 with movie legend John Wayne.

"The Japanese had all the guts in the world," he said. "We dug in every night and circled our foxholes with trip flares. Anything that touched that wire was shot dead, no questions asked. My weapon was a shotgun, and I prayed a lot. It helped having a chaplain close by."

The chaplain was always there, too, when he was assigned to stretcher duty to pick up the wounded and the dead. It was a gruesome job.

"We would pick up a head here, an arm there," he remembered, "and the chaplain would say a few prayers as comfort, mostly for us I guess."

After the flag raising atop Mount Sarabachi and the photo that would serve as one of World War II's most dramatic images, Andros's regiment (and the rest of the 5th Marine Division) was assigned to begin assaulting the network of caves and bunkers that sat farther up the island. Here, his job changed.

Andros receives the Bronze Star in Hawaii after the Battle of Iwo Jima.
(Photo courtesy of Dee Andros.)

"I was told to walk alongside the tanks we were using to lead the attacks," he said.

"The Japanese had a habit of running out of nowhere, hoping to get close enough to throw something underneath the treads so they could blow up our tanks from underneath. I was there to make sure that didn't happen. At first I carried a rifle, an M-1, but later they issued me a BAR [Browning automatic rifle], a much better weapon. I felt a lot safer with the BAR."

Of the 200 men in his company who initially stormed Iwo's beaches that first day, only 40 were alive at the end. His only malady after returning to Hawaii was a bad case of hemorrhoids, caused by going for days without being able to use a bathroom.

Andros credits his survival to pure luck and admitted he would often think about Iwo Jima when he was running onto the football field to begin a game, both at Oklahoma in the late 1940s, where he played guard for legendary Sooner coach Bud Wilkinson, and when, in the 1960s, he finally had a team of his own at OSU. Always the thought was the same, that he was "lucky as hell to have made it this far." He would also remember the 6,821 marines who had given their lives at Iwo. For them, there had been no such luck.

A visit to Andros's office impresses the visitor with its striking collection of photos, trophies and other memorabilia from his highly successful career, both at OSU and the decade of the '50s.

Framed black and white images show a smiling Andros pictured with some of the greatest luminaries the college game has known, at one time all personal friends.

There's one with just Andros and Wilkinson and another with Baltimore Colts Hall of Famer Johnny Unitas. And there's Andros at the East-West Shrine game in the late '60s with Penn State coach Joe Paterno. There are two Hall of Fame certificates, and yes, that photo with "The Duke."

But the one closest to his desk, close enough to reach out and grab still sitting down, is the Joe Rosenthal image of the Sarabachi flag raising.

Even though Andros never personally witnessed that historic moment, he was close by and remains proud that it was his regiment that gave Americans one of the war's most uplifting moments.

22

Back from the Dead

*Not everybody gets a second...or third...or fourth chance. Jess Lewis is
an exception. One of the greatest athletes in OSU history, the All-America
football player and national champion wrestler seemingly had the world at
his fingertips after the 1968 Mexico City Olympics. But it wasn't enough,
and before long Lewis was deep into a life of drinking and drugs. For this
story, a clean and sober Lewis allowed a reporter to follow him to one of his
many motivational talks, where he emphatically and emotionally retold the
story of his perilous journey and implored others to avoid his path.*

The man who was once everybody's All-American, who once sym-
bolized an era of innocence and played to adoring throngs of thousands, is now standing in a darkened barn, holding an entirely different
crowd at rapt attention.

He is doing so not with his teeth-chattering tackles, but with his
gut-wrenching story.

As Jess Lewis speaks, gesturing emphatically with his bear-paw-
sized hands, beads of sweat trickle from his closely cropped blond hair
to the square jaw that once adorned the cover of newspapers, magazines
and media guides.

At first, he talks with the authority and confidence of a man who
made the most famous play for the most famous team in the most famous game in Oregon State's football history.

But soon his voice begins to quake. His Adam's apple clenches. His eyes shift to the trusses overhead in the cavernous barn at Dale Thomas's remote Double D Wrestling Ranch outside of Harlan, Oregon.

His blue eyes begin to water and he pauses, not for dramatic flair but out of necessity.

Forty sets of eyes, most under 16 years of age, are unblinking in the twilight sunlight filtering through the small windows onto the giant wrestling mats. Campers who came to the deep Coast Range woods west of Mary's Peak for a week of wrestling and life lessons are getting a vivid education about choices.

As they watch in frozen silence, they see 22 years of guilt and shame, of pain and suffering, of fear and insecurity, ooze from Lewis's soul to his outer being, just like it has done every time he has given one of his candid presentations over more than a decade.

The former OSU football and wrestling All-American has again uncorked nightmarish memories of unspeakable pain he caused his family, of a financial quagmire and of a cycle of drug and alcohol addiction that had him inching toward death's doorstep.

Lewis, 54, gathers himself and refocuses on his audience, almost apologetically.

"I still feel emotions well up inside of me when I talk about it," he explains. "It's not that I'm an emotional crybaby.

"It's just that it was such a waste of 22 years."

******

Jess Lewis? A drug addict?

Nobody who watched the wholesome farmboy from Aumsville would ever have imagined such a scenario in the autumn of 1967, when Lewis, as much as any player, epitomized the famed Giant Killers.

He was the strong, clean-cut and conservative poster boy for a *Father Knows Best* era that was rapidly evaporating amid the turmoil of Vietnam, desegregation and a general rebelliousness that had permeated nearly every other college campus in the Pacific-8 Conference. The crew-cut Joe College was a solid student, personable and a magnet for Betty Coeds.

Like most college students in his day, he'd sneak an occasional beer or cigarette. But the concept of elicit drugs was utterly foreign to him when he was helping the Beavers defeat No. 2 Purdue and tie No. 2 UCLA before shocking No. 1 Southern California in his sophomore year.

Every Beaver booster over age 40 can recite chapter and verse the tale of Lewis hauling down USC's O. J. Simpson from behind in the slop of Parker Stadium to preserve a larger-than-life 3-0 victory in 1967.

"People always tell me, 'The cops couldn't catch O. J., but you did,'" Lewis frequently jokes, referring to the infamous televised chase of Simpson's Ford Bronco after the murder of his wife, Nicole.

Lewis also was a national champion wrestler at heavyweight, fashioning an 89-1 record over three years. His only loss was in the NCAA final as a sophomore. Few of his matches lasted more than a minute, and wrestling fans came from all over the Willamette Valley for meets, sometimes arriving just in time to see Lewis.

In 1968, he skipped the football season for a trip to the Olympics in Mexico City, where he finished sixth in freestyle competition at 213.5 pounds. He lost his chance to advance to the round-robin portion because of a tie with a wrestler from Turkey, who eventually won the gold medal.

When he returned home from Mexico for the rest of his junior year at OSU, the small-town boy was exhausted, overwhelmed by the Olympic experience and on edge.

A friend offered a solution: a marijuana cigarette.

"I smoked it, I liked it," Lewis said. "It changed my whole mood. I swear to God, I'd be lying to you if I told you I didn't like it."

One joint led to another, and then he moved on to other drugs—uppers, downers, mescaline, cocaine, speed, every illegal drug available at the time except heroin.

He played a football game in 1969 while high on Black Beauties, though he says it was the only time at OSU that he competed under the influence.

That would come later.

"It was mostly afterward, at parties," he said. "Sometimes in the middle of the week."

Upon graduation in 1970, the Houston Oilers of the National Football League drafted Lewis in the 10th round. He estimates that at least one-third of his teammates in Houston used drugs, and the team trainer's open bag was a virtual locker room pharmacy of uppers, downers and everything in between.

Lewis stuffed them in his locker, stuffed them in his pockets, and stuffed them in his dresser drawers at home.

He could've been shipped to Vietnam, and though he was opposed to the war he says he would've gone out of obligation and duty to country. Instead he was classified 4F because of knee surgeries.

"It made me feel funny because I had some good friends go and they didn't come back, and I had some good friends go and come back pretty messed up and they used a lot of drugs," he said. "And I used a lot of drugs with them. I was feeling some of their pain, I guess."

The cycle of abuse had begun, and it would only get worse.

After three years of a life in pro football that was straight out of the script for *North Dallas Forty,* Lewis retired—"the first thing I'd ever quit on," he said—and returned to the family farm in Aumsville, about 40 miles northeast of Corvallis.

He would work high for a few days, disappear for three to five more, return and crash on the couch for a few more days, then work while high again. Unbeknownst to his parents and four siblings, who thought he was simply going through "a phase," Lewis was spending as much as $100 per day on drugs.

Once a year, Lewis and a handful of his former Giant Killer teammates, many of whom were struggling with their own post-glory traumas, would convene at the farm for a ride to the beach on "The Magic Bus," which the family used to transport their berry pickers. The "Beach Ball," near brother Jerry's home in Florence, was an around-the-clock orgy of drugs and booze in which the group sat around a bonfire and laughed, danced, sang, arm-wrestled and leg-wrestled until they couldn't walk.

"We never saw the beach," Lewis recalls. "Everybody just got completely plastered."

Addiction has many phases, and by the mid-1980s Lewis had dovetailed into paranoia. He would hide behind trees in the woods, and he needed to be high to cut firewood or drive to town for groceries.

He pawned his Cascade Union High School class ring, his OSU class ring, his Olympic ring, his fishing rods and all of his hunting gear for drug money. He also used profits from the farm.

In desperation, his parents, who couldn't bear to watch him slowly kill himself and didn't know where to turn, bought him out and, in 1987, threw him out. He avoided all family gatherings, even at Thanksgiving and Christmas.

Lewis moved to a small shanty in the Cascade Mountains at Detroit Lake with his girlfriend Vickie Hayes of Aumsville, a heroin addict herself. He had a couch, a mattress on the floor, a small TV, a coffee pot, a few clothes and a chainsaw to cut enough wood to feed his belly and his addiction. He occasionally sold drugs, though never to kids, he said.

Never had the Giant Killer days seemed so distant.

It was in October 1990, the same year that Lewis was inducted into OSU's Athletic Hall of Fame, that his college wrestling coach, an old-school pioneer of the tough-love approach to life named Dale Thomas, learned of the two-time NCAA champion's struggles.

Thomas drove in his brand-new Mercedes Benz from his ranch on Big Elk Creek outside of Harlan to Detroit Lake, knocked on the door of Lewis's cabin and was horrified to see a former All-American living in squalor.

"You're coming with me to get some help," Thomas said.

Lewis refused. He had things to do, he said.

"Then I'm staying here and I'll sleep on the floor until you decide to come with me," Thomas replied.

Thomas won the war of wills. They loaded Lewis's truck and drove into the valley, where Lewis and Vickie entered a 28-day substance-abuse program called Milestones in Eugene. It would prove more painful than any chop-block or knee surgery.

The first step toward rehabilitation was to sit around a table at the farm and have each family member and friend write Jess a letter explaining how much he'd hurt them in 22 years.

Amid ink-smudged paper and mounds of tear-stained tissues, they shared their stories, until finally Lewis's nephew revealed how he remembered a trip into the woods with Uncle Jess, and how a pill had fallen out of his shirt. He was, he wrote, devastated to learn his uncle did drugs.

"We were all bawling," remembers Thomas, now retired and living virtually full-time in Corvallis. "I'm telling you it's really serious. You don't just go through the motions."

Less than a month later, in November 1990, Lewis was discharged from the program, his body purged of the toxins and his mind rid of the paranoia and hunger for drugs.

Thomas brought Lewis back to the place where he'd known his most success: Oregon State. Lewis earned a master's degree in counseling.

He was hired to oversee the maintenance of the athletic facilities, and he has been there ever since. He is a familiar sight on campus in an old pickup or perched atop a tractor, grooming the fields where he knew his greatest glories.

He is also a familiar sight in OSU's Drugs in Sports class, where he warns current athletes and other students about the perils of addiction and implores them to veer far from the path he chose for 22 years.

Lewis and Vickie, whom he married in 1993, have been clean and sober for 11 1/2 years, and in a sense he has recovered his youth. Though his lineman's appetite is still reflected in his waistline and barrel chest, he still looks as if he could play tackle or linebacker for the Beavers. While once he weighed better than 300 pounds, now he's closer to 250.

And although like all recovering abusers Lewis still describes himself as an addict, he knows he will never go back.

Thomas, who has seen other former athletes suffocate in similar addictive quicksand, knows it, too.

"When I put my foot down with Jess, he had the character to respond," he said. "I think he's a stronger person now. What he's done is beautiful and I never expect him to have a relapse. I'm really proud of Jess."

Of course, the natural question is…why?

Why when he had everything—looks, talent, smarts, fame, glory, women, friends, a loving family, the brightest of futures—would he start down a path of drugs and alcohol in the first place?

He ponders the question thoughtfully, then points out that, contrary to the image he conveyed at OSU, he was more of a follower than a leader, even on the Giant Killers. Some friends led him down a wayward path, he theorizes, and he followed.

But even that doesn't fully explain two decades of "growing backward," as he calls it.

"You know, I was looking for something else, I guess," he says. "I'm still thinking about it. It's hard to explain, but sometimes you're just looking for something else, something more, and that's the situation I got into."

******

Back at the Double D Wrestling Ranch, Lewis is imploring kids to avoid drugs, but more important he is trying to put them on the offensive. Don't just avoid drugs, he said, be proactive—be your own leader.

He talks about how drugs rob a person of their spirit and strength, and how winning the NCAA wrestling championship in 1970 didn't have the same meaning it had the previous year. He warned them to avoid experimenting, because once on that perilous path it is difficult to turn back.

"You do it once and then you want to see if you can get that feeling again, and you're all the time chasing that feeling," he said. "It's like a dog chasing its tail.

"It s fake, it's phony, it's artificial, it's bullshit. Pardon my language, but it is. It all lies to you."

Lewis approaches one of the campers and taps the boy's chest. That, he said, is your seat of power. Listen to it.

"I want you to remember one thing: D.E.A.D," he says. "Anybody know what that stands for?"

A boy in front answers: "Drugs End All Dreams."

"That's right," Lewis replies. "You can use it now, you can tell your friends, you can tell your parents, you can tell your alcoholic uncle if you want. I want you to have some ammunition. I want you to have some offense, some resistance, some resilience to fight this disease, because somebody in here is going to become a drug addict."

Lewis is sweating and gesturing even more now as the program ends. He wings most of his presentations, and they veer in different directions, but they always become emotional.

Dredging up the memories is painful, of course, but a necessary part of recovery, even more than a decade later.

"I'm proud of past accomplishments, yes, but the shame and guilt, you've got to fight that all the time, so some of things you try to do is payback for going in that direction," he explains. "I wish to God I never would've tried it, I wish to God I never would've drank as much as I did, but I did it and now I guess I got to live with it.

"This is repaying society and making it right."

The more he talks, the more he remembers, and the more he remembers the more he is purged of the pain and sadness, the fear and insecurity. The tears sometimes flow, but no longer are they tears of sadness; they are tears of thankfulness.

They are the cleansing of a wounded soul.

"It's OK to do that," he says. "I forgive myself and forgive what I've done and I've made amends to a lot of folks in the last 11 1/2 years.

"And it feels good."

23

Race for the Ages

At one time, football and basketball shared center stage with another collegiate sport in the lower Willamette Valley. There was a time when OSU track and field was a marquee sport, when distance races were king, and when Eugene was considered "Track Capital of the World." And for all the unforgettable distance races played out in front of packed houses at the University of Oregon's Hayward Field, perhaps none is more memorable than the one staged in 1972 between a renowned Duck and a Beaver who, for one day at least, was his equal.

The weather that Saturday, May 6, 1972, was beautiful. The University of Oregon's historic Hayward Field was packed to the rafters.

More than 9,000 people had been lucky enough to get tickets to this long-awaited dual track meet between the Beavers and the Ducks, and when the gates finally opened before noon, everyone showed up in Eugene, right down to the last seat. It wasn't so much because Civil War track meets were always sellouts. It was to witness what was, for that time, the most talked about and most anticipated race in the state's history.

True, it would be shown on live TV, but to the crowd that was irrelevant. To be there was what mattered. The crowd expected it to be the sporting event of a lifetime, a spiritual experience.

Oregon had won three national championships in track and field in the 1960s. Although the Ducks were not so powerful in 1972, they were still considered one of the country's elite programs. Not so Oregon State. Early in the meet, the Ducks began to pull comfortably ahead.

But the crowd didn't seem to care all that much about the score. All eyes were fixed on the stadium clock, eagerly awaiting 2 p.m. That's when the runners for the 1,500 meters (during Olympic years—as in 1972—officials were required to use metric distances at all meets, NCAA or otherwise) would be announced, when all ears would be glued to Hayward's loudspeakers, listening for the announcer to say the names Steve Prefontaine and Hailu Ebba.

Those who knew Prefontaine and saw him compete remember him as a dogged runner who always pushed himself to the limits, on and off the track. His barrel-chested upper body and tremendous strength and speed over long distances, combined with an attitude intolerant of even the idea of losing, fashioned him into one of America's premier distance runners. He was considered unbeatable.

Through the course of his college career, "Pre" won seven NCAA titles, three in cross country and four in the three-mile. His first cross country title was won with 12 stitches in his foot, an injury sustained in a diving board accident. At the close of his tenure at the UO, Pre owned nine collegiate track records. By 1975, he held every American record from 2,000 to 10,000 meters and from two miles to six miles. As a Duck, he never lost a race more of than a mile. He still holds the American high school record in the two-mile, set at Corvallis High School in April 1969.

Besides Pre and Ebba, there were four other runners waiting to race 1,500 meters.

OSU's Keith Munson was there, as was Chris Carey. Mark Feig and Rick Ritchie represented Oregon. Experienced and fast, Munson and Carey looked to Hailu and Pre to be their only competition, both feeling they could easily defeat Feig and Ritchie (they did). To Pre, there was only one person who mattered. The rest were cannon fodder. It was Ebba he wanted to beat. Pre had been planning it for months.

Prefontaine was a predator. Like a gunslinger out of the Old West, he was constantly on the lookout for new prey—the next race to win, that next record to break, and most importantly, the runners he would have to beat to get there. OSU's sophomore Ebba was next in line.

For more than a year, Pre had been hearing good things about the young Ethiopian. And he wasn't shy about remarking on occasion that the two ought to race when the dual meet rolled around.

But the Duck almost didn't get his wish. For two weeks, OSU coach Berny Wagner, now retired and living in Salem, told the press he would probably not enter Ebba against Pre. OSU, he said, needed all the points it could muster. Ebba was a shoo-in to win the 800.

In reality, Wagner had no intention of keeping his star from racing Pre. To let that meet go on without turning Ebba loose would have been like having a fish fry with no fish. His reason for saying otherwise was to keep the press from hounding Ebba. He wanted the young man to stay "focused," not distracted by a million questions, all the same: "Can you really beat Pre?"

Prefontaine had competed a total of 38 times at Hayward Field, losing three races, all in the mile. Beaver fans suspected that if the Pre had any vulnerability, it was at this distance. They knew, too, that he was not a natural miler. In fact, he was "coming down" a notch to race Ebba, an act many Oregon Staters considered equivalent to an athlete thumbing his nose at an opponent.

But Pre had never faced a runner with the speed, talent and intelligence of an athlete like Ebba, and this gave Beaver fans much hope that their guy would prevail. Oregon Staters also knew that Ebba, a better half-miler than anything, was almost as deadly in the mile, using tremendous speed around the final lap to put people away.

Ebba had attended Anderson (California) High as a foreign exchange student. His times at prep meets were so average that no college or university bothered to recruit him. But his dream was to run for his country in the 1972 Olympics. He did. Hearing about OSU from some friends, Ebba wrote a personal letter to Wagner asking for a chance to compete. Wagner, noticing that the young man had finished high school undefeated in cross country, decided to give him a try.

It turned out to be one of Wagner's best gambles. At the end of his freshman year, the young runner had shattered several OSU rookie records. By the spring of 1972, he owned the best time in the mile of any collegiate runner in the country, 3:59.3, recorded on April 15 at Berkeley, California. This also set a record in his native Ethiopia, a country noted for producing world-class distance runners. Now, as the clock crawled its way toward the showdown, the crowd held its breath. Would Ebba run? Would Wagner really hold him out?

As the six competitors left the waiting area to make their way to the starting gate, the answer was suddenly there on the track. The reaction of the assembled 9,000 was explosive. Wagner recalls today that the roar was so loud, Hayward shook to its foundation.

Prefontaine's opinion of Ebba, not generally expressed publicly before the race, became evident once the starter's gun cracked. Three times Ebba tried to pass Pre and three times, with almost Herculean effort and through sheer willpower, the Duck superstar managed to stay inches ahead. For much of the race they were virtually neck and neck, and the outcome was in doubt to the last turn for the straightaway to the tape. Across Oregon, people were jumping up and down, screaming at their TV sets.

Approaching the final turn, the two were even, shoulder touching shoulder. The roar of the crowd was constant and could be heard all over Eugene. Heading into the stretch, Prefontaine, using the experience he had gained racing against European runners, began using his upper body to bump and nudge Ebba to the outside, thus increasing the distance and angle the OSU speedster would have to travel to reach the finish line.

It was just enough to give Pre a one-second victory.

After the race, Ebba was furious, saying his opponent's bumping and shoving around the last turn had been more like "fighting" than racing.

"I can't run and fight at the same time," he told the press. "If I had passed him, there's no way he would have caught me."

Did Prefontaine cheat to win? Wagner says no. Pre was older and more experienced than Ebba, he explained, and it was this experience that began to show as the two made that last turn to the finish. Ebba remained unconvinced. But he had learned a valuable lesson: Never again did he allow himself unknowingly to get shoved around in a race.

Wagner says the Ebba/Prefontaine event in 1972 was one of the greatest collegiate races he had ever watched and added that it was also the personal favorite of Prefontaine's father, Ray. OSU sports information director Hal Cowan said, point-blank: "The greatest race I ever watched." Many OSU alumni remember the race as the sporting highlight of their college days, with the finish still vivid in their memories.

If the defeat affected Ebba in any way, it wasn't for long. He represented his country in the Olympics that same year in the 1,500, but stomach cramps kept him from placing in a semifinal heat.

In addition to the many school and Pacific-8 Conference records he established at Oregon State, Ebba was an All-American in 1973 after his fourth-place finish in the mile at the NCAA championships.

Today, Ebba is an anesthesiologist at the University of Michigan. He lives in Ann Arbor and stays in touch with his old coach.

*Hailu Ebba, Pac-8 mile champion, ran for
his native Ethiopia in the 1972 Olympics.
(Photo courtesy of* The Beaver.*)*

Wagner remains busy at work trying to revive track and field at OSU, while also finding time to help out with the track program at Western Oregon University in Monmouth. In 2002, he was elected to the U. S. Track Coaches Hall of Fame. During his tenure at OSU, Wagner trained 25 All-Americans in 12 different events and was Dick Fosbury's coach the year the high jumper and his "Fosbury Flop" won the Olympic gold medal at the 1968 Olympic summer games in Mexico City.

24

Done Too Soon

The most memorable tales about OSU athletes aren't always provided by stars. Sometimes they come from the far end of the bench, from people who become little more than another name on the lengthy list of letter winners. Such was the case with Tom Huggins, an OSU track athlete whose small gift to the sport would most likely have remained a hidden treasure were it not for a legend and Hollywood.

One was the son of a longshoreman and the other the son of an insurance agent, and yet they were inseparable as kids, joined at the feet by a singular passion.

Tom and Steve. Steve and Tom. They were rarely far apart in the late 1960s. Their legs churned relentlessly and effortlessly on the hardscrabble streets, soggy coastal hills and breezy sand beaches of Coos Bay, the rusty shipping and timber community on the gray central Oregon coast.

Tom and Steve ran and ran and ran, rarely less than 150 miles per week, an average of about one marathon per day.

"In those days I could literally run forever," Tom recalls. "I ran until I got hungry. That was the only thing that could stop me."

One day, just for the hell of it, Tom and Steve ran all the way from Coos Bay to Roseburg, an 85-mile triple-marathon through the Coast Range.

Another day, after dominating yet another high school cross country meet, in Reedsport, the pair told the bus driver they would start jogging home down the Coast Highway. Wait for the other Marshfield runners to finish, they said, and then pick us up when you catch up.

When the bus finally did reach Tom and Steve, two and a half hours had passed and they were crossing the U.S. Highway 101 bridge in North Bend, 27 miles down the road.

Tom would set a freshman state record in cross country and establish other distance-running marks at Marshfield High School. Steve came along a year later and broke almost all of them.

Steve, a cocky and brash sort who always spoke his mind, wasn't always the singularly focused fanatic that he would one day become. Once, Tom caught Steve hiding in the bushes with several teammates who had made a habit of skipping a giant hill in the middle of their training course.

Tom chastised Steve for taking the easy way out. Steve never did again.

"I'd like to think I had some small impact on what he became," Tom says now.

They would soon become perhaps the greatest one-two distance-running punch in Oregon high school history.

Tom was faster in the shorter distance races like the half-mile. Steve was faster in the two-mile run. They were a push in the premier event of the day, the mile, with Tom usually winning on flatter courses because of his superior speed and Steve usually winning on the hills because of unparalleled toughness.

Tom and Steve were so extraordinary by 1967 that University of Oregon assistant track coach Bill Dellinger would bring his stable of Olympic-caliber distance runners to Coos Bay for workouts, ostensibly to one day woo the town's favorite sons to the immodestly named Track Capital of the World.

Tom and Steve would run with Roscoe Divine and Dave Wilborn, and by the time they were upperclassmen at Marshfield they were beating Oregon's freshmen. The state's other major track program, Oregon State, also pursued the duo tirelessly.

They both seemed destined for greatness, until one day, after a routine workout during his senior year, Tom bent down to tie his shoe and felt something pop in his left knee.

He thought nothing of the dull ache at first, and the pain was tolerable, but eventually it worsened. Answers were elusive until Tom was taken to see the same famed Eugene orthopedic surgeon who rebuilt former pro football star Joe Namath's knees.

"Tom," the surgeon finally asked, "have you put on any weight this year?"

"About 20 pounds," Tom replied, noting that he had gone from 135 to 155.

The surgeon nodded knowingly, sadly. He explained to Tom that he had a congenital defect in his cartilage and that the extra weight was more pressure than it could bear.

"I've seen ruptured knees, torn knees and broken knees, and fixed them all, no problem," the surgeon said. "But there's nothing I can do for you."

Tom was told the only way to avoid pain was to forgo his passion. He ran in denial for several months, but always on the day after the pain was so great he could barely walk.

Oregon rescinded its letter of intent. OSU said it would honor its tender by giving partial aid for a year, an offer Tom happily accepted because he dreamt of becoming an engineer.

"I think they did it because they thought I could help recruit my friend," he says with a wry smile.

OSU did recruit Steve, but Tom sheepishly acknowledges that he steered his best friend to Oregon, saying the Ducks were his best bet for a blossoming distance-running career.

And what a career it was becoming.

On April 25, 1969, Steve came to Corvallis to compete in an invitational race against the nation's best two-milers. Tom urged his OSU fraternity buddies to join him at the CHS track, promising that they were about to witness history.

He was right.

Steve outclassed the field with shocking strength and determination, eventually winning by more than 100 yards to shatter the national two-mile record by seven seconds (8:41.5). He earned headlines from coast to coast and become a nationwide cult hero.

Steve eventually made the 1972 U.S. Olympic team, finishing a disappointing fourth in the 5,000 meters, but he never forgot his best friend. After yet another record-setting run, he would hear Tom's voice amid the cheers in the stands and slice through the crowds to greet him.

Occasionally, they would take recreational runs together, and sometimes Tom would join Steve and his U.S. teammates, including Marty Liquori and Frank Shorter.

"C'mon, Hug," Steve would urge.

"You could still do it! You could still run!"

Tom would remember the gray streets, hills and beaches of Coos Bay and briefly flirt with the notion, but then he'd remember the pain. His competitive running days were over.

Eventually, Tom followed in the footsteps of his grandfather and father in the insurance business; then in 1982 he planted a vineyard west of Salem.

Today, Tom Huggins lives in Corvallis, where he commutes daily to his new passion—his job as general manager and principal owner of Eola Hills Wine Cellars.

Steve?

His running star continued to rise on the strength of a psychological drive never witnessed before or since. Every race, he pushed hard to break a record, and he frequently did.

He set 14 American running records and at one time owned all eight marks from 2,000 to 10,000 meters. As a freshman at Oregon, he was on the cover of *Sports Illustrated*.

People from all over the world gathered around television sets and cinder tracks to watch him run.

His potential seemed limitless, and so did distance running's in those days.

But neither was ever fully realized.

At a party one night in Eugene, Steve bid adieu to his friends, including Tom's father and brother, drove Shorter to his home in the foothills, then sped off into the darkness on Skyline Drive in his little MGB sports car.

It was the last time anybody would see him alive.

The rest of the story has been captured in two movies and can be recited by residents of Eugene and distance-running aficionados.

Steve, or "Pre" as he was known to Huggins and the rest of the world, crashed into a rock outcropping and was killed. Steve was 24.

Tom heard the news on his car radio and refused to believe it. He was too devastated to attend the funeral.

Today, his eyes moisten at the memory and he leans forward to reveal goosebumps on his arms.

"I get chills just talking about it," he says quietly. "I still regret not going to his services."

Tom doesn't run much any more, instead relying on his knee-friendly mountain bike for exercise on the streets and hills surrounding the northwest Corvallis home where he lives with his wife, Debbie, owner of The Kid Shop in Corvallis.

He doesn't tell his story often or without prodding, but he thinks of Steve frequently and cherishes a *Los Angeles Times* photo of "Pre" and himself that he has at home.

"I often wonder what he'd be doing now," says Tom, who wonders the same of himself had his knee simply been normal.

Tom and Steve. Steve and Tom.

Distinctly different personalities united by a singular passion, separated by pain and tragedy.

Both done too soon.

25

Before Title IX

Passed in 1972 to provide equality in college sports programs for men and women, Title IX has been hailed by many as one of the most significant pieces of legislation of the 20th century. Women's basketball is a testament to this belief. In the final rounds of the 2003 women's Division I national tournament, games were played before record crowds and impressive TV ratings. The players were outstandingly athletic, the games drew nationwide attention across a broad spectrum of fans and supporters, and sports networks devoted nearly as much time to the women's tournament as the men's. But did Title IX "introduce" varsity-level competition for women to the college campus? The answer is no and certainly not at OSU. A better word might be "reintroduce."

To the college sports historian, a school yearbook is like fine wine. With age comes value. At OSU, nothing illustrates this point better than looking back at old issues of the Orange or Beaver yearbooks to study the evolution of women's athletics at Oregon State.

Compared to the men, write-ups covering past seasons, in most cases, are sparse. But there are photos aplenty, and they reveal plenty about women's athletics and athletes from long ago. No fewer than eight sports were first introduced to the OSU campus by women, including basketball, soccer, tennis, gymnastics, field hockey, volleyball, softball and swimming. For those who liked target shooting, there was a championship rifle team.

So these were "recreational" sports, right? Sound mind and body exercises, the Greek ideal, nothing more?

The yearbooks show otherwise, referring to them in many cases as "varsity" sports. There were uniforms, competitions against other colleges, results of past schedules, championships, and varsity letter sweaters awarded for exceptional performance. Unlike the men, however, it is highly doubtful that these women enjoyed any kind of financial assistance in the form of scholarships, travel money and the like. No records survive to tell us one way or the other.

Another important characteristic of this early period was that women's varsity teams stayed in a constant state of flux. Basketball is an example. First introduced to the OSU campus as a varsity sport in 1899, a full two years before the guys took to the hardwoods, women's basketball by 1913 had been reduced to interclass play and limited to the months of spring. In 1916, the sport was again given varsity status, and by 1919, basketball was so popular that over 300 women tried out for the team.

To be sure, the college campus was a different place before Title IX. Male athletes had facilities, scholarships, varsity teams, generous media coverage, the adulation of fans, money—the works. Opportunities for women were kept to a bare minimum.

Beginning sometime during the 1930s and extending up to the early 1970s, a period of some 40 or more years, participation for OSU women in anything athletic was kept at the level of "student recreation." Gifted athletes were grouped with the not so gifted. Events were scheduled around what were called "Play Days," held once or twice a year and pitting recreational teams from one school against the same from a neighboring institution. Other names used around the country included "Field Days," "Sports Days," or the nondescriptive "Class Days." There were no scholarships, no professional coaches, no travel money, nothing like today. Facilities were generally borrowed from the men's programs. Playing fields were the same. OSU did have a competitive volleyball team in the 1960s that competed on the national level, but the squad had to pay its own way with money earned through such fundraising activities as selling programs at men's basketball games.

The shift from varsity sports to physical activity of a noncompetitive nature began both nationally and at Oregon State in the 1920s. By the early 1930s, the shift was complete.

Once again, yearbook photos provide the evidence. Earlier women's teams, before and just after World War I, are pictured in uniforms,

OSU's first women's basketball team, c. 1898-99,
who competed two years before the men took up the sport.
(Photo courtesy of Orange & Black.*)*

often of the "sailor suit" variety. Athletes from the 1930s wear dresses. In appearance, they look indistinguishable from other women in the student body at large. Something had happened, a fundamental shift in the perception of the public toward the female athlete.

The reasons sporting opportunities for collegiate women began to go dry after World War I are complex and controversial. According to such historians as the University of Florida's Paula Welch or the University of Tennessee's Joan Paul, much of the impetus for change at the time "came from within the ranks of women themselves, who as early as 1922 began to display a growing skepticism that the exploitation and elitism already prevalent in men's sports were also beginning to find their way into women's programs."

This attitude was especially prevalent among the women who sat on the Committee on Women's Athletics (CWA) under the auspices of the American Physical Education Association (APEA). Formed in 1917, the purpose of the CWA was to make, revise, and interpret rules and set standards for women athletes at the high school and college levels. According to Professor Welch, in an article published in 1993 in Greta L. Cohen's (editor) outstanding book, *Women in Sport: Issues and Controversies* (Sage Publications), "[the CWA] was neither a controlling nor legislative body. Nevertheless, women in the physical education profession carefully orchestrated the development of women's sports and worked diligently to advance their philosophy, which emphasized sport for all."

This attitude was further perpetuated by the formation in February 1923 of the National Amateur Athletic Federation (NAAF), a group that came together after a meeting between U.S. Secretary of War John W. Weeks, Secretary of the Navy Edwin Derby and Lou Henry (Mrs. Herbert) Hoover to discuss, according to Welch, "the feasibility of establishing an organization that would set standards for girls' and women's sports programs. As member of the NAAF board, now with its own separate women's division, or the WNAAF, Mrs. Hoover played a key role in establishing certain original resolutions for the group, including condemnation of highly organized and competitive sport for the select few or, put another way, a shaping of collegiate sport away from all forms of elite and varsity competition."

The exact wording of the NAAF policy statement, which came to serve both as the spirit and governing policy for women's athletics nationwide, stated a belief in the "promotion of competition that stresses enjoyment of sport and the development of good sportsmanship and character rather than those types that emphasize the making and breaking of records, and the winning of championships for the enjoyment of spectators and for the athletic reputation or commercial advantages of institutions and organizations."

According to Welch, by 1926, basketball, in particular, had become the bane of several generations of physical educators and had become a "national problem." She continues: "Many collegiate physical educators worked diligently to eradicate the negative aspects of...basketball. In 1927, Blanche Trilling, of the University of Wisconsin, delivered a speech at the annual meeting at the National Association of the Deans of Women and specified the unacceptable practices rampant in interscholastic basketball. She condemned lengthy trips to contests, travel on school nights, male coaches, sending injured players into games, omission of physical examinations, general disregard of participants' well-being, play during menstrual periods, championship tournaments that produced nervous strain, overemphasis on winning and rivalry, derogatory comments from spectators, long seasons, involvement of only a small portion of the student body, and the neglect of other sports and school activities by basketball players."

Welch adds that Trilling also came down hard on the practice of the use of "boys' rules by girls' teams."

"Physical educators [became] convinced that modified rules were the remedy for physical contact and serious injury," Welch says. "They maintained that the welfare of the participant was of paramount importance to women in sports leadership positions."

The result was that by 1940, a national decline in women's interscholastic basketball was in evidence. And because basketball at most colleges was or had been the marquis sport for women, these same negative attitudes spilled over into all other sporting activities.

Part of the triggering mechanism for these new attitudes about competition came from a small group of women athletes whose phenomenal successes in their respective sports brought to discussions within athletic circles both great admiration and great contempt for what these women were doing to the spirit of "womanhood."

Superstars such as Clara Baer of New Orleans, Senda Berenson of Smith College in Massachusetts and Eleanora Sears of Boston dared to break Victorian sporting protocol by venturing into areas previously unknown to women. But they opened few doors for others, receiving little praise from their contemporaries for their amazing athletic talents and achievements.

Sears, in particular, is worth a closer look. The great-great granddaughter of Thomas Jefferson, she won over 240 trophies during her nearly 70 years of competition. But she attracted controversy with every appearance.

Professor Joan Paul explains: "She adopted 'shocking' outfits for figure skating, swimming, sailing and tennis. She was the first woman to ride a horse astride, which the newspapers referred to as 'cross-saddle' because of the 'coarseness' the other term elicited. She attempted to play on an all-men's polo team, but later formed her own when rejected. Her appearance on a polo pony in men's riding breeches caused Boston women's clubs to raise their eyebrows...but it was when a California mother's club passed a resolution against her conduct in 1912 that she really became a national celebrity."

However, no woman athlete of the period shocked the sensibilities of America like Mildred "Babe" Didrikson, arguably the greatest woman athlete of the 20th century. She could drive a golf ball over 300 yards and throw a football accurately for 50 yards and a baseball in excess of 300 feet. She earned two Olympic gold medals and a silver at the 1932 games in Los Angeles and once won a prestigious track meet single-handedly against clubs with many athletes. She was an All-American in basketball and took on her nickname when she hit seven home runs in a seven-inning baseball game in her native state of Texas. She performed at a world-class level in no fewer than a dozen sports. Later, putting all her energies and talents into golf, she was the first American to win the Women's British Amateur Golf Championship. She routinely competed in men's golf tournaments. In 1951, she was voted the Most Outstanding Woman Athlete of the Half Century.

But there was a negative side to "Babe's" fabulous career. "She did much for women in sport," explains Dr. Paul, "but, paradoxically, her crude antics [and coarse language] also helped reinforce and perpetuate the unfair myth that women athletes were not quite women. Because of the conservative attitudes of the times, women athletes lived with that tag from the 1930s through the 1950s."

******

OSU's return to varsity competition in women's athletics took place over many years and was accomplished only through the tireless efforts of a small group of women faculty members and administrators, most of whom are now retired, and all of whom never gave up the dream of returning to the campus sporting opportunities for gifted women athletes.

The names are well known by many Oregon Staters and include Pat Ingram, Sandy Neeley, Sylvia Moore, Nancy Gerou, Margaret Lumpkin and Velda Brust. In the early 1970s, Oregon Senator Edith Green helped in the passing of Title IX legislation and also assisted her home state in its implementation.

Before 1972, when OSU became a charter member of the Association of Intercollegiate Athletics for Women (or AIAW), an organization whose purpose in the beginning was to implement the mandates of Title IX, all women at the university participated in sports under the auspices of OSU's Women's Recreation Association in what was known at the time as the department of health and physical education. Margaret Lumpkin, whose 20 years at OSU in the department began in 1948, remembers how things were when she arrived in Corvallis.

"We didn't have opportunities like the men. Competition was limited to 'Play Days,' a day here, a day there, in which we would play intramural games where one sorority house would compete against another. Afterwards, there would be a 'tea-type' thing for the athletes. There were semi-professional teams for women in Portland but nothing like that here at Oregon State."

Lumpkin adds that what she found particularly surprising during her early years was the extent to which other women on campus were opposed to athletics for women at the competitive level. "They were [simply] not eager for women to get into sports. There was great resistance among some who didn't think girls could compete, and in doing so they sold them short. I remember we had to sell programs at basketball games just to have money to pay the expenses for our 'Play Days.'"

Realizing that money was at least a part of the solution to right the many wrongs, Lumpkin gave a personal gift of $100 dollars to the athletic department to start a scholarship fund for women. "It was returned," she recalls, "because I was told there was 'no mechanism to handle the funds.'"

After the passage of Title IX, OSU established the position of Women's Athletic Director and gave the job to longtime faculty member Pat Ingram, who served for two years, or until 1974. Her office was in the Women's Building. Gill Coliseum was the home of athletic administration for the school, but space there was strictly for the use of men's sports.

"It was a fight," she shares today with no bitterness. "We were made to feel like we were stepping on toes. In 1977, things began to change for the better. We finally had money for scholarships. In 1980, the director was finally allowed to move her office over to the Coliseum."

In fact, it was in 1977 that OSU awarded its first athletic scholarship to a woman, given to a Linn-Benton Community College (Albany, Ore.) transfer student named Donna Southwick for gymnastics. In 1975, she was crowned junior college national all-around champion. Southwick quickly proved she was a good investment for the Beavers by becoming OSU's first-ever All-American in women's athletics at the 1977 AIAW National Championships.

By this time, Ingram had resigned as OSU's first women's athletics director, but she continued teaching. Her successor was Sandy Neeley, who at last report was a faculty member serving at Everett Community College in Olympia, Washington. Together, the two of them brought to Corvallis the AIAW national championship track meet for women in 1975, which proved to be a real turning point for women athletes at OSU.

"We filled the stadium," Ingram says. "We came in second to UCLA that day, but it wasn't important. What was important was that we filled the stands. And President [Robert] MacVicar was there. We proved there was interest in women competing at OSU at an elite level."

Iowa native Velda Brust, who worked in the aircraft industry in southern California during World War II and who came to OSU in 1953, remembers how shocked she was after her arrival to learn that women at the university could not play sports in competition.

"I was never given a real good reason," she recalls. "What I remember is that the women in power at that time didn't believe women students should compete at a higher level." Like Ingram, Brust remembers 1977 as a pivotal year and says that softball and gymnastics were the first two sports to achieve varsity status, complete with scholarships.

After a year as director, Neeley gave way to Sylvia Moore, OSU's first gymnastics coach of the modern era, who headed the program from 1967 to 1975. Moore turned the job over to Nancy Gerou for two years, beginning in 1977, then returned to the post from 1980 to 1982 before becoming deputy athletic director for merged programs from 1983 to 1985. When Dee Andros retired as OSU athletic director in 1985, President John Byrne appointed Moore to serve as interim AD until a search could be conducted for Andros's replacement. Her appointment lasted nine months, and she remains the only woman in OSU history to serve as athletic director for all sports. She is especially proud of the contribution she made during her tenure to a refurbishing of Parker Stadium.

Looking back on that brief moment in her career, Moore says, "The experience was fun. I used to chuckle when I would think about all the mothers and dads out there and what they were thinking when they saw a woman had signed our letters of intent."

She also remembers how she would often sit in her office and think about how far women's athletics at Oregon State had progressed since the 1950s, when women's intramural teams would have to buy classified ads in the student newspaper, *The Daily Barometer*, to get their scores posted; how teams shared warmups; how by the 1980s, women were allowed the use of two locker rooms and a half shower for all sports.

"A rod and shower curtain was all that separated the two halves," she remembers with a laugh. "We got a wall built very quickly."

So that the games could go on in the days before Title IX, Moore had to qualify as a referee in multiple sports, becoming certified in field hockey, gymnastics, basketball, volleyball, track and field, and softball.

"We brought our own officials to our games," she says. "I refereed in all these sports and never received one dollar for the time. It was all volunteer labor."

It would be historically inaccurate to say that the best women's athletes in the school's history are the ones who have competed since the appearance of Title IX and all that this implies. Don't tell this to Oregon Staters Gracie Zwahlen or Jean Saubert, or OSU alumna Dr. Mary Budke.

Developing her talents on her own time and with her own resources, Saubert, '64, won silver and bronze medals in skiing in the 1964 winter Olympics, thus becoming the first OSU woman in history to medal in the world's most prestigious sporting event.

Zwahlen, who is from the class of 1952, won the Oregon State Golf Championship five times, won the Canadian National Golf Championship, was twice a semifinalist in the USGA Amateur Championship and was twice named to the U.S. Curtis Cup Team to play against the British. At a 1952 international two-ball tournament, "Babe" Didrikson became ill and couldn't play. Gracie took her place. In 1986, she was named to the State of Oregon Sports Hall of Fame.

Former Oregon State All-America golfer Mary Budke is still making news, having recently been named the captain of the 2002 Curtis Cup team, chosen by the United States Golf Association Women's Committee.

Budke, a physician, lettered at OSU from 1972 to 1975. She attended school without an athletic scholarship. As a Beaver, she won the 1974 AIAW individual championship and placed third at the team finals, along with current OSU women's head coach Rise Lakowske. Budke has been inducted into the Oregon State (1992), Oregon Sports, and National Golf Coaches Association (1996) Halls of Fame. Budke is an eight-time Oregon Women's Amateur champion.

The Eugene, Oregon, native, who played for the victorious 1974 U.S. Curtis Cup team and compiled a 2-1 record, won the 1972 Women's Amateur at age 18. She then went on to tie for 42nd at the 1974 Women's Open as an amateur.

Budke also won the Hayward Award in 1973, which is given annually to the top amateur athlete in the state of Oregon.

Finally, don't mention this to OSU's women's volleyball team from the 1970-71 season. It competed in the national tournament that year, the collegiate volleyball "Big Dance," and player Patti Perkins from that team recently shared some memories of her own to OSU assistant sports information director Jennifer Lowery via e-mail.

She wrote on October 1, 2002: "I played volleyball at Corvallis High, but it was more of a 'Play Day' atmosphere. I am not sure why I went out for the team at OSU. There must have been a sign-up sheet somewhere.

"As a freshman in 1969, I was not a starter, but there were quite a few tournaments we went to so there was still a lot of playing time [for me]. When we earned our way to the first national tournament, we had to practice at 6 a.m. to have any gym space. We sold See's suckers for 10 cents. We carried them all over and people just recognized us and bought them. Our regular customers seemed to be our instructors in the Women's Building.

"Another offer we had was a chance to play volleyball at a [Portland Trailblazers] game at halftime, for money, but they wanted us to play in bikinis. Our coach, Sally Hunter, turned them down. The football coach offered us $500 if we would dust the trophy case [in Gill], but Sally turned that down also. He gave us the money anyway.

"The whole Title IX stuff was never a big deal, except when we had to do all the fund-raising. I was not aware of how easy the boys had it. I guess I was just having fun doing my own thing. I talk to the kids today about some of the things that went on in the old days, but I don't really think it sets in with them."

Another player from that amazing team, Mary Paczesniak, shared memories of the 1969-71 seasons in a letter in the fall of 2002 to the OSU Alumni Association: "Women athletes were required to usher and sell concessions in the stands at OSU football and basketball games to help raise money for operating expenses. We worked from one hour prior to the game until midway through the second half, at which time we received 80 cents' worth of free refreshments, which could buy a hot dog, bag of popcorn and a drink. If we didn't want the food, we could not receive the 80 cents. Male athletes competing on 'minor' sports teams who were not receiving a full scholarship did the same type of work and earned $5 an hour.

"The volleyball team's 'uniforms' were the physical education majors' uniforms which were worn in PE classes and on which we had stitched felt numbers. Before nationals in Kansas City in 1971, we purchased, at personal expense, long-sleeved white tee shirts to wear with our PE shorts. We borrowed the gymnastics team's warmup suits to wear, and we were slightly larger than the gymnasts!

"We participated in the last two National Intercollegiate Championships for Women in 1970 and 1971. We placed 12th for the 1969-1970 season after having gone 21-0 and winning the Pacific Northwest Championship. OSU paid our way to fly to Long Beach and for us to stay in a motel. In 1970-1971, we finished 17-5 and placed second in the PNW [to Oregon]. However, the OSU athletic department did not deem us 'outstanding,' thus would not help pay for our expenses to participate in the national tournament in Lawrence. We raised our own money for the trip, with a car wash and by cleaning Parker Stadium after the spring football game, for which the athletic department paid us $200.

"Women athletes prior to Title IX played for the pure love of the sport and the love of competition. Times were so simple and honest then, but Title IX was a definite necessity."

26

The Upset

In the history of women's intercollegiate athletics at Oregon State, there have been many defining moments, team victories and individual achievements. All have added significantly to the local lore of what it means to be "Beaver tough": Joni Huntley's American records in the high jump (1975) and her bronze medal in the 1984 Olympics; softball superstar Terrah Beyster becoming one of OSU's rare four-time All-Americans in 2000; Mary Budge winning the U.S. Women's Amateur golf championship in 1972. In the team victories category, there are few that compare to the 1979 basketball squad and what that group did one cold weekend in Bozeman, Montana, in the days before there was an NCAA Tournament for women.

The dates were March 8-10, 1979. The event was the Association for Intercollegiate Athletics for Women Region IX basketball tournament at Montana State University in Bozeman. The winner, to be crowned on the 10th, would advance to Palo Alto, California, for the Western Sectional Tournament, the final regional games before the national championship.

All the strongest teams from the various divisions of the Northwest League were there, including Seattle University, Montana State, Oregon State, Washington State and Oregon.

On paper, the Ducks looked like a sure bet. Led by a talented defense and averaging 86.9 points per game, Oregon entered the tournament 23-0 and ranked No. 20 in the national polls.

First-year coach Aki Hill's Beavers had a 14-5 record, including two not-so-close losses to the Ducks during the regular season. Undefeated and confident, the Ducks drew a bye in the first round, where the Beavers struggled to beat Montana State, 76-73. Against Washington State, OSU fared better with a 71-62 victory, winning the right to advance to the championship round.

As predicted, the Ducks also advanced to the trophy game. The showdown came on a Saturday night, before 120 fans.

Hill's task was huge: Stop a team that hadn't been stopped all year, shut down one of the nation's most potent offenses, and deal with a Duck squad in which everyone up and down the lineup could score.

Final tally?

Oregon State 75, UO 68.

The task was accomplished, the giant felled.

OSU All-American Carol Menken-Schaudt, whose 95 points in three games earned her All-Tournament honors, said she still isn't sure, even after all these years, just how they upset such a talented Oregon team.

"I can't tell you how we beat them," she shared. "Sometimes you just have a game where things start going right for you and it gives you the confidence to think you can win, and things start going wrong for the other team and their confidence begins to fall.

"Against the Ducks, we never let down in the championship game. They were the best team that year during the regular season, but they were our big rivals, and I felt confident we could beat them."

Menken-Schaudt, today an account executive with AT&T in Corvallis, remembers always playing hard against Oregon, no matter what the situation. Her feelings stemmed from the fact that the Ducks had snubbed her during recruiting, had passed along word to her that she wasn't of the caliber they needed for their program.

Whatever incentive she carried into the game, the six-foot-four Menken-Schaudt put up career numbers that night, shooting 14 of 19 from the floor for a percentage of 73.7. Also helping was a tenacious defense that kept the Ducks well below their shooting average, with the ladies from Eugene managing but 28 of 71 from the field. Their normally productive reserves scored six points. In addition, the Ducks did not receive one free throw opportunity in the second half.

"We played a hard, pressing, aggressive defense the entire 40 minutes, and this played a big part in our victory," said Hill, now retired and living in Corvallis. "It was a huge game for us and a huge win. I

All-American and Olympic gold medalist Carol Menken-Schaudt, c. 1979.
(Photo courtesy of OSU Sports Information.)

think this is the game that helped start the intense rivalry that exists between the two programs today."

Hill also emphasized to her players before the game how much turnovers would hurt their chances of winning the championship and how they had turned the ball over a school-record 48 times in their last meeting with the Ducks.

In this third and most important contest with their rivals, OSU would give the ball back to Oregon 18 times.

The Ducks did win the rebound struggle at 50-39. But they had 21 costly turnovers, many late in the game, as Hill's defense began to smell victory and tightened with vise-grip firmness.

At Palo Alto for the Sectional Tournament, UCLA was OSU's first-round opponent. The outcome was never in doubt, as the Beavers lost 105-70.

In the consolation game, OSU defeated BYU 78-74 to end the season at 18-6.

But for Kathy Vanderstoel Campbell, who went on to become an office manager with Superior Lumber in Glendale, Oregon, the upset of Oregon was the one game she remembers more than some of the others.

"Oh yes, we were the underdogs in that game," she said. "What I remember is that we won it on defense. We kept saying we didn't want to try and run with them and that all we needed to do was keep the fouls down and play the defense we had been playing all year.

"It was wild at the end. We were all waiting for the buzzer, trying to hang on. My nerves were really on edge. There were lots of fouls and lots of starts and stops. The Ducks were frantic and then we heard the buzzer, and we were the champions."

27

Old Whiskey Sour

"If you want to interview Ralph, you'd better hurry," the voice on the other end of the phone said. "He's not doing so well." A few days later, in the autumn of 2000, a gracious Jean Miller greeted visitors at the door of the picturesque retirement home at Black Butte, Oregon. For the next three hours, legendary former OSU basketball coach Ralph Miller, aka "Old Whiskey Sour," regaled guests warmly with raspy and vivid tales ranging from his memories of Dr. James Naismith and Phog Allen to the Beavers' ill-fated bid for a national championship in 1981. Eight months after this final interview, in May 2001, he was gone.

The Legend has quietly faded into this serene setting in Central Oregon, where his privacy is preserved amid a labyrinth of twisting roads, fairways and ponderosa pine.

Once a household name in Oregon, Ralph Miller is just another resident at Black Butte Ranch, where he has lived with his wife, Jean, since bidding adieu cold turkey in 1989 to the dynasty he built and the game he, in many ways, invented and reinvented.

Here, the former Oregon State basketball coach can sit all day in his favorite reclining chair in the dining room, smoking his ubiquitous More cigarettes while absorbing a stunning view of Black Butte and watching golfers play the 12th fairway at Big Meadows.

Miller, 81, greets visitors cheerfully and remembers his Hall of Fame coaching career in vivid detail, but the earthy split-level home offers precious little evidence of the accomplishments, plaudits and trophies he accumulated in four storied decades.

At the bottom of the lower stairway, which features an electric escalator-style chair so the emphysema-weakened Miller can access his other favorite spot—the recliner where he watches sports, *Walker: Texas Ranger* and *La Femme Nikita*—is "The Wall."

On The Wall is all of his most cherished memorabilia: Letters of commendation from former presidents Reagan and Bush, a photo that includes his former Kansas University professor and mentor Dr. James Naismith, and plaques commemorating college basketball's 17th winningest coach of all time.

The lone exception is a giant framed poster featuring Miller and a handful of his best players posing on a train outside Gill Coliseum.

That single poster hangs alone on a separate wall, a tribute to the team that, for Miller and the university, stands alone.

The 1980-81 Orange Express.

Twenty years earlier, Miller's Beavers were at the top of the national polls for two glorious months. They galvanized the state and captured the nation's fancy en route to winning their first 26 games.

Students slept overnight on the steps of Gill Coliseum for tickets. The likes of Steve Johnson, Lester Conner, Ray Blume, Mark Radford and Charlie Sitton became household names. Hundreds of fans joined the team on charter flights and celebrated victories with the Millers in their festive hotel suites.

The national media descended on Corvallis in unprecedented numbers to unlock the mystery of a program that had unseated mighty UCLA as the Pacific-10 Conference's perennial power.

"It was wonderful," remembers Radford, an All-Conference guard who is now a real estate agent in Portland. "I don't think we had any doubt that something special would happen. We didn't expect anything less than perfection. We expected to win every game."

At the hub of the maelstrom was Miller, a Kansas native who absorbed what he learned from cohorts Naismith, the game's inventor, and a fellow legend, Phog Allen, and then devised a system of full-court pressure defense that revolutionized the game in the 1950s.

Miller's teams were elegant and brilliant in their tactical simplicity.

He recruited quick, fast and strong athletes who typically weren't highly touted coming out of high school, then molded them to fit his system. The only other requirement was a love of defense. In a precursor to today's famed "40 minutes of hell," Miller was the first coach to have his players press full-court after every possession.

Offensively, he ran only two sets and dared opponents to stop either. Few could. To this day, Beaver Believers have vivid images of Johnson tossing a back-door bounce pass—the one circumstance where the otherwise worthless pass was allowed—to a sharply cutting Blume, Radford or Conner for an easy layup.

"It was like taking candy from a baby," Miller says now, barely masking his pride. "A thing of beauty."

The Beavers carved up the opposition with such monotonous ease that they often felt like workers on an assembly line. In January 1981, after top-ranked DePaul was upset, OSU moved into the No. 1 spot for the first time in school history.

The roll would continue for nearly two months. The Beavers were 17-0 in the Pac-10, with only six of the victories coming by fewer than 10 points, heading into a gala season finale at Gill Coliseum against No. 4 Arizona State.

Meanwhile, Miller was steadily moving up in rankings for career victories, eventually passing legendary John Wooden of UCLA to move into sixth place before he retired in 1989.

Not bad for a coach who got into the profession purely by accident.

******

Miller rises gingerly from his chair, extends a firm hand and gestures to his visitors to sit.

The hallowed former coach, whose perpetual scowl earned him the nickname "Old Whiskey Sour," is smiling warmly. The irascible Hall of Famer, whose gruff voice and disdain for silly questions once reduced young sportswriters' knees to quaking jelly, beckons with a gentle, throaty "Welcome."

A man who could send rumblings through packed arenas with public dressing-downs of players who played lazy defense or—gasp—threw a bounce pass, greets the latest in a steady stream of visitors with a friendly, grandfatherly persona.

Miller returns to his chair just as carefully as he rose, plants a leg on the table and fingers a pack of More cigarettes, his constant companion for 35 years.

As he begins to talk cheerfully and with the blunt candor on which his reputation was built, memories pour out in sharp detail. It is as if it all happened yesterday, from his sharing a classroom at Kansas with

Naismith to his ill-fated bid for a place on the 1940 U.S. Olympic team as a decathlete to OSU's unforgettable 1980-81 season.

Miller is largely confined to this corner of a house his son Paul designed and built 11 years ago, but he has few complaints.

Sure, the need to walk with a cane forced him to give up his cherished golf game two years ago. The 30-step walk to the bridge room at Black Butte Ranch means he can no longer play a game he once rarely lost.

Respirators in several corners of the home are a reminder of the price he has paid for smoking most of his life.

Small matter.

Doctors have finally solved the medication-induced summer tailspin that recently had Jean, his college sweetheart and wife of 58 years, fearing his days might be numbered in double digits—or less. He is sleeping fitfully and no longer needs a wheelchair or walker to get around.

Miller is once again accepting what the fates give, or take away, with a shrug and a wave of the hand—with two or three notable exceptions that haunt him to this day.

"Life's not bad," he says, smiling again. "I'm alive. That's better than the alternative."

******

Ralph H. "Cappy" Miller was born in Chanute, Kansas, and became the state's top high school athlete of his time.

He set the state record in the low hurdles in 1937. He was All-State for three consecutive years in football and basketball. By 1940, he was beating '32 gold medalist Jim Baush in seven of 10 events in the decathlon and seemed a cinch for a berth on the Olympic team.

Fate intervened.

"Mr. Hitler got in the way and tried to blow up the world," Miller recalls. "So I never got to participate."

In the fall of 1937, while at Kansas University, where he was an All-Conference basketball player and a standout in football, he took a physiology class. The students were seated alphabetically. Next to him was an attractive coed from Topeka named Emily Jean Milam.

They were married five years later.

The year before they said their vows, Miller was asked in a pinch to coach boys' basketball at Mount Oread High School in Lawrence. The team consisted primarily of professors' sons.

"They were smart as hell, but they didn't have much physical talent," Miller says. "I'm not sure we won a game. I think we lost every damn one. When I got out of that, I really didn't think too much about coaching. I thought there were better ways to make a living."

Miller didn't have to go overseas during World War II because of knee problems that began at KU. He enlisted in the U.S. Air Force and held desk jobs in Florida, Texas and California.

After the war, he became an assistant director of recreation and oversaw a swimming pool and playground in Redlands, California. Soon, he joined a friend in the business of hauling fruit.

"They thought they'd make a fortune stocking grocery stores," Jean recalls, "but everything went wrong."

In 1949, eight years after his ill-fated first attempt at coaching, a friend from Wichita, Kansas, named Fritz Snodgrass sent Miller a telegram asking if he might be interested in returning to guide his son's team at East High School.

Reluctantly, the Millers left sunny California and returned to their native Midwest.

At East, Miller became a student of the game. He was fascinated by the full-court zone press defense that had been developed at Kansas in 1930, but he wondered why it was only used after a basket was made. Nobody could give Miller a solid answer, and so he began tinkering with ways to press after missed shots, too.

His idea was to assign each player a man to guard, and when an errant shot went up, they were immediately to pick up their man.

It worked.

In three years at East High, Miller's teams finished second, third and first in the state using his system of execution and pressure basketball.

"The experience at East more or less changed my whole philosophy about coaching," he says. "It made me cocky. I could coach with these guys, and I spent the rest of my life doing it.

"All of a sudden I had my own system. I used my system for 40 years without changing the concept, so it was worthwhile."

In 1951, the president of Wichita State University offered him a job.

The rest is the stuff of legends.

******

Miller spent 13 years at Wichita State, winning 220 games, earning three National Invitation Tournament berths and a spot in the NCAA Tournament in 1964. That spring, the Millers left for the University of Iowa, where he built one of the greatest offensive juggernauts in NCAA history.

The Hawkeyes averaged more than 100 points a game in 1970 and went undefeated in the Big Ten Conference en route to an NCAA Tournament berth.

Miller seemed destined to build a dynasty in Iowa City. He and his wife cherished their home in the hills and the fans offered unconditional support.

But one element was too much to bear.

"The last year we won them all—we were 20-0—but it was the worst weather you could imagine," Jean Miller remembers. "It was below zero. Students had to cover their faces to avoid frostbite. That year, there was hail that killed cattle. We had to take the kids to the coliseum basement when the tornado sirens sounded.

"When we got to the Final Four that year, I said, 'Find a place with an opening that has a moderate climate.'"

That place was Oregon State, where Paul Valenti had just stepped down as coach five seasons after succeeding another Beaver basketball legend, Slats Gill.

It's difficult to fathom now, but Miller's first three years in Corvallis were so rough that the family contemplated returning to Kansas.

One of his players, Mike Keck, was killed in a car accident on a trip to Reno, Nevada. The Beavers went 12-12, 18-10, 15-11 and 13-13 in the first four years. Less than a decade removed from Slats Gill's 1962 Final Four team, fans were getting restless.

"We don't look back at those first three years happily," Jean Miller says.

"Ralph would've gladly left after two years."

Part of the issue was the perception of Miller as a demanding, harsh and militaristic leader, an image that dogged him even through the glory years. Friends who knew him as a caring father with a kind soul would plead his case, but it fell on deaf ears.

Another vivid image among OSU fans was of a player making a mistake and getting benched. Once the player sat down, usually as far away from the coach as possible, Miller would slowly rise from his chair, walk slowly down the bench and tower over the offending party with pointed gestures and words.

A chorus of nervous "oohs" would flow from sellout crowds of 10,000 as they watched the theatrics.

Miller acknowledges that he was a demanding perfectionist. It was his way or the highway.

"I had one basic concept: I am one person, the squad is many," he says. "It's easier for many to adjust to one person than for one person to adjust to 20. So you adjust to me. You either do what I want you to do, or you don't play.

"My weapon was simple: You want to play? It's your choice."

Further perpetuating the "Grinch" perception were sportswriters who melted in his presence. Miller had as much tolerance for inept questioning as he did for the bounce pass.

One of his favorite "stupid question" stories involves another OSU legend, broadcaster Darrell Aune. Miller recalls that when they first conducted postgame radio shows together, Aune would shuffle papers and neglect to pay attention to the coach's answers.

When Miller would finish talking, it was Aune's cue to ask another question. One time, Aune asked a question that Miller had already answered.

On the air, Miller said, "Darrell, that's a stupid question because I just got through answering it!"

Says Miller: "We never had any more problems for the rest of my career, because he listened and we would have nice conversations about the game."

Nevertheless, his image was sealed, and with a glint in his eye, Miller says he was acutely aware of sportswriters' dread.

"That's the way I liked you to be," he says, smiling impishly.

Yet largely unseen was the relationship Miller had with his family, friends and players. He rarely had disciplinary problems with his players, most of whom policed themselves on and off the court.

Epitomizing this scenario was former point guard Gary Payton, whom Miller now says was the best player he ever coached, slightly better than former Wichita State standout Dave Stallworth.

Fans assumed that Miller and Payton were two stubborn stars who constantly had clashes of wills and weren't shy of displaying them in front of 10,000 spectators.

Truth was, Miller says, that he and Payton never had a disagreement in the three years they were together. Payton recruited himself by showing up one day at a pregame shootaround in Berkeley, California, and, after an unknowing Miller was informed by assistants Jimmy Anderson and Lanny Van Eman that he ought to take a chance on the Oakland high school star, Payton never gave the head coach trouble.

"Gary had a strange demeanor, and when he talks he always looks like he's jawing," Miller says. "People used to be concerned that I was having trouble with Gary because he'd come over to the bench and jaw at me. Well, all he ever wanted to know was, 'What do you want to do next, Coach?'"

And it's also worth noting that of the dozens of sportswriters who covered Miller during his 40-year career, he lists many among his friends today.

He recalls only three sour media memories: A rocky relationship with a former *Oregonian* columnist, the *Corvallis Gazette-Times'* investigation into allegations of NCAA violations in the early 1980s, and a newspaper story out of Wichita in 1994 that suggested Miller had racist tendencies.

Like most other painful memories, Miller has let those slide, but Jean, who always wore the stress more than her husband, still bristles when reminded—particularly about the story from Wichita, for which Miller was never contacted.

"You could say a lot of things about my husband except that he was a racist," Jean says. "He once asked his [high school] principal if he could put five black players on the court at one time. He was a young and volatile coach, but he's literally color-blind. I don't know many coaches who did more for black players than Ralph. If one player couldn't eat in a restaurant, they all ate somewhere else."

Indeed, Miller was recruiting black athletes at Wichita State long before it became fashionable at many of the major southern universities. His 1980-81 OSU team that was ranked first started four black players, who still maintain contact with him.

The Millers toughed out their first few years in Corvallis, in part because they loved having the two youngest of their four children living there.

They are grateful that they did.

＊＊＊＊＊＊

Miller had only two losing seasons in 19 years at OSU, but even by his perfectionist standards the 1980-81 Beavers were extraordinary.

The veteran team revolved around Johnson, a mobile six-foot-10 center with a wide body and a soft touch around the basket. His eye-popping 74.6 shooting percentage, an NCAA record, was a function of not only his talent but of a disciplined offense that OSU ran with such precision that it established a school record for shooting (56.4).

Johnson, Blume and Radford were chosen All-League in the Pacific-10 Conference. Conner, a junior college transfer who was the final piece to this remarkable puzzle, and Sitton made the All-Rookie team.

Everybody who played for Miller had to operate within the system, and those who didn't eventually disappeared, but no team embraced his concepts like this one.

"We completely believed in Ralph's system," Radford says.

"It was a very simple system to master, a system where he really allowed us to groove and become very proficient at one way of playing. And we were able to master it based on a certain amount of skill level and a certain amount of hunger."

The Beavers were so focused and businesslike that they couldn't always enjoy their achievements as much as the screaming denizens who packed Gill every night. They were almost robotic in their work. Smiles were infrequent, high-fives rare, chest-thumping nonexistent.

"One of my disappointments personally was that it wasn't as fun as it could have been," Radford says.

"It was too businesslike. You'd beat somebody by 20 and it should've been 30. That was the perfectionist in Ralph, but it could've been a little more fun."

Miller's teams usually ran themselves and he rarely had to do much coaching once seasons began, but with this group he virtually became one of 10,000 appreciative spectators. At practice, he rarely had to say a word.

"I just sat in my chair and smoked," he recalls, adding: "We rarely had any trouble scoring. Everybody knew exactly what we were going to do, but we went ahead and did our thing."

Heading into the season finale against Arizona State, the Beavers were 26-0 and had earned a first-round bye in the NCAA's West Regional at Pauley Pavilion in Los Angeles.

By then, OSU seemed invincible. The players believed it, and even opposing players seemed to believe it. In those rare close games, the Beavers found a way to win—and the opponent found a way to lose.

"That's a certain rarity to achieve in athletics—and in life," Radford says. "People don't think they can beat you."

Certainly nobody expected it at Gill Coliseum, but that's exactly what happened in the final game. Fourth-ranked Arizona State, which featured five starters who would wind up in the NBA, was the one team

Former OSU basketball coach Ralph Miller (1970-89),
with longtime assistant Jimmy Anderson in the background.
(Photo courtesy of Barry Schwartz.)

that had the talent to overcome the crowd noise, the precision offense, and the tenacious defense.

The Sun Devils shocked the basketball world by blistering the Beavers 87-67 at Gill, shattering the perfect season.

Up next was Kansas State, which had won its first-round NCAA game over San Francisco and had exorcised tournament jitters. OSU had earned a first-round bye in the event, which featured 48 teams then.

The Beavers immediately felt the pressure, and it didn't help that crank phone calls to the starters' motel rooms near the UCLA campus kept them awake until 1:30 a.m. the day of the game.

Still, the Wildcats couldn't stop Johnson, and the Beavers built double-digit leads in the second half.

There was no reason to think their magical journey to the Final Four would end on this night, even though they had suffered first-round exits at the hands of Lamar in the NCAA Tournament the previous year and Nevada-Reno in the NIT the season before that.

Then Johnson was called for two second-half charging fouls, negating two baskets, giving K-State four free throws and sending OSU's most formidable player to the bench permanently. The Beavers began committing rare turnovers. They missed free throws.

Amazingly, with time ticking away, the game was tied and Kansas State had the ball.

Every Beaver fan over age 25 knows what happened next.

K-State's Rolando Blackman pulled up for a jump shot with Radford flying at him. Radford, who had perfected the art of "snakebite"—tapping a shooter's elbow hard enough to alter the shot but lightly enough to not get called for a foul—ticked Blackman's elbow precisely the way he wanted.

Yet when he looked back, the ball was dropping through the net, giving K-State a shocking 50-48 victory. The Beavers couldn't believe it.

"The shot was incredible," Radford says. "I got him and he still made the shot, and in my mind if I'd not done that, he'd have missed it."

The shot wound up on the cover of *Sports Illustrated.* Afterward, Miller said little to the players. He usually returned to the team motel with the team, but on that night he walked the streets of Westwood alone, trying to purge the sick, empty feeling.

It remains the most vivid basketball memory of his stay in Corvallis. And it's the second most painful experience he's known, exceeded only by the death of his son, Ralph Jr., or "Cappy," in 1986.

"I was devastated," Miller says. "That trip was a bummer."

It was his last best hope for a national title. He would coach eight more years, finishing with 657 wins in 38 seasons.

In 1989, when he was the same age at which his former mentor Phog Allen retired, he'd had enough.

"Hell, I was 70," he explains. "I don't think I ever knew anybody in the coaching business who worked at 70. I looked at it this way: What more could I accomplish? I was in every Hall of Fame wherever I was associated. A high school gym in Chanute is named after me. There is a Ralph Miller Court and a Ralph Miller Avenue. What's left?

"When I got to 70, I was very happy to step out, and I've had no regrets whatsoever."

But he left a legacy that'll never be forgotten in Corvallis and around Oregon.

"I never had a better coach, and I think he prepared us as good as he could and we achieved huge success," Radford says. "He had his moods and his temperaments, but he was very fair and you knew what you'd get day in and day out. There were very few surprises.

"I respected him, but what I liked about playing for him was that it was a challenge. A lot of players left, so it wasn't for everybody, but I started every game for four years so obviously I had certain success with him. Not every player had what I had, and obviously it was challenging, but I don't think there's anybody quite like him.

"Overall, he's a rare breed in the game."

******

Today, Miller still follows college basketball on television and chuckles when he sees variations of the offenses and defenses he created and honed a half-century earlier. He is certain he could win with them today, and he wonders why full-court pressure has largely disappeared.

"Most people complicate it," he said of the offense. "They try to add a few more wrinkles, and that just confuses it."

Most of his time is spent watching television while Jean visits with neighbors or participates in activities at the ranch. They often play gin rummy well into the evening.

It requires an effort to get Ralph out of the house, but the motorized chairs in both stairwells get him up and down. Once a week the couple will drive to Bend to see doctors and stop at The Gallery Restaurant in Sisters for breakfast. For a scenery break, they'll drive to their other home on Yaquina Bay, which they've also owned since 1989.

They rarely reminisce about the glory days, though occasionally Jean will play tapes of games or interviews and they'll listen together.

That he can't coach or golf or even play bridge hasn't affected his demeanor.

"There are things that happen and you can't do nothin' about it," he said. "So I just more or less take it in stride."

Miller takes another puff on a cigarette and shifts carefully in his seat. He is content to live whatever life he has left in this picturesque setting on the 12th hole.

After all he has accomplished, he has reduced his life's goals to this: "Just one," he says, smiling. "Stay alive."

28

Down for the Count

No Oregon State coach ever did so much for so long with so little. Dale Thomas won 616 dual meets as the Beavers' wrestling coach from 1957-90, giving him 17 more victories than legendary basketball coach Slats Gill. A feisty, give-'em-hell country boy in the Harry Truman mold, Thomas fused irascibility with a giant heart that would help any wrestler or coach gritty and determined enough to pull his own weight. Weakened from an always-fatal liver disease and other age-related ailments, he was presiding over the last of his renowned summer wrestling camps when he sat down for a conversation in August 2001 in the old wrestling barn at his Double D Ranch near Harlan.

This much he can still do.

At 78, Dale Thomas can still get down on the mats in his shadowy wrestling barn and demonstrate moves to his last group of campers. He still has the feistiness and dexterity to show proper leg positioning, takedowns and holds.

He still chews out youngsters who lose focus or fail to be considerate or dog it on the daily 6 a.m. hike/run on the wooded ridge above Big Elk Creek deep in the Coast Range.

If only that were enough.

Thomas can't climb ladders to clean troughs or trim alder branches. He can't cut windfall for more than a half-hour because his anemia fatigues him. He could get hurt tending to his cattle. He can't even fathom butchering a bull or castrating a goat himself the way he once would in front of wide-eyed country kids.

The cherished acreage he once traversed at ease on foot or by ATV has become a monster too big and unruly to tame to his satisfaction.

The diseases he has defied for the past 15 years—first pancreatitis, then cancer, and now, for the past eight years, the deadly primary sclerosing cholangitis—have slowly gained an upper hand and, he grudgingly admits, are ever closer to taking him on his final fall.

And so this is it.

After 26 years, this is his last go-round with his Double D Wrestling Camp, which has taught thousands of kids about wrestling, nature and life.

He and his wife, Nadine, who already spend most of their time in Corvallis to be closer to Dale's doctors and medicines, are selling their vast acreage of meadows, creeks and timber west of Mary's Peak.

The place has been on the market for several years, yes, but this summer clearly is different. When the Double D is sold, the wrestling camp may continue, but it will do so without its founder and guiding light.

Thus, a hint of sadness hangs over the rustic wrestling barn and cook shack, which like its creator and builder are showing signs of age and wear on their remote perch above the creek and the winding, gravelly Big Elk Road.

"It's tough, but I've got to face the reality that I can't work," Thomas said earlier in the week while observing his final group of one camp and 31 kids—a far cry from the eight camps with more than 250 budding grapplers in its heyday in the 1980s.

"It's not easy for me. I'm going to miss running the camp, but it's too dangerous."

To those who know Thomas, it seemed this day could never come.

Ever since he hitchhiked west in 1942 with a group of Cornell College (Iowa) students called "The Red Hats" and fell in love with Oregon, he has been a fixture at Oregon State, in Corvallis and in the coastal forests.

He coached OSU's wrestling team on a shoestring budget from 1957 until 1990, winning 616 dual meets and building a respected national power. He won 22 conference titles, finished among the top five nationally seven times and molded 60 individual All-Americans.

Twice he was chosen NCAA Coach of the Year.

Along the way, he became renowned—notorious in some circles—for doing things his own way, for speaking his mind without fear or favor, and for demanding the utmost of his athletes on the mat, in the classroom and in the community.

He took teams to South Africa when such travel by sports squads was banned because of apartheid. He defied his own cost-conscious administrators and took his OSU teams on East Coast swings—and actually *made* money for his program on the trips.

He openly challenged the win-at-all-cost attitudes increasingly adopted by the NCAA, athletic directors and coaches, and says he was resented because he produced more postgraduate scholarship winners than all other OSU sports programs combined.

Administrators told him he had "created a monster" and, with the Beavers playing to 6,000 fans at Gill Coliseum, reluctantly acknowledged that Thomas had created a winner.

"That's not a compliment," he'd reply coarsely. "I'm an educator."

Amid the demands and occasional controversy, Thomas also became known for his giant heart, which provided the impetus to start the Double D Wrestling Camp in 1975.

Thomas and a few friends in the wrestling community built the 50'x100' barn over two summer weekends. Using a brand of tough love that occasionally made campers and their mothers quiver, he taught wrestling, social skills and other life lessons.

They would rise at 6 a.m., go hiking, identify trees and return for breakfast. At other times campers would pull weeds, cut firewood or look for evidence of cougar, bear, elk and deer in the fir and alder forests surrounding the Double D. They would wrestle 20 to 30 matches in a day under the watchful eye of counselors.

Evenings consisted of meals—nothing was to be left on a plate—and life skills seminars.

Then it was lights-out at 9:30 p.m. in the barn, where sleeping bags, pillows and blankets were scattered on the mats amid walls covered with moose racks, deer antlers, cougar skins and dusty memorabilia dating back to the 1940s.

"It takes a special breed to come here," said counselor Jeff Smith, who wrestled for Thomas at OSU in the mid-1960s, lives in Sisters and commutes weekly to a teaching job at Cal State-Dominguez Hills.

"And it's pretty intense for us, too."

Sometimes kids would get scared or homesick. They weren't allowed to call home, and parents weren't allowed to visit. Only in case of injury or illness would the camps be cut short.

When kids returned home after five days, sometimes their parents would barely recognize them.

Former wrestling coach Dale Thomas.
(Photo courtesy of Barry Schwartz.)

"I had one mother ask me, 'What have you done to my kid? He's telling *me* how to cook!'" Thomas recalled wryly. "There's so much this camp does. It changes kids' attitudes, changes their lives. It's more like a military camp. I don't see how a society can create boys and girls without adversity. We create some adversity here."

Said 13-year-old camper Abe Hogel of Walterville, whose grandfather migrated west with Thomas from Cornell in 1942: "I get a good experience here. It teaches me about nutrition, life and wrestling."

In the end, all the proceeds from the camp went not to Thomas but toward scholarships for wrestlers and opportunities for coaches.

The journey to this final chapter in the camp's story began in 1987, when Thomas experienced severe pain on OSU's flight to Minneapolis, Minnesota, for the NCAA championships.

Doctors discovered gallstones, and he was sent home for surgery to remove his bladder, which was found to have cancer. In 1993, he was diagnosed with potentially lethal pancreatitis, and in the process he was found to have sclerosing cholangitis, a progressive disease that's always eventually fatal.

It's the same illness that killed former Chicago Bears star Walter Payton within months of diagnosis.

Thomas was put on a waiting list for a liver transplant, but was told he wouldn't get one until he was free of cancer. He was told he might not last a year; as of this summer, it's been eight—and he's free of cancer, not certain whether he'd accept a liver transplant because of the other health complications it might cause.

He has received dozens of calls from other sufferers of the disease who wonder how he's lasted so long. He describes himself as the "poster boy" for sclerosing cholangitis.

Indeed, last week, his doctor extended a hand and offered congratulations.

"What for?" Thomas asked.

"Because we were all betting you'd be dead by now," the doctor replied.

One day, Thomas knows, the disease will kill him, too.

Its progression has moved him to set up a trust fund for Nadine. He has lowered the price of the Double D for sale. He leaves Corvallis only to tend to matters at the ranch. And he is stepping away from the camp.

Smith said he and fellow counselor Tommy Phillips hope to negotiate with the new owners to continue the camp there as a tribute to Thomas, but it's doubtful the founder would be a part of it.

"I hate to see it," said former OSU All-American Jess Lewis, who participates in Thomas's seminars on drug abuse. "A lot of kids have come through here."

Thomas hates to see it, too.

He contemplates the impending loss every time he walks his acreage. He laments the cruelty of a sharp mind trapped inside a deteriorating body.

"There's never a good time to die," he said. "I'm as enthusiastic about life today as I've ever been. Here I am 78 and I'm still trying to figure it all out because you can always improve. I hate to leave it, but you've got to leave things progressively anyway.

"You don't live forever."

29

A Local Legend

The Ides of March, 1980. It had been 19 years since Oregon State's Gill Coliseum had hosted such a wrestling tournament. This was the big one, the finals of the NCAA Division I national championships. By the time of the last match, featuring the heavyweights, the mostly partisan crowd of 7,128 had already seen quite a show. But the best was yet to come.

Up to this point, it had been the University of Iowa's night. Long before the heavyweights, Hawkeye coach Dan Gable's grapplers had won enough points to cruise to their third consecutive national championship and their fifth title in six years. The word "dynasty" showed up in a lot of sports stories the next day.

Ah, yes, and then there were those other two guys, diminutive Joe Gonzales at 118 pounds and John Azevedo at 126, both from Cal State-Bakersfield.

Gonzales made history that night at OSU's Gill Coliseum. His became his school's first national champion in wrestling.

In his junior and senior seasons, he had compiled a winning record of 98-1, with an astonishing 440 takedowns. He was 54-0 before his victory in the finals, an NCAA record for most wins in a single season (held formerly by OSU's Larry Bielenberg at 51-1).

Teammate Azevedo became Bakersfield's second national champion a few minutes later, easily defeating Jerry Kelly of Oklahoma State, 17-9.

He finished the season at 52-0 and would have had the single-season record had it not been for Gonzales.

Now it was time for the heavyweights. The largely OSU-backing crowd felt pleased the evening would end with a performance by one of their own.

And he was local, had gone to school just to the north at McNary High in Keizer. Most felt he was probably the best two-sport athlete to ever play for any team in Oregon's capital city, winning all-state honors in both football and wrestling.

On his OSU wrestling questionnaire, when asked what name he preferred to be called, he wrote down that people should call him "Howard" or "Harris," one was as good as the other.

As he moved his six-foot-four, 190-pound muscular body toward the center of the mat to face an extraordinary young heavyweight from Indiana State named Bruce Baumgartner, Howard Harris was poised to make some history of his own.

At 45-0 for the season and 168 total wins, he was tied with Bielenberg for the OSU record for most career victories. His 40 falls his senior year also set a record. To put this number in another perspective,

All-American Howard Harris dominates another opponent.
(Photo by Robert Griffith, The Beaver.*)*

Howard Harris had more falls in his final year than all his teammates combined.

Harris was what wrestling coaches refer to as a "thrower," a man who could throw and pin an opponent so fast, a match was sometimes over before fans had a chance to open their popcorn boxes.

In round one of the tournament, for example, it took him 32 seconds to dispose of Craig Newberg of Ball State.

He also pinned his next three opponents, a feat that had wrestling experts scratching their heads in wonder. No one could ever remember seeing anything like that in the national finals.

A few Beaver fans that night had memories of their own. Watching Howard Harris prepare to cap off the tournament, they remembered a single phone call made four years earlier, one that changed, in a small way, the course of wrestling history at Oregon State—the call that kept Howard Harris home.

As we have seen, Harris was an amazing competitor in high school. His career record of 86-4 did not go unnoticed nationally, especially in the wrestling-crazy state of Oklahoma.

The Sooners flew him down for a visit. He returned the day before letter of intents were to be signed and announced Oklahoma was where he wanted to go.

But Jerry Lane had other ideas. He had coached Harris for four years at McNary and knew him to be an elite athlete, the kind you don't let leave the state if you can help it. So Lane got on the phone and called coach Dale Thomas. He told Thomas that if he had any chance of keeping Harris local he would have to act quickly. That evening, Thomas, accompanied by OSU wrestling greats Greg Strobel and Bielenberg, traveled to Keizer, where they convinced the young star that Corvallis was where he needed to be.

The next day, Strobel told *Corvallis Gazette-Times* sports editor Roy Gault: "He was going to Oklahoma, no doubt about it. I told him that if he went to Oklahoma, who will care if he's a national champion?

"I could have gone to Oklahoma, too, and that's fine if I wanted to spend the rest of my life living in Oklahoma. But I wanted to live in Oregon, and Oregon people care if you win an NCAA national championship for Oregon State. We sold him on that idea. In one night, he changed his mind."

Asked later why he cared so much where Howard Harris attended college, Lane replied he did so because he had a lot of respect for Dale Thomas's program and that he knew that Thomas cared about whether his players graduated.

He also said he was convinced Howard Harris was a major college wrestler.

So was Bruce Baumgartner, who entered the tournament as one of the most talked-about young wrestlers in NCAA history, sporting a 27-2 record.

Their match began.

For a while, Harris was in trouble, hovering on the edge of losing it all.

To begin the second period, Baumgartner chose the position of advantage and rode Harris until the Beaver star escaped with 43 seconds to go.

This was a true Clash of the Titans, each wrestler looking for the other to make the slightest error. Baumgartner blinked first, by not reacting fast enough when Harris suddenly back-tripped him. Down went the 255-pound super sophomore, and Harris was on top in a flash, pinning him at the 4:35 mark.

Bedlam reigned in the stands, and everyone stayed around to watch Harris be named the tournament's outstanding wrestler. The victory was also the 169th of his career, an NCAA record, breaking the old mark of 168 wins by OSU heavyweight and national champion Bielenberg in 1975.

Bielenberg was at Gill Coliseum that night, cheering Harris on. Afterward, the jubilant OSU alum, his arms around Harris's neck, had this to say: "Howard scared the heck out of me tonight because I'd watched this [Baumgartner] kid wrestle in the first two rounds, and he's a powerful guy. I didn't like it when he was riding Howard because a powerful guy like that can tire you out. But he escaped. With Howard you never know. All things are possible."

But Thomas wasn't worried.

"The fight wasn't taken out of Howard because I had confidence in his conditioning. He was the best-conditioned wrestler at the tournament and I knew he'd be all right if he didn't get psyched out. I didn't read panic in his face; worry maybe, but not concern."

Howard Harris was immediately selected an All-American and became one of the elite few in OSU's history to win this honor over all four years of eligibility. In the last 20 years, only three other OSU athletes have been so honored.

On March 15, 1980, the honor was Howard Harris's, and fans will always remember this great moment in the history of Gill Coliseum.

30

They Were No. 1

For longtime Beaver loyalists, Oregon State's stunning drive to the Tostitos Fiesta Bowl in the autumn of 2000 stirred memories of another time and another sport. Twenty years earlier, the OSU men's basketball team captured the hearts and imaginations of an entire state during an unprecedented rise to the top of the college basketball world. Only this was no one-year magic-carpet ride from the outhouse to the penthouse. This was no unlikely fairy-tale orchestrated by an ingenious coaching staff and athletic administration that pushed all the right buttons. This was the real thing, and for Beaver Believers it's never been any better—except for that fateful final moment in March.

Oregon State was the fourth winningest basketball program in NCAA history entering the winter of 1980-81, only 78 victories behind all-time leader Kentucky at the onset of a season that held special promise.

The Beavers' crusty coach, Ralph Miller, had improved on what he had learned from the game's inventor, James Naismith, and built powerhouses at Wichita State, Iowa and OSU. The Beavers were coming off a 26-4 season in which only a shocking first-round loss to Lamar in the NCAA Tournament had short-circuited an anticipated run at the title.

Every key player was returning, and Miller had recruited the final two pieces to an elegant, immaculately fitting puzzle: All-America junior college guard Lester Conner and All-America high school forward Charlie Sitton.

Yes, before Dennis Erickson, Fiesta Fever and a budding football juggernaut, there was the Orange Express, and in 1980-81 The Express was, in the immortal words of broadcaster Darrell Aune, "Red Hot and Roooolllllling!"

Sellout crowds of 10,000 were the norm, and the fire marshal looked the other way as every nook and cranny of creaky old Gill Coliseum was filled with hot-blooded Beavers. Students slept overnight in the cold rain on the steps of Gill to get prime seating. Boosters traveled with the team by the hundreds, even thousands, in the longest continuous athletic party in school history.

Corvallis was bathed in orange.

The Beavers carved up opponents with precise, almost monotonous ease en route to a 26-0 start. It was, even by OSU's lofty standards, an extraordinary team—certainly the best in school history and, according to the pollsters, the best in the nation for nearly two months.

They were so good that tortured Beaver Believers were certain that OSU would escape the first-round postseason jinx that haunted the program two years earlier against Nevada-Reno in the National Invitation Tournament and the previous year against outmanned Lamar in the NCAA Tournament.

"I really thought that team would make the Final Four," Miller recalled 20 years later at his retirement home in Black Butte, Oregon, where he lived until his death in May 2001 at age 81.

Indeed, in the winter of 1980-81, Corvallis and the rest of the state was caught up in a sports frenzy matched only by the Portland Trail Blazers' march to the NBA title four years earlier.

As they headed to Los Angeles for their first NCAA Tournament game at UCLA's Pauley Pavilion, the Beavers were poised to roll to the first basketball title in school history and second NCAA championship in any sport.

What happened next remains frozen in infamy, forever etched by a dull ache in the hearts and minds of 40-plus OSU boosters, most of whom can remember precisely where they were and what they were doing the moment Rolando Blackman rose for his fateful shot.

******

They were an eclectic group with diverse backgrounds, brought together by a legendary coach who took less touted players with heart and smarts, then molded them into refined basketball players.

There was Mark Radford, the studious and elegant senior off-guard from Portland's Grant High. There was Ray Blume, the street-smart and rough-hewn senior wing from Parkrose. There was Charlie Sitton, the folksy freshman farmboy from McMinnville. There was Lester "The Molester" Conner, the tireless junior point guard from Fremont-Chabot (California) Junior College, who was the final piece to the puzzle.

And at the hub was Steve Johnson, the one blue-chip recruit in his class. The once-troubled six-foot-11 post from San Bernardino, California, had turned his life around by finding religion—and then he started finding the basket like no other player in NCAA history.

"The finest post man in the country," Miller called him.

The Beavers first showed flashes of greatness during the 1978-79 season, when sophomores Johnson, Blume and Radford led the team to an 18-10 record and gave eventual national champion Michigan State, with Earvin "Magic" Johnson, all it could handle in a 65-57 loss in the Far West Classic.

A year later and wiser, OSU threatened to steal the reins from previously unchallenged Pacific-10 Conference powerhouse UCLA, which was five years removed from its streak of 10 national titles in 12 years.

Both seasons were tainted only by the inexplicable first-round postseason losses, 62-61 at home against Nevada-Reno in the NIT in 1979 and 81-77 to Lamar a year later after the Beavers had earned a first-round bye in the 48-team NCAA field.

The players were an orchestra and Miller was their conductor. The 61-year-old Kansas University graduate loved pressure defense and hated the bounce pass, with one notable exception. He loved disciplined offense and hated showboating.

He ran a tight ship from the sidelines, where he alternately growled and smoked his familiar More cigarettes in practice, and he ran off anybody whose view of the basketball world differed from what he viewed behind his wide-rimmed glasses.

"He's a great guy when he's not around the game of basketball, but when it comes to basketball he's realistic about the game," Blume said. "He's going to tell you what's going to win the games and what's going to lose them. He's not going to pat you on the back if you make a great play. He'll tell you you'd better go back and play some defense.

"That kind of sums the man up."

Agreed Miller: "For me, it all boiled down to this: You either do what I want you to do, or you don't play; make up your mind. And I didn't argue with them. Either you learned it or you didn't. If you didn't, you sat on the bench forever."

*Lester Conner led OSU to two NCAA tournament wins in 1982.
(Photo courtesy of Barry Schwartz.)*

Miller rarely had any issues with the 1980-81 edition.

Conner was the point man in an aggressive defense that suffocated opposing offenses. The Beavers' 1-4 offense ran in remarkable synchronicity. Without a shot clock, OSU patiently worked the ball until defenses tired or eventually ran into one too many screens. The most vivid memory of longtime Beaver loyalists is of Blume, Conner or Radford cutting back door and taking a pass from the wide-bodied Johnson for a layup.

"So watch closely," wrote Curry Kirkpatrick of *Sports Illustrated*. "The unselfish, quick-witted folks in the backcourt will spread the floor, whirl the ball around the horn like berserk infielders turning triple plays and then, suddenly, shoot the lights out, forcing the opposition to focus its defense on the perimeter. Then it will be time for Johnson to go to work inside and…well, who were those masked men?"

Joked Miller at the time: "This is some bunch. I can't even show them game films of themselves. All they do is clap."

Teams tried everything in those pre-shot clock days in a futile attempt to stop the Beavers. Stanford even attempted an all-out stall the previous season. OSU won 18-16.

Once the Beavers took the lead, it was over. And with their pressure defense, no deficit was insurmountable.

Their average margin of victory was 15.8. Johnson set an NCAA record with a 74.6 field-goal percentage, which still stands. The team shot a whopping 56.4 percent. And on Jan. 13, 1981, after top-ranked DePaul finally stumbled, the Beavers rose to No. 1 for the first time in school history.

Fans celebrated, and the party would continue for two months, all the way to the regular-season finale against fourth-ranked Arizona State, a team the Beavers had dispatched 71-67 two months earlier in Tempe, Arizona, on the one night where they had to break a sweat.

The Beavers had clinched the Pac-10 title two nights earlier with a trouncing of outclassed Arizona, but there was no lack of incentive in facing the Sun Devils. It was Senior Night, and a packed house paid an emotional tribute to a group that had fashioned a 52-4 record over two seasons.

Thus it was an ominous salvo fired when Arizona State—with a gifted starting five of Byron Scott, Fat Lever, Alton Lister, Kurt Nimphius and Sam Williams—overwhelmed OSU 87-67 in front of a stunned crowd.

Afterward, during a somber Pac-10 championship presentation, commissioner Wiles Hallock tried to ease OSU's pain.

"I'd rather be involved in this under more pleasant circumstances," Hallock said.

"But let me tell you this. This loss is not the end of the world, and it may be a blessing in disguise."

Indeed, for several weeks fans had wondered if the pressure was mounting, and some suggested that a loss would do the Beavers well.

"Maybe Lamar came early this year," *Corvallis Gazette-Times* sports editor Roy Gault wrote.

Huffed Miller: "I don't know that I buy the idea that we should lose a game. Everyone keeps telling me it would be nice to lose one, and I've been hearing that for two months. I never said I agree, but now we've lost one. We'll see."

Five days later, the Beavers were en route to UCLA's Pauley Pavilion, where they would watch Kansas State meet San Francisco in a first-round game. OSU had earned a bye by virtue of its league title.

At the time, a bye was considered a reward. Within a week, serious debate had begun as to whether it was a reward or a hindrance.

******

Kansas State and San Francisco squared off on Thursday in the tournament's equivalent of an eight-seed taking on a nine-seed, and the Wildcats won 64-60.

Beaver Believers weren't concerned, thinking that if OSU simply played its game, either team would be dusted easily. The odds were 45-1 on the Wildcats winning the tournament, 7-1 on OSU.

"Kansas State has a great capacity to make a team think it just played the worst game of the year," OSU assistant coach Lanny Van Eman cautioned. "There have been 14 or 15 teams shake their heads and say they didn't play well against the Wildcats."

Kansas State was indeed a dangerous opponent to those in the know.

The coach, Jack Hartman, came from the same tree that produced Miller. Hartman was coaching at Coffeyville (Kansas) Junior College when Miller was down the road at Wichita State in the 1950s.

The Wildcats thrived on precision offense and pressure defense. They had a go-to guy in Blackman, a sturdy inside player in Ed Nealy and a strong guard named Tim Jankovich, who had started his career at Washington State. The one element they didn't have was an answer for Johnson, the wide-bodied center.

The good news for the Beavers was that they didn't have to worry about Pac-10 officiating in the tournament. Miller had spent much of the season fuming about the league's referees, particularly the attention they paid to Johnson, who had fouled out of seven games.

The bad news was that UCLA students learned the Beavers were staying at the Westwood Holiday Inn, and they spent much of the Friday night before the game calling the players' rooms to keep them awake.

"The night before the game was a nightmare," recalls Jean Miller, Ralph's wife of 58 years. "Somebody was harassing us with a fictitious story."

The clerk at the front desk was a foreign student who spoke broken English. It was nearly 3 a.m. before the Millers could get the phones turned off.

Still, the Beavers played well enough to keep the Wildcats at arm's length most of the way. K-State did a solid job of limiting Johnson's touches, but OSU led by 10 in the first half, 26-19 at intermission and 42-32 with 11:30 to play.

In those days, with OSU's discipline and precision as well as lack of a shot clock, a 10-point lead might as well have been 30.

Nealy scored on a rebound basket and was fouled for a three-point play and Blackman hit a 12-footer on which Johnson was whistled for his third foul. But Blume hit a layup and guard Jeff Stoutt buried a 17-footer for a 46-39 lead.

"They were moving away from us and I was thinking, 'Oh, oh, it's over,'" said Hartman, who died in 1998.

Yet it was far from over.

Stoutt's basket was OSU's last, and still eight minutes remained.

Johnson hit a baby hook at 5:20 to apparently give the Beavers a 48-44 lead, but it was waved off and the big center was called for a charge, his fourth foul. Then, with the score 48-46, Blume got a steal but missed a layup in traffic.

Johnson was called for his fifth foul going for the rebound.

The Beavers were getting anxious. The UCLA students were noisily hopping on K-State's bandwagon.

Nealy made both free throws to tie the game 48-48 with 3:23 to play; then Sitton went to the line at 2:03 to put OSU ahead. He missed the front end of a one-and-one.

K-State rebounded and killed nearly two minutes. With 14 seconds on the clock, Blackman faked a back-door cut and came to the top of the key to retrieve the ball. He dribbled toward the right baseline and went up over Radford, who tapped Blackman on his right elbow as he shot.

The ball swished through the net, bringing down the collective hopes and dreams of an entire state with it. Final score: KSU 50, OSU 48.

The Beavers frantically called time out, but the best they could muster with less than two seconds was a 45-footer by Stoutt that fell way short.

They stood on the floor afterward in stunned disbelief.

"You have to say what we did," said Stoutt, who now lives in Amity. "We choked."

Said Johnson: "We just didn't play like a championship team."

Just like that, the season—and the dream—was over.

******

"It was very hard on Ralph," Jean Miller said.

"You wouldn't have known it then, but he was very disappointed because that was such a great team and they were so beautiful to watch. I still hate to watch close games."

What went wrong? How could OSU have stumbled again in the first round?

Some suggested that the Beavers were too tight under Miller's direction. The debate would become more intense in future years as OSU would become renowned—like the Buffalo Bills and Minnesota Vikings losing Super Bowls—for falling in the first round of postseason tournaments. Though the Beavers would win two games and make the Sweet Sixteen of the NCAA Tournament a year later, they were first-round failures in 1984 (West Virginia), 1985 (Notre Dame), 1988 (Louisville), 1989 (Evansville) and 1990 (Ball State).

They haven't been back since.

Others thought OSU simply didn't match up in talent once it reached the NCAA Tournament. Miller had milked the most that was possible out of average talent.

Still others, including the feisty Sitton, suggested the Beavers lacked killer instinct.

"This is the nicest bunch of guys I've ever been around," Miller said. "Maybe they're too nice."

Other attention was focused on the tournament format. The bye hurt the top teams because it enabled lower seeds to get first-round jitters out of the way. Indeed, eight of 16 teams that had a bye lost that year. The NCAA Tournament has since expanded to 65 teams, leaving nobody with a bye.

"There's not logic for this," Miller said then. "But this is the way the pickle is squirting."

The reasons hardly mattered.

The pain was excruciating. Beaver Believers still remember where they were the moment Blackman's shot fell.

"Maybe if we had won it all, we'd look back and say, 'Gee, it was fun,'" Radford said. "But sacrificing as much as we did and not to achieve our goal..."

The Millers stayed for several days in Los Angeles. When addressing a group of about 150 boosters afterward, "Old Whiskey Sour" nearly broke down.

"You might feel bad, but you don't feel nearly as bad as I do," he said then.

"I don't feel for myself because I've lost a lot of games over the years. Nothing in the world could dull the ache and the hurt in the hearts of these young men who represent Oregon State University."

Today, the game is indelibly etched in memory banks at OSU and K-State. Tell the sports information department in Manhattan that you're a sports reporter from Corvallis, and they know exactly what you want.

Most of the key participants have become remarkable success stories.

Blackman became a Hall of Fame player for the Dallas Mavericks of the NBA and later became an assistant there. Jankovich is an assistant at Vanderbilt University in Nashville, Tennessee. Nealy is a successful businessman in San Antonio, Texas.

All five Beaver starters went on to careers in the NBA, with Johnson having the most success. Many still live in Oregon, and those who live in the Portland area—Johnson, Radford, Blume, Bill McShane and Sitton—still play some ball together.

Sitton, who would play with Blackman for two years with the Mavericks, runs a hotel in Tualatin. Blume works for the Multnomah County Road Department. Conner has been an NBA assistant and owned a Legends restaurant in southern California. McShane, who remembers himself as the "President of the Pine [bench] Club," is a financial adviser.

Some like to remember; others try to forget.

It seems so long ago at a school that now cherishes success in another sport in another era, but in many ways it seems like yesterday.

Radford has never watched a tape of the game.

"I still can't tell you what happened," he said.

Neither can Miller, a Hall of Fame coach who acknowledged eight months before his death in May 2001 that the most vivid memory of his 19 years at OSU "is one of disappointment."

"It's about as empty as I've ever been," he said, "at least in basketball."

31

Thanks, A. C.

If the success of a university's athletic department is measured not just in wins and losses, but in character and values, ethics and generosity, admiration and respect, then Oregon State truly has itself a champion in A. C. Green. The Beaver basketball great (1982-85) was an iron man on the court, where he set an NBA record for consecutive games played, and in his heart, which has earned him a place in the Humanitarian Hall of Fame. Green didn't know it at the time, but his memorable NBA career had come to an end when he was interviewed in July 2001 while operating the scoreboard clock for his annual summer camp at Concordia College in his hometown of Portland.

Silence engulfs the cozy gym at Portland's Concordia University and some 75 teenage basketball hopefuls freeze as the towering presence at midcourt starts to speak.

"Team One," he says, "talk to me."

More silence. The dozen members of Team One, standing in a single row along the baseline, squirm. The others are motionless as they watch. The leader had asked for 15 jumping jacks from the group. Somebody on Team One lost focus and did 16. Nobody wants to confess.

"What have we talked about honesty and character?" the leader prods, firmly but gently.

At last, acknowledgement comes from the guilty party.

A. C. Green smiles.

"All right, honesty—thank you," he says. "You were being honest even though there was a lot of pressure on you."

Everybody claps, and the A. C. Green Leadership Camp continues, with its namesake soon to be involved in everything from calisthenics and operating the scoreboard to participating in skits and sweeping the floor.

For 16 years, the most durable player in National Basketball Association history and Oregon State University Hall of Famer has returned to this old brick gym in the neighborhood he still calls home, not so much to teach basketball but to share bigger-picture convictions with an increasingly troubled generation of kids.

Honesty. Character. Compassion. Courage. Fairness. Integrity.

A. C. Green doesn't talk the talk. He simply walks the walk.

At a time when many pro athletes lend their name to a camp, show up for the introductory first day and then disappear with a fat paycheck, Green has missed one day of his Portland camp in 16 years. That happened when he left abruptly to attend the funeral of a cousin who was killed in a car accident in Los Angeles. He paid for his entire family to fly to L.A., and then returned to Portland the next day.

Along with brothers Steve and Lee, A. C. is one of the first to arrive and the last to leave his camp. He has been known to ride a bicycle past the neatly manicured lawns and older homes in his northeast Portland neighborhood to the quiet Lutheran campus that has been the oft-troubled area's anchor for several decades.

He high-fives the kids, wrestles playfully with his nephews and remembers names of campers from years back.

He doesn't receive a nickel.

"He's willing to invest his time back into his neighborhood, but it's the way he does it that's special," says Joel Schuldheisz, Concordia's athletic director and a longtime friend of Green's. "You can see he's here for the love of the game and young people."

To Green, it all seems so natural—as natural as lacing up his sneakers for a record 1,192 consecutive NBA games over 16 years, reading the Bible at 5 a.m. and steadfastly resisting the urges to relinquish his renown as the league's only known virgin.

This, he says, is the plan God had for him and the reason He bestowed upon him a special gift called basketball.

"It's just a reflection of our hearts flowing," Green says. "It's a part of me. I could complain about all the problems coming up with kids, but rather than complain I'm trying to find solutions.

"It's a message bigger than me."

For all that he stands for, all that he's been and all that he hopes to become, A. C. Green—his father, A. C. Sr., won't say what the initials stand for, if anything—credits his faith, his family and, in no small way, the four years (1981-86) he spent at Oregon State University.

******

In 1981, Green arrived on the OSU campus sporting kinky Shirley Temple locks, a gaudy basketball resume and a reputation unfairly sullied by a gambling debt skirmish that actually involved his gregarious older brother Lee.

Never did anyone imagine that one day he would become one of the finest players the school has ever produced, the NBA version of Cal Ripken Jr. and a worldwide poster child for humanitarian efforts.

Even in the family, only his dignified and gracious mother, Leola, knew of his extraordinary basketball talents until his sophomore year at Benson Tech in Portland, when Lee decided to take a detour from his usual stop to look longingly at cars at Lou Williams Cadillac. Lee noticed a full parking lot down the street at Benson and ventured inside in time to see his brother swooping for a dunk and hear the PA announcer gush.

"I didn't think of anything like this happening," Lee says of his brother's fame.

A. C., who never pined for an NBA or collegiate career while growing up, merely wanted to graduate from high school so that he might one day leave a neighborhood that remains an inextricable part of his fabric.

"I didn't have that fire in my belly," he recalls. "That wasn't me. Basketball was just something I enjoyed. I didn't plan on going to college. My goal was to make it out of my particular situation to the next. Get a nice job—that would've been cool with me. But God had a bigger plan.

"Proverbs, 18th chapter, says, 'A man's gift will make room for him.' The gift of basketball has opened up a lot of doors for me."

Green, who turns 40 on October 4, 2003, parlayed his gift into a solid NBA career in which he has played with hardscrabble elegance and stoic grace.

The fourth leading scorer and second leading rebounder in OSU history never missed a game after November 18, 1986, his second year with the Los Angeles Lakers.

Yet for all of Green's on-court exploits, he is even better known for his commitment to community in Portland, Los Angeles and Phoenix—the three cities other than Corvallis that figure most prominently in his life.

He oversees the A. C. Green Youth Foundation in Phoenix. He operates numerous leadership camps. He is an outspoken advocate of sexual abstinence and has unflinchingly discussed his virginity on the *Oprah Winfrey Show*.

On September 25, he was inducted into the World Sports Humanitarian Hall of Fame in Boise, Idaho.

"Yeah, he's an athlete, but he's an athlete with a brand," says Rob Michaels, his agent. "He's the real deal."

Adds his mother, Leola: "I'm very proud. I see a humble person, a beautiful person, a spiritual person. We are blessed to have him represent the young people. He doesn't put on airs. It's just what he stands for.

"He's just himself."

******

A. C. Green Sr., who grew up in El Centro, California, and maintained cars for a Portland dealership, and Leola Green, a switchboard operator at Nordstrom, already had given birth to three children when the last Green arrived on October 4, 1963, in Portland.

The first three were named Vanessa, Lee and Steve, but as soon as Leola saw No. 4 she knew.

"He looked so much like his daddy that I said I'm going to name him A. C.," she said.

Hence, while the rest of the world has known him as A. C., at home it's always Junior.

Junior split much of his youth between school, church and the courts at John Jacob Aster Elementary School and Woodlawn Park, where Lee was as gentle as a pit bull.

"If it wasn't for me taking him down to the park every day and putting it on him, he wouldn't be where he is today," says Lee, 41, the family character. "I shouldn't play ball against him now because he'll get his revenge. He might have flashbacks."

A. C. was an ordinary five-foot-11 ninth grader, but by his senior year he was six foot eight, averaging 26.0 points per game and earning state Player of the Year honors. He committed to join an OSU basketball team that had been ranked No. 1 nationally for nine weeks the previous winter.

Christianity had become a distant part of Green's life, and he had even quit going to church. Then a friend in the Fellowship of Christian Athletes asked him to join a group driving to Hermiston, Oregon, for a religion class taught by a Benson Tech faculty member.

Green hesitated, relented and, on August 2, 1981, became a Christian for life. At OSU, he joined the Maranatha ministry and could frequently be seen on campus reading aloud from a Bible.

Green's years in Corvallis were pivotal in his personal, professional and spiritual development. He fondly remembers his pastor, his academic advisor, his coaches and other families guiding him through difficult transitions.

"That's when habits start developing," he says of his college years.

He recites the names of the most significant contributors as if they were guiding him today: best friend Lee Johnson, legendary coach Ralph Miller, assistants Lanny Van Eman and Jimmy Anderson, pastor David Elliott, and the Fenner family of Corvallis. He even remembers the names of the advisors who helped turn a naïve kid into a conscientious student who earned a degree in four years.

"They helped me focus on school," Green explains. "I didn't want to come back to school when I got done playing."

Of the crusty Miller, his legendary basketball coach, he says: "Ralph played a strong role in my life."

For all that his four years in Corvallis has provided him, he is giving back.

Green has established a fund at OSU for ethnic minorities. He says he eventually plans to start youth programs in Corvallis with Johnson, who today works for the state in drug prevention and gives speeches at Green's camps about the evils of narcotics.

"We just talked about it—what can we do around the city of Corvallis?" Green says. "We owe a lot to our time there. A lot of people there helped me along the way. Most of what I've learned, I learned in Corvallis. It's where I learned the difference between conviction and opinion."

To this day, he gets misty-eyed when he hears OSU's alma mater.

A. C. Green makes a pass at Gill Coliseum.
(Photo courtesy of Barry Schwartz.)

It was at OSU, at a time when the sexual revolution was in full bloom, that Green made his first public stand for sexual abstinence. Twenty years later, he beats the abstinence drum so tirelessly that he is at least as famous for his virginity streak as he is for his consecutive games played.

Indeed, in a recent mainstream movie called *The Brothers*, about four African-American friends who are forced to confront issues with honesty and commitment after one marries, one of the characters decides to abstain from sex until marriage.

"Who do you think you are," a third says incredulously, "A. C. Green?"

Green, described by *Sports Illustrated* as "The Only NBA Player Who Has Never Scored," has never seen the movie, but former Miami Heat teammates told him the story. Once they might have kidded him, but now they relate the tale with respect for a man who lives his convictions but refuses to browbeat others into following his lead.

To Green, the movie is an indicator of the role, however small, that he's had in altering cultural mindsets.

As a longtime player in Los Angeles, a glittery city that embodies much that he stands against, he has used his stage to coax makers of movies, television shows and videos to include unmarried characters who save sex for marriage.

In a league where some players have more kids out of wedlock than cars in their garage, Green was once almost a freak show. He was the butt of jokes on Letterman and *The Tonight Show* with Jay Leno.

But he's seeing a slow evolution in the NBA, too.

"You would think of him as a goody-two-shoes from the outside looking in," Heat teammate Anthony Mason once said. "It was something to make fun of when you weren't there, but to see it up close, to see how his life has benefited, you realize that's the way you're supposed to live."

Green didn't waver in 20 years despite flocks of female groupies hoping to snap one of his famed streaks.

"It's a message to a culture that has a lot of confusion from a lot of sources," Green said of sexual mores. "Parents tell kids one thing and live by a different standard. Churches do the same thing. They pass out condoms and teach about alternatives. I'm challenging personal behavior.

"If that's the biggest part of my legacy, that's fine. I've got to try to work on it and keep it a focal point. That's why I've stayed so long."

It isn't that he sees sex as "dirty." Nor is it all about his religion; he notes that he was a steadfast virgin long before he was a devoted Christian, though he sheepishly admits that in high school he bragged about sexual conquests he never made.

"Sex itself isn't a bad thing," he said. "That's the most crazy and ludicrous thing. But there is a time and place for it."

For Green, that time and place is marriage. He dated seriously only twice, but he always knew one day he will bring a special gift to a union.

After all, abstinence makes the heart grow fonder.

Or, as brother Lee put it with a hearty laugh, "I don't know when or where he's going to find the right one, but boy, boy, boy—somebody's going to be in big trouble."

That somebody is Veronique Green. They were married April 20, 2002, in Los Angeles.

"I have waited a while for marriage to take place, but my beautiful wife has been well worth the wait," Green said.

Said Veronique: "A. C. is the man I have waited for my whole life. To know that he has also been faithful in waiting for me is the best wedding present I could ever imagine."

Green's life remains a whirlwind.

The two weeks he spends at his camp at Concordia each summer in his old neighborhood provide a rare opportunity for a deep breath.

Now that his NBA career is over, he has a variety of business interests and humanitarian efforts under way.

He owns 12 Denny's restaurants in the Portland, Salem and The Dalles areas, a company he chose because has always liked the food and it was one place he could afford growing up. He has a company called Integrity Media, which produces movies, TV shows and videos, including an upcoming film called *The Final Solution* about an Afrikaaner man in South Africa coming to grips with his oppression of blacks.

He also owns Bio Sport, a sports drink he says is healthier than the others out there. And he has a Hyundai auto dealership in Huntington Beach, California.

When he's finished with basketball, he plans to immerse himself even more into community work and spend more time with his nephews and nieces. His world could involve just about anything—except basketball.

"Anything around organized basketball other than watching the kids...forget about it," he said.

Whatever he does, he says, will be another step in the pursuit of spiritual perfection. This much he knows: The equation will include family, children and God, whom he calls his "head coach."

Certainly Green will continue to return to the old neighborhood, where well-to-do and at-risk kids alike gather for pearls of wisdom about accountability and responsibility from a true modern-day hero. He will be there every day, with broom in hand, scoreboard clock at his fingertips and a high-five for any focused camper who isn't wearing a Duck T-shirt.

"It's like an NBA career—you've got to prove who you are and what your game is all about," he says. "I can say anything, but you have to show it."

32

Eating Crow

There's no gentle way of saying it: In the early 1980s, the Oregon State football team was a national joke, awful even by the standards of a program that was in the process of establishing a benchmark for futility with a string of losing seasons that would reach an NCAA record of 28 straight. OSU won six games from 1980 through 1984. The 1983 Civil War was re-named "The Toilet Bowl" after the "Meager Beavers" and equally woeful Oregon Ducks played to what likely will forever remain the last 0-0 tie in NCAA Division I football history. So there wasn't a doubt in anybody's mind what would happen when the battered Beavers traveled north to play powerful Washington in 1985. As a century's worth of football games drew to a close in 1999, one game above all others stood tall in a program known for being a feisty underdog rising to knock powerhouses from their thrones.

Traveling to Seattle on the team bus that Friday, October 19, 1985, Oregon State's players and coaches tried to forget their last three games and concentrate only on the one just ahead.

It wasn't easy.

The Beavers had been greatly embarrassed. And it hurt.

Against Washington State the week before, the score was 34-0. Before that, Southern California humiliated them 63-0. In OSU's long and storied football past, no team had ever given up 97 points in back-to-back games.

Before USC there had been Grambling, an NCAA Division II school out of the Southwest Athletic Conference in the Deep South.

The Tigers from north Louisiana showed no mercy, whipping OSU 27-6. Six points in three games. The defense had allowed 124 points. Only two OSU teams, in 1954 and 1974, had done worse over a three-game stretch.

And it wasn't just the mounting losses that hurt. Across the board, negative numbers on the program were piling up.

By 1985, the Beavers had suffered through 14 straight losing seasons, a school record. It had been 20 years since they had gone to a bowl, and that one had ended in a 34-7 Michigan rout in 1965. From 1972 through 1985, the Beavers had won but 21 games, with seven victories coming before 1974.

Directing the '85 team was first-year head coach Dave Kragthorpe, an older, experienced mentor who had won a Division I-AA national championship a few years earlier at Idaho State. He was considered an offensive whiz.

Using a Brigham Young-type passing offense that seemed to confuse opponents at first, OSU started the season 2-0, its best since 1967. But by the Grambling contest on September 28, the new "Air Express" offense was having trouble getting back off the ground.

Now it was time for the Pacific-10 Conference-leading Washington Huskies. The players let their minds move forward to the friends, family and fans waiting for them in Seattle. No one was ready to admit he was probably living through the lowest moment of the century for OSU football—a bottoming out.

But light sometimes has a way of penetrating even the darkest corners of a room. Before the weekend was over, Kragthorpe and his team would establish for all time an example of what it means to be Beaver proud.

All during the week the OSU coaching staff had stressed that the UW game would not be about winning and losing. It would be about becoming a better team. Kragthorpe said he wanted everyone to play well enough to move the program up another notch. It was the kind of coach's pep talk you hear when you play for a school on the rebuild.

For the Beavers to move up, they would have to do so with their two best offensive weapons riding the bench with injuries: quarterback Erik Wilhelm (out for the season) and Reggie Bynum, the Pac-10's leading receiver.

In Wilhelm's place would be freshman Rich Gonzales, a backup quarterback who had taken nine snaps with the first unit the entire year.

When the betting line came in on the game in Las Vegas, everyone had a chuckle. Oddsmakers had the Huskies as 38-point favorites. As the spread hit the newsrooms of Seattle, insults began flying off typewriters. One sportswriter after another rushed to see who could fire off the next insult at the visiting country cousins from Corvallis.

As soon as OSU stepped off the bus at the hotel, fans began passing around a newspaper, folded to an editorial in the sports section of the *Seattle Post-Intelligencer.*

"Oregon State plays football pretty much the way Barney Fife played a deputy sheriff on Mayberry. They have ceased being a joke. They are not only an embarrassment to themselves and their fans…they are an embarrassment to the Pac-10."

The words of columnist Steve Rudman cut into the team's pride like a butcher knife.

More Rudman: "If Dave Kragthorpe can just make the Beavers halfway competitive, he will be doing the whole conference a very big favor. Beaverball, after all, is a blight that has gone on long enough."

That night, as OSU's players settled into their hotel rooms for the evening, local TV sports shows continued the barrage.

On one station, UW head coach Don James was saying he expected the game against the Beavers to offer his reserve quarterback Chris Chandler a chance for some playing time.

Another sportscaster, referring to Washington's bye the weekend after OSU, slyly remarked it was as if the Huskies had two weeks off to prepare for the rest of the season, a campaign they fully expected to cap off with a trip to Pasadena on New Year's Day.

By the time of the game, everyone from Corvallis knew Rudman's editorial by heart. Kragthorpe used it to good effect in his pregame pep talk. On this day, OSU's new coach would not need any extra emotion in his voice to get his players ready to rumble. Rudman had taken care of that. Beaver radio announcer Darrell Aune kept his listeners entertained (and stirred up) before kickoff by sharing large excerpts of Rudman's prose over the air.

To add insult to injury, the Huskies seemed reluctant during pregame drills to do anything but watch OSU. To the guys from Corvallis, the message was subtle but clear: We don't have to warm up to beat you.

As the Beavers at last jogged down the ramp and out onto the field at huge Husky Stadium, the home team, using the same entrance and bunched in a group just to their rear, began barking at them like dogs.

It was the final straw. As OSU took the field for the kickoff, everyone, from the water boy on up, was ready for war.

Even so, Washington struck first in the opening quarter with a field goal to take a 3-0 lead. It was a prize of sorts for the Beaver defense. Washington had started this series of downs with a first and 10 from the Beaver 27. The defense that had allowed 97 points in two games had held, at least for now.

Then Gonzales went to work, stunning the highly partisan crowd of 56,544 with a 43-yard touchdown strike to Darvin Malone for a 7-3 OSU lead.

Receiving the kick, Washington marched 80 yards in 15 plays for a score, putting the home team ahead 10-7. Now it was the Beavers' turn to answer. The best they could do was a fourth down and 20 from their 28. A strong Husky rush forced punter Glenn Pena to make a desperate run for a first down. He was tackled 10 yards short, and Washington had the ball on the Beaver 38. OSU fans braced for an onslaught.

Sometimes in a game, a little thing can happen to give an underdog hope. With first and goal from the eight, Washington tried blowing OSU off the ball—loss of two. On the next play, safety Reggie Hawkins intercepted a pass in the end zone and the Beavers were back in business. Taking over on its 20, OSU drove 80 yards on seven pass completions and finished the drive with a spectacular 20-yard touchdown scamper by Gonzales. OSU 14-10.

At halftime, a Seattle sportswriter in the press box turned around to a Beaver contingent sitting nearby and asked, "When's the real Oregon State gonna show up?"

The third quarter produced a Husky touchdown and the lead, 17-13. The Corvallis country cousins still had a chance, but somebody was going to have to step up big.

Again, the defense did the trick, and it happened with 1:32 remaining in the third quarter. UW was sitting pretty with first and goal from the one. A score this late in the game would probably cause OSU to cave in. If ever there was a time for the Huskies to make good the brag of their local sports scribes, it was right now.

Washington tried twice to ram the ball down Oregon State's throat. The Beaver defensive front proved impenetrable. On third down, tailback Vance Weathersby fumbled, and OSU's Lavance Northington recovered. Beaver linebacker Osia Lewis had delivered the knockout blow, one of his 19 tackles. Yes, a knockout blow—Weathersby had to leave the game.

With 7:59 remaining in the fourth quarter, UW upped its lead again with a field goal, 20-14. From this point on, OSU's defense would rise up and play some of the most historic minutes ever put in by an Orange and Black team.

At 1:29 left in the game, the Huskies were deep in their own territory, out of downs and forced to punt. Always taking great pride in their special teams play, they anticipated nothing out of the ordinary.

OSU's Andre Todd didn't see it that way. Tearing into the backfield and rushing straight for the ball, Todd extended his arms and felt his hand pulsate. He knew instantly what he had done. He watched the pigskin fly back toward the end zone to his left.

The problem was, it was heading straight for the *back* of the end zone. If it skipped over the line, the Beavers were dead and everyone knew it. The most they could get would be a safety, two points. They needed six.

Hearts stopped.

Time stood still.

A giant gasp rose in the air from 55,000 mouths.

Please don't let it go out of the end zone.

Pleeeeaasse…

…and then suddenly, as if hitting an invisible wall, suddenly, as if the invisible hand of an F. S. Norcross or a Wes Schulmerich or a Jess Lewis had reached out to deflect it, the ball did what footballs sometimes do: it took this funny dart and became a traitor to the Husky cause. Northington pounced on it and that was that.

Touchdown Beavers!

Do you believe in miracles?

The extra-point by Jim Nielsen was good and proved to be the winner. One last Washington try for a score ended at midfield. Then the game was over. Pandemonium reigned as the Beavers left the field. "You can blame this one on your media," jubilant OSU players yelled as they filed into a locker room building to chaos.

It didn't take long for the local news, now singing a different tune, to tell the Beavers exactly what they had done.

This wasn't just another big upset. It was the biggest ever. No team in the history of college football, as far as the experts could tell, had ever beaten a 38-point spread.

Somehow, this didn't seem as important to the Beavers as the statement they had just made with their never-say-die play: the statement that they *belonged*, that on any given Saturday they could compete with the big dogs.

Beaver players raise their hands in triumph as they score the winning TD over the Washington Huskies, Oct. 20, 1985, in Seattle. Rated 38-point underdogs at kickoff, OSU's stunning win was the biggest upset in Division I football history up to that time.
(Photo courtesy of The Beaver.*)*

A few doors down from his players, Kragthorpe sat at a table staring out at a room full of empty chairs. He was waiting to answer questions from the Seattle media.

They never showed up.

Could be that crow tastes better to the vanquished when eaten out of sight of the victors.

33

The Miracle Worker

He arrived in Corvallis in 1999 with a gaudy college resume, a love of the Pacific Northwest and a burning desire to erase a forgettable NFL tenure—a combination that had OSU football fans giddy with anticipation. Yet not even the most starry-eyed Beaver Believer could envision what Dennis Erickson accomplished in his first two years as head coach. When 2001 dawned, Erickson's Beavers, just one year removed from halting a 28-year losing streak, had finished 11-1 and demolished fabled Notre Dame in the Fiesta Bowl. By the fall of 2002, after guiding OSU to its third bowl game in four years, he was on a pedestal like few other coaches in school history. Who is the man behind the miracle?

You'd think the man behind one of the most remarkable turnarounds in college football history, a man who ranks among the winningest coaches of all time, a man who has won two national championships, would be shrouded in a mystique thicker than coastal fog.

You'd think that TV cameras would lock onto his every movement, that analysts would fawn over his every word, that fans would bow in his presence.

You'd think he'd at least have a nickname like "The Wizard of Corvallis" or "Magic Erickson" or "The General."

But no.

Except for one extraordinary gift—an innate ability to coax young men to commit their unwavering support and then follow him into passionate battle on the football field—the most striking aspect about Dennis Erickson is that he's a strikingly regular guy.

Always has been.

And, in all probability, always will be.

The 55-year-old football coach, the architect of Oregon State's stunning march to an unprecedented 11-1 record in 2000 and 41-9 Fiesta Bowl rout of Notre Dame on January 1, 2001, has been mellowed by age, hardened by stinging criticism, bolstered by success and humbled by his own mistakes.

Yet he remains largely the same boy-next-door sports junkie who left Everett (Washington) High School with a solid B average, a sizeable heart, a dry sense of humor and a powerful gravitational pull with people that mystifies his admirers to this day.

"He's just a square guy, not a big shot," says Norm Lowery, Erickson's basketball coach at Everett High from 1962-65. "He's an honest guy, but he's not squeaky clean; he's had his problems like everybody else.

"He's just an ordinary guy, but he's so damned loyal and he's a hell of a coach."

A hell of a coach indeed.

His 144-56-1 record placed him among the top five active coaches in winning percentage when he suddenly and surprisingly left for the San Francisco 49ers in February 2003. He has been Coach of the Year in three different collegiate conferences. He has had two losing seasons in 17 as a head coach, including a 5-6 mark at OSU in 2001, even though four of his five stops—including Oregon State—were considered coaching graveyards until his arrival.

He won two national championships at Miami. He rebuilt a horrendous program at Idaho into a winner two decades ago, and the Vandals are still riding his coattails to success. He needed only two years to lead downtrodden Washington State, where he had his other losing season in 1988, to a bowl game.

And then came Oregon State, where he accomplished what many thought impossible: a No. 4 national ranking only two seasons after the program completed its NCAA-record 28th consecutive losing season.

To this day, Erickson's remarkable success story is something of a marvel in Everett. It isn't because the three-sport athlete wasn't liked or respected, because he was. It's just that, except for that gravitational-pull thing with people, he was, well, so average—even on the playing field, where he was a good high school quarterback but not flashy enough to be courted by any NCAA Division I-A program.

"I wish I could say, 'Yeah, I did,'" Lowrey says of seeing a star quality in Erickson. "But I didn't know that then."

Even Erickson's father, Robert "Pink" Erickson, who coached against his only son (Pink and Mary Erickson have three daughters) in high school, admits he never envisioned Dennis advancing beyond a solid high school coaching career in Montana.

"I'm completely surprised," Pink Erickson says of Dennis's success story. "I just hoped that when he went to college and entered athletics that some day he might get himself a good high school job. Anything beyond that was beyond any dreams I might have had."

Now, with enough trophies and plaques and rings to fill a spare bedroom in his home, Erickson still doesn't have a mystique that reaches out and grabs the sporting world by the lapels. He hasn't carved a niche as a great innovator, a phenomenal recruiter or a studious Xs and Os man.

Indeed, consider that Everett High School gives a Man of the Year award to a distinguished alum every year at a charity banquet in Snohomish County.

Former Washington football coach Jim Lambright won it once. So did former Washington State coach Mike Price, whose offense was a gift from Erickson. Even Pink Erickson has won it.

Dennis Erickson didn't get it even after winning two national titles.

Always, there was somebody flashier, more flamboyant, more charismatic.

Erickson is just a regular guy who drives an SUV, listens to country and '70s music and enjoys a round of golf with the boys. He also has a disarming wit and likes to yank out his fake front tooth to get a laugh or two.

What separates him from the masses is what happens between the lines on Saturdays. He wins wherever he goes.

Those who know him best are still trying to analyze what makes this average guy such a phenom when he steps onto the sideline and dons headphones.

A decade ago, Lowrey and former Central Washington coach Tom Perry were standing on the artificial surface in Pullman, Washington, watching Erickson orchestrate a warmup about an hour before a game at Washington State, when Lowery posed the question.

"Tom, what does he do differently than you?" Lowrey asked of Perry, a successful coach in his own right. "What the hell is it that makes Dennis such a good coach?"

Perry paused thoughtfully before responding.

"I think he's the best game-day coach I've ever been around," Perry finally said. "He seems to be able to sum up a situation and respond. If you check games he's been in, they come from behind to beat clubs, and when it looks like they might be outmanned, he comes up with something. He doesn't just throw up his hands."

And, of course, he has The Gift.

From the time Erickson was very young and carried in a blanket to his father's games at Ferndale High School near Bellingham, people gravitated toward him. He was always the leader of the neighborhood sports events, which included baseball, football, track, basketball and a game called "rat-flogging" in which he and friends would wander to the city dump and chase the rodents with baseball bats and 9-irons.

Lowrey first noticed The Gift at Everett, where young Dennis, the second of the four Erickson children, would mind his own business and find the sons and daughters of the school's loggers and longshoremen following him as if he were the Pied Piper.

Erickson's three sisters looked after him and cleaned his room without expecting anything in return. Dennis was so quiet, so studious and of such high character that an English teacher broke her hard-and-fast rule about not attending football games just to watch the Seagulls' Boys Club president.

Erickson's innate leadership qualities and feistiness made him a natural at quarterback, where he was two-time All-League, and at point guard, where he was a three-year starter.

Erickson won two of three games from his father's team, Cascade High, and ran the option with proficiency, but he wasn't heavily recruited in any sport. Among NCAA Division I-AA schools, only Montana State coach Jim Sweeney, who had befriended Pink Erickson at high school clinics years earlier, took an interest and asked for some film.

"I don't know," a skeptical Pink told Sweeney. "He's not very big, but I think he's tough. I think he's going to make a good defensive back for you."

Three years and dozens of accolades later, Erickson had graduated from Montana State with school records for career total offense, career passing yards, single-season passing yards, passing yards in a single game and the longest pass.

"Dennis had some players on the team who absolutely worshipped him," Sweeney said later.

Along the way, the sports junkie who rarely had time in high school for so much as a date went on an outing from Bozeman to Great Falls one weekend with a college friend. It was there that he met a charming University of Montana student named Marilyn.

They would eventually be married.

Without a car of his own, Erickson had to be creative to make this long-distance relationship work—Bozeman and Missoula are about four hours apart on Interstate 90. Often as not, he would hitchhike, and occasionally he'd thumb rides all the way back to Everett.

Though he had abandoned his lifelong crew cut for a more contemporary '60s shag that shocked his father, he never had trouble coaxing a ride home, even in conservative rural Montana.

His hair, like his personality, hasn't changed much in the ensuing 30 years, except for the tufts of gray.

Erickson started coaching instantly upon graduation, first as a graduate assistant at Montana State under Tom Parac and then as a graduate assistant under Sweeney at Washington State. He took his first head coaching position at Billings (Montana) Central High School in 1970 and led his team to the state championship game before making the leap back to MSU in 1971.

Perhaps his most significant stint came as offensive coordinator at San Jose State from 1979-81 under head coach Jack Elway, who had just adopted a unique one-back/no-back offense created by Granada Hills High School coach Jack Neumeier in the 1970s. It was there that Erickson had the good fortune of watching a rifle-armed quarterback who happened to be his boss's son, one John Elway, overwhelm hapless defenses with a wide-open passing attack at Granada Hills.

"Dennis took a look at his attack spreading the field out and went right for it," Pink Erickson recalls. "He put it in for Jack at San Jose State, then spread it out a little more when he left for Idaho."

Erickson took his first head coaching job at Idaho at 1982. He coaxed NFL-caliber quarterbacks and small, darting receivers—including future OSU assistant Eric Yarber—to the Palouse with the promise of wide-open offenses unlike any they'd ever known.

Within four seasons, the Vandals had their first Big Sky Conference title in 14 years. In 1986, his Wyoming team was second nationally in passing. In 1988, he took WSU to the Aloha Bowl.

In 1990 and 1991, he won national championships at Miami.

But after leaving Idaho, Erickson was never fully able to savor his accomplishments.

He was branded a traitor and a liar in Laramie, Wyoming, and Pullman, Washington, for abruptly leaving what he had termed "dream jobs." In Miami, the Hurricanes' penchant for overly passionate play, silly penalties and an NCAA investigation that eventually exonerated him took a toll on Erickson's reputation and personal life.

Turmoil dogged him from 1994 through 1998 when he left the collegiate ranks for an NFL coaching job close to home, with the Seattle Seahawks. He recalls his four years there as a mostly miserable experience, topped off by a DUI charge in 1995 that's a taboo topic for any reporter.

"People have perceptions of me that aren't true," Erickson says. "You just have to live with it."

The experiences have hardened him some, and he has a reputation for being gruff with overly probing media, but only for so long.

The insulated heart that has drawn people to him for five decades eventually returns to his sleeve.

"He may talk a tough game, but he's got a soft heart, like his mother," Pink Erickson said. "I would say he's a very big-hearted man."

Which would explain why players originally attracted to his offense are so eager to leave their blood, sweat and tears on the field for him. Or why he has such affection for a lunch-pail walk-on like quarterback Jonathan Smith.

Behind the stern taskmaster exterior and a reputation for refusing to play baby-sitter is an ordinary guy who connects with his players in a way most coaches can't. His devotion to his assistants also has created a loyalty matched only by such legends as Penn State's Joe Paterno.

None want to let down, or disappoint. His is a personality with extraordinary staying power.

People in Everett who watched Erickson as a high school player still travel the nation to his games. Often as many as several hundred— most in a group of Seagull alums called The Poker Club—would make the cross-country trek to Miami or Laramie to support their favorite son.

"He's a kid who commands a lot of loyalty, and I don't know what it is," says Lowrey, his old basketball coach. "It's an intangible quality. He commands a lot of respect for his loyalty because he's so loyal to every guy who ever worked or played for him."

Erickson will never have the flash, the charisma and the charm that many of his brethren. In fact, many people believe his lack of a commanding presence contributed to his inability to have a winning season in four tries with the Seahawks.

Dennis Erickson led the Beavers to their best-ever season in 2000—an
11-1 record and a 41-9 Fiesta Bowl win over Notre Dame.
(Photo courtesy of Barry Schwartz.)

All of which may partially explain why he was so enamored with
Corvallis. It's a place where he blended in and could just be a regular
guy with a gift.

Erickson signed a seven-year contract after the Fiesta Bowl and
gave no hint of a desire to leave. But his experience with the Seahawks
gnawed at him like a sore that wouldn't heal, and so when the perfect
professional job with the 49ers beckoned, he ultimately left his perfect
collegiate job.

Too bad, too.

Had he stayed long enough at a school renowned for such greats as
Amory "Slats" Gill, Dee "The Great Pumpkin" Andros and Ralph "Old
Whiskey Sour" Miller, he might even have his own nickname.

34

The Greatest Fan

Behind every athletic program there is that one loyal fan who stands above all the rest, a person whose devotion is unparalleled, whose knowledge is unmatched and whose love affair transcends the scoreboard. At Oregon State, that person was Cliff Robinson, a Corvallis native old enough to remember watching Slats Gill play for the basketball team. A regular at basketball practices into his 90s, Cliff would find a way to attend practices and games until ill health forced him to miss a game for the first time in years in late December 2001. This story was written by co-author Jeff Welsch on Christmas Eve of that same year, the night the greatest fan he ever saw died at the age of 93.

The greatest fan I ever saw never booed a player or a coach in 93 years.

The greatest fan I ever saw didn't see good guys and bad guys on the floor or the field, only a delightful treasure trove of names and faces and families and stories and dreams.

The greatest fan I ever saw would never let such minor inconveniences as rain, sleet, snow or gloom of night keep him from his appointed rounds at Gill Coliseum practices—and that was when he was 90 years old.

In his days of youthful vigor, way back when he was in his 70s and 80s, Cliff Robinson would drop whatever he was doing—including sleeping—and drive his trademark white Volvo to the arena to greet the Oregon State basketball teams upon their return from road trips.

It didn't matter whether it was two in the afternoon or two in the morning. Cliff was always there, win or lose, with his familiar fedora and scholarly black-rimmed glasses, to offer a friendly handshake and a"job well done" to travel-weary 20-year-olds.

Sometimes, when the team bus would pull up in the lonesome quiet of the wee hours, assistant coach Jimmy Anderson would tap on the car window to rouse Cliff, who often dozed off along what is now Ralph Miller Way.

The Corvallis native's love of Beaver basketball is so passionate that they rank a close third in his heart, trailing only his family and the students who, for half a century, he urged to achieve more than they dared imagine.

Yet the term "fan"—short for fanatic—doesn't fit Cliff in the traditional cultural sense.

He is a fanatic about OSU basketball, all right, but only in the way that Plato was fanatical about math, Socrates about philosophy, Thoreau about the environment.

He has savored the nuances, the intricacies and the personalities ever since watching Slats Gill play for the Beavers in the 1920s.

For Cliff, the scoreboard is an accessory, merely one way among many to measure performance—much the way grades were merely one way to measure performance when he was educating students, first as a teacher, then as a principal in Albany and Ashland, then as a superintendent in Coos River and, finally, as a professor at California's Chico State University.

He studies the game the way he studies the world's religions: not as an active participant but as a keen observer. He is not a Christian, he often likes to say, but Christianity fascinates him.

Others smarter than I also saw what I see.

Legendary coach Ralph Miller made Cliff an honorary assistant coach. Successor Jimmy Anderson considered him a *de facto* part of the staff. Eddie Payne made a singular exception to his rigid closed-practice rule.

Cliff always viewed his revered status as a privilege and has always refused to reveal any inside secrets to those who seek his keen insights, including his son, Roy, and daughter, Ann Patterson.

"We'll just have to wait and see what happens," he'd say.

While others at Gill boo and jeer teams like powerful UCLA and Arizona, Cliff sits back quietly with arms folded and admires the precision, elegance and grace even when the Beavers are getting trounced.

While others groan at OSU turnovers and missed shots and defensive lapses, Cliff empathizes with young men who are struggling with math or arguing with girlfriends or pining for home.

He doesn't see robots in uniforms representing institutional prestige; he sees hearts and souls that require nurturing and unconditional support.

At practices, he doesn't ask players about statistics, the one-four offense or upcoming opponents; he inquires about family members, studies and social experiences.

A few years ago, when declining eyesight and mobility forced him to give up driving, an undaunted Cliff would grab his fedora and raincoat, wave to the nurses at Timberhill Place and head for the nearest bus stop.

He would walk slowly through the rain, whenever bus and practices schedules meshed, lamenting every year in his tired body but determined to provide continued support.

"Golden years?" he'd say in recent seasons, rare negativity creeping into his persona. "Don't let anybody kid you. These golden years aren't so golden."

Saturday afternoon, before the Beavers were to play Arizona State at Gill, I walked down press row and stopped cold in my tracks in front of where Cliff usually sits. In his place sat his daughter, Ann.

A wave of trepidation washed over me.

A Beaver basketball game without Cliff Robinson is like a stream without water. Only under the direst of circumstances is it not there.

"Where's Cliff?" I asked apprehensively.

Ann and Cliff's longtime companion, Eleanor, pulled me close. They uttered the words I never wanted to hear, but knew eventually I would.

The tumor in his lungs is growing. His breathing is labored. Hospice is moving into his room.

The pained look in their eyes finished the story.

It could be weeks, it could be days, it could be hours.

All too often, particularly in this business, we wait until it's too late to pay tribute to those we admire, honor and treasure. Those left behind cherish the words, but they go unheard by those who deserve to hear them most.

I stopped by Cliff's room at Timberhill on Sunday morning to say good-bye and tell him how much I value his friendship, how much I admire his tireless thirst for learning and how much I appreciate his perspective on life.

I wanted to tell him that he's a chapter in a book about the history of OSU sports and that I want the first copy off the press to be his.

I wanted to tell him that every sports fan who has cursed a referee or hurled a plastic beer bottle or booed a fresh-faced 18-year-old should've been required to watch at least one game with him.

I didn't get the chance because he wasn't up to company, but I'm fortunate to have another venue here.

From my heart to yours, have a restful, comfortable and warm Christmas, Cliff.

This is for you—the greatest fan I ever saw.

Bibliography

In the bibliographical discussion that follows, only those sources that were of most importance in the preparation of this book have been cited. Also, the inclusion or absence of a source is not to be considered a reflection of its overall importance to students of OSU history or fans of its athletic programs.

All photographs chosen by the authors to illustrate the book's feature stories were secured, unless otherwise noted, from various collections housed at the OSU sports information office, or were selected from either the pages of the university's student yearbook, known from 1907-1916 as *The Orange*, and thereafter as *The Beaver*, or OSU's alumni magazine, known variously as *The OAC Alumnus* or the *Oregon Stater*.

Printed sources used by the authors included the following OSU publications and Oregon newspapers: *The Barometer, Benton County Democrat, Corvallis Gazette, Corvallis Times, Corvallis Gazette-Times, The Oregonian, Oregon Journal*, the Salem *Statesman-Journal*, the *McMinnville News-Register* and *The Newberg Graphic*. Oregon State student yearbooks included *The Hayseed* (1894), *The Orange* for the years 1907-08, and *The Beaver* from 1916-1999. Use was also made of documents, newspaper clippings and other materials housed within the collections of the OSU Archives. Until the introduction of electronic record keeping in the 1980s, the OSU Alumni Association kept track of alumni for almost seven decades through the use of an elaborate index card system that today sits in storage at the CH2M Hill Alumni Center on the OSU campus. It remains one of the historical treasures of the university for finding out detailed information about graduates and former students of OSU before 1970 and was used extensively in researching many of the athletes and individuals featured in this book.

Several of the stories featured in this book originally appeared in the *Oregon Stater* and are used here with the permission of the OSU Alumni Association, including "Eating Crow," "Andros at Iwo," and "The Greatest Fan."

Chapter 1: Birth of Football
The authors believe this opening chapter to be the first attempt to pull together in specific detail the personalities and events that led in 1893 to the establishment of football at OSU. The school was officially

named State Agricultural College at the time, but fans, students, faculty, and particularly sports writers preferred the more popular Oregon Agricultural College or "OAC."

Unlike the other stories in this book, certain liberties were taken in the writing of this first chapter, in much the same way historian Michael Shaara produced his Pulitzer Prize-winning novel, *The Killer Angels*. Events happened just as they are outlined, but the narrative has been occasionally embellished to help the reader (we hope) understand the climate of the times. The approach also infuses the participants with a depth of personality that makes for a more entertaining story. This is true in our description of the first game, particularly as it pertains to the dialogue between participants and how the crowd reacted to activity on the field. The scarcity of eyewitness sources for the years 1893-98 led us to this approach.

For background on OSU President John McKnight Bloss (1892-1896), his Civil War record and the role he played in the finding of "Lee's Lost Order," see Stephen W. Sears, *Landscape Turned Red: The Battle of Antietam*, Ticknor & Fields (New York), 1983, pp. 112, 208 and 350. Bloss shared credit for the find with Corporal Barton Mitchell. Both soldiers were members of the 27th Indiana Regiment. For a detailed description of the 27th Indiana during the battle, particularly as they were engaged in "The Cornfield" on the morning of September 17, 1862, see John M. Priest, *Antietam: A Soldier's Battle*, Oxford University Press (New York and Oxford), 1989, pp. 71, 85 and 94.

For events surrounding President Bloss's decision to grant permission to the student body to conduct the sports of football and baseball, and for the role played by Professor Bruce Wolverton of Monmouth, Oregon, in establishing the spirit of athletic competition among institutions of higher learning in the Willamette Valley, see John E. Smith, *Early State Colleges of Oregon: Corvallis College*, published by the author in 1953, pp. 40-41. For many years, Smith was historian of the Benton County Pioneer Historical Society and in 1953 was president of the Oregon State College Golden Jubilee Society.

Members of the first team, their names and positions, are included in *The Hayseed*, a small yearbook-type pamphlet published by the senior class in the mechanical arts in 1894, pp. 41-43. Copies of this rare publication are available through the OSU archives and the OSU Alumni Association. Information regarding what happened to members of the first team later in life can be found in Zelta Feike Rodenwold's *Alumni Directory of the Oregon Agricultural College*, published by the OAC

Alumni Association in November 1925. See also *The Orange*, 1908. The pages in this, the first yearbook in Oregon State history, are not numbered but information regarding the cheers, coaches and scores for the 1893 season are located in a chapter titled "Athletic History." The *1909 Orange* includes a tribute to the 1893-94 football team in a section on athletics. Two photos of the team are shown. Again, the pages are not numbered.

The game was played on the afternoon of November 11, 1893, and covered by the *Corvallis Gazette* newspaper in several stories published just before and just after this date. The remaining games of that first season were also covered by the newspaper and had wide readership throughout the town and Benton County. An account of the first game has also appeared more than once in past issues of the university's alumni publication, known variously since its founding by E. B. Lemon in 1915 as the *OAC Alumnus* or *Oregon Stater*.

According to the *OSU Fact Book* for 2001, OSU's official name from 1888-1896 was State Agricultural College of the State of Oregon. Off campus, as early as 1889, Frank Conover, editor of the *Corvallis Gazette*, was using Oregon Agricultural College or OAC in his reporting. The same is true for stories appearing in the Salem *Statesman* in 1891. By February 1892, the name OAC was very popular on campus and in wide usage.

Chapter 2: Birth of Basketball

The best published source issued to date covering the early years of OSU basketball is James C. Heartwell's *The History of Oregon State College Basketball: 1901-1953*, Cascade Printing Company (Corvallis), 1953. The anecdotes that appear in this chapter were gleaned from Mr. Heartwell's highly entertaining book. That male students at Oregon Agricultural College considered the game of basketball a "sissy" game during its first appearance on campus in 1899 comes from a June, 1951 interview done with a writer from the *Oregon Stater* during an Alumni Association Golden Jubilee Reunion. The remarks were made by William Beach, OSU's first basketball coach, and one of his former players, Fanny Getty Wickman, both of whom were on campus for the reunion.

Chapter 3: The Wall

The story of Oregon State head coach F. S. Norcross and his immortal defensive teams from the years 1906-1908 had to be pieced together from a variety of sources, including the 1907 and 1908 *Orange*

yearbooks, the 2000 *OSU Football Media Guide*, various web sites out-
lining the career of Fielding Yost of the University of Michigan, for
whom Norcross was a starting quarterback at the turn of the century
and who gave the young OAC mentor his knowledge of the game, and
a special publication issued by the OAC *Barometer* student newspaper
in late 1907 celebrating the play of the '07 football team, which finished the season undefeated and unscored upon and which defeated St.
Vincent's of Los Angeles for the "unofficial" title of West Coast Champions. The publication, a copy of which is housed in the OSU archives,
is titled simply "Champions." The account of Curtis Coleman's four-
point field goal against the Agrics to end the 1906 season, which represented the only points scored on OAC over a span of approximately 18
games, was put together through newspaper articles written at the time
in the *Corvallis Gazette* and from a telephone interview with the archives department at Willamette University.

Chapter 4: Hitless Wonder

The 1912 OAC student yearbook, *The Orange*, has a brief feature
on the tenure of Fielder Jones at Oregon State. For the major league
baseball career of Jones, any good baseball encyclopedia has the story of
Jones and his 1906 "Hitless Wonders." Also see Fielder Jones story and
obituary in *The Oregonian*, March 15, 1934, the day after he died. Among
the baseball luminaries at his funeral was William "Billy" Sullivan, catcher
for the White Sox during their immortal 1906 series against the heavily
favored Chicago Cubs. Sullivan, who lived to be 96, died in Newberg,
Oregon, in 1964. His obituary in *The Newberg Graphic* has bits and
pieces about Jones.

Chapter 5: The Greatest Ever

Stories about Robin Reed, from both his student days at Oregon
State and his achievements in the 1924 Paris Olympiad, are available in
The OAC Alumnus in various articles dating from 1923-26, as well as
numerous wrestling Internet sites. Further information was received via
interviews with Reed's widow, legendary former OSU wrestling coach
Dale Thomas and longtime fan Cliff Robinson.

Chapter 6: Schissler's Boys

The basics of Schissler's coaching career are covered in any current
OSU Football Media Guide printed before each football season by the
sports information department of the OSU athletic department, pre-

pared by director Hal Cowan. For the story of Webley Edwards and his role during the December 7, 1941, attack on Pearl Harbor, see Gordon Prange, *At Dawn We Slept*, (Penguin Books), 1982, p. 561. As announcer aboard the USS *Missouri* at ceremonies to mark the end of World War II, see *From Pearl Harbor into Tokyo: The Story as Told by War Correspondents on the Air*, Columbia Broadcasting System (New York), 1945, pp. 290-292.

Chapter 7: The Bare Facts

Material was gathered through an interview with Cliff Robinson less than a year before Mr. Robinson's death in 2001, OSU men's basketball media guides and James Heartwell's *History of Oregon State Basketball: 1901-1953.*

Chapter 8: Knute Was Here

Rockne's trips to OAC to teach summer school are covered extensively by the *OAC Alumnus* from issues produced between 1924-1927. Also the *Alumnus* mourned his death in 1933, with a small article done the next issue after receiving word of his tragic accident in a plane crash.

Chapter 9: Starting Point

Material was gathered from *The Beaver* yearbooks for 1933 and 1934. See also James C. Heartwell's *The History of Oregon State College Basketball: 1901-1953*, pp. 43-54; Roy Gault's "OSU to retire jersey No. 25" in the Salem *Statesman-Journal*, 3-1-99; telephone interviews conducted by George Edmonston Jr. on February 6-7, 2003, with Ed Lewis of Salem, Oregon, Ralph Hill of Walla Walla, Washington, Merle Taylor of Albany, Oregon, and Clarence James of Tillamook, Oregon.

Chapter 10: First Lady of Basketball

This chapter was based on interviews by Jeff Welsch with Slats Gill's widow, Helen Gill, interviews with former OSU athletic director Mitch Barnhart and former athletic director/basketball coach Paul Valenti. Further information was gleaned from accounts in the *Corvallis Gazette-Times.*

Chapter 11: Iron Immortals

The "Iron Man" game against No. 1-ranked USC at Portland's Multnomah Stadium on October 21, 1933, took on almost historic proportions almost immediately after it was played and was covered extensively by every newspaper in Oregon and the Pacific Northwest.

Accounts from the *Corvallis Gazette-Times*, *The Oregonian* and the *Oregon Journal* were used to write this story. The from-the-field description of the fourth quarter included in this chapter was drawn from a series of interviews conducted with Bill Tomsheck, starting right guard for the team and last surviving member of the starting 11, during the fall of 2000 at his home and at the CH2M Hill Alumni Center. Tomsheck's personal scrapbook of the 1933 season, which includes clippings from newspapers around the Northwest, was also a priceless resource for details of the game and the 1933 season and is now housed in the OSU Archives.

Chapter 12: War of the Roses
Accounts from the *Corvallis Gazette-Times*, *The Oregonian* and *The Beaver* yearbook were used for this story, along with interviews and correspondence in August 1993 with members of the team, including Quentin Greenough and coach Lon Stiner.

Chapter 13: Thrill Kid
Written using information gathered from interviews with Paul Valenti on December 15-16, 1998. Valenti was an assistant coach for Slats Gill. As a player in the early 1940s, Valenti was a teammate of Lew Beck's during Beck's first year at Oregon State College and had played against him during the team's practice sessions. Another Beck teammate, "Red" Rocha of Corvallis, also provided valuable information into the basketball style of play and talents of Beck in a 1998 telephone interview on December 16. See also Lew Beck's "My Outstanding Basketball Memories" in Jimmy Heartwell's *History of OSC Basketball*, p. 105.

Chapter 14: The Day Harlem Came to Town
Much of this story was written from interviews conducted the first week of January 1999 with former OSU basketball coach Paul Valenti, who worked with Slats Gill in the fall of 1952 to assemble the team of former OSC greats and who actually issued the invitations to the participants. Valenti also played in the game. An interview with Alex Petersen on January 13, 1999, one of several key players for Oregon State in the late 1940s and a starter on Slats Gill's 1947 "Thrill Kids" team also supplied valuable information about the game. Another participant, Bob Payne, was also consulted on January 13 for his account of the

evening. An excellent story of the game by sportswriter Brian Storm of the *Corvallis Gazette-Times* on January 14, 1953, gives a description of both the action between the two teams, crowd reactions, anecdotes about what he observed from the OSU bench, and a description of the half-time entertainment.

Chapter 15: Kidnapped!

Eyewitness accounts used for the writing of this chapter were derived from telephone interviews conducted November 16-17, 1998, with prank participants and University of Oregon alumni Steve Anderson of Gig Harbor, Washington, and Jim Grelle of Gearhart, Oregon. From the OSC Homecoming Court, Verle Pelling Weitzam of Sisters, Oregon, was interviewed. Additional accounts of this notorious prank are found in most of the major newspapers of the state the week following the incident, especially *The Oregonian*, the *Corvallis Gazette-Times* and the Salem *Statesman Journal*. The *Seattle Times* was also consulted for its version of the story.

Chapter 16: Beginner's Luck?

Most of the information used to write this chapter came from telephone interviews conducted between November 12-14, 2001, with cross country team members Dale Story of Wallowa, Oregon, Cliff Thompson of Kings Valley, Oregon, Bill Boyd of Coeur d'Alene, Idaho, and Jerry Brady of Norman, Oklahoma. Head coach of the team, Sam Bell, was also consulted by phone from his office at Indiana University, where, at the time this story was written, he was working a few hours a day and enjoying life as an emeritus track coach.

Chapter 17: Heisman Hype

This chapter was based on personal interviews with Terry Baker in 1993 and 1999 and interviews with Kerry Eggers, the son of John Eggers and sportswriter for the Portland *Journal*, and Hal Cowan, OSU sports information director, both in August 2001. See also "Heisman Hype," *Corvallis Gazette-Times*, September 2001. See also Kerry Eggers, "A Son Remembers His Dad," *Oregon Stater*, September 1992, p.20.

Chapter 18: A Beaver and a Duck at the Top of the World

The story of America's first successful attempt to conquer Mount Everest has been written about many times and in many publications and remains one of the most talked-about expeditions in the history of mountaineering. The principle sources used by the authors in this chapter included newspaper articles written at the time in *The Oregonian* and the *Corvallis Gazette-Times* and a series of stories that appeared in *National Geographic* magazine in August and October 1963. See, for example, writer Melvin Payne's "American and Geographic Flags Top Everest," in the magazine's August issue, p. 157; see also these three articles in the October issue: Norman Dyhrenfurth's "Six to the Summit," pp. 460-473; Barry Bishop's "How We Climbed Everest," pp. 477-507; Thomas Horbein and William Unsoeld's "The First Traverse," pp. 509-513. A photo of Oregon Stater Willi Unsoeld posing with a photo of an Oregon State College Mountain Club triangular-shaped flag at the summit of Everest can be found on pp. 501-502 in the Bishop account. Also, Unsoeld was probably not the only Oregon Stater who served as a member of the expedition. John E. Breitenbach is honored on page 345 of the 1964 *Beaver* as having lost his life on the Khumbu Ice Fall during the team's initial assent of the mountain. It is assumed he was at some point an Oregon State College student, but nothing was found during our research of Alumni Association records regarding his attendance or year of graduation.

Chapter 19: The Flop

The account of the most revolutionary change in track and field history was gleaned through a 1991 interview with Dick Fosbury in Ketchum, Idaho, a 1999 interview with former OSU track coach Berny Wagner and stories in the *Corvallis Gazette-Times, The Oregonian,* the *Oregon Stater* and *The Beaver.* See also *Corvallis Gazette-Times,* "Beavers Make Their Mark in the Olympics," September 2000.

Chapter 20: Giant Killers

Numerous historical accounts of this famous 1967 game appeared in the *Corvallis Gazette-Times, The Oregonian, Oregon Journal* and other publications. Sources for this story were interviewed in 1993 and 1997, including Dee Andros of Corvallis, Skip Vanderbundt of Sacramento, California, Steve Preece of Portland, John Didion, Jess Lewis of Corvallis, Gary Houser, Mike Haggard and Tom Greerty of Martinez, California.

Chapter 21: Andros at Iwo

Based on interviews with Coach Andros in his office in Gill Coliseum the first week of March 2002. Secondary sources used for details of the battle for Iwo Jima included: *Iwo Jima: Legacy of Valor,* by Bill D.

Ross, The Vanguard Press (New York), 1985; Ronald H. Spector's *Eagle Against the Sun*, The Free Press (New York), 1985; and Samuel Eliot Morison's *The Two Ocean War: A Short History of the United States Navy in the Second World War*, Little, Brown and Company (Boston), 1963. See also James Bradley's *Flags of Our Fathers*, Bantam Books (New York), 2000.

Chapter 22: Back from the Dead

This story was written after the author joined Lewis on one of his campaigns against drugs, at former wrestling coach Dale Thomas's camp in Harlan, Oregon. Lewis was interviewed along with Thomas, several coaches at the camp and numerous wrestlers. Lewis also has been interviewed on numerous other occasions and accounts of his athletic exploits are in many newspapers, including the *Corvallis Gazette-Times*, *The Oregonian* and the *Portland Tribune*.

Chapter 23: Race for the Ages

An excellent account of the race can be found in the *Corvallis Gazette-Times*, May 7, 1972, along with stories filed several days before the May 6 race, all of which help set the stage for the historic event. Telephone interviews conducted August 13-14, 1999, with retired OSU track coaching legend Berny Wagner and OSU sports information director Hal Cowan, among the thousands who were eyewitnesses to the contest, were also valuable in telling this story. Regretfully, Olympian Hailu Ebba could not be reached to contribute to this story and Steve Prefontaine was killed in a one-car accident in Eugene, Oregon, the night of May 30, 1975.

Chapter 24: Done Too Soon

Based on interviews with OSU graduate Tom Huggins, who was Prefontaine's best friend at Marshfield High School in Coos Bay, Oregon, and, like Pre, held many school records. Huggins was a track athlete at OSU, is currently a major supporter and owns Eola Hills Winery in Rickreall, Oregon.

Chapter 25: Before Title IX

See Joan Paul, "Heroines Paving the Way," in Greta L. Cohen's (editor) *Women in Sport: Issues and Controversies* (Sage Publications), 1993, pgs. 27-37; also, Betty Hicks, "The Legendary Babe Didrikson Zaharias," in Cohen, pgs. 38-48; Paula Welch, "Governance: The First Half Century," in Cohen, pgs. 69-78; see also *The Orange* and *The Bea-*

ver yearbook editions for the years 1908-1939, published by Oregon State University student media; interviews with former OSU faculty members Sylvia Moore, Velda Brust, Pat Ingram and Margaret Lumpkin conducted February 19-21, 2003; Patti Perkins e-mail to Jennifer Lowery sent October 1, 2002 at 3:36 p.m. and used with permission; letter by Mary Paczesniak to George Edmonston Jr. dated August 27, 2002.

Chapter 26: The Upset

Telephone interviews with former OSU women's basketball head coach Aki Hill and team members Carol Menken-Schaudt and Kathy Vanderstoel Campbell were key resources in the writing of this story. See also stories filed in the *Corvallis Gazette-Times* during and after the tournament, March 7-11, 1979.

Chapter 27: Old Whiskey Sour

This chapter was based on an interview with the ailing former men's basketball at his retirement home in Black Butte, Oregon. Also interviewed were his wife, Jean, and numerous former players, especially Mark Radford. Numerous published accounts of Miller's career were used for background, including stories from the *Corvallis Gazette-Times* and *Oregon Journal.*

Chapter 28: Down for the Count

This chapter was written from numerous interviews with former OSU wrestling coach Dale Thomas after he learned he had a lethal liver disease. Interviews took place in 1999, 2000 and 2001.

Chapter 29: A Local Legend

This chapter was based on a telephone interview with former OSU wrestling coach Dale Thomas, February 8, 2000. An excellent account of the March 15, 1980, national championship tournament can be found in the *Corvallis Gazette-Times* for March 16. Also see *OSU Wrestling Media Guide* for 1980. Attempts to interview Mr. Harris for this story proved unsuccessful.

Chapter 30: They Were No. 1

Numerous accounts of the top-ranked OSU men's basketball team can be found in the *Corvallis Gazette-Times, The Oregonian, Oregon Journal, The Register-Guard* and Salem *Statesman Journal.* In addition, former coach Ralph Miller, his wife, Jean, and several players were interviewed for this story. The authors also gratefully acknowledge Kansas State University's sports information department for their assistance.

Chapter 31: Thanks, A. C.

This chapter was based on an interview with the former OSU basketball standout during a camp at Portland's Concordia College after his final season in the NBA. Also interviewed were members of Green's family: his mother, Leola, his father, A. C., and brothers Lee and James. Also interviewed was Concordia athletic director Joel Schuldheisz. Information was also gleaned from Green's web site, www.acgreen.com.

Chapter 32: Eating Crow

Based on interviews with "Voice of the Beavers" Darrell Aune (announcer for the game) and former Beaver defensive standout Osia Lewis, December 28, 1999. Also interviewed was former OSU football player Erin Haynes, who attended the game. See also stories recounting play-by-play action in *The Oregonian*, the *Corvallis Gazette-Times*, *The Seattle Times* and the *Seattle Post-Intelligencer*, all appearing on October 19, 1985. Steve Rudman's "Barney Fife" column can be found in the *Seattle Post-Intelligencer*, October 17, 1985.

Chapter 33: The Miracle Worker

Written from interviews with OSU's former football coach as well as his father, Pink Erickson of Everett, Washington, his former high school basketball coach Norm Lowery of Everett and former Montana State football coach Jim Sweeney. Published feature stories about Erickson in the *Corvallis Gazette-Times*, *Seattle Post-Intelligencer*, *The Oregonian* and the *Portland Tribune* were also used.

Chapter 34: The Greatest Fan

This chapter was based on numerous conversations and interviews with Cliff Robinson, a devoted OSU fan for nearly a century. Robinson, whose memory remained sharp until his final days in December 2001, was a resident of Corvallis when Slats Gill was a player for the Beavers. Robinson was considered the foremost living historian on OSU basketball and provided a written journal of his years in Corvallis for the authors.

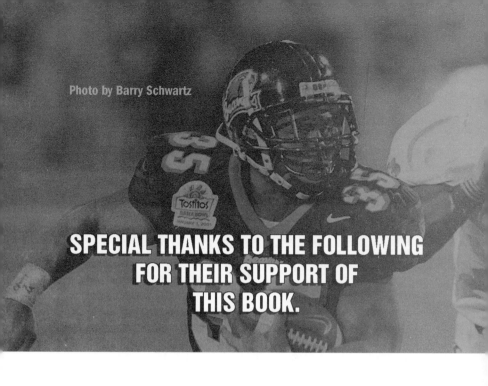

Photo by Barry Schwartz

SPECIAL THANKS TO THE FOLLOWING FOR THEIR SUPPORT OF THIS BOOK.

RESTAURANT & PUB

137 SW 2nd

CORVALLIS, OR 97333

GO BEAVS!!!

- 16 DRAUGHT BEERS
- LARGEST BACK BAR IN TOWN
- FULL SERVICE LUNCH & DINNER
  FEATURING N.W. CUISINE
- DAILY SPECIALS
- LIVE MUSIC

Congratulations to all! past, present, & future Beaver Athletes from the staff at A.J.'s!